ROCK
AND A
HARD
PLACE

ROCK
AND A
HARD
PLACE

STEPHEN J. MARTIN

MERCIER PRESS
WHAT YOU NEED TO READ

MERCIER PRESS
Douglas Village, Cork
www.mercierpress.ie

Trade enquiries to Columba Mercier Distribution,
55a Spruce Avenue, Stillorgan Industrial Park, Blackrock, Dublin

© Stephen J. Martin, 2006

978 1 85635 549 0

10 9 8 7 6 5 4 3 2 1

Mercier Press receives financial assistance from
the Arts Council / An Chomhairle Ealaíon

Printed and bound by J.H. Haynes & Co. Ltd, Sparkford.

For

Brian Dolan, Eric Persson and Jonie Hell ...
... who had more than one foot in The Grove

One

JIMMY'S MORNING was turning to shite on him. He was in his office with one of his engineers and in the process of explaining to her that, despite the promises that had been made earlier and the fact that she had worked her arse off this past year, weekends and all, there just wasn't much in the way of bonus to go around. Cathy wasn't taking it very well. She went pale and swallowed a couple of times. Then she looked down at her feet and told Jimmy very quietly that she had promised to bring her Mam to Fatima. She looked up and he saw her bottom lip begin to tremble. She was going to cry. Oh bloody marvellous, thought Jimmy. Second one this week and it only Wednesday. Now what? At least with your sister or friend, or even your bird, you could give her a hug or squeeze her arm or some bloody thing, but when it happened here in the office he never knew what he was supposed to do. A pat on the shoulder was just plain condescending, and as for sitting her gently on his lap with some soft words and burying her sobbing face into his cologne-splashed neck – well, he was pretty sure there was a special section in the employee manual about that kind of thing.

And he remembered now. Cathy's Mam had something wrong with her heart. Something pretty bad. The first big tear welled up in her eye and started to make its way down her cheek. Jimmy watched it for a second and then decided, fuck it, to go for the pat on the shoulder. He stood and was about to move around to her side of the desk when the jaunty air of '99 Red Balloons' suddenly exploded from his trousers. He winced and grabbed the phone from his belt, looking at the caller id and cursing inwardly. For a drummer, Aesop's timing could be bloody awful. He had to answer it. Aesop would just keep ringing until he did.

It had seemed like a good idea at the time. Jimmy would buy Aesop a mobile phone for his birthday and the increasingly frustrating problem of never being able to find the bollocks when he needed to would go away. Simple. Since their first single, 'Caillte', had made the Top Ten in Ireland, the band was in almost constant demand for gigs, interviews and even the occasional record store signing on a Saturday; but Jimmy also had a real job here in Eirotech Solutions and things were starting to get seriously stretched. Taking phone calls all the time during the day from Dónal, their manager, was starting to take its toll on his work. His regular boss knew that things were starting to happen for The Grove and was pretty cool about it, in a bemused kind of way, but really he didn't give a shite about all that – Jimmy Collins ran Eirotech's Information Systems and that was about all he was interested in. Jimmy figured that giving Aesop a phone would also mean that he could take half the calls from Dónal or do some of the interviews and Jimmy would be left alone during work hours.

Unfortunately though, his brilliant plan backfired. What happened was that, while Aesop had actually figured out how to make outgoing calls, he'd gotten bored with the gadget's advanced phonebook features after putting only one number into the bastard thing – Jimmy's. He called all the time. All the time. Stray thoughts would occur to him and he'd just call and call and telling him to fucking give over was a complete waste of breath. Jimmy answered it.

'Yeah?' he said, quietly. He could hear AC/DC in the background and put his spare hand over the phone. Cathy already looked like she was on the Highway to Hell and didn't need reminding. She was sniffling away now, a tissue balled up in her fist, her nose red and her eyes puffed and brimming. She had her bottom lip in her teeth and was staring miserably at the lucky orange Gonk on his desk, wondering how she was going to tell her poor mother the bad news about their pilgrimage to Our Lady of Fatima.

'I was thinking of shaving me balls Jimmy,' said Aesop. 'What do you reckon?'

Jimmy closed his eyes.

'Not now, Aesop.'

'What? No, I mean next week or something. After Shiggy's gig. What do you think? I'm reading in one of my gentleman's magazines here that Tommy Lee had it done and if it's good enough for Tommy, Jimmy, well then obviously I thought …'

'I'll call you back, Aesop, right?' said Jimmy. Cathy was getting up to leave. The last thing he needed was her going back out there in front of everybody in that state. He had five more people to talk to this morning.

'All right so,' said Aesop. 'Well listen, I'm meeting yer woman from the dry cleaners at lunchtime and I'll be bringing her back here, assuming she's up for it, so don't call till about two or half-two, right?'

Jimmy squeezed his eyes closed again and hung up. That girl wasn't a day over nineteen.

Cathy had the door open and was gone, head down, before he could do anything. He went to go after her and then stopped. What was he supposed to say? He looked at the door for a second and then sat down again and opened the bonus spreadsheet on his computer, staring at it for ten minutes and chewing on the end of his pen. Was there anything at all he could do? There wasn't. It was impossible. There just wasn't any dosh in the pot this time round. There was no way. Fatima? Not a chance.

'It's fucking Knock again for you this year I'm afraid, Mrs Clarke,' Jimmy said, clicking the window shut. He felt pretty crap about it, but he was stumped. Things had turned around again but Eirotech were still a long way from firing money at people like it was holy water, the way they used to.

He remembered Cathy arriving into a gig once and coming up to him during a break, her face flushed from the few vodka and Red Bulls. She gave him a big hug and told him he was the coolest boss in the world. Later on he dedicated a song to her and her mates and waved down to them. Cathy had been mortified but delighted and all her friends dragged her up and they spent the rest of the night dancing and laughing right in front of the stage. The following Monday in the office she was all shy – probably because of the hug – but that didn't last. Jimmy thought she was great. Always smiling and talking to everyone. Even if she wasn't a really good engineer – which she was – she was still worth a top bonus because the office was a nicer place to be when she was around. Jimmy thought that was important even if his bosses didn't.

And Jimmy had just made her cry. Fuck it anyway.

He went to the window and looked out over the car park where it was lashing rain. His pale green Peugeot was squatting there between two huge jeep things. He'd chickened out of buying one himself a couple of years ago. Probably a good thing. He knew some of the lads were in a bit of shit now trying to pay for theirs. The stereo in the Snot Mobile, as Aesop called his 206, was worth more than the engine. But then again, music was more important than mobility to Jimmy. It was more important than most things.

JIMMY COULD remember the very first time that music had an emotional effect on him. The occasion was 'Bohemian Rhapsody' being Number One on Top of the Pops and the emotion was sheer terror. That video, all those long-haired heads flying about the place and singing gospel, was worse than anything that Doctor Who could have thrown at him as he hid behind his Dad's armchair and peeked out at it every now and again. His sister Liz thought Freddie was gorgeous. Jimmy thought he was a scary bastard, but he wasn't allowed change channel. He had his cartoons and Swap Shop on Saturday mornings and Liz had TOTP on Thursday nights. As luck would have it, 'Bohemian Rhapsody' was Number One for nine bloody weeks, Christmas and everything. It had gotten to the stage where Jimmy just climbed behind the chair with a few toy soldiers as soon as Jimmy Saville or Dave Lee Travis started counting down the Top Ten, without even waiting to see if it was still Queen in the top slot. It was 1975. Jimmy only remembered two things about 1975. Those disembodied heads on Thursday nights and his Dad telling Liz that he once saw Jimmy Saville wrestle a bloke from Fairview in a fight club in Leeds. He didn't think much of it at the time, but twenty-five years later it was this latter memory that sometimes visited him in the small of the night to fuck with his head rather than Freddie's black nail varnish and massive choppers.

Liz loved Kate Bush more than anyone in those days. After Kate came Abba and the Brotherhood of Man and Boney M. It was about then that Jimmy started to hang around with Aesop, who to this day maintained that it was only he and his brothers that had saved Jimmy from homosexuality given the kind of music he'd been exposed to during the first eight or nine years of his life. The Murrays were all into Thin Lizzy and Black Sabbath and AC/DC and so Jimmy discovered Rock and decided almost immediately that he wanted to be a rock star. He wanted long hair and a guitar slung low around his waist and sweat on his face and a wry grin and a mike stand. He wanted to be cool. He stopped thinking of Kate Bush's limber ankles and starting thinking of Angus Young's stomping feet. When the eighties came along, he found himself loving Madness and Bad Manners and felt like he was betraying Aesop and his super-cool brothers. He bought *Colour By Numbers* on the sly with his confirmation money but didn't even show it to his best mate until about three years later. His very ownership of that album, with the picture of Boy George on the cover, all sultry and pink, would have been like a kick in the crotch to Aesop.

He wanted to be a rock star, but even at the age of twelve he didn't want to box himself into any one kind of music. Aesop had rules – real music had to have guitar solos for instance – but

Jimmy thought that was just stupid. He wasn't going to stop liking a bit of Spandau Ballet now and then just because Aesop said they were only a shower of queers. In 1984 he got his Mam to buy him a pair of pointy grey shoes, grew his hair into a mullet like Nik Kershaw's and told Aesop to fuck off annoying him. He wanted to listen to everything. He wanted to figure out how it all worked.

A rock star would need to know these things.

BACK AT his desk, Jimmy looked down the list of other people he had to talk to this morning. Out of all of them, only Marco Fellini would be no bother. He actually had some good news for Marco, Cathy's project manager. Tony Fitzgerald had left the company and decided to stay out in Tokyo where he had been on a six-month fact finding mission. That left a hole in Marketing and, despite being a really talented software engineer, Marco had been pushing for a move into the business side of things for ages. He was a natural too. Tall, dark, handsome, charming – he was basically a smooth Sicilian bastard and Marketing suited him right down to his shiny black handmade loafers. He was also one of Jimmy's best mates and it had been Jimmy who pushed all the buttons to get him transferred. He had just gotten a call from Simon, his boss, to tell him that everything was approved and that he could go ahead and offer Marco the new position. Marco would be over the moon. Besides anything else, he had always reckoned that his very expensive Italian wardrobe was wasted in a department full of engineers, the scruffy bastards. At least the Marketing lot shaved.

'Heya, Marco. Sit down there. Do you want a cup of coffee?' said Jimmy.

'Hi Jimmy. Coffee?' said Marco, looking at him. Marco had adjusted to life in Ireland to the point where he could actually be in the same room as boiling cabbage, but while he would now try the house red if he couldn't find any Contessa Entellina Rosso

Riserva on a menu – which in fairness was most of the time – he absolutely drew the line at shite coffee. In a restaurant, at home or here in Jimmy's office, if it wasn't in bean form five minutes ago, he just didn't want to know. The Irish should stick to their tea. They could do tea.

'Oh right,' said Jimmy. 'But it's the Roasters Choice, look.'

He held up the jar. Marco just sat and smiled and said he was fine. Poor Jimmy. He'd bring him to Palermo one day.

'Right so,' said Jimmy. 'Anyway, listen.' He clapped his hands together. 'I've just been onto Simon and he said it's all cool. You can start with Marketing next month. Wotcha think of that? Who's the best manager in the world?'

'Oh Jimmy, that is so great. Wow! Thank you!' Marco was standing again, reaching over to shake Jimmy's hand. Jimmy shook and grinned at him.

'Nah. Sure, I only suggested it to them. You were the one who sold yourself to them, so you deserve it. That was the hard bit. Martin can be a terrible gobshite sometimes with his handwriting tests and his bleedin role-playing interviews.'

'Well, maybe it's not all bullshit, Jimmy, you know? Studies have shown…' said Marco.

'Oh God. Fucking listen to you! You're one of them already! Look, have you anything on for lunch? We should probably all get together – me, you, Simon, Martin – and have a chat. Make sure we all know what's happening.'

'Yeah, great,' said Marco. 'But if we're going out somewhere, I have a tie in my desk you should borrow. You know, one that matches your shirt …'

Jimmy looked down at his tie and laughed. Marco had come a long way since that first day he arrived into the office a few years ago, afraid of his own shadow.

'I'll be grand with this one,' he said. 'Anyway, no one will be able to see my tie with the shine coming off the grease in your head.'

After lunch, Jimmy and Marco went back to his office to clear up some of his transfer details. It was just about the last thing he needed on his plate right now, but Jimmy would be taking over responsibility for Marco's project team for the moment. They were talking about an upcoming deadline and the fact that the client was a grumpy bastard when Jimmy's phone rang.

'Hello?'

'Howya Jimmy.' It was Aesop again. 'Did you know that bird doesn't speak English?'

'What? What bird?'

'Down the dry cleaners. Turns out she's from Czechoslovakia. Only knows how to say "shirt ready tomorrow" and "thank you sir, five euro please, bye bye".'

'You didn't …' said Jimmy.

'Of course I did! And I'll tell you something Jimbo, Czechoslovakia is gone way up in my estimation since about half an hour ago. She has an arse on her you want to bite lumps out of. Smashing young one. I think I can feel an encore coming on.'

'Christ, Aesop, she's a bit young isn't she?' said Jimmy. 'And don't call me Jimbo you fucker.' He was looking at Marco and shaking his head.

'Believe me, Jimmy, I'm not the first boy she's kissed. Blabbering away in Russian so she was, telling me I'm brilliant or whatever. It was like being in a porno movie. Look, I'd better go. She's pulling at me here.'

'She's there?!' said Jimmy.

'Yeah. She's lying here next to me. Do you want to say hello?'

'No, I fucking don't want to say hello! What are you doing talking about her like that and she there listening to you?'

'I told you, Jimmy, she doesn't speak English. It's grand. Here, hang on a sec …'

'Wait! Aesop! I don't have time for …' Jimmy said, but Aesop was gone.

He heard him whisper something to her. It was all muffled. She whispered back. They repeated a few times and then she came on the phone.

'Hallo?' came her voice in a throaty drawl. She sounded like Dracula's sexy little sister.

'Eh, yeah. Hello,' said Jimmy, shaking his head. He looked at his watch. For fuck sake …

'Aesop has a masseef peeenus,' she said, slowly.

'Does he? Does he really? Well, good for you,' said Jimmy. He looked over at Marco. 'Christ, you wouldn't want to be trying to get a bit of work done in here, would you?'

Aesop was back.

'Wotcha think, Jimmy? I had her telling me I was "hong like a moooose" earlier. Irish women are crap like that. They'd never give you a pat on the back and you putting in the effort after a night on the gargle. What's a moose anyway? Is it a type of cow?'

'Aesop,' said Jimmy. He was rubbing his temple now. 'You know I work, right? I have a job that I go to every morning and work at until the evening. You know that, right? It hadn't escaped your attention this last dozen years, had it?'

'No,' said Aesop.

'Well then will you *please* stop fucking ringing me during the day? Please? It's awful distracting, so it is. I'm here with Marco trying to …'

'Oh, is he there? Put him on a minute,' said Aesop.

'No, I bleedin won't put him on! We're busy, Aesop, y'know? I'll talk to you later.'

'Did he get the promotion?'

'It wasn't a promotion, but yeah he did. Now piss off, right? I'll seeya later. Oh, and Czechoslovakia isn't a country anymore, Aesop. And they don't speak fucking Russian there either, right?'

He hung up. Marco was doubled over laughing. He'd gotten the gist of the call.

'I'm glad you think it's funny, Marco, cos you're marrying into it,' said Jimmy.

He tried to remember what they'd been talking about and couldn't. Then he started to laugh too. Bloody Aesop ...

BY AROUND four in the afternoon, Jimmy was done with the performance reviews for the day and stretched out his back, yawning. He looked around the desk. There were two messages from Dónal Steele. They had a big gig in town this weekend – a farewell gig for Shiggy the bass player – and Dónal had arranged for 'some heads' to be there. That's what he called people in the music industry. Jimmy had been nervous at first about handing things over to Dónal. The Grove had always been his band inasmuch as it was anybody's, and having someone else call so many shots didn't come naturally at all to Jimmy. But he also knew that he couldn't possibly capitalise on the success of Caillte himself. For starters, he didn't have the time. Or the experience. And anyway, Dónal was a good bloke. He was the one who had produced the song with his engineer, Sparky, and he'd been in the business in Ireland for years. Jimmy trusted him and that pretty much sealed the deal.

There was only one problem. Jimmy knew he couldn't keep his job and The Grove both going at this level. Something would have to give. Music and rock stardom were all he'd ever wanted, but it was supposed to happen to him when he was seventeen, not in his thirties. Now he was up to his neck in a real career that paid him pretty good money. This was where the secure future was. But if he never gave the music a chance after all these years of waiting for something to happen ...

While all this was going on he found himself now, on top of everything else, with Marco's team to supervise because there was no budget and with a bass player to find because Shiggy was going back to his job with Kyotosei in Japan. Jimmy hadn't been sleeping well recently.

And as for bloody bass players. Nothing but trouble.

Their previous one, Beano Ward, had 'left' the band after Jimmy's then girlfriend Sandra started shagging him and then broke up with Jimmy to move in with the dickhead. Jimmy hadn't taken it too well. His faith in womanhood went down the toilet and his opinion of bass players followed. Of all people, it had been Marco who'd come to the rescue on the latter issue. Shiggy had joined Eirotech on secondment from Tokyo and Marco naturally became friendly with him, as he did with just about everybody. It turned out that Shiggy was a shit-hot bassist and during the seven months or so that he'd spent in Ireland he'd become one of their close mates as well as one of the band. But now his stint was up and next week he was out of there. Jimmy would miss him. They all would, the whole gang. Shiggy was a great bloke. It would be an emotional gig on Saturday, especially since it was only during Shiggy's tenure that the band had gone from being one of any number of pub bands in Dublin, to suddenly being on the telly and radio and newspapers. It had all pretty much come out of the whole Superchick thing, but Jimmy tried not to think about that. Superchick was something he was trying to put behind him. Not that the lads would fucking let him, the slagging bastards.

Suddenly he had a brainwave. Something Aesop had said about Marco.

Wages and headcounts were frozen, but salaries in Eirotech Solutions were still tiered. A project manager always earned about four grand more than an engineer and that was the case irrespective of budgets. He didn't want to do Marco's job, but he didn't have another project manager and he wasn't allowed hire one. Fine. But no one said he couldn't promote someone. He picked up the phone and dialled. He was pretty sure this would work.

'Heya Cathy, could you come in here a minute, please?'

He sat back in his chair and waited for her. Christ, actually being able to tick a box for a change would be fucking great. All he ever seemed to do these days was draw more boxes. His eyes felt dry and heavy and his lower back always seemed to ache when he had time to stop and think about it. Every now and again he felt a little like he was losing control. A little panic in his chest and blood thumping around in his head. He sat back down again and noticed that his email inbox had over a dozen unopened messages. There were documents all over his desk. He shut his eyes tight and rolled his neck. He was starting to fall behind. That had never happened before.

Cathy knocked and walked in and then his phone rang. He sighed and turned it off.

Two

AFTER WORK, Jimmy headed into Temple Bar where Dónal and Sparky owned Sin Bin Studios. They'd planned to do a light rehearsal for the gig on Saturday night, but as it was to be Shiggy's last time practising with the band, they'd probably just doss about and then head to the pub. Sparky let him in and they joined Aesop, Shiggy and Dónal upstairs.

'Howyiz lads,' said Jimmy, putting down his guitar case and taking off his coat.

Sin Bin was almost like a second home to Jimmy now. He'd recorded 'Caillte' and six other songs there at this stage and he often came in now to help Sparky mix them or just to watch and learn. Sparky was a genius. Mad as a fucking hatter and he did tend to smell a bit like a wet dog on Wednesdays and Thursdays for some reason, but when it came to music production there was no one in Ireland who could touch him. He seemed to understand exactly what Jimmy wanted even before Jimmy did himself. Working in the studio with him was like having an extra brain in his own head from which he could draw inspiration. A deranged brain, true, and one with a nasty dose of Tourette's Syndrome when it got annoyed, but one that seemed to effortlessly appreciate those aesthetic subtleties in music production of which Jimmy himself could catch only the occasional glimpse. Jimmy would watch Sparky eating his banana sandwiches, hunched over a bin so as not to drop crumbs on the equipment, and wonder what was going on inside his big grizzled head. He'd asked Dónal once, but Dónal just laughed and told him that they were probably both better off not knowing.

Jimmy walked over to Shiggy and clapped him on the back.

'Hey Shiggy. All set for the big gig?'

'Sure, Jimmy. No plobrem. We swap guitar?'

Jimmy had told Shiggy that they could swap over so that Jimmy played the bass and Shiggy played lead for one of the sets. They'd been meaning to do it for ages, just for a laugh, but just hadn't gotten around to it with everything else that had been going on. Shiggy wasn't just a bass player. He was also a pretty hot jazz and blues guitarist and no slouch on the saxophone either. Sax didn't really suit the type of music that The Grove played so he rarely got a chance to play it with the lads, but Jimmy had told him that it was his gig on Saturday night and he could do whatever he wanted. Shiggy told him that he'd like to do a guitar set and one song on the sax.

'Grand, so. You play guitar for that middle set, right? We'll have a laugh. Dónal, what about these people you were talking about? Will they be there?'

'Yeah. Should be there for the first half of the gig anyway,' said Dónal. 'But listen, you don't want to be messing about with Shiggy on guitar and all when they come in. Keep an eye on me. I'll give you a nod when they get there and then you go straight into the set we talked about and play your arses off.'

'Who are they anyway?' said Aesop, who was eating a donut and reading *Kerrang* with his feet up on the bass drum. He didn't really give a shite about all this business stuff. Things had gotten a little bit more complicated since they'd released the song, but his was a simple existence. He just wanted to play the drums, drink beer and ride as many women as possible in the time God had given him.

'Just a couple of executives from one of the record companies,' he said. 'Don't worry about it.'

Aesop nodded and went back to his magazine and donut for a minute, then stopped chewing and looked up again. There was sugar and jam all over his face.

'Blokes?'

'What?'

'Are they blokes?'

'Now, Aesop …'

'What? I'm just saying. Ye never know, right? I might be able to get us a better deal if I give some young one from the record company a quick stab. Isn't that how these things work?'

'Not in bloody Dublin it isn't,' said Dónal. 'And even if it was, I don't think a "quick stab" from you would get us very far. Anyway, it probably will be a couple of blokes so don't go getting excited. And let me worry about any deals. You just play the drums and smile at the girls in the crowd. That's your job.'

'And I'm good at it, amn't I?' said Aesop.

'Yeah, you're brilliant.'

'Can I have a raise?'

'No.'

'Why?'

'Cos I spent all the money on donuts. Now shut up a minute, will you? I'm trying to talk to Jimmy.'

Dónal and Jimmy sat down at the table they used to take notes and started to talk about the set they'd be playing on Saturday night. Dónal didn't usually get involved in that end of things, but this was important. One of the guys who was coming in to see them had a finger of some description in the Senturian Records pie and, as Dónal told Jimmy, that was a very tasty pie.

'I'm talking rhubarb here Jimmy,' he'd said solemnly, and Jimmy had nodded. He was a bit partial to rhubarb himself.

While this was going on Shiggy was letting rip on his sax, playing 'Baker Street' by Gerry Rafferty and standing right next to Aesop where he could annoy him properly. To Aesop, the saxophone wasn't even a musical instrument. It was Satan's big golden knob and anyone who blew it was blowing Lucifer himself. There wasn't a sax solo in the world that wouldn't have been much better had it been a guitar solo.

'Shiggy, will you get that fucking thing out of my face before I hop it off the wall, will you? It's doing me head in.'

'Aesop,' said Shiggy, 'This is my rast gig! I can pray whatevah I want, everybody say. So brow it out your arse, *ne*, jamface?'

'Fucking abuse he's giving me now,' said Aesop, wiping his

chin and looking at his fingers. 'Breaking my bollocks this last six months, being nice to him, trying to make him feel welcome in this country. Making sure there's always a couple of women around for him to play with, and all I get is bleedin potty-mouth smart answers off the fucker now.'

Shiggy laughed and put one foot up on the bass drum. He broke into 'Annie's Song', jazzing it up with a load of fills and loops. Aesop jumped up with another curse and walked off to the toilet where he could smoke out the window without everyone bitching at him.

'So much for the Japanese having a bit of manners,' he muttered on the way out. 'Fucking disrespectful fucker playing that shite in here. I suppose we'll be doing 'Greensleeves' on Saturday night, will we?'

He hadn't told Aesop yet, but Shiggy had actually elected to do 'Rat Trap' by The Boomtown Rats on Saturday evening for his sax spot. Aesop and Jimmy loved that song, but there was no fun in letting Aesop know too soon. Let him think he was going to have to sit and play through something awful. Do him good.

'What's that shitebag whinging about now?' said Sparky, who'd wandered in from the mixing desk in the other room with a cup of tea. Sparky and Aesop were always at each other. Well, Aesop was always at Sparky. Especially over the bananas. He kept winding him up, calling him Mr Tally Mon and stuff, hiding his sandwiches on him. With the amount of drugs that Sparky had taken before he cleaned himself up, it was amazing that he was able to function at all, but in fact the only real physical health problems he had were that his liver was shot and that he needed a lot of potassium for some reason. Since he refused to take any pills at all anymore, except the liver ones that kept him from dying, he tended to eat bananas by the crate load.

'He not rike sax,' said Shiggy.

'Doesn't he? Well, you just keep playing it then Shiggy,' said Sparky. He raised his voice so Aesop could hear him. 'And maybe he'll stay out there in the shitter where he belongs!'

They heard Aesop doing Harry Belafonte through the open door.

'Day-o! Dee da day-ay-ay-o!'

'I'll bleedin kill him,' said Sparky. 'The cheeky bastard never lets up, does he?'

'Just ignore him,' said Jimmy. 'Believe me, if you ignore him he'll just get bored and stop eventually.'

'Eventually my arse, Jimmy,' said Sparky. 'He'll find a banana up his hole one of these days and we'll see him sing his song then, so we will. Two bananas maybe. Anyway, listen, I'm off now, right Dónal? I've … eh … a bloke to see.'

'Right Sparky. I'll seeya tomorrow,' said Dónal.

He smiled at Jimmy as Sparky went to put on his coat. They both knew what Sparky was doing. It was Wednesday and he was going home to watch Pop Idol. Every week he did it, and every Thursday he came in like a bear with two sore arses, raving about the state of the industry. That show drove him absolutely insane but he couldn't stop watching it. It was like he used it as a focus for all the latent fury that swilled around inside him day to day, and directing it at the show meant actual real people were, for the most part, spared. The bananas may have helped with his potassium deficiency, but they did fuck all for his anger management issues. Jimmy didn't know where it all stemmed from, but since meeting Sparky he rarely even touched weed anymore. There was obviously some dangerous shit out there.

Still, for all his dementia, Sparky was brilliant. He was even cool to be around once no one was taking the piss out of him.

'Ah, Sparky,' said Aesop, coming back in the door and seeing Sparky with his coat on. 'What, has daylight come and you wan go home?'

He just had time for a big grin before he ran back out to the toilet and locked himself in. Sparky banged on the door and cursed Aesop till he was purple-faced and shaking and then he went home, promising to rip his spleen out through his arse the next time he saw him.

'Sparky's in good form tonight,' said Aesop, sauntering back out to the lads and shoving another donut in his mouth. 'Off to his yoga class, is he?'

NORMAN MET them in the pub in town afterwards. He was all excited. After four years of working in a bank he was finally getting out of it. The work killed him. He'd been in the army for ten years before that and now wearing a suit and dealing with moany bastards and their money all day long was seriously starting to wear him down. He'd been putting away as much as he could afford over the last year or so and was going out on his own. He was going to be a landscape gardener. It wasn't quite the same as running a farm in his native Cork – his ultimate fantasy job – but it was outdoor work and he was good at it. He'd just given his notice. Six weeks and he was gone.

'That's brilliant, man,' said Jimmy. 'Congratulations!'

They all clinked glasses with him. He was beaming.

'I'll tell ye lads,' he said, 'I feel like a weight has been lifted off me. It's going to be great. Up and out early in the morning, working all day on the land, coming home in the evening like I've actually achieved something. God, I won't know meself. Heaven.'

'How early?' said Aesop.

'As early as I can. I'll be up with the sun most days, please God.'

'Jesus. Were you dropped on your head?' said Aesop. He picked up his pint and scanned the room quickly for gee. There was none. He turned back to Norman.

'Sure, you've a grand job now. Sitting on your hoop all day. Getting well paid in a nice warm office. Why do you want to go out and work in muck and shite and the pissings of rain? That's really fucking hard slog, that is. I had to weed me nanny's back garden once and I couldn't stand up straight for a week. A poxy fiver she gave me. Big fuck-off spiders and yokes with millions of legs chasing me down the yard and everything. And Grandad Murray fucking laughing at me from the kitchen, the bollocks, and only half his face able to move.'

'Aesop, of course a big city poof like you wouldn't know what it's like to get out into nature. They could put you in a glass bubble and you wouldn't move as long as they pushed the occasional bag of chips through the flap and let you watch telly.'

'At least I'd be warm. And I wouldn't smell of gick. So, c'mere, will you be wearing your wellies at work?'

'I will sometimes I'm sure. I'm after buying a lovely new pair at the weekend.'

'Unbelievable. Lovely wellies. Only you could say that and mean it, you big bleedin mulchie. Would they fit me do you think?'

'Well I'm pretty sure I could fit one up your hole, Aesop, which is where you're heading at the moment.'

Norman took a big slug of his pint and winked at Shiggy. Shiggy was well used to it at this stage, but Norman still liked to show him that he was only joking. He wasn't a violent man. Well, technically, he was a trained killer who had spent five years in the Army Ranger Wing and he could easily have broken Aesop's head off his shoulders and thrown it over a wall ... but that was different. The thing about being able to beat seven colours of shite out of absolutely anyone was that you never actually had to.

'So Shiggy,' said Jimmy. 'Are you looking forward to going home?'

'Ah, yes Jimmy. My famiry also happy. Japanese food ... I miss that tsoo.'

'Will you miss us?'

'Sure. Hey I come back sometime, yes? Horiday or maybe work?'

'Of course you will. We can do a big reunion gig and everything. But we'll miss you as well though. It was fucking great having you here. I don't know what we're going to do for a bass player.'

'You famous now, Jimmy. No plobrem. Everyone want to pray with you.'

'Ah, I don't know about that. Anyway, what if we want to do some jazz for a change?'

'Well then you'll be looking for a new drummer as well,' said Aesop. 'Listen Shiggy, before you go, I want you to tell me something. Japanese women. What's the story?'

Shiggy looked at him, puzzled.

'No story.'

'There is a story,' said Aesop. 'There must be. Are they all, like, y'know, bowing and bringing you tea and washing your jocks for you and all? I heard that.'

'Where did you hear that shite?' said Jimmy.

'I read it.'

'You read it?' said Jimmy, laughing. 'Where was that, then?'

'It was in a magazine.'

'Jaysis. Let me guess …'

'Japanese girl different from Irish girl, sure,' said Shiggy. 'But Japan different from Ireland, *ne*? Guys different too. Everysing different. But girls tsoo.'

'Which is better?' said Aesop.

Shiggy thought about it for a minute. He shrugged.

'Aesop, different is not better. Different is different.'

'Spot on Shiggy,' said Norman. 'If more people saw things like that, then we wouldn't have the shite and killing going on in the world that we do today.'

'Ah, for fuck sake Norman,' said Aesop. 'Don't be changing the subject. This is important. Go on Shiggy. Do they make the tea?'

Shiggy nodded.

'And do they bow?'

Shiggy nodded again, but he was frowning.

'And the jocks?'

'Aesop, I sink you don't understand.'

'Well, tell me then.'

Shiggy didn't really have the English for this type of conversation. And he wasn't sure that Aesop would get it anyway. He sat looking at his pint on the table in front of him for a minute.

'In Japan,' he said, 'woman is more … quiet. Than Irish girl.' It wasn't quite what he wanted to say, but he thought that it said a lot on the off-chance that Aesop took the trouble to think about it. 'But,' he went on, 'she is also very … very … ahh … strong. Inside.' He put his hand on his chest. 'Here.' Then he slowly moved it to the front of his head, thinking. 'And here.'

Aesop looked blankly at him for a minute.

'And … so … eh … you wash your own jocks, is it?'

Shiggy laughed. 'No Aesop,' he said, winking at Jimmy next to him. 'In Japan all jocks are disposaburu. We just wear and throw away.'

Aesop sat up straight and looked around at the others, blinking in surprise: 'That is a fucking *brilliant* idea! Why don't we have them?'

Shiggy nodded at him seriously, tapping his head.

'Ah! Japanese, *ne?* Smart, *ne?*'

'Can you send me some when you get home? Jaysis, that's terrible clever.'

They carried on along those lines for the rest of the evening. Jimmy looked around at them, his mates and himself in a bar getting a bit too drunk than was good for them on a school night but loving every minute of it. They had the gig on Saturday night but they probably wouldn't get to spend a quiet evening in the pub together again before Shiggy left. This would be the last time and he was a bit sad. Shiggy was a great bloke. The Grove would be a bit stuffed without him, but he had to admit that having him around was about a lot more than that. He knew he was getting a

29

bit shitfaced when he found himself realising that Shiggy was the coolest person he knew. Jimmy had always thought that Jimmy was the coolest person he knew.

The rest were fairly pissed too.

'So, anyway, how many people did you kill?' said Aesop to Norman.

Norman looked around in surprise.

'What?'

'In the army. Ever shoot anyone?'

'Aesop, I was in the Rangers. I can't tell you what I did. You know that.'

'Ah c'mon, ye fucker. Give us an oul story. Did you ever drive a tank?'

'Aesop …'

'Did you ever jump out of a helicopter and land on some fuck-er's head?'

Norman laughed.

'Yeah, we couldn't afford parachutes so it was the only way to get down safely.'

'No really, c'mon. Tell us a story. Did you ever get shot at or anything? You must have, all those mad places you went.'

Norman just grinned at his pint, shaking his head. Even if he wanted to tell them, he couldn't. Most of what he did he never actually officially did at all. He wasn't there. No one was. It was that kind of job. He'd made a longer paper trail in his first two weeks as a bank clerk than he did in those five years of being a Ranger. But he liked it. He only left because his Mam was on her own and getting on a bit. She worried.

'Must have been scary sometimes, though,' said Jimmy. 'Even for a Rambo like you.'

Norman thought about it for a minute.

'Well … there was this one time …' said Norman.

All the lads put down their drinks and leaned in to listen. He laughed.

'I wasn't a Ranger then. But I was on patrol one night in the jungle in Cambodia …'

'Brilliant!' said Aesop. 'Fuck sake, why do none of my stories start like that? What were you doing in Cambodia?'

'I was looking for cheap wellies. Shut up, will you? So anyway, I came on this young lad with an AK47. Wasn't a day over twelve years old. He jumped out from behind a tree and stuck it in my face. We just stood there for a minute, not a word out of either of us, and eventually I just reached up and pulled the barrel away from my nose and pointed it down at the ground. Then I looked him in the eye and very slowly took it off him. He ran away into the bush.'

'Fuck,' said Jimmy and Aesop together.

'And were you scared?' said Aesop.

'Aesop, I was so scared I nearly pissed in your pants.'

'Jaysis,' said Aesop to the others. 'And I wasn't even there!'

They all roared laughing. Jimmy loved nights like this. He stood up to go to the bar and his phone went off.

'Ah for fuck sake!'

It was work this time. Could he spare five minutes to talk to the Head of Infrastructure at a New York client? Jesus, he was after having five pints. That prick knew what time it was in Ireland. And getting his secretary to call him. On his mobile!

'Tell him I'll call him tomorrow, will you?' he said to her. 'I'm not at home and I've nothing in front of me. I'll call him tomorrow.'

He hung up and went over to Dave at the bar for some pints. The lads were howling at something Shiggy had said and he turned around and smiled, but he could feel the buzz leaving him now and the taste of pizza from the studio bubbled up hot and sour into his mouth. It was the phone call. Even what little time he had to himself wasn't his own anymore.

Bastards.

Three

ON SATURDAY, they went back to McGuigans. That was their home turf and where it had pretty much all started. The manager, John, from Mayo, was a good mate now and had helped them out a lot back when they were getting started. Jimmy was only too glad to pack out the Sound Cellar there with pint-drinkers for Shiggy's last gig. People enjoyed themselves in McGuigans and didn't give a shite who was looking at them – not exactly the norm in Dublin these days. They'd have a laugh playing there and Jimmy needed a laugh after that bloody week in work. This would be like old times.

They headed in good and early and had a pint and a chat with John.

'It's going well anyway, Jimmy,' said John. 'Herself was saying there the other day that she heard you on the radio. Sure you're never off it now, are you?'

'Ah it's good, yeah, John. We've got a bit of momentum. Just riding it now, like, y'know? See what happens. It could all go tits-up tomorrow.'

'Not at all, Jimmy. I've been in this lark for thirty years and I'm telling you yiz are ripe for it. Even my young one was talking about you last week, and she doesn't even like live music. She prefers a "live DJ", she says. Whatever the fuck that means. She'll be in tonight.'

'How old is she, John?' said Aesop.

'We had her twenty-first last month,' said John. 'Out in Howth.'

'Twenty-one,' said Aesop, adjusting his pint on the bar. 'That's a lovely age.'

John threw his head back and roared laughing.

'You'd be dead before you left the place, boy!' he said. 'She's seeing a big Yank. Body builder. Muscles on his face, so he has. Keeps calling me sir and shaking me hand. Every time I see him he does it. Grabs me and starts pumping away like he's looking for me to vote for him. Polite cunt, y'know? But it's like sticking your hand down the back of a couch, the size of him. Anyway, I wouldn't like to annoy him Aesop, and you're a great man for annoying some blokes when they're out with their women.'

Aesop just grinned and made a show of fixing his hair in the mirror behind the bar. He had no intention of going near John's daughter. Despite what Jimmy and everyone else thought, he did actually have a bit of self-control. Except, of course, when it came to winding up Yanks.

Jimmy always got a bit queasy before a gig, but this was worse than normal. It was supposed to have been a celebration and a party for Shiggy, but now Dónal had these people coming in to look at them and the way he was talking it was the most important show they'd ever do. So much for having a laugh. The only good thing was that the fuckers had arrived early. At least they'd probably piss off after half an hour and they could get on with it. The place was full already and they weren't on for another twenty minutes. Wonky Sheehan, Aesop's cousin, was up there doing an acoustic set for the punters. He was pretty good. Funny fucker too, like everyone else in that family, and he had the punters in a good mood. He even had Shiggy up to jam with him on the sax for Moondance and that got everyone going.

'Fair fucks to you, Wonky,' said Jimmy to himself. The crowd would need to be all over them tonight, Dónal had said.

Rather than drag it out, Jimmy had them all ready to go at nine on the button. He wasn't able to enjoy himself, standing there at the bar with the lads and looking over at Dónal's table. There were three of them. A bloke his own age, another one about Dónal's age and, un-fucking-believably, an extremely pretty black woman with huge knockers who seemed to be the boss. As soon as they'd walked in, Dónal had grabbed Jimmy's arm in shock, the other hand on his mouth.

'Oh Jesus. Keep Aesop the fuck away from us, will you? That's Alison Greene. She's married, kids, Christian. Takes her job very seriously but hates all the shite that goes with it. Goes mad when men try to ride her. Everyone has a go.'

'I'd say they do,' said Jimmy. 'She's fucking gorgeous.'

'She must have flown over from London for this. Oh Christ … where is he?' Dónal was scanning the room desperately. He was practically wringing his hands on Jimmy's shirt.

'Fuck sake Dónal, it's all right. I'll get him up on the stage and out of the way.'

'Do. And if he sees her, tell him she's … eh … a lesbian.'

Jimmy laughed.

'That won't work. Aesop loves lesbians, Dónal. And a gorgeous black lesbian with a rack like that? No, I'll just tell him she's a man in a dress. He won't believe me but he'll be too scared to take the chance.'

'Good thinking. Look, I'd better go. Good luck up there, Jimmy. Seeya later.'

Jimmy smiled and watched him go over and start talking to the three of them, leading them to a reserved table by the mixing desk. He drained the last of his pint and looked around. Shiggy and Aesop were now at a table with Marco and Norman. Jennifer, who was Aesop's sister and Marco's fiancée, was there too with some of her friends. He could see that he knew at least half the people in the place. That was good. They knew the songs and would be up for it tonight. There were even a couple of people there from work. Shiggy had been very popular in the office and this would be a much better farewell party than the more formal one on Thursday night had been, in that wanky bar off Stephen's Green. Cathy was sitting by the side of the stage with some of her mates. She gave him a wave and he wandered over. He was the best manager in the world again now that Portugal was in the bag at last for Mrs Clarke. They were going in a couple of months. Jimmy reckoned she probably had a lot on her plate these days, but the Blessed Virgin could still do a lot worse with her heavenly influence than have a quick word with Himself about Cathy and her Mam.

THEY OPENED the set with a new one that they'd been working on in Sin Bin called 'Bush Whacked'. It was a bit political for The Grove, or at least it could be read that way, but it started with drums, then bass and then a big fuck-off power chord and lights explosion. It was fifteen minutes and three non-stop pounding songs later before Jimmy grinned out at the crowd.

'All right?' he said.

They roared back.

He picked up the Ovation acoustic he'd borrowed off Sparky and strummed it a few times. Dónal had told him to do something to show he was able to really play. That there was more to him than just 'the leather pants and the face', he'd said, the cheeky fucker.

'This is an old Lightnin' Slim song,' Jimmy said, once he got a bit of quiet. 'This one's for Rory.' He paused and spoke again quietly. 'Twelve years gone now ...'

He bowed his head and the lights went down, leaving just a spot on him. It was an old blues number. 'Very Delta'. They'd talked about that one for ages, him and Dónal. It wasn't very The Grove, but Jimmy reckoned it would be okay and he really wanted to play it. This venue? This crowd? Should be no problem. This was a home game.

He was right; they loved it. They weren't expecting it, sure, but they shut up and let him play, punctuating the song with the odd whistle or shout and cheering during the intricate licks of the slide solo. The solo was another reason he was doing it. To show those three down there what he could do. And that he could play a song like that in a place like this and pull it off. He couldn't see Dónal's table with the light in his face, but he could make out Sparky at the bar when he was done and got a thumbs-up. That was good enough for Jimmy. He took a little bow, looked up and pointed at the ceiling for his hero Rory Gallagher and then put the guitar back on a stand behind him, picking up his Strat.

He came back to the mike and smiled back and forth around the room.

'And here's one for you.'

Big cheer.

They ripped through 'Landlady Lover' and 'Alibi', which everyone knew and sang along with from the tables and the dancefloor.

Shiggy was bopping and grooving like his life depended on it. Winking at girls and grinning his big happy grin at anyone who caught his eye. At one stage he jumped from his monitor, two feet off the ground, straight down into the splits. Aesop missed half a bar because he stood up in surprise to check that Shiggy hadn't broken his bollocks, but caught up again once he saw him rolling over onto his back and doing a little backwards tumble up into a standing position, left fist in the air as he thumped on the open E string with the right. He'd timed the whole thing perfectly. Fuck sake, thought Jimmy, who'd nearly dropped a load himself with the shock. Did he practise this stuff or was he made of rubber fucking bands? They'd be calling for the priest if he tried that. Aesop wouldn't have even made it up the monitor.

But the crowd roared.

Next, it was time for 'Meatloaf's Underpants'. The punters knew the intro and starting cheering straight away. Jimmy let them start the song and sing the whole first verse on their own. It sounded – and looked – brilliant. Aesop was like a man possessed all the way through. He'd recently expanded the drum solo section, incorporating a little light show during which he'd put on a miner's lamp and search out the prettiest girls in the audience with the house lights turned off. When they went into the miniature bass solo that introduced this little bit of cabaret, the lights went off on cue and he pulled off his shirt and stuck on a yellow workman's helmet to which he'd now attached his lamp. 'Cos I'm on the job,' he'd said to Jimmy with a grin. He'd also gotten his Da to paint one of his pairs of drumsticks with luminous paint. Out they came too.

It was even more electric than usual. All you could see was his head lashing about like it was only tied to him with string. The sticks blurred into ghostly blue clouds and his lamp flashed across the drumkit, the ceiling, the stage and the front row of moshers. It was one of the most amazing things Jimmy had ever seen on a small stage like this. He was never one hundred per cent behind this whole thing. It was corny and Glam – a bit fucking stupid, really – but for some reason it worked. And they hadn't seen it in McGuigans before. The floor was shaking under him and he actually had to put his hands over his ears at one stage.

He heard his cue to come back in with a roaring chord and pounced on it. The drums stopped and out the light hopped into the audience, jumping from table to table and scanning across the bar. Jimmy glanced out as he kept thrashing away on the guitar, Shiggy doing the same on the bass on the other side of the stage. The light panned across Dónal's table and did an actual double-take.

'Fuck me!' he heard Aesop say behind him, and looked again to see Alison Greene's cool dark eyes sparkling in the glare, her perfect white teeth glistening behind scarlet lips.

Aesop was about to grab at the mike on his snare to say something to her, but then Alison's features were replaced with a panic-stricken Dónal, who was leaning in and throwing daggers right back up the light at him. Aesop tried to move the beam around Dónal, but Dónal kept following it with his head, mouthing warnings and obscenities, his tie flopping around in his pint on the table. Eventually Aesop gave up and continued along that row. He found another cracker. She was sitting beside a bloke the size of two blokes. Had to be John's daughter; the fucker next to her looked like he had a calf strapped to him under his plaid shirt. Definitely American. He might as well have been sitting there with a big camera hanging around his neck and eating a hotdog.

Aesop pulled the mike off the snare and found her again with his light.

'Howzit goin'?,' he said, smiling his smile, like there was just the two of them in the room. 'Guess what I'm thinking.'

'Oh fuck,' said Jimmy, trying to make out the ape sitting next to her to see if he was going to storm the stage. Bollocks to this. He upped the volume straight away, prompting Shiggy to do the same and finally, laughing his hole off, Aesop wrapped it up on rolling, thunderous cymbals and toms to wild cheering and whistling. The lights blared on again.

Aesop stood up to take the applause and pointed over to John's daughter, winking and doing 'let's have a drink' and 'call me' motions with his other hand. Everyone was laughing except Bud, who was just sitting there with his fists clenched on the table and his seething face like a great big square plum.

Jimmy stepped back to get his acoustic guitar again.

'You've done it this time, you fucking eejit,' he said to Aesop behind him as he leaned over to pick it up. 'That bloke's going to batter the shite out of you, so he is.'

'What bloke?' said Aesop, throwing his sticks up into a loop and catching them. He wasn't finished with Bud yet.

'We're going to take a break for a minute,' said Jimmy, back at his mike. 'So we'll leave you with this one. I hope your ears aren't ringing too much after all that!'

He'd been working on a new solo arrangement of Caillte on the guitar and slid into it now as the spot came on and the stage lights went down again. They didn't usually follow Meatloaf's Underpants with something like this, but he wanted to make sure Dónal's table got to hear it before they took off. There were some tricky bits, but he made sure he only tried to play them between verses. The crowd picked up on the new version and sang along. It actually worked better in the higher ranges and the girls obliged. It was that kind of song anyway. The last chorus was sung twice and he let them sing it on their own. He didn't even play the guitar, just closed his eyes and smiled as they carried it home like they owned it. Which they probably did, now that he thought about it. Fuck it. Why not?

'Absolutely perfect,' he said as they faded out, and then the spot snapped off and they screamed themselves hoarse again.

DURING THE break they all had a quick pint and mixed it a bit with the punters. It was almost impossible to actually talk to anyone the way people kept coming over and saying hello. Jimmy and Aesop eventually escaped out onto the street for a bit of fresh air and a smoke. Shiggy wanted to lap it all up while he could, so he stayed down with Norman and Marco, looking around at all the people and waving at the faces he knew. They were playing Tom Dunne's Irish CD over the house system and the atmosphere in the place only got wilder. The Frames were on now and the dance floor was full of slowly twisting and grinding girls, with guys playing air guitar. Pints were whipped off the bar and passed back to waiting mates as John and his staff sped back and forth, taking orders two and three at a time to keep up with everyone's thirst. Shiggy looked on, loving it. He'd miss Ireland. What an incredibly strange place.

Up on the street, Aesop was still laughing about Bud.

'But Aesop,' said Jimmy. 'What are you going to do if he decides to kill you and put you in a fuckin protein shake?'

'Ah Jimmy, you worry too much,' said Aesop. 'Didn't John say he was all polite and all? Anyway, he'll get a laugh out if it, watch.'

'He'll get a laugh out of you asking his bird for her phone number? That big fucking gorilla in there is going to find that funny, is he?'

'Sure, aren't Americans known for their excellent sense of humour and appreciation of irony?' Aesop said.

They both laughed.

'Yeah, I forgot about that.'

'But c'mere,' said Aesop. 'More importantly, who was that absolute fucking goddess sitting next to Dónal down there? I'd marry her tomorrow, so I would, and never leave the house again.'

'Jaysis, will nothing do you tonight only getting your arse kicked?' said Jimmy. 'She's from the record company and Dónal told me to tell you to keep away from her.'

'Why? Is there something wrong with her?'

'Yeah. She's married, has kids, loves God and has no time for sinners trying to get the jocks off her.'

'Ah. I see. But Jimmy,' said Aesop. 'Aren't we all sinners? I mean, I'm not the one going around the place with perfect cherry lips and long curly eyelashes and tits like space hoppers, am I? Look at her!'

He was looking over Jimmy's shoulder at the stairs, where Dónal was leading his guests out.

'Dónal!' he said.

'Eh, howya Jimmy. Eh, Aesop. Eh … actually it's good that you're here,' said Dónal. 'I was hoping you'd get a chance to say hello to the crew from Sultan Music here.' He'd actually been trying to sneak them out. 'Alison Greene, this is Jimmy Collins … eh … and Aesop Murray …'

He made the introductions quickly, stepping between Aesop and Alison and putting one hand on Aesop's shoulder so he could give him a discreet dig if he needed to. The two guys chatted to Aesop and Dónal for a minute, Jimmy making small talk with Alison and telling her about the origins of Caillte. Then Aesop cleared his throat.

'Well, it's an absolute pleasure to meet you Alison,' he said, leaning in to her. 'And tell me this, now, did you enjoy the show?' He'd caught her accent and was giving it a bit of blarney.

'Very much, Aesop,' said Alison, smiling at him. 'And I loved your drum solo. Very imaginative! Aesop … not a very Irish name, is it?'

'Ah no. Well Mam, Lord rest her, used to call me that. You see, I was the oldest of twenty-one children Alison, and me poor Mam used to be run off her feet with the little ones. So to help her out, I used to make up stories to keep them quiet and she started calling me her little Aesop. It kind of stuck, so it did. I'm really Paul. After Saint Paul.' He glanced at Dónal. 'Of Tubber-curry.'

Dónal jumped in before Alison could say anything and back-handed Aesop on the ear quickly.

'We're off to get some dinner now, lads. Youse better be getting back down there to your adoring public. I'll see you later, okay?'

He started to guide the others away from the awning and down the street, glaring back over his shoulder at Aesop.

'Seeya now,' called Aesop after them, rubbing his ear. 'God bless.'

He turned around to see Jimmy looking at him.

'Hmm?'

'Twenty-one children?'

'Too many?'

Jimmy pursed his lips and shrugged.

'And this Saint Paul of Tubbercurry … a chaste and holy man, was he?'

'In my mind Jimmy, I see him as a tragic kind of figure; roaming the countryside, converting culchies, y'know? He probably struggled a lot with doubt. God, she has a lovely arse on her too, doesn't she? Look.'

THE REST of the evening was brilliant. Shiggy did the whole next set on the guitar, stomping around the stage and throwing shapes like he was in an eighties hair-metal band. Jimmy sang and played the bass and Aesop tied his shirt around his head like a bandana. Jimmy sprinkled another couple of their own newer songs around and then, about ten to twelve, he called Shiggy to the centre of the stage and told the crowd that it was his last gig. They knew that anyway but they still roared as he beamed out into the lights and bowed again and again, tears swirling in his eyes at the noise they made for him.

Jimmy went to Shiggy's mike at the right of the stage and called for Wonky. Wonky got up and took Shiggy's bass, positioning himself at the back next to Aesop. This left Shiggy on his own, front and centre, his sax slung low around his legs and his hair hanging down his face. The crowd hushed up, not knowing what to expect, and then Jimmy played the guitar intro to 'Rat Trap' and they went crazy, loving that Shiggy was singing on his own at last with his brilliant Japanese accent. It was such a hard song too. So many lyrics for him to try and get his tongue around. At the sax solo, which Shiggy made at least four times as long as the original, a spotlight shone down on him, the rest of the stage plunged into darkness, and he blew that horn like never before, filling the rest of the song out with trills and licks until it ended in a storm of cheering and stamping feet.

For an encore they did their normal version of 'Caillte' and then they were done; exhausted and drained, but feeling like they'd nailed another one.

They got down off the stage and went over to the lads. Aesop immediately sat down, drained a pint, burped and then stood up again.

'Now, where was I?' he said, and looked around. He spotted John's daughter moving towards the bar. 'Ah, yes.' Off he went.

Jimmy shook his head, laughing. It had been a good night. Dónal was due back in before the place closed and he'd get all the gossip then. But he was sure they'd done what they needed to do. They'd been on fire. Everything was perfect. Everything. The sets, the crowd, the performance. Everything.

Except … now they were losing Shiggy. How the fuck do you replace someone like that?

Four

JIMMY WOKE up the next morning with a bag of twisted ankles where his head used to be. It was those fucking Tequila Suicides that Aesop had insisted on them all doing later on, after Dónal had told them the good news. Squirting the lemon in his eye was painful enough, but snorting salt up his nose was easily the most stupid thing Jimmy had ever done while drunk. He'd already thrown up twice by the time he'd gotten to bed and could vaguely remember staving off a third chuck by planting one foot on the floor as he lay there watching the ceiling do cartwheels. Now that he was awake and squeezing his throbbing skull between two pillows, he found that he could also devote some attention to the bubbling and rolling in his stomach. Lovely.

An hour later he staggered into the bathroom, took care of business and then stepped into the shower, shutting the door and sitting down with his legs crossed and his head bowed as the boiling hot water stabbed at him. It was only after ten minutes of this that he registered all that Dónal had told them when he'd returned to McGuigans. That crowd from Sultan had been well impressed. They wanted The Grove to do a couple of London club gigs. Based on the reception they got there, they might consider signing them for an album. Hence the tequila.

This was what Jimmy had been dreaming about for most of his life and now it seemed to be right there in front of him and giving him the wink. He couldn't believe it. It felt like it was happening to someone else. Was this really it? Dónal had told them not to get too excited but then started on about doing a tour of Europe to support the album and wondering who they'd get to direct the video of the first single – he knew just the man for the job. Then there was a festival in Germany at the end of the summer. If they could get into that it would be amazing. It went on … people they'd get to meet, the budget they could expect for the album, famous London venues they'd play, parties they'd go to … the whole thing was discussed in an increasingly drunken, surreal haze. All they needed was to do these three gigs in London, blow everyone away, and then they were off.

Except they weren't. Jimmy checked out his bloodshot eyes in the bathroom mirror as he dried himself. He was sober now and in a lot of pain still. The euphoria of the previous evening was evaporating like the steam off his back and Jimmy knew that the churning in his stomach wasn't just because of the kebab he'd had on the way home. Two weeks in London was one thing. He had holidays. But a six-week tour of Europe, playing festivals and plugging an album? How the fuck was he supposed to get that past Simon, not to mention HR?

Jimmy had begun to sense that this day might come. He'd been dreading it and wanting it more than anything else all at the same time. What would a chance at his dream cost? Most people never got to find out, but now Jimmy knew. He had a career he'd spent the best part of fifteen years, including college, working his arse off to build. It was sixty grand a year, plus bonus. Options. It was a nice house, cool holidays, a decent car once he got around to buying one. Security. Lots of golf when he packed it in at the end. The best for his kids, whenever they turned up. It was a future. A real one. Could he risk that, going off to chase butterflies with Aesop and Dónal? His Da would fucking murder him for starters.

He shook himself out of it. He didn't have to worry about it yet. It hadn't actually happened. It was all just talk.

He was pulling on his jeans as the phone rang. It was his Mam.

'Hi love,' she said. 'Did I wake you?'

'No Ma,' he said. 'I'm just out of the shower.'

'Oh that's all right so. How was last night? Did Shiggy have a good time?'

'He did, yeah,' said Jimmy, smiling to himself. The last thing he remembered seeing of Shiggy last night, the mad little fucker was up on the stage on his own after all the punters were kicked out, miming to 'Don't Stop Me Now' on the house system for them and doing a pretty convincing ballet routine of some sort. Freddie would have loved it.

'That's great. Listen pet, I'm after forgetting the cream. Your father was rushing me out the door of the shop after mass because he got a new Celtic video off one of the lads and nothing would do him only to get back and watch it, so didn't I forget to pick the cream up with the nectarines. He won't budge now from the telly and I can't drive this week with my back.'

'I'll pick it up on the way around. No problem. How much do you want?'

'A pint should do. Do the lads like Irish coffees after their dinner?'

'Eh, I'm sure they do.'

'Yeah, a pint so. I have that squirty cream if we run out, but I'm not putting that on the pavlova. Sure, it's only full of air, that stuff. It's only good for decoration.'

'Right. Well, I'll see you about three so, right?'

'Grand. Oh, do you know who I saw at mass this morning?'

Jimmy lay down on the floor, putting a hand over his eyes. His head was pounding and he didn't know how long this would take.

'Who did you see, Ma?'

Twenty minutes, as it turned out.

PEGGY COLLINS had invited all the lads around to dinner to say goodbye to Shiggy. Cooking for her husband was fine and all, but she loved nothing more than having eight or ten people squeezed around her dining table on a Sunday afternoon, laughing and eating and enjoying themselves. And it was a special occasion today, so they'd be getting the works.

She was in the kitchen when Jimmy arrived, with things bubbling on all the rings of the hob, the oven on, the microwave on and the fridge full. Everything under control. She was sipping a glass of wine from one hand, stirring the cheese sauce with the other and singing along to Barbara Streisand on the radio when Jimmy walked up behind her and kissed her on the cheek.

'Howya Ma.'

'Jimmy!'

She turned around and gave him a big kiss, linking an arm through his. Jimmy grinned. No matter what happened – ever – his biggest fan was right here. She ooh-ed and ah-ed at the dozen daffodils he'd picked up with the cream and found a vase for them, chatting nineteen to the dozen about her morning as she peered into steaming pots and prodded at the ducks in her custom-built oven.

Aesop arrived next. He had an enormous bunch of flowers with him, the bastard, and Peggy beamed and giggled like a schoolgirl at all the attention. Aesop had practically grown up in the house and Peggy loved him like her own. Marco, Jennifer, Norman and Shiggy arrived soon enough and they stayed chatting in the dining-room off the kitchen rather than risk going into the lounge. They all knew Seán Collins well enough at this stage and weren't about to barge in to say hello when he was watching football.

'What game is it?' said Jimmy.

'The UEFA cup final,' said Peggy, shaking her head. 'Porto ...'

'Ah Ma, no! Not that one. Why didn't you hide it until everyone was gone?'

'He wouldn't let it out of his sight. I told him to watch the Inter game from sixty-seven because we had guests coming, but he watched that last week. Poor Jimmy Johnstone ...'

Peggy handed him two bottles of wine. There was another roar from the lounge. The referee was getting terrible abuse in there.

'Do you hear that?' she said to Jimmy, nodding at the wall.

'And he only after receiving communion. I've to put up with this now till the end of July when the league starts again. A big suitcase full of tapes he has.'

THE RELATIVE significance of any celebratory meal that Peggy prepared could be gauged not by the number of courses, but by the number of different types of potato dishes she served. In this respect, Shiggy was accorded the highest possible honour – it was a Five Spud meal. One of the starters was prawn cocktail in a bed of shredded lettuce, set off with a discrete pat of home-made potato salad. The plates Peggy used for the main course were like bin lids. Along with the clutch of roasties that everybody naturally got, a generous helping of scalloped potatoes in cheese sauce was balanced between the broccoli and the cauliflower. A steaming dish of parsnip colcannon was placed at either end of the table for easy access and, when they were all done with their roast duck, a small beaker of chilled potato, ginger and coriander soup was placed before their disbelieving eyes.

'To clear your palate,' said Peggy, smiling at Aesop.

'I cleared mine before I came out,' whispered Aesop to the table, as she disappeared again to start fetching desserts.

'Are you being cheeky in there, Aesop Murray?' she called from the fridge. 'I'll give you a clip on the ear, so I will.'

'Sorry Peggy. I was just saying that I don't know where me palate is, but I think it's going to need all the help it can get after this feed. I swear I won't be able to eat again till Wednesday.'

Norman was leaning back in his chair, one hand on his belly, groaning. Then Peggy arrived in with a four-inch-high pavlova topped with fresh fruit and he glanced around with a resigned look on his face.

'Stand back lads. This mightn't be pretty …'

They were sitting around later, sipping on Irish coffees and nervously eyeing the apple slices when Jimmy tapped a spoon on his glass.

'Can I just say something quickly, while everybody is here?'

They all looked at him, glad to be distracted from the straining buttons, zips and clasps on their trousers.

'Just a little something about someone here who I know we all think a lot of.'

'Jaysis, Jimmy,' said Aesop, hiding his face behind his hand. 'Don't embarrass me now in front of everyone.'

Jennifer gave him an elbow.

'Will you ever give over and let Jimmy speak.'

'Thanks Jen. Give him another scone there, might shut him up. Well, I just wanted to say Shiggy, from all of us, it's been great to have you here and I wanted to wish you all the best when you head back to Japan. We'll miss you as mates and, of course, in the band and I hope we all get together again some time and have a laugh, play a couple of gigs and all that. Eh … so how about you pick up all your glasses there … Right? Everyone got one? … To Shiggy! *Sláinte*!'

'*Sláinte*!' they all said, raising glasses in the air.

Shiggy beamed red and bowed at everyone.

'That was a great speech, Jimmy,' said Aesop. 'How long have you been working on that?'

'Don't make me swear in front of my mother, Aesop,' said Jimmy.

Shiggy stood up with his glass of coffee.

'Sank you Jimmy. Sank you berry much.'

He put down his glass and paused to clear his throat.

'When I come to Ireland, I leave my famiry behind. In Japan, famiry so important. And I leave my friends. Pretty scary. Engrish not so good. Don't understand many things when I get here … big dinners like this, big beer in pub tsoo! Many things berry difficult for me.' He bowed his head again. '*Honto ni*.' He looked up. 'But then Marco come and say harro in work and he such a nice guy. I have a friend then.' He looked at Marco and smiled. 'Sank you Marco. And I wish that you and Jennifer will be happy for all of your lifes together. You will be, I know. Two special people rike you. You always smiling. Always happy to see me. I will miss you.'

He turned to Norman and Aesop.

'And you two! I learn many things. I know everysing about Cork, even though I never go there. I sink it best place in the world, *ne* Norman? One day, we go together. Play crazy hurling game? Aesop, I also learn many things, but … hmm … cannot say in front of Mrs Corrins-san, *desho*? We have good times with Grove and in pub. I miss that tsoo. I try to teach you, with jazz, but you say it only devil-music. But one day I will teach you!

'Jimmy, praying music with The Grove was the best time in my rife. Really. So sorry to reave, but must go home to Japan. When I sink of the most special time, I remember you write a song for a girl you love. That song, "Caillte", I will always pray when I sink of you in Japan. Because a guy who can write song like that … so much bad trouble in world today … people need song like that. Write more. You have special talent, and special heart. Never forget that when rockstar, *ne*? More important than rockstar.

'Mr Corrins-san, Mrs Corrins-san, I already say I have no famiry here. But you always welcome me in your house. Give me such dericious foods and always make sure everysing okay. Ask how I am and how is work. How is everysing back in Japan. Always …'

He wiped away the tear that spilled over and ran down his cheek.

'… Always I feel rike this is my home when I come here. Many times now I come. So now, I sink, I have famiry here. I hope it is okay. You all are my famiry. Irish parents, Irish brother and sister. When I go home tomorrow I will be sad again, because I am leaving my famiry again. But, *ne*, I am rucky tsoo. Because now I have two famiry.'

He bowed low.

'*Domo arigato gozaimasu. O-tsukare-sama deshita.*'

He looked up. They were all staring at him, stunned. Jennifer and Peggy were blubbing.

'*Domo,*' he said again, with a small smile.

Norman was the first out of his chair, smothering him in a big hug. The rest of them all took turns. Peggy went off to clean up her face as the others sat down again, happy and sad.

Aesop clapped his hands and looked around.

'Now let's hear Jimmy's speech again!'

THEY HEADED to the pub later.

'God, Shiggy,' said Norman. 'Are you sure you're going home tomorrow? Because I can't take too many more of these farewell parties. This is the last one, right?'

'Yep. Rast one. Rast Guinness before I go home.'

It was a good night. Probably a bit too good for a Sunday, considering the early start in the morning, but worth it. There was a trad band on and Jimmy knew the bodhrán player from school. He got up and sang 'The Blower's Daughter' with them. He hadn't done this type of thing for ages, just playing very casually for fun, and actually thought that he was going to upstage the lads on the stage, he'd done such a cool job on it. But then one of the lads sang 'The Lakes of Ponchartrain' unaccompanied, dedicating it to the people of New Orleans. It was soaring and haunting and beautiful and Jimmy had to sit there and admit to himself that the guy had blown him out of the water. The entire pub listened in rapt silence as his eerie voice and those plaintive, despairing lyrics teased the hairs on the back of Jimmy's neck like an evening breeze. The song over, he just thanked everyone and picked up his guitar for the next number. No fuss.

Jimmy watched and felt like a complete prat. That's what happens when you go around thinking you're God's gift to music! He smiled to himself and made a few mental notes about not turning into an arsehole if The Grove ever really took off. Then he bought the CD that the lads were selling, to balance out the karma, and got back to enjoying his pint.

Aesop came back with a round of drinks. He had a puzzled expression on his face as he slowly put the glasses on the table and sat down, glancing back towards the bar. Then he turned around.

'Where's your prostate?' he suddenly said to Norman.

Norman picked up his pint and looked sideways at him.

'It's up me hole, Aesop. Where's yours?'

'Oh is it? I was just wondering. There's a couple of oul lads up there and one of them was giving out about his. It's enlarged apparently. What does it do?'

He looked around. No one seemed sure.

'I read that a bloke's G-spot is in his prostate,' said Jimmy.

'Up his … ?' said Aesop. 'But what bleedin use is a G-spot up your arse?'

Jimmy shrugged.

'It was in a book about the War. Apparently, military medics used to give prostate massages to soldiers who hadn't had any in months. So they'd clean their pipes and not be thinking about gee the whole time.'

'You're taking the piss!' said Norman. 'I never heard of that in the army.'

'Well, it's true.'

That was food for thought. They all took a drink, looking off into the distance.

'I wonder do girls have prostates?' said Norman.

'Nah. I don't think so. Isn't it something to do with, y'know, your load?'

'Is it?'

'I think it is.'

'But doesn't that not come from your balls?'

'Maybe not all of it.'

They hadn't noticed that Jennifer was back from the toilet

and standing there looking at them with her arms folded. She picked up her vodka and finished it without sitting down, then grabbed her coat.

'Thanks guys. Thanks for that. I was hoping we'd finish the evening off with a nice chat about your balls.'

She kissed Marco on the cheek.

'Seeya later, babe. I'll leave you with these gobshites and go home to my *leaba*. Seeya tomorrow.'

She gave Shiggy a big hug and a kiss to say goodbye and turned around to them all.

'There's a feckin library across the road, you know. Would it kill you to learn what's going on inside your own bodies, would it? How old are you all now anyway? Eejits.' She lifted her bag onto her shoulder. 'And just for your information, the prostate gland is where some of the semen is made. It can cause problems in older men, you're supposed to get it checked out every year or so and, no, we don't have them.'

She left them all looking at her, swung around and went out the door.

They turned back to the table and looked at their pints for a minute.

Aesop looked up.

'See that Shiggy? And you going on about Japanese women? Irish women can be strong fuckers too. She loved that and then the big exit with her head in the air like we're all dopes. Did you see? Fuck sake, I wouldn't mind but she was wrong.'

'Are you sure?' said Jimmy.

'Positive,' said Aesop.

He took a slug of his pint and pointed out the window with his thumb.

'That's a school.'

Five

JIMMY HAD lunch with Dónal on Tuesday. Sultan were after coming back with two bookings for London in a month's time and needed to confirm with Dónal and the lads. They were paying for everything – flights, accommodation, meals, the works. There'd probably be another couple of gigs organised once they got there. The trip would take in two weekends. It was up to The Grove whether they flew back and forth or just stayed in London for the ten days.

'They're serious, Jimmy,' said Dónal. 'I can't remember the last time they did something like this. I've got a feeling that the whole Sultan angle is just playing it quiet. I think I know what she's up to. This is Senturian money, Jimmy. Has to be. I think this could be big. If it is Senturian … and they want you …'

He tapped a coaster on the table.

Jimmy looked down at his sandwich. He'd stopped eating almost as soon as Dónal had started talking. The bit he'd had was stuck in him and taking big gulps of water wasn't doing much to budge it.

'Fuckin hell Dónal,' he said, twirling the little flag that was stuck in the top slice of bread. 'That's brilliant. But … I don't know what to say. This is just … it's all getting mad.' He sat back and folded his arms, looking at him.

'You don't know what to say?' said Dónal. 'Okay. So we've got a problem, do we?'

Jimmy sighed.

'Kind of.'

'It's not Shiggy is it? We've got two blokes ready to audition, Jimmy.'

'I know. I know. It's not that. Dónal, all I ever wanted is exactly what we're talking about. But it was like winning the lottery, y'know? It was never actually going to happen. And now it might. Only might, though. Jesus, I'm thirty fucking two years old. This bastard phone has rung twice since we sat down. I've a budget meeting in an hour to discuss how we're going to come up with a million euro for a development centre we're setting up with Kyotosei in the middle of bleedin India somewhere. I've staff problems and deadline problems and a prick in New York that calls me up in the middle of the night to talk about fucking documentation standards. I'm working sixty-hour weeks most of the time, and another thirty or so on the band. I'm starting to fucking lose it, Dónal. I'm cocking things up in the office and by the time I meet you lot for a gig or rehearsal my head is bleedin wrecked with it all and I can't concentrate on what we're doing. Y'know? It's like real life is getting away from me because I'm on the doss and living half of it in fucking La La land.'

'What does Aesop say about it all?'

'Aesop? Dónal, Aesop is having a bad day if the binman wakes him up before ten o'clock. I told him last week exactly what I told you now and he just looked off into the distance and said he always wanted to ride a girl from India.'

Dónal smiled. 'But all this affects him too.'

'I know,' Jimmy sighed. 'And that doesn't fucking help either.'

'All right,' said Dónal. 'Look, why don't you just take the rest of the week off? No rehearsals or anything. Just try and relax and I'll talk to you at the weekend, okay? Jimmy, I know what you're saying. I do. You know what I think you should do, but it's not up to me. This business is a real fucker and I'd be lying to you if I said otherwise. Let's just take it step by step. We'll do London and see what happens, right? Maybe they'll give us a million quid to make the album and then none of us has to worry about it anymore.'

He looked at his watch and gathered his coat from the back of the seat next to him.

'Sorry Jimmy, but I have to get out of here. Listen, for what it's worth, I think you've got as good a chance of making it as I've seen. And I think the only regret you'll have is not giving it a go. But I think you know that already. Give me a shout if you need anything.'

He headed off out of the café, leaving Jimmy to stare at the small mound of salt he'd poured onto the plate in front of him.

'I KNOW what you need,' said Aesop.

He was scabbing dinner at Jimmy's because his Dad was out with his golf mates and Jennifer was at the cinema with Marco and he didn't feel like eating beans on toast.

'I'm sure you do,' said Jimmy. 'Does it involve a woman?'

'At least one. Will we go out?'

'I'm too tired Aesop. I was in work early today and yesterday, and yesterday was a killer after those pints on Sunday.'

'Poor Jimmy. When was the last time you had a portion?'

'Piss off Aesop.'

'When was it?'

'I don't know.'

'It was Sandra, wasn't it?'

Jimmy nodded.

'Ah, sure then it's no fuckin wonder you're all messed up in the head, Jimmy. That was ages ago. Your lad is screaming out to be cuddled and you're too busy checking your messages. You need a woman, man. I know you can be a terrible sap about relationships and deep-and-meaningfuls and fuckin getting to know people, but it doesn't have to be as complicated as you always want to make it. Like fuckin Superchick ... God, what a load of ...'

'Ask me arse, Aesop. Anyway, I'm not even thinking about that stuff now. How can I? Amn't I after telling you how busy I am? Where am I supposed to fit a girl into all that?'

'Fuck sake, I'm not telling you to start clearing a shelf in the hot press for her knickers, am I? Why do you always think women are so different from us? There's plenty of women out there who're more than happy just for a bit of company. They're all out working their bollocks off too, y'know. Where are they supposed to get the time to date some fucker for six months and meet his Ma and his dopey mates and put up with all his shite as well as their own and then maybe – maybe – find out that he's actually an all-right bloke and worth getting serious about? If it happens it happens but most of the time they're only interested in going out for a pint and a laugh with their mates. And a half-decent jant on a bloke that seems to like them is a lot better than a taxi home on your own to an empty gaff and a fucking big bowl of ice cream.'

Jimmy stared at him over his spaghetti.

'Where in the name of fuck did you come up with all that? Are you telling me now that you have the whole thing sussed?'

'Jimmy, get your head out of your pipe, will ye? It's all over the place! Do you never watch the telly?'

'I don't have time for the fuckin telly.'

'Well make time! You might learn something. Times are changing, Jimmy. That's why I'm a metrosexual now. Look …'

He pulled a packet of tissues out of his pocket and held them up.

'See?'

He pointed to the pack and winked.

'Infused with emu oil. You know what these tissues say to chicks?'

'You hate emus?'

'No. They say that I'm on the same wavelength as they are. We're all grown up now. Women our age dig tissues, man. They're always spilling things or cleaning their fingers or crying. Pull these babies out in the pub and hand them over, and the next thing you know she's looking for her handbag and kissing her mates goodnight. Subtle, but effective. I'm all about subtlety now, Jimmy. But here you are, acting like you're bleedin twenty years old. Do you think women in your position are all out there playing hard to get and looking for true fuckin love? They're not that stupid, Jimmy. They've got jobs and gaffs and cars and they'll settle down when they're good and fuckin ready to. In the meantime they're going out and enjoying themselves and doing what they want to do and taking things as they come. Well, at least until they hit about thirty-five, thirty-six. Then they start shitting themselves and marry the next fuckin eejit who buys them a drink and … eh … what were we talking about? Oh yeah. Your problem is that you're not looking after yourself properly and you're going to make yourself sick.'

Jimmy shook his head and pushed the plate away from him.

'My problem, Doctor fucking Phil, is that I'm up to my tits. I can't sleep properly, me back and neck are killing me the whole time, the bastard phone won't stop ringing all day and I can taste everything I eat for about six bleedin hours afterwards. In the meantime I'm being asked to give up twenty years of hard work to make a fucking record that maybe no bastard will want to listen to.'

Aesop sat forward suddenly and pointed at Jimmy.

'I wonder do you have an enlarged prostate as well? Y'know, because yours must be at bursting point at this stage, mustn't it? If it's where you keep your spadge, like.'

'It wouldn't surprise me, Aesop,' said Jimmy, sitting up straight to stretch out his back and wincing. 'But I don't have time to do anything about that just now.'

'Jesus, look at the state of you.'

'You don't need to tell me.' He was rocking back and forth with his arms up above his head. 'Ma goes and gets these massages every couple of weeks. You know the way her back is. Says she feels brilliant after them. I was thinking of giving it a go. Y'know? A massage and then a big sauna and all that with a nice cold beer. No phone or anyone annoying me.'

'A weekend thing? Sounds brilliant. We'll all go!'

Jimmy laughed. 'A weekend away with you, the state I'm in? Are you mad? No, just me and some big fucker beating the knots out of me back.'

'A bloke? Bleedin hell. What if he's a shirt lifter?'

'Yeah, well I'll see if I can find one that isn't. I'm sure they have them.'

'Hmm. Not sure I'd be into that. Some fucker touching me. You wouldn't know where he's been.'

'Where would he have been?'

'Ah, there's some strange people out there, Jimmy. What if he's the kind of bloke who goes home at night and makes model airplanes out of his dog's shite or something?'

'What?'

'I'm just saying, like. Then he comes into work the next day and starts rubbing your back. You see what I mean? Or maybe he likes his missus to piss on him, y'know? Like them Germans.'

'What? What Germans? Aesop, why the fuck should he be into something like that?'

'Look what he chose to do for a living, Jimmy. Is that normal? What did he say in school? He goes into his career guidance counsellor and says, "I'll tell you what I'm after. I want a job where men take off all their clothes and let me rub oil into them." "Right so," says yer man, looking down his list of requirements. "This might suit you. Do you like the smell of piss by any chance?"'

Jimmy started to laugh.

'I'm sure I'll be all right. I'll ask him beforehand.'

'Yeah, well. Better you than me. Just don't get too relaxed lying there or you might fall asleep and the next thing he'll be wearing your jocks on his head and pushing raisins up your hole to nibble on later. I'm telling you Jimmy, I've seen magazines …'

'Aesop, on balance I think I'd be pretty unlucky to go in there for a massage and end up being the bloke's gimp.'

'Maybe so, Jimmy. But do yourself a favour and if the bloke comes over and introduces himself as Gunter, you kick him in the cherries and run like the fuckin wind out of there. Now, c'mon to fuck and we'll go for a pint. Give Norman a call and we'll meet him in the pub.'

'Aesop, I'm tired.'

'And I'm tired of looking at the moany fuckin head on you. Now get your coat and let's go and have a scoop. And leave that bleedin phone here, will ye? You're not the only one who has to listen to the fuckin thing going off all night long when you're trying to enjoy your pint. You're not a doctor or a fireman or ... or that bloke that drives the boat out to dopey cunts that can't swim.'

'The coastguard?'

'Yeah. You're not him either. So whatever it is, it can wait till tomorrow, right?

Jimmy shook his head, stood up and looked around for his coat.

'Isn't it well for me that I have you here to sort out my life for me?' he said.

'You're blessed,' said Aesop, grabbing Jimmy's half-full plate and shovelling a few quick forkfuls into his mouth. He drained his glass of milk and looked over at the press next to the fridge. 'Do you have any buns?'

'Fuck sake. How are you fixed for jocks?'

JIMMY THREW up again that night. They only had about four pints each and then headed home, but about three in the morning he woke up to feel the beer and meat sauce squirming its way into the back of his throat and he jumped out of bed and into the bathroom to relieve himself of it. He washed and dried his face and went back to bed, thinking that things were starting to get a bit strange. He often made a huge pot of meat sauce and froze the excess in small plastic bowls for some other time, but what he'd eaten today had been absolutely fresh. Even the spaghetti was straight from the shop. And he'd never had a bad pint in the Fluther in fifteen years of drinking there.

Four hours later, when his Weetabix came burning straight up too, he called in sick and went around to the doctor. He hadn't been to the doctor in years.

She asked him some questions and then got him to lie on the bed as she prodded his belly and felt around his neck. Then there were more questions.

'Do you skip meals?'

She had a faint accent. European. Italian or Spanish or something.

'Kind of. I don't eat lunch most days. Just a sandwich if I do.'

'Smoke?'

'Not really. A few at the weekend maybe. And, eh, a spliff now and again, but I haven't had one in about a month.'

'Other drugs? Prescription?'

'No.'

'Alcohol?'

'Yes.'

'How much do you drink?'

'Eh … well …'

'In a week. How many drinks?'

Jimmy started counting in his head.

'Eh … I suppose I might have about twenty pints. Maybe more if I'm on a big one at the weekend. A bottle of wine the odd time. A few whiskies or brandy if I'm playing poker. Eh, I had some tequila at the weekend, but I don't drink that if I can help it. Awful stuff. That's about it. Maybe a beer at night if there's something good on the telly and I can't sleep, but … God, it sounds like a lot when I say it out loud, doesn't it?'

He smiled but she didn't smile back.

'In other countries, Mr Collins, you'd be considered an alcoholic. Here, though, you're only slightly above average. But you need to cut down. Drastically. I'll be sending you for blood tests after this to see just how much damage you've done to your liver. Among other things.'

Jimmy swallowed and felt a cold rush up his back. For fuck sake. Was he really sick?

'Sports? Are you a member of a gym?'

'No. I don't really have time.'

'Allergies?'

'No. Well ... just Slime I think.'

'Slime?'

'Yeah. You know that stuff when you're a kid? It's purple and has these rubber worms in it. There was a green one too.'

She shook her head, frowning at him.

'Comes in a little plastic bin. I got it off Santy one year and it gave me a rash on my fingers. And my leg as well, actually, because I lost the bin and used to keep it in my pocket until it went hard and Ma threw it out.'

She tapped her pen on the pad for a minute, looking at him.

'Mr Collins, have you had an allergic reaction to anything in the last twenty-five years?'

'No. I don't think so.'

'Thank you.'

Jimmy sat and answered her questions, but now he was starting to get a bit worried. This fucking doctor was way too serious. Did she suspect something was up or did she just like being a scary fucker to all her patients?

'Are you sexually active?'

Jesus fucking Christ.

'No. Not really. Not in the last few months. Eh ... you mean with someone else, right?'

Eventually she stood up and put on a latex glove. Jesus, thought Jimmy two minutes later, as he gripped the table, some fucking G-spot. It must work differently in women.

'I suspect, Mr Collins, that you have a peptic ulcer,' she said afterwards. 'I'll have a better idea after the blood tests, but in the meantime I want you to stop drinking alcohol and caffeine. Stop smoking too. Take your meals regularly and sleep at least eight hours a night if you can. Avoid aspirin and ibuprofen and other nonsteroidal anti-inflammatory drugs. It will say on the box. I don't believe there are complications at this point, but we'll just have to see. Avoid stressful situations at work and at home if possible. I'll call you when the results of the blood tests come back.'

She stood up to shake his hand.

'Goodbye Mr Collins.'

She still wouldn't fucking smile at him.

'Thanks Doctor. Bye.' He took the slip of paper that she gave him for the blood tests and walked out of the surgery into the cold morning light, feeling numb from the shoulders up.

When he was done at the blood place, he headed into the office and did a Google on 'Peptic Ulcer'. He read about perforations and peritonitis and pyloroplastic surgery and just knew that he had the works. Every poxy little thing that could invade his guts had done so and now it was only a matter of time before he was going to have to live the rest of his life shitting out a tube. He'd never be able to drink again or eat steak again and if his sex life was a bit slow this weather, what the fuck would it be like if he had to hide a plastic bag of shite under his shirt when he was down the pub? He closed the door of his office and sat there with his face in his hands. Not to mention the fucking slagging he'd get from Aesop.

The phone rang. He was going to ignore it, but saw from the caller id that it was Simon.

'Hey Simon.'

'Hi Jimmy. Listen, can you come into me for a minute. Bit of a thing here, I'm afraid, and I think you might be able to help.'

'No problem. I'll be there in two minutes.'

Jimmy sat back and looked at the ceiling. A bit of a thing is fucking right.

In Simon's office, Jimmy sat at the desk and waited until Simon got off the phone.

'Jimmy,' said Simon, 'Brad Kowalski has been on to me.'

Kowalski was that fucking eejit in New York. The one who thought people were only put on this planet to listen to him talk through his hole all day. Jimmy sighed and nodded.

'You get on with him, right?'

'Only because I have to. He wouldn't take the time and materials contract and now he's holding back payment on the analysis deliverable until we supply the documentation in some bloody format that even his head of IT thinks is ridiculous. We never even said we would. I've been back and forth with him all month. That's a five-hundred page document, Simon, and he just wants us to code it up into his intranet for free and cross reference the whole thing to what he's already got. I don't have the time for that Simon. And anyway, he's just chancing his arm.'

'Yeah. He sounded like a bit of an eejit all right. But still, that's an important contract, Jimmy. It's a small one, but a foot in the door of a couple of those banks in New York and we're suddenly looking very good, you know?'

'I don't know what to tell you, Simon. I'd have to put someone on it for three weeks and I don't have anyone. What was he in your ear for anyway?'

'Well that's just it. He seems to think you're the best thing that's ever happened to him, Jimmy. We talked about the documentation and I got the impression that he'll let it go if he can have you for a few days to show off to his people over there. He was talking up that Margin project too.'

'What do you mean "have me"?'

'Have you in New York. He wants you to fly out for a week, brief them on Eirotech Solutions and present the proposals for phases two and three in person. Said he wants to show you around too.'

'But Billy's already out there!'

'I know, but he wants you. He's pretty impressed with you, Jimmy. I don't know what you've been telling him.'

'You should hear what I haven't been telling him. Christ Simon, I'm already up to my eyes. A week in New York? Marco's going to Marketing and I'm trying to get Cathy up to speed on his stuff.'

'Yeah. Actually, I was going to say to you that we hold Marco back here for another little while. Till things cool down a bit, you know?'

Jimmy looked at him. This was just fucking typical. He was about to say something else but saw that Simon was straightening papers on his desk now. That meant they were done discussing.

'When?' he said.

'In a couple of weeks. I told Brad you were busy, so it'd take a couple of weeks to sort it out.'

Ah right. So it was already all fucking decided then, was it?

'And Marco?'

'Can you let him know the score? Tell him it'll just be another two or three months. I already spoke to Martin at lunch and he's fine with it. Listen Jimmy, I know you're already working real hard but this is top priority. Keeping Kowalski happy could get us a lot of business in the States and I really appreciate you going out there and doing your thing for him.'

'No problem,' said Jimmy. You geebag. And I suppose you appreciate me having to break the news to Marco too, cheeky fucker.

Back at his desk he closed the page that was still open on his computer. He didn't want to know anymore about the horrors that could be visited upon him by ulcers and infections and damage to his liver. He'd had enough good news for one day. He was about to start looking through his email when a sour burp made him wince and hold two fingers in against the top of his belly to relieve the burning pain. He went down to get some antacids and munched at them back at his desk, the afternoon dragging on for what seemed like ages as he tried to catch up on the morning he'd spent having a grumpy fucking Italian lady's finger up his arse and being told he was a dipso.

'Avoid stressful situations at work and at home,' the doctor had ordered. She'd bloody kill him if she could see him now.

He left the office early and headed around to his Mam's for dinner. He wasn't about to tell her that he was sick – Christ, no – but he decided that he needed someone to make a fuss over him and not ask for anything in return. Peggy was the only person in the world who did that. She'd talk about anything and everything and feed him spuds and buns and make him sit down with the paper in front of the telly with his feet up and annoy his Dad into having a conversation with him. She'd laugh and joke with him about whatever was going on in the world and get excited about his sister's wedding, which was coming up next year. She was the only one who wasn't constantly at him to do stuff. It was brilliant.

And a bit fucking sad too, now that he thought about it.

Six

JIMMY WENT back to Dr Santos on Monday morning and sat in the waiting room with two women and their bored, sniffling brats. His stomach was in knots but it was nothing to do with being sick. He was shitting himself about what she was going to tell him. One of the women tried to talk to him but he couldn't muster up more than a few pleasantries and then just sat there morosely looking at a magazine and wondering how they could 'scientifically prove' that a conditioner could make your hair up to six times softer. How the fuck did you measure softness? It was putting him in a bad mood. And fifty per cent more bounce? Get fucked.

He threw the magazine onto the seat beside him and was about to pick up one about sailing when the light went on over the door to say it was his turn. He stood up with a lurch, fit to puke with the nerves, and made his way into the surgery.

'Hello, Mr Collins.'

'Doctor,' he nodded back, and did a quick scan of the desk to see if there were any rubber gloves sitting there ready to go. His hands were cold and wet.

'Well, your tests came back this morning.'

Jimmy nodded again. His mouth was dry and sticky. Christ, why was it so cold in here? The walls, ceiling and floor were all in white tiles. It was like a bleedin morgue.

'It could be an ulcer ...'

'Shit,' said Jimmy, under his breath.

'... but I don't think so.'

'No? Okay. Okay. Well, that's good, right?'

'Mr Collins, have you ever heard of Gastro Oesophageal Reflux Disease?'

'Oh holy fuck. No. What's that?'

His balls suddenly felt like marbles.

'You might be suffering from a mild case.'

He took his hands away from his mouth.

'A mild case?' Mild cases were good. 'Of Castro Essogelle …'

'Gastro Oesophageal Reflux Disease.'

'Gastro Essofigal … Gastro Ess …'

'Or it might just be heartburn.'

He stopped trying to pronounce it.

'Heartburn?'

Was she fucking winding him up?

'Yes. You're quite healthy, actually. I'm more concerned about your drinking habits. Your liver seems fine, but you really should cut down. You see …'

'Eh, Doctor?' He held up his hand.

'Yes?'

'This horrible disease you were talking about? The one I might have a mild case of?'

'Gastro Oesophag …'

'That's the one. What is it?'

'Well, the acid in your stomach is ejected back into the oesophagus. That's the pain you feel. It can get quite nasty in chronic cases, but in your case I think you just need to watch what you eat and drink and try to relax a bit more. It's really very common and not something you should get too worried about as long as you look after yourself. In any case, there are treatments …'

'And you're sure it's not an ulcer? So there's no risk of perforations or gastric obstruction?'

The doctor sat back.

'You've been on the Internet, haven't you?'

Jimmy nodded.

She sighed.

'I'm pretty sure you're in the clear, but I'm going to give you a prescription anyway and I want you to come back to me in a couple of weeks.'

'But no upper endoscopy? Did you check for peritoneal leakage?'

She looked at him.

'Discovery Channel,' he said, with a small shrug.

'Mr Collins, I attended medical school to become a doctor. Some people find that the best way. I can assure you that I know what I'm talking about. If you're unsure about any of my diagnoses, I could easily schedule you to be examined again by Dr Mugabe. He is an excellent doctor.'

'No. No, it's fine …'

'Are you sure? Let's see, what did we do … blood, endo, rectal …'

'No! It's fine. Thanks doctor, I'm good. Just happy that I'm not sick. I was having visions of eating pea soup for the rest of me life. I'm just excited. I'm really okay?'

'I wouldn't quite say that, Mr Collins. You appear to have more than a few stress-related symptoms. You need to slow down. Reduce your alcohol and caffeine intake. Stop smoking. Go out and take a walk in a park in the evenings or something. Now please, take this fact sheet, bring this one to the chemist and try and take some time off from work if you can. It seems to me that a holiday would do you good. I'll see you next month.'

'Sure. No problem. No problem at all.' He paused. 'Oh, by the way, how is … eh … y'know …' He leaned to one side and made a small, embarrassed pointing gesture at his arse.

'It's fine Mr Collins.'

'It's not too … y'know … it's not too full or anything, is it?'

'Full?'

She put down her pen and took off her glasses.

'Full? Mr Collins, please stop reading up on these things unless you're prepared to do it properly. You'll only upset yourself. It's fine. I'll be only too glad to take another look for you next year, but right now I've got other patients.'

'Grand, grand. God, that's great though, isn't it? I thought I was on me way out there for a minute.'

'Goodbye Mr Collins.'

'Seeya, Doctor. And thanks.'

'You're welcome.'

He walked out the door laughing to himself.

'Heartburn … for fuck sake.'

He checked his watch when he got out on the street and cursed. He was gagging for a pint after all that but it was way too early. He turned and headed into work instead, wondering as he did exactly what medical school she went to where they taught you to tell patients all about diseases they didn't fucking have.

HE GOT confirmation that afternoon. He'd be in New York for the first London gig. It wasn't even work. They'd be finished work on the Friday but Kowalski had that weekend lined up to show him the sights and Simon 'couldn't impress enough' on Jimmy how important it was that he keep the stupid fucker happy. He'd be flying back to Dublin on the Monday morning … Eirotech Solution's bitch.

Jimmy called Dónal and Dónal got onto Sultan. It turned out that one weekend wasn't enough to get a feel for The Grove and they'd decided to cancel both London weekends and re-schedule.

'Except, Jimmy,' said Dónal. 'They haven't re-scheduled. There's no date. It's on the long finger now and we'll just have to wait and see. I'll keep at them to see that they don't forget about us, but there's a lot of bands out there, y'know? I really don't know what's going to happen. At least we've time to find a bass player, but …'

Jimmy was still relieved to know that he wouldn't have to be fitted for a colostomy bag, but he felt like he was letting the lads down in a big way and he hated the situation he was in. He started to check the Web for holiday ideas. He hadn't really gone away in years. A long weekend in Prague with Aesop and Norman just after Christmas and one in Boston on his own in March to meet up with his sister who'd flown in from Chicago with her fiancé. But the last proper holiday he'd had was eighteen months ago in Spain with Sandra.

He still missed Sandra. The fact that she'd left him for Beano, one of the biggest plonkers in Dublin, had really hurt him at the time, but that was mostly gone now. The edges to it were anyway, leaving just a kind of numb sadness when he thought about her, something he didn't really do too often anyway. But when he was down – and lately that was a fair bit – and on his own at home, he'd think of her then and remember that he'd really loved her. Maybe things had gotten a bit routine, a bit settled, near the end. Maybe that's why she dumped him for that other tool. But, fuck it, they'd had some good times.

He missed walking around with a babe and knowing that they made a great couple in everyone's eyes. He missed their quiet nights in when neither of them had something on. He missed stupid things like arguing over whose turn it was to empty the dishwasher. And of course he missed the intimacy a lot too. Love-making. Knowing her so well that way. The physical side of it, sure, but not just that. The stillness afterwards, when they were just lying there. All the shit going on in the world around them and all the shit going on in their own lives … it was still going on but when they were together like that, it was like ducking into a cave and taking shelter from it. That's what he missed most about his time with Sandra. There was just no fucking escape anymore. Music and gigs and chanting crowds came close when it was happening, but they were also part of the problem. They added to the pressure because he had to follow them up with more gigs and more performances. He never got to switch off. He never … he never got to unload any of his shit on someone else. Although that's probably not how they phrased it in the magazines.

On the upside, Greenpeace, Amnesty and Médicins Sans Frontières had stopped sending shit to his address and making him feel guilty. She'd been into all that.

He settled on Greece. He was up to his goolies, but decided

that he wanted to get away on his own and chill out on an island somewhere and if that didn't suit everyone, they could talk to his doctor. She'd said he had to go. That was his excuse and he was sticking to it. This place he'd found, Mykonos, sounded like the bollocks. He'd never been anywhere like that. Spain was lovely but it was full of noisy fuckers, frantically having a good time and getting pissed and sunburnt. He was after somewhere quiet and different where the weather was good and there was no reception on his phone. Sun, beaches, wine, old ruins. It looked perfect. He checked what was coming up in work and decided that two weeks after New York he was off. Ten days of relaxation. Then he went in to see Simon.

It was the day before he was due to take off for JFK and he figured that it would take Simon by surprise and there wouldn't be time for him to try and *plámás* him out of it, which he'd probably have a go at anyway.

'Jimmy,' said Simon, when Jimmy knocked and came into his office. 'Just the man. Listen, bit of good news for you!'

'Great. What's the story?'

'You're not going to believe it. Sit down there.'

Jimmy sat down.

'Kowalski's gone,' said Simon.

'Gone?'

'Yep. Apparently some big bonus came through for him yesterday and he packed up his desk and walked out. Do you know what he's doing?'

Jimmy shook his head.

'He's opening up a health food shop. Getting out of the business altogether. Isn't that gas?'

Jimmy just looked at him. This better not fucking mean …

'So, obviously, the trip is off. That's the good news. I know you weren't keen on the idea. Billy's arranged meetings all next week with his replacement to get him up to speed, but we're pretty much starting from scratch as far as the client relationship goes. Luckily, they're tied in to the contract for the moment so it should work out, please God. Anyway, I just wanted to spread the gospel myself. Wotcha think?'

Jimmy thought of all the work that Dónal and the band had put in to get as far as they had with Sultan. He felt sick. They'd heard nothing back from Sultan in over a fortnight. Jimmy had put it all on the line and now some tofu-selling bastard had decided to jack it all in and leave him with no business trip, no gigs, no contract, no album.

'I need a holiday, Simon.'

Simon blinked at him. 'A holiday?'

'Yeah. I'm going to Greece. For ten days. I'm booking it this afternoon and I'm going in about two weeks.'

Simon frowned and started going through his desk diary.

'Jimmy, it's really not a good time, y'know? There's so much on at the moment. You've got that week in New York back again. I thought we'd keep Marco as planned and you could start working on that proposal for Merrill and leave him to …'

'No.' Jimmy put up his hand. 'I'm going to Greece.'

Simon saw the hand and closed his diary.

'But Jimmy, why don't you just wait till September? By then …'

'In September there'll be something else, Simon. I'm tired and I've been a bit sick and I need to get away.'

'How sick?'

'Sick enough. Sorry Simon, I've just had too much on my plate and I want a holiday.'

'Is it the band?'

'Part of it is, yeah.'

'God, Jimmy, y'know we've talked about this before. That's not where your future is. You know that, don't you? I know it's been going well and all, but it's not all it's cracked up to be. You know what the chances are of making it big at that lark? You're on the fast track here. In three years you'll be doing my job. In

72

ten years you'll be running the shop. I'm telling you. If the band is putting pressure on you …'

'Simon, you're right, okay? I know all that. It's all getting a bit much and that's why I'm going to Greece. To get my head straight. I'm going.'

Simon sat back, fingering his moustache.

'Jesus, Jimmy, if it's like that then of course you should go. Have a rest. Is ten days enough?'

Jimmy looked at him. He wasn't expecting that.

'Eh …'

Simon smiled.

'Listen, I'm not an eejit. You've worked your arse off here since day one and if you tell me you need a holiday, then off you go. I was in Florida for two weeks in April. It was brilliant. I played golf every day and ate about a million lobsters. Go. Enjoy.'

Jimmy suddenly felt lighter.

'Thanks Simon.'

'There's nothing to thank me for Jimmy. This place would be in the shit if it wasn't for the work you put in. I mean it, Jimmy. You deserve a good holiday. Actually … you know something … ?'

He sat up and stared off into space for a couple of seconds, tapping his pen on the desk. Then he looked back at Jimmy, frowning.

'You haven't booked Greece yet?'

'No.'

'Can you hang on for a couple of days?'

'Simon …'

'Jimmy, I have an idea. Listen, just let me make a few calls, right? I'll talk to you in a couple of days.'

'What kind of idea?'

'Just hang on, right? Trust me.'

Simon was smiling.

'It's just an idea. C'mere, why don't you go home for the afternoon? It's Friday. You might as well. Go on. I'll talk to you on Monday, right? Have a good weekend. At least Brad won't be bugging you.'

Jimmy looked at him and then stood up.

'Okay. Seeya Monday. You want to tell me what your idea is?'

'Need to check a few things first. But listen, either way, the holiday is on us, right? A bonus. You deserve it. I'll have the letter on your desk on Monday morning.'

Jimmy walked to the carpark. It was a bright, warm afternoon and he was feeling extremely good about himself. Suddenly he felt all special and appreciated. Fuck sake, was that all that was missing in his life?

Seven

JIMMY HAD a great weekend. Norman and himself drove to Cork on Saturday morning for no other reason than to go on the piss. They didn't even pretend to themselves that there was another reason for going. Aesop had to stay in Dublin for his granny's eightieth birthday. Since Jimmy was supposed to have been in New York there was nothing on anyway, and when Norman suggested Cork on Friday night it seemed like a brilliant idea. Out of the blue and spontaneous and a good laugh. Perfect.

They set off first thing and Norman practically sang all the way down in the car. He loved going to Cork. Even though he was from way out in the countryside, his Mam used to pack him off to Cork City for a few weeks every summer to stay with his cousins. After he moved to Dublin he still made the trip at least twice a year, and then got himself based there in Collins Barracks afterwards when he was in the army. For Norman, there was nothing about living in Dublin that held a match to Cork, city or country. Seeing the change in him as they got closer to the county border was like watching a superhero get closer to the source of his power. He wouldn't shut up talking and kept laughing and pointing out things through the window.

'Look Jimmy!' he suddenly shouted, the car swerving as he cocked his head to follow the flight of a bird to their left. They were just outside Mitchelstown.

'Fuck sake Norman,' said Jimmy, grabbing the dashboard and pushing himself back against his seat. 'Will you watch the bleedin road?'

'That was a White-winged Black Tern.'

'That's brilliant. What's that then? Are they rare?'

'Are they rare? Do you know fuck all, Jimmy?'

'I know fuck all about seagulls, Norman.'

'Seagulls?! Jesus, Jimmy, you need to get out more. What's that tree over there? The one hanging over the road.'

'Eh … an oak tree?'

Norman looked at him. The car wobbled again.

'Holy fu …' said Jimmy, the tree looming large in the windscreen before he managed to squeeze his eyes shut.

'An oak tree?' said Norman. He looked back to the road. 'Are you taking the piss? Did you not see it?'

'See it? Norman, I was nearly fucking in it! I don't know trees, okay? I don't know trees and I don't know seagulls or badgers or pheasants or bleedin White-winged Black Tits, okay? Will you stop asking me, will you, if you're going to crash the car every time I fucking give a wrong answer?'

'It was a hawthorn,' said Norman.

'Good. I won't forget that so.'

'It's the most common tree in Ireland.'

'Is it? Right. I'll remember that.'

'What's that one?'

'Ah Jaysis, Norman …'

'One more!'

Jimmy looked out the window.

'It's … eh … a Scots pine.'

'It's a rowan!'

'Norman, please. Unless it's covered in fucking tinsel and has the baby Jesus being born under it, I'm not going to know what kind of tree it is, right? They all look the same.'

'But a Scot's pine, Jimmy? It had berries on it!'

'Oh Jesus. Are we nearly there?'

They stopped in Fermoy for an early lunch. Jimmy murdered a pint and felt much better. The sooner Norman started his new job the better. He was far too excited.

Norman kept up the nature lesson all the way into Cork City, but at least he'd stopped asking Jimmy questions. It was cool, in a way. He was so happy and enthusiastic that it was easy to get caught up in it, and Jimmy didn't mind learning a thing or two once he wasn't being driven into a ditch.

They booked into a B&B near the university and dumped their bags, heading straight back down towards Patrick Street in search of a good pub. They got about two hundred metres before they walked past a cool-looking old place with no one in it. Jimmy checked his watch. It was half-past two. Time for a couple of scoops.

'Guinness please,' he said to the landlady.

'Murphys for me,' said Norman.

'Actually, I'll have a Murphys as well,' said Jimmy. 'Why not?'

He looked around as the pints were settling. There was a hurling game on the telly and Norman had already turned his stool around to face it. Jimmy knew he wouldn't be getting much conversation out of him until it was over.

The top two inches of Jimmy's pint slid down his throat. He gave it a second and then looked up at Norman, who was grinning at him.

'That's fuckin gorgeous!' he said.

Norman nodded.

'I knew you'd like it. Welcome to Cork, Jimmy.'

They clinked glasses and put two more pints on straight away.

Half an hour later Jimmy was feeling just fine, but was getting bored with the match. He looked at his watch.

'Why don't Cork just beat them?' he said to Norman. 'It's only Kilkenny for fuck sake.'

Norman glanced over at him.

'Yeah. Not the keenest student of the sport, are we Jimmy?' he said.

Cork did beat them in the end and Norman turned back to the bar with a huge grin. He decided that they should conduct a little experiment.

'Two pints each of Guinness, Murphys and Beamish, thanks very much,' he said.

The landlady didn't bat an eyelid. Up came six pints and she lined them out on the bar, three in front of each of them.

'Actually, you'd better give us a couple of small Paddys too,' said Jimmy, winking at Norman. 'To clear our palates, as Ma would say.'

The landlady put two small ones up and went off into the kitchen behind the bar. She came back with a loaf of homemade brown bread on a plate with a knife.

'Take a bite of this after the whiskey and before the stout,' she said, cutting up a couple of slices. She put down the knife. 'Ye might as well do it properly if you're going to do it at all.'

Two hours later and the lads were well on the way to being shitfaced, but happy in the knowledge that it had been an afternoon well spent. They'd educated themselves.

'Right, that's it. So what do we have?' said Jimmy, swaying on his stool.

Norman squinted down at the beer mat they'd been writing on.

'Guinness,' he said. 'Creamy, smooth, hoppy.'

Jimmy nodded.

'Murphys,' Norman went on. 'Creamy, nutty, oaty. Is oaty a word?'

'Don't know. Is hoppy?'

Norman shrugged and burped. The beer mat fell onto the ground and he went after it.

'Beamish,' he said when he reappeared. 'Milky, burnt, toasty.'

'Jaysis, that could be your breakfast stout. But I'm not sure about toasty. It means warm. I meant it to mean "tastes like toast".'

'Toast-like?' said Norman.

'Perfect. Toast-like. Go on.'

'Right. Paddy. Eh … I can't read that …'

Jimmy peered at the beer mat.

'Earthy.'

'Oh right. Earthy. Earthy, peaty, raw.'

'Peaty. You know Aesop's Uncle Petey? Did you know that's how Wonky got his name?'

78

'No. How?'

'Cos his Da, Uncle Petey, had polio. Left him with a terrible limp.'

'Oh, right,' said Norman. 'I was wondering about that. Wonky doesn't limp though?'

'No. Just Petey. Or Gammy, his mates call him.'

'Bushmills Single Malt. Smooth, creamy, delicate.'

'That's a bit like the Guinness. Can we change smooth to something else? Eh … silky?'

'Nice one Jimmy.'

Norman scribbled it in.

'Powers. Gravelly, mucky, peaty.'

'Yeah. But it sounds like we're being a bit hard on Powers. I liked it.'

'I did too. But we were running out of words, Jimmy.'

'Yeah. Still, but, we'll have to try again.'

He called the landlady over.

'Can we have another Powers, please? Just one is grand. And do you have any more of that bread? That was deadly.'

The landlady nodded and walked off.

'Oh fuck,' said Norman.

'What?'

'Look up there.' He was pointing to a high shelf above the cash register. 'I thought we were done.'

There were three more Irish whiskeys up there. Jameson and two he hadn't even heard of.

'And two more pints of Murphys please,' he called out. He turned to Jimmy. 'We're going to have to line our stomachs if we're to get through them all or we'll be hammered.'

Jimmy nodded solemnly. Then he pointed at the beer mat.

'Change that to peat-like, will you? I keep thinking of Wonky's Da now and it's putting me off.'

He looked around the bar and grinned at his distorted reflection in the mirror behind the bottles.

This was just the kind of stupid weekend he needed. Cork was deadly.

ON MONDAY morning Jimmy checked his desk when he came in to see if there was some kind of letter there from Simon, but there was nothing. He was too ropey after the weekend to start looking for things to do, so he just turned on his computer and made himself a cup of coffee while it booted up and then he read some email and the news headlines while he drank it. His desk inbox was empty because he'd cleared it for the New York trip.

He was just daydreaming about Mykonos when Simon called him to his office. Two minutes later he was sitting there, stunned.

'Are you taking the piss?' he said eventually. He stood up and put his hands in his pockets.

Simon shook his head and stood up too, leaning against the wall behind his desk and grinning at him.

'Nope.'

'How long would I be gone for?'

'I'm thinking probably ten weeks anyway. Maybe three months.'

'Thailand?'

'Yep. Two weeks. Then two months in Tokyo. Then back here again.'

'Jaysis.'

'What do you think?'

'Three months? But what about this place?'

'We'll manage. I was hoping Marco would fill in for you before he goes over to Martin. Would do him good actually. He's been tech-centric since he got here and some exposure to management is probably just what he needs before Marketing get him. Anyway, I'll be keeping a close eye on things. And of course, it's not like you'll be out of touch completely. We'll conference once a week at least. It'll be fine.'

More thoughts than Jimmy could grab hold of were flying through his head. The band, Dónal, Sultan, Shiggy, Japan, his Mam, Thailand … it was all just too much.

'That's only the beginning, Jimmy. This is a big opportunity for you. Eirotech are expanding. We'll have a New York office this time next year. London will follow on. Going in with Kyotosei on this India thing could open up the whole Far East financial services market. I'm talking Hong Kong, Singapore, Tokyo. China's going through the roof. We're doing okay here, but it's only Ireland. It's a drop in the ocean, Jimmy. Between you and me, if things work out, we're looking to sell the whole kit and kaboodle in between three and five years. Fiona's already done the numbers. We'll all be buying castles. Retired. What'll you be then, Jimmy? Forty? Less? You'll be forty and sailing around the Caribbean on your big yacht. Your folks will be going first class on safari for their holidays whenever they like.'

Jimmy tried to imagine his Dad stalking a giraffe in a pair of baggy shorts.

Would you look at the head on that lanky fucker?

He shook his head.

'Jesus, Simon, when did all this happen?'

'It hasn't happened yet. Me, Fiona, Martin … this has always been the way we planned it, but it's only now that it's starting to come into play. The States and Japan have opened the door and now we've got to barrel through it before it closes again. This particular trip I'm talking about, we were going to get a consultant to do it for us. It was going to cost an arm and a leg – that's one reason the bonuses were the way they were this year, that and setup costs – but we figured that nailing Kyotosei into that India deal would set us up for Asia so it'd be worth it. I won't bullshit you, Jimmy. I had to bend a few arms to get them to agree to letting you take this on. It's a big ask, y'know? You haven't had exposure at this kind of level before. But I thought about it and I figured that if you knew what was at stake then you'd come through for us. You're the only one outside the Board who knows what I've just told you, and I'd appreciate your discretion by the way. But that's where I see you going with Eirotech. Next March I'll be proposing to have you on the Board. Pull this off in Asia and you're there. We're all married with kids. We need someone at our level who can get on a plane to the States or Asia at the drop of a hat and fix problems, make deals. Someone we trust.'

Jimmy stared out the window.

'Jimmy, are you thinking about the band?'

He hadn't been, but he was now. He nodded.

'Thought so. That's why I'm telling you all this now, Jimmy. I need you to focus. You're slipping on me. MTV and Top of the Pops and all that? That's only bollocks. This is real. Get your head out of your backside, Jimmy. By all means play your gigs at the weekend if that's what you want, but don't throw this away. You'll never have this again. You need to buy in now. Right now. All the stuff you've done so far; the engineering, the project management, the staff management – all that day-to-day work – that's only baby stuff. You need to step up now and get serious. I'm telling you that this time next year you'll be a partner in this company. In the meantime you'll be grooming someone for your job. Cathy maybe? Marco would be in line if he wasn't going over to Martin. Maybe you can talk to him about that when you get back? You don't have to tell him everything, obviously. I'm not messing Jimmy, this will take over your life in many ways, but the reward will be everything anyone could want. Now, go on. I'll talk to you tomorrow. If we're going to do this thing, we'll need to start prepping you straight away for the trip.'

Jimmy sat for a minute and then stood up.

'Thanks Simon.'

'You don't have to thank me, Jimmy. If you're on board, then you'll be working for yourself as much as anyone else. Eirotech Solutions will be your baby. Think about it.'

Back at his desk, Jimmy wasn't able to think about anything else. The implications were enormous. Being one of the Eirotech directors? Christ, he was only hitting his mid-thirties! This was huge. Being the guy who flies to New York to meet with fund managers and the heads of desks? Jetting around the world, doing the Richard Branson and cutting deals. Tokyo this week, Frankfurt next week, Singapore the week after. It wasn't just a promotion, it was a whole new life.

But he knew The Grove was history too if he took it on. At least, they weren't going to go anywhere. Even casual gigging would be tough if he was going to be this jetsetting businessman all of a sudden. Going to Asia now for three months would kill any Sultan deal for starters. But it'd be amazing to see all these places around the world that Simon had talked about. Jimmy didn't know if he wanted a yacht – they looked really hard to drive – but poncing around the Caribbean sounded like a pretty fucking cool way to spend his holliers if he felt like it. Retiring at forty with a million quid in the bank … Christ, that kind of money didn't even seem real.

There was so much to think about. It affected so many people. If he was honest with himself, Simon had pretty much convinced him to take the new role and effectively ditch The Grove. But if he talked to Dónal about it, he'd probably convince him to do the complete opposite. He mulled it over at lunch on his own, going through everything in his head, all the different ways things could turn out depending on what he decided.

Eventually he was sure he knew what to do. He couldn't turn down this opportunity with Eirotech. He'd be a fucking lunatic if he did. He called Aesop in the afternoon and arranged to meet him for a pint later. He had no idea what Aesop would think of it all, but it was only fair that he be the first person to know.

'How much money are we talking about?' said Aesop.

'I don't know exactly. A lot, assuming it all worked out.'

'I see. And how much do I get?'

He was being completely cool about the whole thing. Jimmy laughed.

'Listen Jimmy, you're the one who went to college all those years and studied and had fuck all money and then got up at seven every morning to go into that bleedin office. I don't even know what you do, for fuck sake. It's none of my business. If they're talking about a deal that you can retire on, then of course you should take it.'

'But The Grove ...'

'Ah, The Grove me bollocks. We play music because we like it. That's always been the reason, right? We can still do that. We'll gig whenever we can and that's good enough for me. Since last November I've got a bank account for the first time in me life, man. They gave me a plastic card to get money out of the wall and I forgot me number the next day. The fucking place is always closed – when I get up anyway – so the money for "Meatloaf's" is still in there. I don't even know how much it is. What'd happen if we went with Dónal and became big rock stars? We'd get rich? So fuckin what! I'd only drink it and smoke it. We'd end up doing it cos we have to, not cos we want to, and what's the point of that? Christ, look at the bullets on yer one ...'

Jimmy followed his gaze.

'Aesop, are you sure about all that?' he said. The girl had disappeared into the Ladies.

Aesop turned back to him.

'What?'

'Are you sure?'

'Of course I'm bleedin sure, Jimmy. Listen to me a minute. It's quite simple. It's like you're playing two hands against the house. You can see one of them. It's a full house. Aces and kings. The other one is face down. You've no fuckin idea what's in it. Now. You're only allowed bet on one of the hands. You've to pick the hand you can see or the one that's face down. Which hand do you run with? I'm a dopey bastard, Jimmy, and I know the answer to that one.'

'You're right,' said Jimmy. It was true. There was no question. 'But, oh man, Dónal will be disappointed.'

'He'll get over it. And Sparky will be fuckin delighted with himself that I won't be there to pull the piss out of him. C'mere, remind me to send him a fruit basket when we quit, will ya?'

Jimmy laughed.

'And don't forget, when you're loaded you're going to buy me loads of shit, aren't you?'

'I thought you weren't interested in money.'

'I don't mind having it, Jimmy. I'm just not interested in having to earn it.'

Jimmy laughed and headed to the toilet. He felt like a load was lifted off him. It was going to be a huge step, but for the first time in ages he actually felt less pressure.

Aesop watched him weave between tables and then he turned back to the bar and watched his fresh pint settle.

He was gutted.

Eight

DÓNAL DIDN'T talk so much as listen at first. Jimmy met him for dinner on Tuesday night and told him everything. Dónal leaned back in his chair and took it all in, his face giving nothing away. When Jimmy got through the new role he was being offered, he started into the repercussions for The Grove. Then he told Dónal that he'd already been over it with Aesop and that everything was okay there. The Grove would carry on, but there was just no way Jimmy could commit to the kinds of things that Dónal had in store for them. For the first time, Dónal nodded. Jimmy was pretty much done and sat looking at him, but Dónal just picked up his fork and put a cherry tomato in his mouth.

'I'm sorry Dónal,' said Jimmy. The silence was killing him.

Dónal gave him a small smile.

'Don't be, Jimmy. I'm running a business. Shit happens. Looks like your own business is taking off and that's great. I'm happy for you.'

'I feel shite.'

'Yeah. Well, don't feel shite for me. I've a studio, other bands. I thought you might be my Mike Oldfield but there'll be someone else. Don't worry about it. If you're going back to McGuigans then you won't be needing a manager, will you? We can settle up the contract we signed. Not much to it and there's no point in dragging it out. A few quid to hand around. Most of that's been done already. No sweat. There's some residual rights issues to keep an eye on, but I'll sort that out and keep you in the loop. Get Aesop to give me a call and I can fix him up too.'

Jimmy put his head in his hands.

'Fuck sake, I feel like I'm breaking up with a bird.'

Now Dónal really did laugh.

'Will you stop. It's cool. I wish you all the best. Really. Maybe we'll do some stuff together some day.'

'That'd be great.'

They got through their salads and then the mains arrived. Jimmy had ordered fish because he knew he wouldn't be able to stomach a steak. He'd been feeling much better recently, but had a pocketful of antacids ready to go in case it all flared up. Nothing was happening in the conversation department. They talked about the last U2 album and how cool Mama's Boys used to be, until that fizzled out too. Dónal was looking sombre and Jimmy was feeling like someone had died.

'Ever been to Thailand?' said Dónal eventually, looking up.

Fair fucks to him. He was trying.

'Thailand? Jaysis, no. Have you?'

'Yeah. Back in seventy-two when I had hair you could hide a kilo of gange in.'

'Really? What was it like?'

'Can't remember much to be honest with you. Sparky says we had a good time. Mind you, he's not exactly reliable in the recollection department. I do have a vivid image of him falling backwards off an elephant, though, and landing on his head. Which might explain a lot. Having said that, I could have sworn I didn't meet Sparky till around seventy-six when Horslips were doing *The Book of Invasions*. But then, that's acid for you. Sparky doesn't remember the elephant. Stay away from acid, Jimmy. Fucks you up.'

Dónal must have told Jimmy that a hundred times. He was actually starting to get curious.

'Anyway, only drink bottled water and don't eat salads. You'll get a dose of the trots like you wouldn't believe.'

'Thanks.'

'You'll have a ball though.'

'Yeah, I've been looking it up on the Internet. I'm going to a place called Koh Samui. Supposed to be deadly. Two weeks on the beach drinking Pina Coladas.'

'Brilliant. You should bring Aesop. Sounds like his thing.'

Jimmy laughed.

'Yeah. A whole new continent of women for him to corrupt.'

'From what I hear about Thailand, I don't think that dirty little bastard will be anything new to them. Have you told Shiggy about Japan? He'll be chuffed.'

'Just on email. He's all excited. Dying to show me around. The music scene in Tokyo is supposed to be brilliant. He's got all these clubs lined up for me. Wait'n you see, he'll try and convert me to jazz if he gets me on his home turf and I've nowhere to run away to. He's back playing the sax already. Some crowd he used to gig with before he came here. Loving it. Did you see him doing "Rat Trap" in McGuigans? Man, I've never seen a bloke so happy.'

'No, I missed it. Was off with Sultan.'

Jimmy looked down at his coffee. Sultan. That was gone now.

'All right Jimmy, all right. Forget about it. Look, something like this was going to happen anyway one way or the other. You can't spread yourself around like you were doing. You've made your choice, so just get on with …'

He stopped suddenly and looked at Jimmy.

'What?'

'Eh … nothing. I just thought of something. Doesn't matter.'

'No, what?'

'It's nothing. I just had an idea. About something else. It's grand. Do you want another coffee?'

Jimmy did. He felt like they were cool now. Dónal was obviously disappointed but he wasn't laying any shit on him, which he definitely had a right to do after all the work he'd put into The Grove in the last eight months. Jimmy was grateful for that.

'Actually,' he said. 'What about a scoop? McDaids?'

Dónal looked at his watch.

'Yeah, why not? Just one.'

After three pints, Dónal was starting to get fidgety.

'Do you need to head?' asked Jimmy. Dónal had kids and the

hours he kept were bad enough without Jimmy dragging him out to the pub.

'No. No, I'm grand. I'm just … eh, Jimmy, this new job you've got … do you need to sign a contract or anything?'

'A contract? No. It's the same job. They're just grooming me for a promotion next year. I suppose I'll have to sign something if they do put me on the Board. I'll be a principal then, so I'm sure all that needs to be on paper.'

'Right. Right …'

'What's up?'

'Nothing. Just … if … just say Sultan called me up tomorrow and said they were going to record an album and here's a cheque for a million quid.'

'But that's not going to happen, is it?'

'Fairly unlikely. But, in theory, you don't have to make your final decision until next year when that Board thing comes up, right?'

'Ah fuckin hell, Dónal …'

'Just listen a minute. Hypothetically speaking, you don't have to officially jack it in yet, that's all I'm saying.'

'Hypothetically speaking, yeah. But I'm working my bollocks off now, Dónal. That's the problem. I can't tour or record to a schedule or anything like that. You sign us up for an important gig in Belfast or something, and ten minutes before we go on I could be called up to fly to the States. It won't work. Anyway, I'll be away for the next three months.'

'I understand that. But I just had an idea. If there was no pressure to do anything except when you had the time, would you be willing to just let things ride for a while?'

'No pressure? That'll never happen! Something will come up and the next thing I'll be up to me bollocks in it all over again. Dónal, it was really hard for me to do this. You're messing with me head, man, come on.'

'Okay Jimmy, okay. I'm not trying to make it any harder, I

swear. If I promised not to put any pressure on you at all, would you let it tick over for the time being?'

'Dónal …'

'I swear to God, Jimmy. We only do stuff when you're available. No questions asked. And when the time comes, you go and join your board of directors and we all go out and get pissed and then move on.'

'It's not your best idea ever, Dónal.'

'That wasn't the idea. I just need you to stay with me for another little while.'

'For what?'

Dónal drained the pint and looked up.

'Jimmy, what if I was able to get you a gig in Tokyo?'

Jimmy laughed.

'With who?'

'The Grove of course. Shiggy's already out there.'

Jimmy thought about it. Playing Tokyo with Shiggy? Oh man …

Dónal went on. He was chewing his thumbnail now, talking quickly.

'I could sort out a drummer. Or get Shiggy to find one. He'd know what we need. We could …'

'Hang on Dónal. Before you go into Paul McGuinness mode … I'll be really busy in Tokyo.'

'Same deal, Jimmy. Only if you're free to do it. No pressure.'

'But why go to all that trouble? What do we get out of one gig?'

'Let me worry about that. But we have a hit song here, remember. Actually, I could get CDs pressed for you to bring. Or send them out. Or …'

'And how would we get this gig? It's Japan for Christ sake.'

'Yeah, I know. But I have an idea there too. I might know someone.'

'Who?'

'Don't worry about that for a minute. You gave me the idea a second ago when you were talking about Shiggy playing in McGuigans. So, what do you think?'

Jimmy shrugged.

'Sounds brilliant. Once you realise that I'm not in Tokyo on me holliers, Dónal. They work long hours over there and I'll be doing the same. And I'll be working even later so I can still talk to Eirotech here when they get in in the morning.'

'No problem Jimmy,' said Dónal. 'That's fine.' He was back to his old self. Grinning and thinking a hundred miles a minute.

Jimmy shook his head and went to the toilet. What the fuck was Dónal up to? He came back to see two pints waiting on the bar.

'Jesus, Dónal. These are the last ones, right? Mags will bleedin batter me if I send you home on your ear.'

'Jimmy, I'm after having another idea.'

'Oh Jesus. What now? You want me to do a quick tour of Mongolia while I'm out there, is it?'

'No. I was just thinking. Why not send Aesop out to Japan too?'

'Aesop?'

Jimmy did a quick count but they were only on their fourth pint.

'Are you mad?'

'Why not? He's got some money, right? It's not like he spends it on anything. I could help out with the flight. Write it off. He could stay with you in Tokyo and …'

'Me?' Jimmy roared laughing. 'No fucking way! I'm not living with that mad cunt while I'm out there on the most important job of me life. I'd get nothing done!'

'You won't be working at home will you? You'd only see him in the evenings. It'd be good to have someone out there with you. You and him and Shiggy could hang around together at the weekends. And anyway, it wouldn't be for the whole time. Just a few weeks.'

Jimmy looked at him. He was serious.

'But Dónal …'

He couldn't think of anything to say.

Dónal grinned at him.

'Come on. It's not that shite an idea is it? Think about it.'

Jimmy did. His first reaction had been like a firewall going up in his head, but now it didn't seem quite so mental. He was trying to think of a downside and, besides the massive unpredictability that went with living under the same roof as Aesop, he couldn't. He thought of standing on a stage in Tokyo with the lads. Fucking hell, as long as new experiences were popping up in front of him, why not? That'd be one for the grandkids. Dónal was pointing a finger at him, bending down to catch his eye.

'You're smiling, Jimmy. I can see it. Look at you! Come on, ya boya! You want him to go now, don't you? You do. You know it'll be brilliant.'

Jimmy scratched his head, smiling. For fuck sake, an hour ago he was packing it all in. But, seriously, he was going to be up to his goolies out there.

'Dónal …'

'Once more, Jimmy,' said Dónal. 'For the road. One more big gig for your Uncle Dónal, before you come home and stitch that suit to your back.'

'Dónal, of course it sounds cool. But you won't even be there. I don't understand what you're getting out of it. And firing money at it to have Aesop there as well? What's the comeback?'

'Jimmy, business is about taking risks. My business, your business … they're all the same. Actually, there's a little nugget for you, for when you come back. But for every risk there's an opportunity. That's the point. Now, are you on?'

'Tell me how you're going to get us a gig out there.'

'I told you. I might know someone.'

'Who the fuck do you know in Japan?'

'Just someone I used to know.'

Nine

JIMMY WAS in Aesop's bedroom. Aesop wasn't leaving until the weekend, but he was packing already. Jimmy had put the idea to him the previous week in the pub and his reaction had sealed the deal as far as Jimmy was concerned.

'You fucking *what*?!'

'Would you be up for it? It'd probably just be for a few weeks. You'd be staying with me in Tokyo. They're putting me up in some apartment yoke. We'd hang out with Shiggy, maybe do a gig if Dónal can set something up. What do you think? I was thinking about it, and you could meet me in Thailand beforehand and we could fly to Japan together.'

He'd actually meant that they'd meet up in Bangkok airport off Jimmy's connecting flight from the island and fly straight on to Tokyo, but that's not what Aesop heard.

'Thailand as well?! Jesus, Jimmy, keep talking man. I'm there. I'm fuckin there with bells on!'

'Eh, Aesop, I didn't mean …'

Aesop called the barman.

'Hey Tommie? I'm going on me holliers.'

'Where are you off to Aesop?'

'Thailand and Japan! What do you think of that, ha? You and your bleedin Algarve. Asia's where it's at, man. The Algarve? Jaysis, Tommie, sure Spain is only for the tourists.'

Fuck, thought Jimmy. That two weeks was supposed to be for taking it easy.

'So you're back in the game then Jimmy?' said Aesop, turning around. 'What about the big job and all that?'

'Not really. I just told Dónal that we'd do a gig out there if he wanted and that I didn't mind doing some stuff here for the next while if I have the time. I'm still going with Eirotech. Listen Aesop, about …'

'Ah, whatever Jimmy. The important thing is, I'm going on me holliers. Thailand! Jaysis, I can't believe it. You know that Andy was out there a couple of years ago with Elaine? Loved it. Said it was the best holiday of his life. Hang on, I'll just give him a quick call.'

Aesop talked to his brother for ten minutes and was beaming when he got off the phone.

'He says the gee is amazing, Jimmy! Fuckin hell, this is going to be brilliant.'

'Yeah,' said Jimmy quietly. 'Brilliant.'

Now, in Aesop's bedroom, the usual mounds of clothes on the floor had been kicked into different corners depending on Aesop's idea of their suitability for a trip to Asia. He even had a list made out on a writing pad.

'I don't think you're going to need jumpers Aesop,' said Jimmy, nodding towards one pile.

'Is it not winter there?'

'Winter?'

'It's the other side of the world, Jimmy. It's winter.'

'Eh, right. I checked on the Internet, Aesop. Thailand is in the thirties. Japan is as bad.'

'Thirties?'

'Very hot.'

'Yeah. But it might get cold at night.'

'I don't think so, Aesop.'

'How many pairs of jocks are you bringing?'

'I haven't really thought about it. A dozen?'

'A dozen? What are you planning on doing to them for fuck sake? Anyway, didn't Shiggy say they have disposable jocks in Japan? That's what I'll be wearing. And I'll be bringing a few boxes back with me too. Fuck this washing-me-jocks lark. Oh look, Jennifer said I could take her camcorder. I'm going to record everything we do. It'll be great for when they do a documentary of the band later, won't it?'

'Aesop, will you relax? Did you get your injections?'

'Yeah, on Tuesday. I've a bruise on me arse the size of a frisbee. The fucker said he'd count to three and then he went and stabbed me on two. I screamed like a baby and called him an evil bastard. I don't think he was expecting that, the head on him.'

'I'd say he wasn't.'

'The nurse had me in some kind of arm lock for the second one. A big girl she was, and giving me the hairy eyeball. I was afraid to move.'

'Right, well that's everything sorted, right? Tickets are booked, I'll see you on the island. You'll get there a day before me because of that cheap flight you got. Now, I have to go and see Ma. She's all worried that I'm never coming back.'

'I know. I was doing the Meals on Wheels with her at lunch-time yesterday because her back was bad again. She was all upset. You're the last one left in the house, Jimmy. That's going to be fuckin hard on Peggy, y'know?'

'I know. But fuck it, what can you do? Anyway, it's only for a couple of months.'

'Are you going for a pint this week?'

'I can't. I'll be working late every day. I'm so fucking busy with this trip you wouldn't believe it.'

'Yeah. Me too.'

'You're busy? What has you busy?'

Aesop looked around the bedroom.

'Well, I need to pack, don't I? And Jennifer has me looking after her bleedin goldfish while she's in Galway. I have to feed the fuckers twice a day and she said if any of them die I'll be on me own in the ironing and dinner-making department. That's a lot of responsibility, man.'

'God, the stress.'

'Who are you telling? I found one of them floating on the bottom of the tank yesterday morning. Me heart. He was only asleep though. You can't tell, Jimmy. They don't have eyelids, y'know? I poked him with a drumstick and all of a sudden he's tearing around the place looking for his breakfast, the bastard. Séamus. She has names for them all. Séamus fancies himself as a bit of a comedian, the sleepy fucker. One o'clock in the afternoon it was. And when he's not pretending to be dead, he's biting lumps out of Nemo. This morning he was making out like he had a sore paw and kept going around in circles. He has me tormented. I was thinking of getting him a little ball to play with.'

'It's not fucking Flipper you have in the bowl, Aesop.'

'Well I have to do something. It's not like I can give him a kick in the arse for himself to sort him out, is it?'

'I don't know, Aesop. But I'm pretty sure fish don't have paws.'

'Paddles?'

'I'll seeya in Thailand, right?' said Jimmy. He headed for the door.

'Yeah. Oh, Jimmy?'

'What?'

'Dónal said I shouldn't bring any weed on the plane. What do you think?'

'What do I think about crossing international borders and arriving in a place like Thailand with a month's worth of skunk in your suitcase? I think it's a fucking great idea Aesop.'

'I was only asking.'

He picked up his pad and scribbled it off the list.

PEGGY WAS very quiet. Jimmy hadn't seen her like this since Liz had left Ireland for the States with a Green Card and no real idea if or when she'd be coming back. They were in the car to the airport. Seán was worried about Peggy and so was doing all the talking. It wasn't a familiar role for him and he took to it with no great degree of concern for the interests of his audience. Jimmy found himself rocking in the front seat, trying to make the car go a bit faster. They'd moved onto landmark games in Scottish soccer. Seán had spent a lot of time working in Glasgow as a young man.

'I'm not condoning it, like,' said Seán. 'I'd never condone that kind of carry on. But you can see why they were all fired up. Two-one in Wembley? There was no call to go ripping up the pitch and the goalposts, but. That was out of order. McQueen scored that day. And Dalglish of course. I remember Macari came on for Joe Jordan. Didn't Archie Gemmill come on as well, Peggy?'

He looked at her in the rearview mirror.

'Love?'

Peggy was gazing out the window.

'Gemmill, pet. Who did he come on for in that game in 1977?'

'Was it not Masson?'

'That's right, it was, yeah. Sure Gemmill was the better of the two anyway, but he played in Derby. That's what that was all about. But didn't they both play against Argentina two weeks later?'

'Ma,' said Jimmy. He couldn't take it anymore. 'Are you all right back there? You're very quiet.'

'I'm grand love. Just looking at all these new roads. Sure every time I come out here now I don't know where I'm going. I tried to get to Swords there a couple of weeks ago and I ended up in Malahide. I was all confused. You could graze sheep on the roundabouts they have these days. Remember we used to cycle out here Seán when we were coortin'? We'd stop and pick blackberries, Jimmy, and then eat them on the beach in Baldoyle. Your father would have a pint then in Graingers and I'd have a glass of orange and we'd come back by Dollymount way. It was all fields out here then. Do you remember that Seán? Or we'd pick mushrooms and your Nanny Collins would stew them in milk when we got home. Sometimes we'd stop in St Annes and ...'

Jimmy groaned inwardly and rested his head against the seat. He wished Aesop was here. Aesop loved talking to his Mam about this stuff. Still, at least this story was better than the Archie fucking Gemmill one.

Things got worse in the airport. By the time the three of them stood in the check-in queue, his Dad had stopped trying to fill the silences. Jimmy just wanted to get going but he could tell that his Mam was in a bit of trouble and the last thing he wanted was to rush off and leave her in that state.

Once he had his boarding card they headed upstairs for a coffee. His Mam was upset because he was going so far away for so long. His Dad was upset because his Mam was upset and now Jimmy was starting to get upset because he knew she'd spend the rest of the day crying. Fuck it, he had to get out of here. There was no point in dragging it out. He looked at his watch and drained his cup.

'I'd better head.'

That did it. Peggy's eyes were suddenly red and brimming and then the floodgates opened. She wasn't wailing or anything, but she clung to his arm as they went back down the escalator, telling him to be careful out there and mind himself and to call her and for God's sake to be careful out there.

'It's only a couple of months, Ma. It'll be grand. Come on.'

'I know it is love, but it's so far away. Japan. God. We used to read about it in school, but sure you might as well have been talking about the moon.'

'Aesop will be there. And Shiggy will look after us. We'll have a laugh. I'll have loads of stories for you when I get back. Anyway, it's for work, right? It's not like I'll be going mountain climbing or anything.'

'I know, love. Look, go on. You'll be late for your plane.'

They were at the sliding doors where only passengers could pass through. Jimmy looked around. Peggy wasn't the only heartbroken mother in the area. At least two more were standing there, distraught and leaning against their pale husbands as they tried to catch the last glimpse of a wave from the son or daughter who was going away on them. Jesus. This was even worse than when Liz left, and he was coming back for fuck sake!

She gave him another big kiss and hug and then Seán finally took her arm, looking up at Jimmy.

'Will you go on, for fuck sake. Take care of yourself, right?'

Jimmy nodded and gave him a hug as best he could with Peggy hanging off him and two bags in his other hand. Then Peggy turned and walked off, not able to stay any longer.

'Jimmy?' said Seán, before turning to follow her. 'Call your Ma, right?'

'Course I will,' said Jimmy.

Seán nodded.

'Good luck.'

And then they were gone.

Jimmy took a deep breath and joined the queue just inside the door. Christ, that was fucking traumatic. He felt awful. The security guard on the door smiled at him.

'It's always terrible hard on the Mammies,' he said.

'I'm only going for three months,' said Jimmy.

'It won't feel like that for her though,' said the guard.

Jimmy looked at him. Was he getting therapy now off this fucker?

'C'mere,' the guy went on. 'I'll give you a bit of advice.'

Jesus, he was.

'What's that?' said Jimmy.

'Take your shoes off now. Save you queuing up to do it at the table over there. There's a terrible hum around that table. Some people are nervous flyers, y'see? They sweat. Some of them are sweating in a bus all the way from Galway. Then they line up at that table and take off their shoes. That's why I'm over here at the door.'

'Thanks for that.'

'No problem. And make sure and call your Mam when you get wherever you're going.'

'For fuc … right. I will. Anything else?'

The guard thought about it for a minute.

'Don't eat yellow snow.'

Ten

JIMMY HAD to stuff himself into a small seat from Dublin to London, but he was flying business class after that. He thought he'd have three hours to kill in Heathrow, but since the Aer Lingus flight arrived into the absolute remotest corner of the airport, half of that was spent finding the gate for his next flight. He found a small bar close to where he had to be and sat down. It was only mid-afternoon but he was bollixed tired already. He took a sip out of a pint of Guinness and sat up straight in disgust. What the fuck was that? It looked nice. It was all delicate curves, the head standing proud and the glass beaded with icy droplets, but it tasted like someone had dropped a pocketful of coins into it. Everyone around him was drinking yellow beer, so he ordered a bottle of Corona and drank that instead and munched on a tiny sandwich, eyeing the still-full pint next to him suspiciously.

He'd never flown business class before and was looking forward to it. The other passengers queuing up were mostly Asian, some of the men in long shirts that came down to their knees and the women in brightly-coloured sarees or sarongs. Gorgeous kids with dark skin and gleaming white smiles ran between the milling crowd, laughing and shouting. Jennifer had bought him a book on Japan and he was going to read it on the plane and learn all he could before he got there. He didn't want to look like some gobshite westerner in front of everyone. He had the book out as soon as he was sitting down in his nice big seat. There was an Indian businessman beside him, immaculately turned out in a grey suit and brilliantly starched shirt, and Jimmy smiled at him and nodded. The man smiled back and got back to the English language textbook he was studying.

A stunning airhostess handed Jimmy a glass of champagne and a steaming towel for him to freshen up with. Jimmy took them with what he hoped was an air of polite nonchalance, but a bloody big grin made its way onto his face and he couldn't stop it. This was cool. She was utterly gorgeous and the smile she was giving him … well, Jimmy knew that smile. This was going to be a brilliant nine hours.

He was going to go for the chicken when mealtime came around, but decided at the last minute to give the vegetarian curry a go – just to get in the mood. It was lovely. A bit too vegetarian, maybe, but the vegetables were nice and crunchy and although it was hot, he was well able for it. No bother. Then he crunched down on what he would later swear was a small bendy tomato and almost immediately thought he was going to die. The pain radiated out from his tongue until it encompassed his whole head and stretched down into his sweat-soaked chest. His eyes streamed tears and his face was suddenly slimy with the heat. His throat started to clog up and he began to cough and lean forward, knocking his glass of water onto his lap and putting his elbow into a bowl of blancmange. As he struggled to catch a breath, a bolt of snot flew from his nose and stuck to the back of the seat in front. A gob of vomity dribble fell from his mouth as he belched loudly, but he could only barely make it out through his bubbling eyes. He wouldn't have been able to stop it anyway. He'd totally lost control of his numb lips. He was starting to struggle desperately with his seatbelt, trying not to knock the tray onto the floor, when the Indian beside him tapped his arm and gestured for Jimmy to listen to him.

'One must be most wary,' he said slowly, 'of unfamiliar victuals.'

'You get fu … fuc … get fu …' sputtered Jimmy, but his tongue was too swollen to form the words and trying to only made him dribble more. He really thought he was on the way out.

The airhostess noticed him at last and swept the tray away as it teetered on his knee. Then she had his seatbelt off and pulled him to his feet. Still coughing and spluttering, she led him to the toilet, pushing a bottle of water into his hands before pulling the door shut. She was still smiling that same smile as it clicked, the fucking cow. That was just her airhostess smile. She didn't want to ride him at all.

Jimmy coughed and belched into the toilet bowl for five minutes, spitting and clearing his throat and washing his mouth out with the water. When he finally managed to take a look at himself in the mirror, he was aghast. His hair was completely sodden and stuck to his head. His pale blue shirt had huge saucers of sweat under the arms and on his chest, and he was covered in curry, blancmange and bits of his breakfast. The crotch of his pants was soaked and stained with runny food too. He leaned against the tiny sink and was about to start washing his face when there was a knock on the door.

'Mr Collins, are you all right, sir?'

It was smiley-arse.

'I'm grand.'

'I'm sorry?'

'I'm fine. I'm okay. I'll be out in a minute.'

'Can I do anything for you, sir?'

'No, I'm grand.'

'I'm sorry?'

'I'm bleedin grand, I said. I'll be out in a minute.'

'Are you bleeding, sir? Have you hurt yourself?'

'What? No. No, I'm fine. Just give me a minute.'

'I can get you some more water, Mr Collins.'

Jimmy opened the door a crack. She took one look at him and then a step back.

'I'm okay,' said Jimmy. 'Can you just give me a minute?'

'Of course, sir. If you need anything, just let me know.'

'Thanks.'

He shut the door again.

It took another ten minutes before he was ready to come out but a final look at himself in the mirror revealed the improvement to be marginal at best. The stains on his clothes were replaced by yet more damp patches where he'd tried to rinse them, and his hair was stuck flat against his scalp. His face was finally losing the scarlet tint it had taken on and he was able to breathe again. He grabbed some tissues from the dispenser on the wall and opened the door, stepping into the aisle.

All of Business Class was looking up at him with various expressions of concern, fear and amusement.

'Eh …' he said. 'Sorry about that.' He pointed to his throat. 'Went down the wrong way.'

He made his way back to the seat, nice and red again as all those eyes followed him, and sat down next to his pal. The man was smiling at him.

'What a most exciting episode,' he said.

'I'm glad you enjoyed it,' said Jimmy, buckling his belt and sitting back against the pillow with a big sigh.

'Although personally I would venture that the incident verily smacked of pathos.'

Jimmy closed his eyes.

'I know another thing that'll be getting verily smacked if he doesn't shut his hole,' he muttered.

He eventually dozed off and slept most of the rest of the way.

THAILAND

Eleven

JIMMY STARED out the window of the plane as it circled and then came down to land on Koh Samui. He'd never seen anything so beautiful in his life. It was like flying over where they filmed the Bounty and Timotei ads. Blue-green water, dappled with darker purples and steel greys, lapped at the brilliant white beaches out of which sprung huge palm trees. All of this was a halo to the lush greens of the middle of the island. It was utterly stunning and by the time the plane sunk down and the ground became almost close enough to jump out, he'd left a grubby wet patch on the glass where he'd been stuck to it in amazement.

Before he left, he'd been on the phone to Aesop's brother and gotten the lowdown. Thailand was a brilliant place, but you needed to keep your wits about you. Compared to the average IT manager in Dublin, they earned fuck all and most of them would do their best to balance things out a bit. The thing was not to let them sucker you.

He picked up his bag and walked out of the arrivals area. Almost immediately there was a guy in front of him, full of smiles and advice.

'No thanks. I'm grand,' said Jimmy, instinctively walking the other way.

'Please, sir, that way.'

'No really. I'm fine. My friend is waiting for me. I don't want a car.'

'But this way ...'

'I'm not going that way. I'm telling you, I'm grand. Will you get away from me?' Jimmy pulled his bags closer and shook his head.

'But ...'

'Will you leave me alone? I already have a car.'

'Sir. I am a police officer.' He showed Jimmy his gun. 'The exit is over there.'

Jimmy looked. Everyone else was walking over there.

'Oh bollo … I'm sorry. I thought you were a taxi man.'

The policeman looked at him and tapped the 'Tourist Police' badge on his brown shirt.

'No. Enjoy your stay on Samui.'

'I will. Eh, good man. Thanks.'

Jimmy followed the rest of the crowd, burning red, his head down. He wasn't in the continent an hour and he was already after making a tool of himself.

Three minutes later he was in the middle of a circle of shouting men, each of them explaining that theirs was the best, fastest and cheapest taxi on the island and trying to grab his suitcase off him. He clung onto it for dear life and looked around desperately for the copper, who was nowhere to be seen. Other tourists were getting the same treatment, but they seemed to be handling it fine, talking to the taxi men and arguing over money. Another hand lunged at him, going for his duty free bag this time, and Jimmy had enough. He sat down on his big case and glared around him.

'Will yiz leave me alone for a minute, will ye? Jesus, I don't even know the name of me hotel.'

He took out his travel pouch and found the page with all the details. The taxi men all looked at him, waiting.

'Eh … Chaweng … Sawadee Grand?' he said, and looked up.

There was an explosion of noise and they all started grabbing at him again. He was all hot and bothered now. He stood up, took hold of his bag and legged it back into the airport where it was air-conditioned. They weren't allowed follow him into the building and he stopped and turned around. He took out his travel details again and looked between it and all the signs that pointed off in different directions. He was stumped. Eventually a small girl with blonde hair and baggy pants smiled at him and walked over.

'You look like you're having problems there. Were the nasty men ganging up on you, you poor lad?'

Bloody hell. She was Irish.

'Howya. Yeah, I'm not sure what I'm supposed to do. They're all trying to grab me stuff. Are they going to take off with it?'

'Not at all. Who told you that?'

'I just heard they're a bit mad.'

'Ah sure it's not that bad. Just smile at them and haggle. It's a laugh. They only want the few quid to bring you to your hotel. Where are you staying?'

'Eh. The Chaweng Sawadee Grand.'

'Ooh. Very posh. That's new, that one. Lovely.'

'Do you know where it is?'

'Yeah, I'm going to Chaweng too. C'mon, I'll sort you out. Hey Pablo?'

She called to a guy who was standing with a few mates.

'Pablo, are you right? Let's go.'

Jimmy walked out with them. They were all wearing loose shirts and tie-dyed pants and sandals. Jimmy looked down at his polo shirt and chinos and felt like he was after walking into the wrong party. Plonker.

Linda did the haggling for all seven of them and they caught a minibus for the bumpy ride to Chaweng. She sat next to Jimmy, chatting all the way.

'So, how do you know Koh Samui?' asked Jimmy.

'I've been here a few times. I used to live in Seoul and it's as handy to go away here as anywhere for a few days. I learned to dive here. Do you dive?'

'Dive? With parachutes, like?'

'Parachutes, yeah,' she laughed.

'No, never. Seoul. Korea, right? They had the Olympics.'

'That's the one. Anyway, I'm doing a bit of travelling before I

107

head home. This is the last stop before Europe.'

'Been anywhere nice?'

'Well, Pablo and me started in Beijing, made our way down to Xian and then on to Hong Kong. Then we headed back up into Yangshuo and Guilin. A few weeks in Laos and then over to Vietnam. Flew into Hanoi and then down the coast to Saigon. Then overland to Cambodia. Then here to relax a bit. It's taken four months so far.'

Jimmy stared at her.

'Bleedin hell. That sounds amazing.'

'Yeah,' she said, smiling. 'It was.'

Jimmy looked out the window at the coconut trees. He turned around to Linda again.

'Four months?'

She nodded.

'But what about work?'

'Ah, I just quit. Had enough of all that for a while. Decided to take a big break and start again at home. Or maybe the States or Europe if something comes up. Sure fuck it, you're only young once.'

Jimmy shook his head again. Who just pissed off like that for four months?

Linda looked him up and down.

'Are you here on business or something?'

'What? No. Not really. I'm meeting a mate here for a couple of weeks.'

She laughed.

'Well, I hope you brought other clothes. You don't want to get sand in your loafers there, do you?'

He smiled. Linda and her mates looked like they danced naked around bonfires at night and here was him dressed up like a Jehovah's Witness, the fuckin eejit. He'd do some shopping once he got to the hotel. He started thinking of Aesop being there in the hotel when he got in and then smiled to himself. He probably wouldn't have to worry too much about being able to escape from real life for a couple of weeks if he was spending it with Aesop. Aesop didn't do real life.

THE BELLBOY led him out of the lobby and down some steps into beautifully floricured gardens.

'Doctor Aesop is your friend?' he said, turning around. He was laughing.

'You know him?' said Jimmy. Doctor?

'Oh yes. Very funny guy. Aesop. Very funny. Ha ha.'

He turned back around and kept walking down the path. Jimmy could see his shoulders bouncing as he chuckled away to himself. Aesop had only been in the place a day. Jesus, what had he been up to?

Jimmy kept catching glimpses of the sparkling sea between the buildings in front of him and soon enough the path branched off to his apartment, a detached hut right on the beach. It seemed to be made of bamboo and sticks and had a small veranda in the front. Two coconut shells decorated with orchids sat empty on a tray on the glass table. The bollocks hadn't wasted any time getting into the swing of things, had he?

The guy opened the door for him and Jimmy walked into the most luxurious bamboo hut he'd ever been in in his life. It was immaculate and beautifully decorated in white tiles, pink and purple flowers and rattan furniture. He walked through and saw sliding doors out to the back veranda. The sand and sea were right there beyond a small garden with low walls and four coconut trees that stretched up past where he could see them. Hanging from the coconut trees were two hammocks and, sprawled in one of them, a bone-white hairy leg thrown out over the side, was Aesop.

He was wearing just a pair of green flowery shorts with a beer balanced on his chest and his hand pulling on a string to swing the hammock.

Jimmy pulled open the door.

'The fucking state of you, Murray,' he said.

Aesop craned his neck back.

'James! About bleedin time! What do you think of me back garden? All it needs is two bare-diddied servant girls waving palm leaves at me and I'd be laughing.'

He swung around and stood up.

'Prem, would you ever get meself and Jimmy here another couple of Singhas, please? And another few for the fridge. *Khab khun krap*. Have one yourself sure. What time are you off?'

'Kap crumb what?' said Jimmy, watching Prem giggle and leave. 'What's that?'

'I just said thanks in Thai,' said Aesop. 'Jesus, look at you in your sensible trousers. Were Trinny and Susannah on the plane, for fuck sake?'

'Who?'

'Who?' Aesop roared laughing. 'Man, you need to get a life.'

Five minutes later Jimmy was in the other hammock in a pair of denim shorts and they were both slurping on their beers.

'Wotcha think?' said Aesop.

'Aesop, I think I've died and gone to heaven. Jesus, this is paradise.'

'That's nothing, man. The whole place is teeming with gee! Look, see that bird coming out of the sea? The cutie?'

'Yeah.'

Aesop stuck two fingers in his mouth and let fly. The girl, forty metres away, looked up and Aesop gave her a big wave. She waved back. Aesop gestured for her to come over and she stopped drying herself and wandered over the sand in their direction.

'Fucking hell, Aesop. What are you doing?' Jimmy sat up in his hammock and looked over at Aesop in a panic.

'I told you. This place is mental. They're all gagging for it.'

'She's coming over!'

'Sure why wouldn't she?'

The girl was at the small wall now. She was gorgeous. Pink bikini and long wet hair. Straight out of the Bounty ad.

She stepped over the wall.

'Oh Jesus, Aesop …' muttered Jimmy, trying to hide behind his bottle.

She walked over, gave Jimmy a big grin and then bent down and kissed Aesop, her lovely arse about two feet from Jimmy's shocked head. He didn't know where to look. Then he couldn't help it.

'Jimmy,' said Aesop. 'This is Marie. Marie, this is my mate Jimmy that I told you about.'

She turned around.

'Hi Jimmy. Hey Aesop, I'm just going in to take a quick shower. Back soon, okay?'

She slid the door open and was gone inside.

Aesop just lay there, swinging in his hammock and smiling his big fucking smiley head off.

'Fucker.'

'Man, I wish I'd me camcorder. That was brilliant. You'd swear she was coming to rob your handbag.'

'Who is she?'

'Ah, just some bird. She's Dutch. Met her in the bar last night. We were chatting and she said she was out of here tonight and could never sleep on planes. So naturally, being a doctor, I told her I had something back here that would do the trick. Now don't be looking at me like that, Jimmy. I was only lying about the doctor part. She'll sleep like a baby tonight, wait'n you see, so it wasn't like I was bullshitting her. Dutch birds are brilliant, aren't they? So fuckin sexy. Out in the sea and everything we were at four o'clock this morning. Ever do it in the sea Jimmy? It's like being up in space or something. Floating around, weightless, everything wet and slidey. I have to tell you, Jimmy, I've a feeling we're going to be enjoying ourselves here. And, being the mate I am, I consider it my holy duty to make sure you clean your pipes before we leave this island. You're all bent out of shape.'

'Aesop …'

The door slid open and Marie came back out with two more beers from the fridge for them. She was all cleaned up and ready to head back to her hotel. Kiss for Aesop, two cheek-kisses for Jimmy and then she was over the wall and off down the beach with a small wave. Jimmy looked over at Aesop who grinned and held out his bottle. They clanked their drinks together and lay back on their hammocks, watching a red and green parrot yoke hop from branch to branch across their coconut trees. Jimmy let a huge sigh out. He hadn't felt like this in years. If ever. He was on his holliers.

'Man, I needed this,' he said.

'Yeah. Me too,' said Aesop.

'What, were the fish getting to you?'

'Fish?'

'Jen's fish.'

Aesop laughed.

'Oh yeah, right. Da's looking after them. Do you know what Séamus did last week? He bit the top off Nemo's tail, the mean bastard. And me looking at him doing it, not a bother on him! I had to take him out of the tank. I put him in a glass of water under the bed, teach the fucker a …'

The squeaking hammock stopped. Jimmy looked up. Aesop was staring at his beer bottle, frowning.

'Aesop?'

'What day is it today, Jimmy?'

'Sunday.'

'Sunday, right.' He started counting days out on his fingers and then looked up. 'Eh, Jimmy, does your phone work over here?'

CLOUDS ROLLED in later in the afternoon and it rained for about four hours solid. The lads sat in the apartment and Jimmy tried to teach Aesop how to use his laptop to play music. He'd bought proper speakers for it on the plane and it sounded great.

'You've a lot of gayboy music on there, Jimmy, but it'll do.' He squinted at the screen. 'What's … tell me that doesn't say Enrique Iglesias, you big jessie.'

'I just bought it for the rhythms. I was trying to play along with that whole Spanish thing. Remember when we were …'

'All right homo, if you say so. Well, at least you've got Maiden.'

'I've got everything Maiden ever recorded! I'm telling you Aesop, all you need to do is type in … will you pay attention?'

Aesop was checking to see if the rain had stopped. He looked around.

'What? Ah fuck that. I don't know computers.'

'It's easy. You just click here and …'

'You do it. I can't be arsed learning all that stuff. I like me vinyl.'

'But if you just look …'

'I might as well be looking up a bull's hole, Jimmy. Listen, you be in charge of the music, right? Just don't play any Enrique fucking Iglesias and we won't have any rows about it. How do you work the volume?'

Jimmy pointed to the knob on one of the speakers.

'Grand so. That's all I need to know.'

'But Aesop, I was going to set you up with an email account and everything.'

'Email? For what? Who would I write to?'

'Well, me or …'

'But you're here.'

'Yeah, but … you could … if you had email you could … ah fuck it.' Jimmy closed the top of the laptop. 'Get me a beer you fucking useless gobshite. You're worse than me Da.'

THEY GOT cleaned up and headed out for dinner at about eight. There were loads of cool restaurants right on the beach, tables laid out in the sand with candles and soft piped music. They stopped at one place where a Thai guy in a colourdy shirt was playing guitar and singing about life on the island. There was a huge spread of fish next to him, arranged over crushed ice on a bed of palm leaves. Jimmy wandered up to the display and suddenly felt very hungry. He saw a lobster. He'd never had lobster. He bent in for a closer look and the guy nodded at him.

'Excellent lobster,' he sang, beaming at Jimmy and strumming on the guitar.

Jimmy looked around the restaurant, but no one seemed to notice the improvised lyrics. He smiled back and turned to find Aesop, but Aesop was already sitting at one of the tables on the beach, having a smoke and videoing a group of girls who were walking by and waving at them. He went out to join him.

'They have fish.'

'Do they? Do they have hamburgers?'

'You can't eat hamburgers in Thailand.'

'I did last night. Lovely it was. Pineapple and everything. Very tropical.'

The waiter came over and Jimmy brought him up to show him the lobster he wanted. Aesop ordered a cheeseburger and they got a couple of beers.

'Do you want a bit of me lobster,' said Jimmy, when it arrived in front of him, steaming and smelling great.

Aesop looked at it like it was a disembodied head.

'I do in my fuck.'

'It's lovely. Here, have a bit.'

'Me hole. That thing arrived here in a fuckin flying saucer, the state of it. Do you want some burger?'

Jimmy shook his head.

'Are you going to be eating chips and burgers until you get back to Ireland?'

'And after I get back.'

'But the fish here is lovely. They probably caught it this morning.'

'I don't like fish.'

'What are you going to do in Japan?'

'I'll just eat the curries.'

'Curries? I never heard Shiggy talking about curries.'

'Well, whatever. I don't like fish.'

'Yeah, I think Séamus is testament to that, the poor fucker. Jen is going to murder you.'

'Ah stop Jimmy, I feel bad enough.' He rubbed his eyes. 'Anyway, it was his own fault.'

'Yeah. Can I be there when you explain that to her? How he brought it on himself?'

'Da said he'd buy another one before she gets back next week.'

'She's not fucking seven, Aesop. She'll know it's not him.'

'I know, I know,' said Aesop, his head in his hands. Then he looked up over Jimmy's shoulder, annoyed. 'Jesus, how many songs about coconuts does that fucker know? C'mon, hurry up with ET there and let's go for a pint.'

They ate their dinners and drank three beers each. It was lovely. There was a big storm out to sea and the lads watched the lightning show for a while when they were done eating. It was like something on the telly, the black sky suddenly flashing with views of thick cloud as though God was taking pictures up there. On the island, though, there wasn't even a breeze.

'Right, enough fuckin nature-watching,' said Aesop. 'Beer. And we need to find you somewhere to park your lad while you still remember what it's for.'

They paid the bill and Aesop led the way through the restaurant and onto the street outside. The road was alive with bars and shops and lots of young people out for the night. The place was buzzing.

'Where are we going?' said Jimmy.

'We'll have a couple of quick ones in Christy's first. Then maybe Austin Powers and then we'll head into the Green Mango. I was on a pool table in there for an hour and a half last night. I ended up losing it to an English bloke cos Marie walked in and started dancing and I couldn't concentrate. He thought he was brilliant cos he'd beaten me. I betcha he wasn't laughing this morning when the sun came up, but. I saw the state of the yoke he walked out of there with, and the face on her like a dropped pie.'

THEY WERE on a pool table in the Green Mango at midnight when a troupe of scantily clad Thai girls walked out from behind the bar with trays of shots. It was the kind of thing that had been happening all night. Jimmy and Aesop were smashing all-comers at pool and laughing and joking with each other like they were sixteen again. It was turning into the best night they'd had out in as long as Jimmy could remember. Aesop insisted that they give up the table after a while to see what else was going on. The girls with the shots had obviously stirred something in his shorts.

They stood next to the hopping dance floor and watched the revellers. Aesop went to the jacks and, almost straight away, a drop-dead Thai girl walked up to Jimmy and said hi.

'Eh, hello. I'm Jimmy.'

'I am Jessica,' she said, holding out a hand with long slender fingers to him, like he was supposed to kiss it. He almost did too but caught himself in time and shook it instead. Close one, Jimmy, he said to himself. It's okay *not* to make a gobshite of yourself as well sometimes, y'know?

She laughed, showing off perfect teeth and as she turned to swish her long straight hair out of her face, Jimmy was able to take in the full length of her model's body. She was incredible. Like some bird you'd dream about. Tall and graceful with an easy smile and eyes you'd nearly fall into. They chatted for a few minutes. He told her he was from Ireland and she hung on every engrossing syllable. She was from the north of Thailand. She was a dancer. Jimmy could believe it. Jessica was her stage name, but her real name was too hard for him to pronounce. Fair enough. Could he buy her a drink? She said she didn't drink, but a glass of sparkling water would be superb. That was the word she used. Superb. Jimmy was shaking as he stopped a waitress walking past and ordered. He chatted on, not even knowing what he was talking about, until the waitress came back with the drinks. He'd ordered a vodka tonic for himself, as though drinking beer in front of an angel like this would have been uncouth.

A finger tapped his shoulder.

'Meet someone nice, Jimmy?'

'Howya Aesop,' Jimmy smiled. 'Yeah, actually, I did. Aesop, this is Jessica. Jessica, this is my friend, Aesop.'

Jessica gave a little bow, her palms together just below her chin with the fingers pointing up, and then raised her eyes up coquettishly at Aesop and smiled her spellbinding smile.

'All right Jack,' said Aesop, nodding towards the exit. 'Here's your glass of water. Now rev up and fuck off. He's not interested.'

'Aesop!' said Jimmy. 'What the fuck are you *doing*? Shut up, you rude cunt!'

Jessica looked shocked and linked an arm through Jimmy's, her huge eyes gazing up at him, hurt. Jimmy turned to her, his other arm going to her shoulder protectively. She stepped a little closer, brushing his crotch with her side.

'What's the fuckin matter with you?' he said to Aesop.

Aesop shook his head.

'Dopey bastard.'

'What?'

Aesop lit a smoke and blew it over his shoulder.

'She's a bloke.'

'What the fuck are you talking about?'

'She's a bloke.'

'What do you mean "a bloke"?'

117

'I mean she's not a girl. She's a bloke. She has balls. She pisses standing up. She can't parallel park. How many ways do you want me to say it?'

'Fuck off!'

'I thought you were only being polite, cos that's the kind of spa you are, but when I saw you buying her a drink I had to come over. She's a bloke, Jimmy. Drop the hand on Jessica here and you'll spend the rest of your life scrubbing it with Brillo Pads.'

Jimmy looked around at Jessica, who was still staring pitifully at him and clinging onto his arm. Then he turned back to Aesop.

'You're fucking mad!'

'Ask her.'

'I can't just …'

'Hey Jessica,' said Aesop, 'Are you, or were you ever, a man?'

Jessica didn't answer. She wouldn't even look at Aesop.

'You ask her,' he said to Jimmy.

Jimmy was starting to feel a bit queasy. This was kind of Aesop's department after all.

'Eh, Jessica, sorry … I mean … are you … eh … what he said?'

Jessica shrugged her shoulders and frowned. She didn't understand.

'Ah right,' said Aesop. 'Can't speak English all of a sudden?'

Jimmy wasn't holding her shoulder anymore and tried to extract his arm from hers. He looked at Aesop.

'Are you fucking sure?'

'How many women do you know with Adams apples?'

Jimmy turned back again slowly. She had one. A cold shiver ran up his back and into his hair. A closer inspection revealed more details. It was nothing obvious, but there was a certain strength to her jawline. Her make-up was so, so perfect, but a little bit caked on there. Those long slender fingers grew from Packie Bonner hands. He suddenly had a vision of her with short

118

hair and a fag sticking out the corner of her mouth and knew Aesop was right. He'd just had his first woody over a bloke. Well, he didn't anymore. He wasn't sure he'd ever have one again.

Jessica knew the game was up. She slapped Jimmy on the arm, still frowning and looking like she was pissed off that she'd been wasting her time, and pulled herself away from him. She took the glass of water that Aesop was still holding and turned and walked away, head high and back straight and with more dignity than Jimmy could have cobbled together right then in a fit. He watched her go and then took a sip of his vodka.

'Are you okay, Jimmy?' said Aesop.

Jimmy nodded at him, saying nothing.

'C'mon, don't feel bad.'

'I'm fine.'

'To be perfectly honest with you, Jimmy, I don't think it would've worked out. She'd be working these mad hours and all …'

'Shut up Aesop.'

'I'm just saying, y'know? She'd be out in the clubs till late, you'd be wondering who she was with, what she was doing, who'd been blowing her cock …'

'Aesop …'

'Then there'd be all these fights over not putting the toilet seat down.'

'Will you fucking shut up? I'm going for a piss. Where's the jacks?'

Aesop pointed over beyond the bar.

'Hold that.'

Jimmy gave him his drink and walked off. He wasn't even embarrassed yet, just furious with himself. And Aesop would never forget this in a million years. This was only the beginning. Everyone at home would find out about it. Now he started to feel it, the heat in his face. Fuck. He turned the corner and found himself with his hand out to push open the door of the Ladies.

He looked around and saw the Gents on the opposite side of the dancefloor. He turned quickly and walked over, firing a quick finger back at Aesop, who blew him a kiss and waved at him from behind his camcorder.

Twelve

'JAYSIS,' SAID Aesop, the next morning. 'Look at the arse on yer man.'

He was nodding at the waiter.

Jimmy looked down at his banana pancakes and sighed.

'Are you going to be winding me up for the next two weeks? Cos I'm fucking bored with it already.'

'Jimmy, there's some things in life that you don't get to see very often, and seeing you go all googly-eyed over a bloke in a dress is one of them. You'd have no respect for me if I didn't remind you of the depths of your shame every now and again.'

'I have no respect for you anyway, you fucker. You had me all fired up about scoring. How was I supposed to know that a bloke in a dress can look like that? She wasn't exactly carrying a parasol and going "But I'm a *lady*", for fuck sake, was she?'

'I thought you talked to Andy before you came out?'

'I did! But we were only talking for a few minutes and then he had to drop the kids to swimming. Elaine was the one who was telling me about Koh Samui, and we were talking about water-falls and the snake farm and some fucking big Buddha yoke. She didn't mention anything about men doing themselves up as birds and going around trying to … I mean, what the fuck was she trying to do, even? What was going to happen if I brought her home? I'm not exactly going to take one look at her bollocks and go, "Sure fuck it, I'm on me holliers", am I? What was I meant to do?'

'Well you could start by going for someone with a little less banana in the trouser department. Look, I don't know how it works, Jimmy. But will you do us all a favour and stay away from Thai women? The only ones you're going to score with are either blokes or brazzers. The nice girls wouldn't touch you with a bamboo pole.'

'Why not?'

'I don't know. I mean, they see the shite that blokes get up to when they're in a place like this, don't they? You think they want to have anything to do with that? Would you, if you were a girl? Which you nearly were last night, by the way. Anyway, there's plenty of other women here for two weeks worth of vadge. You've no reason to be going native.'

'Well you don't have anything to worry about on that score. I'm not touching any women from now on that I haven't seen in a bloody bikini first.'

'Sure that's only common sense anyway Jimmy. You didn't have to humiliate yourself to come up with that, did you? Anyway, what'll we do today?'

'Want to see the snake farm?'

'Snake farm? What's that?'

'It's a fucking farm with snakes on it.'

'For what? Do they keep the birds away or something? Whatever. And let's try that Islander place next to the Mango later for dinner. They have fish and chips, s'posed to be brilliant.'

'I thought you didn't like fish.'

'Once they aren't carrying fuckin laser guns I'll give it a go.'

JIMMY COULDN'T help himself. He'd been walking through the lobby of the hotel when he noticed a sign that said 'Business Centre'. He stuck his head in the door and saw three computers and a fax machine. Before he could ask the Thai girl sitting at a desk if there was Internet access, he saw another sign. The Chaweng Sawadee Grand was proud to be the first place on the island to provide wireless Internet access. He was sitting back in the hut, frowning at his laptop, when Aesop came in from the bank.

'Jesus, there was some queue out at the ATM,' he said. 'I swear, one of the fuckers must have been trying to get a mortgage. What are you up to? It's very quiet in here.'

'I'm just checking me mail,' said Jimmy.

'What? You're s'posed to be on holidays. Turn that yoke off and get ready. We're going out. I'm having a shower after that python crawling all over me. I notice that you weren't rushing to help, by the way, when he started wrapping himself around me legs.'

'I'm not good with snakes.'

'And I'm Tarzan now, am I?'

'Just a minute Aesop, I need to check this.'

Aesop stood at the bathroom door for a minute, looking at Jimmy, and then went and had his shower. When he came out, Jimmy hadn't moved.

'Jimmy ...'

'I know, I know. I just need to write one more and then I'm done.'

He was still sitting there when Aesop came out of his room and went to the fridge to get a beer.

'Do you want a beer while you're doing that, or will I call reception and ask them to send down a secretary to take notes for you?'

'I'm nearly done.'

'Jimmy, for fuck ...'

'Aesop, I won't be long. Just give me a minute, will you?'

'I'm going down to the Islander for some grub,' said Aesop. 'I'll see you there when you're done. Or will I wait? Are you ready now?'

'Aesop, I have to work!'

'Ah, fuckin work then, Jimmy. Enjoy yourself. Sure that's what we're here for, right?'

Aesop took his beer and walked out.

Jimmy looked at the door closing behind him and sighed. But he had to get this done. He couldn't leave anything hanging, knowing it needed attention.

He eventually caught up with Aesop in the bar of Islander, where Aesop was just finishing off his dinner. Jimmy ordered a beer and sat down next to him.

'How was your day at the office, dear?' said Aesop.

'Grand.'

'Are you having dinner?'

'Nah. I'm not hungry.'

'Pint next door?'

'Yeah.'

They took it easier compared to the first night. No dancing this time and they left at around midnight. It had all been a bit subdued after their little spat. They'd had a laugh, but it wasn't the same. It reminded Jimmy of having a row with Sandra. It wasn't resolved, but they were just letting it blow over. Except Aesop wasn't Sandra.

'You're a terrible arsehole, Jimmy,' he said.

They were lying in their hammocks, watching the moon out over the sea.

'Aesop, I just needed to sort a few things out. No big deal.'

'I don't give a wank about that. You came out tonight and you looked exactly like you do back in Dublin. Staring into space and scratching your head. Last night you were the old Jimmy, having a good laugh, and then one hour of that fuckin computer and you might as well have been at home again, the big worried smig on you. I know you have a big job and all, but everyone needs to get away from it. Does your boss check his email when he's on holidays?'

'He does sometimes.'

'Well then he's a fuckin eejit as well. And don't think no one sees you eating them little white tablets all the time either, or sticking fingers into your belly.'

'It's just heartburn.'

'How many people on this island have heartburn, do you reckon?'

'I was sick a few weeks ago. I'm just getting over it now.'

'A relapse is what you'll be getting if you don't cop on.'

'It's nothing, Aesop. A few emails. You're fucking giving me

124

heartburn now, sure. What do I have to do for you to shut your hole?'

There was silence.

'Jaysis, that was easy,' said Jimmy, looking over at the other hammock.

'I'm thinking. Are you going to be working while we're here?'

'Maybe, yeah. But just a little bit. Less than an hour a day.'

'Right. I'll make you a deal.'

'What?'

'I won't give you grief if you do one thing for me.'

'What?'

'If you score some time in the next three days, I'll leave you alone.'

'Bleedin hell, Aesop …'

'But!' said Aesop. 'But … there's one condition.'

'What?'

'The person you score with isn't allowed have a bigger mickey than you.'

'Ha fuckin ha.'

'Okay? Is it a deal? We go out, have a laugh, find some women and you take the skin boat to Tunatown. For free, now. She can't be a brazzer either.'

'Why is me having sex so important to you?'

'It's not the riding, Jimmy. The riding is only symbolic.'

'You're some bollix.'

'Are we sorted?'

'Okay. Jesus, okay. If it'll shut you up.'

'Excellent,' said Aesop. 'We'll start tonight.'

'What? It's nearly midnight!'

'Come on you lazy fuck. Get up. We're going out.'

THEY MET two English girls in the Green Mango and ended up asking them if they wanted to go back to their place for a beer when it was closing. The girls were on for it. Jimmy felt an almost-forgotten jump in his chest and tried to keep the smile off his face. God, how long had it been since he'd done this? Years. He was shitting himself, thinking about what might happen later.

They were both about twenty-seven. Amanda with the green eyes and the freckles and Susan with the incredible body and pouty lips were from just outside London somewhere. They were all chatting as a group as they walked back to the hotel, but Aesop caught Jimmy alone when they ducked in to get a pack of cigarettes. The girls stayed near the door, browsing through the bikinis hanging there.

'You can have Susan. Go on. I'll take the other one. That's how nice I am.'

'Shush. Shut up. Anyway, what about what they want?'

'Well, they'll both want me, won't they? But go on, spoil yourself. I'll introduce Amanda to The Cannon in the bedroom after we have a beer or two and you'll be free to work the old Jimmy magic on Susan out in the hammocks.'

'Shut up. They'll hear you.'

'I betcha they're talking about the same thing we're talking about.'

'I doubt that.'

'That's why we're in here! I have duty-free smokes back in the hut, sure. But you need to give the girls a chance to huddle. That's only manners. God, do you remember nothing? Just relax. Anyway, that wasn't so bad, was it? They're nice enough for you, right? Nothing sleazy going on, right? Nice and cool. Everyone's on their holidays, out for a good time. No sweat. And look at the cheesy grin on your beak! That's more fuckin like it, you big homo.'

'Shhh. Christ, you have me all wound up.'

'That's exactly why we're doing this, ye tool. You've lost your way. I'm here to lead you back to the path of the righteous.' He raised a hand in a blessing. 'Now go forth, my son. The oil is yonder. The wick is dry. Dip deep and be merry.'

'Ever the poet.'

'Doctor, Jimmy. This week I'm a doctor. Try and keep up, will ye?'

They got back to the hotel and Jimmy got four beers out of the fridge while Aesop gave them the grand tour, which effectively meant steering them out to the hammocks. When Jimmy stepped through the doors he found them all at the low wall at the bottom of the garden, looking out over the moonlit sand and up at the stars. Aesop was naming out constellations to them.

'That's Capricorn,' he was saying softly, one arm around Amanda's shoulder and the other pointing up at Perseus.

Jimmy shook his head and walked out to them.

'I'm just telling the girls here, Jimmy,' said Aesop, 'how I studied astronomy in college.'

'I thought you studied medicine, Aesop.'

'Yeah, but that was afterwards. Did I not tell you that, Jimmy? You see, Amanda, I always loved the stars. When I was growing up in Cork, we lived way out in the country. There were no street lights of course, and the sky would be like a black silk sheet stretched out over the house at night, with those flecks of silver dust speckled across it. As a young lad, me Grandad Miley, Lord rest him, used to bring me out into the fields when he was babysitting us, and explain to me all the different names of the stars and the stories that went with them. Most people know the Greek stories, but we had our own stories in Ireland, from way back in the old days.'

Jimmy stepped next to Susan and handed her the beer. She smiled at him and looked back up into the sky. Jimmy looked up too. Aesop was talking through his hole, but they seemed to be enjoying themselves.

'Tell us one of the stories,' said Jimmy. Let the fucker work for it for a change.

'I will so, Jimmy. You see that star there, Amanda? The one with the faint orangey tint? Well that's not a star at all. That's the planet Neptune. Of course, we didn't call it Neptune back home. We called it *An Madra Beag*, which in Irish means The Lonesome Boatman.'

Jimmy took a huge gulp of beer to hide his face. Aesop was shite at Irish.

'The Boatman used to have a girl. A beautiful young flower she was and her name was … Orla. *Orla Sé do Bheatha Abhaile*, which means Orla of the Flowing Fair Hair. But Orla's old man …'

'What was his name, Aesop?' said Jimmy.

'The Dad? He was called *Báidín Fheilimí*, Jimmy. Anyway, he didn't like the Boatman. You see, being out on the water was an awful dangerous job in the old days. There'd be terrible fierce storms, and monsters too they'd say, and no man was safe if his luck turned on him. Her Dad didn't want his daughter to be falling in love with someone like that. Someone that might break her heart by going out and never coming back to her. So anyway, didn't he forbid that they see each other, not even at mass, and kept a close eye to see that he wasn't disobeyed. But of course, this broke her heart too. One night, mad with the pain of not being close to her love, she crept out of the house and down to the shore to see if she could find the Boatman. But Madra Beag was out fishing. You see, it was winter, and the Langer Crab spawned in the winter, but would only move about at night. If you wanted to catch them, that's when you had to go looking. Ireland was full of Langers in those days. There's still loads of them today, down around Cork especially.'

'Anyway, as she scoured the sea to catch a glimpse of him, didn't a big wave come in and sweep her away. When the Boatman came back to land, he saw her orange shawl washed up on the sand and knew immediately what had happened. With a fierce cry, he got back in his boat and went out looking for her. But the luck turned even more on him then and he got caught up in the storm and was never seen again.'

Aesop paused to wipe an eye with the back of his hand.

'And so now, when you look up at Neptune, that's the Lonesome Boatman you see. He keeps searching for his love, *Orla Sé do Beatha Abhaile*, up there in the heavens, criss-crossing the sky and calling her name in the wind … *Orrr-la … Orrr-la*. You can hear him still when it's stormy and blowing out over the ocean. It was winter when he lost her, and so cold that he wrapped up in her orange shawl as he sailed off that night to try and find his darling, the girl that first her Dad and then the sea took from him. That shawl was all that was left of her.'

Aesop took a sip of his beer and then looked up again.

'And that's why Neptune is that colour up there still. He wears it still, hoping to give it back to her one day when he finds her.'

No one said anything for a minute. The girls gazed skywards, Amanda leaning against Aesop and Susan now holding Jimmy's hand. He'd barely noticed it happening he was concentrating so much on not snorting out loud.

'And is Orla up there as well, Aesop?' said Jimmy.

You're not done yet, you chancer.

'She is Jimmy. But she's not a star. Nor a planet, nor a moon either.'

'Is she not?'

'No. Orla became even more special than that. She became a comet.'

Jimmy let go of Susan's hand and pretended to look for a lighter so she wouldn't feel his shoulders shaking.

'A comet?' he managed, cupping his smoke to light it.

'Yes. And a well-known one. You've heard of Halley's Comet? Well in Ireland we call that comet The Face of Orla. Or *Liath-róidí Orla*. And the long beautiful tail of the comet? That's Orla's long beautiful fair hair, being blown away from her face on that awful stormy night as she stood on the beach looking for her Lonesome Boatman.'

Jimmy looked over. Aesop was still facing the sky, his eyes

glistening and his mouth fixed in a tiny, sad smile. The fucker was good. You had to give him that. He actually ad-libbed this shite. Jimmy could see goosebumps on Susan's neck and decided that he'd better change the subject before she started to cry. Although fucking Pinocchio over there probably had a contingency plan for that as well.

'Such a sad story,' said Amanda. Her eyes were shimmering.

'We have a lot of sad stories in Ireland, Amanda,' said Aesop, looking around at her. 'We're a troubled people.' He reached into his pocket. 'Here, do you want a tissue?'

Oh for fuck …

'Another beer?' said Jimmy quickly.

'I'll get them, shall I?' said Susan.

'I'll help you,' added Amanda.

The two girls disappeared into the hut and slid the door closed.

Aesop was still standing there, looking back up at the sky wistfully.

'They're gone, Aesop, you can give over. Jesus, did you ride the Blarney Stone? What a load of shite.'

'To you and me it's shite, but to them it's the reason they flew halfway round the world instead of going to Butlins. Any dopey bastard can buy them a few drinks and then try and prise their legs open with fumbling, stupid fingers and beer-soaked words of empty meaning and …'

'Aesop, for fuck sake …'

'Sorry. I was on a roll. Anyway, my point is that you have to know your audience. Just like a gig. Every woman is a souf-flé, Jimmy. Remember that. You'll only get one chance at her and if you fuck it up, no dessert. That pair wanted something special. They're not a couple of slappers out for a quick root and some free gargle. Blokes are probably trying that every Friday night with them, down the Fox and Wanker or wherever they go to relax at the weekend. They're your kind of women, Jimmy.

Nice, like. And now they think we're nice too! No need to thank me.'

'But I am fucking nice!'

'Yeah, but right now it's only because you're reflected in the glow of my shining sensitivity, y'see? They're aroused by the fact that they've hit the jackpot. All the drunk spas on this island, and they managed to hook up with two fantastic, charming, interesting, warm Irishmen who'd rather gaze with them at a beautiful sky than paw at their tits like a couple of schoolboys.'

Jimmy finished his drink and rattled the can. He could see the girls talking at the fridge.

'You think they're aroused?'

'Jimmy, if they were any more aroused they'd be speaking in tongues.'

'Hmm … you're some lying bastard though. I don't care what you say.'

'Fair enough. But Jimmy, all I did was give them a night to remember. They haven't even gotten to the good part yet, but they won't be forgetting the evening they spent with us, here, and the story of poor, sad *Orla Sé do Bheatha Abhaile*.'

Jimmy shook his head and laughed.

'*Orla Sé do* …what are you fucking like? Did you spin this crap for Marie as well?'

'Marie? A Dutch bird? Christ, no. Sure they have no interest in all that rubbish. She had the twins out before the front door was closed.'

The girls stepped back into the garden with the beers. Amanda went straight to Aesop and Susan stepped up close to Jimmy, handing him the can with a big smile. She was looking right into his eyes, her own big and bright in the moonlight. That wasn't an airhostess smile. No mixed messages there, thought Jimmy.

They adjourned to the hammocks, the lads in first and then the girls curled up next to them. It was quiet, only the small waves lapping at the shore. The four of them chatted about stuff for a little while, laughing about Aesop being terrorised on the snake farm and how Jimmy nearly killed himself with the chilli on the plane, and then gradually that died away too until Jimmy was just talking to Susan in a low voice. He heard Aesop and Amanda murmuring away too, but it was all becoming a bit more private. Intimate.

Eventually there was some movement from the other hammock and Jimmy looked around to see Aesop and Amanda push themselves up and stand there, hand in hand.

'Going to hit the hay, Jimmy,' said Aesop.

'G'night so.'

'See you in the morning,' said Amanda.

She came over and gave Susan a quick hug and then she and Aesop walked back into the hut. It got even quieter. The amazing sky, the swishing water, the palm leaves waving overhead. Jimmy felt like he was dreaming as Susan nestled in closer to his chest, her leg curled around one of his. He was glad that Aesop had left them. He didn't want to talk shite anymore. He just wanted to lie here with this beautiful girl, who smelled of flowers and tropical oils and was clinging to him like she needed him. If only she knew.

'Jimmy?' she said.

'Yep?'

'I really ... I ... it's just so nice out here.'

'Yeah. Isn't it?'

'I'm glad we met you and Aesop.'

'So am I.'

'We came here for a break. Amanda just got out of a messy situation with a guy. It was hard on her. She really needed this. They'd been together a long time.'

'I know what that's like.'

'Do you? Want to tell me about it?'

'Eh ... well ... no, not really. I broke up with someone a while ago. That's all. It hurts, but you just have to get on with it.'

132

'Did you love her?'

'Yeah. I did.'

'I'm sorry.'

'Ah, stop. It's gone now. I tried to figure out what it all meant, but in the end things just happen, right? You can't spend the rest of your life torturing yourself over it.'

'I know. That's what I tried to tell Amanda, but she was so down. In the end, we figured that if we went away for a while, somewhere different, she'd be able to let it go. We've been friends forever. I hated seeing her like that. We didn't come here to meet guys.'

Jimmy said nothing.

'Really, Jimmy. I don't want you to think that we're just here for … you know. We're not like that.'

'I don't think that.'

'It's important to me that you don't. I know we just came along tonight without even knowing you, but you seemed nice. Especially you, Jimmy.'

She got up on one elbow and looked at him.

'Are you nice, Jimmy?'

'Eh … well, I try and call me Mam once a week …'

She laughed.

'That's good. Is Aesop nice?'

'He's great.'

Jimmy shifted in the hammock. This was dodgy territory and he could feel himself blushing in the dark.

'Because Amanda needs nice. Can Aesop give her that?'

If I know Aesop, he's giving it to her right now.

He swallowed.

'Aesop will look after her.'

Which wasn't a lie, strictly speaking.

'Good.'

Susan turned his face to hers with her hand and kissed him. He shifted again in the hammock so that he could put an arm around her waist and they lay there kissing and cuddling and wrapped up in each other.

Another hour went by and they got to know each other little by little. Jimmy was annoyed that he had to keep an eye on himself so that he didn't give away the fact that almost everything Aesop had said earlier about his job, his family, the sky and his time with the Peace Corps was utter bollocks. He didn't want to bullshit Susan. He told her something about his own work and the band and the fact that he was giving it up to concentrate on his career. She wanted him to sing her a song, but he didn't want to. It was too quiet. He thought about singing 'Caillte' to her softly in the darkness of the garden, but the rockstar in him thought that he wouldn't be able to do it justice after all the beer and smokes. Instead he went in to get a bottle of water and came out with the laptop, opening it on the small table between the hammocks and standing next to it, looking out to sea and telling her what it was about as the guitar intro started. When he looked back into the hammock at the end of the song she was staring at him, her eyes the only thing he could make out in the shadows.

'Tell me what it means. The lyrics.'

Jimmy translated the song line by line as he played it again.

She got out of the hammock and took his hand.

Jimmy's heart was thumping.

This was it. And it was perfect. He felt so close to this girl, a girl he'd really only just met. All this time he'd been feeling hurt by Sandra and made a fool of by Kayleigh, who'd come later, he'd always imagined that the next girl would probably be something meaningless. Something to get him past it all in his mind, before he could move on properly. But it wasn't like that at all. Susan was intelligent and beautiful and there was an understanding in her eyes that made him feel like they recognised each other. His belly seemed to collapse a little as he looked back at her. This was it.

'Will you do something for me, Jimmy?'

'Sure. Anything.'

'Will you watch the sunrise with me?'

'The sunrise?'

She turned and pointed out over the water, where the horizon was now splashed with indigo and deep pinks.

'Do you know, I've never actually seen the sun come up over the ocean.'

'Neither have I,' said Jimmy.

He hadn't. But, Jesus, who the fuck cared?

She led him down the garden and over the wall as he tried to grapple his thoughts back into sync with what was happening.

They stood with the water swirling around their ankles for the next hour, her arms wrapped around him and the distant clouds seeming to shift and pulse as berry colours glanced off them and the fiery ball of the sun finally peeked above the edge of the world and rose into the sky.

'So beautiful,' she said.

Jimmy nodded.

'And you're a beautiful man,' she added.

Beautiful? Ah, fuck this. Jimmy was getting tired. It was one thing to have magical thoughts cruising through you as you hung from a coconut tree on a tropical island paradise in the dead of night, but there was a natural progression to these things, surely, and she was fucking taking the piss now.

'Do you want to see if anywhere is open for breakfast?' she said.

Do I fuck.

'Actually, Susan, I'm kind of tired. How about we just head back to the hut.'

'Hut? Where I'm staying is a hut, Jimmy. Your place is gorgeous.'

'What do you think?'

'Okay. I'm kind of pooped too.'

They went back to the garden, but she climbed back into the hammock and held her arms out for him to join her.

He looked at her. Fuck it. At this stage a kip was all he was good for anyway.

He got in and they dozed off.

Thirteen

WHEN JIMMY opened his eyes later that morning, he lifted his head to see Prem smiling at him from the other side of the wall. He had a rake and a bucket and was cleaning bits of flotsam from the sand in front of the hotel.

'Good morning, Mr Jimmy.'

'Howya Prem.'

Jimmy shifted sideways to get his arm out from under Susan and groaned. It was gone asleep on him and his neck was stiff and sore from the hammock.

'Would you like breakfast? I can bring it here for you and Dr Aesop and your friend.'

'Eh, yeah. Why not? What time is it?'

'It's nearly eleven o'clock. What would you like?'

'Jaysis, I don't know.'

Susan was starting to wake up.

'What do you want for breakfast?' Jimmy asked her, when he saw her eyes open and squint in the morning sun.

'Fruit,' she mumbled.

'Fruit. Right. Prem, we'll have a load of fruit and some bacon and eggs. And coffee.'

'Okay, Mr Jimmy. I will have it for you very soon.'

'Good man.'

He got out of the hammock and stood on the sandy dry grass, stretching and turning to get the kinks out of his body. Back in the hammock, Susan was taking advantage of the extra space and seemed to be going back to sleep. He looked at her. She was pretty cute, lying there. Her gorgeous lips were all big and still red even though he'd been stuck to them for the best part of three hours last night. He wasn't pissed off anymore. It would've been crap, bringing her to bed at that hour of the morning, half drunk and knackered. It had been so long since he'd done it, God knows what kind of performance he would've put in in that state. He picked up a piece of palm leaf from the ground and tickled her nose with it. She wrinkled up her face and Jimmy smiled. She looked like a disgruntled little pixie when she did that. He kissed her on the lips and she opened her eyes.

'Morning,' she said, rubbing her eyes.

'How do you feel?'

'Cosy.'

'Ready for a swim to wake up?'

'Hmm. Okay.'

She stumbled out of the hammock and the two of them walked hand in hand to the water. She was wearing a bikini under the short cotton dress she'd had on last night. Jimmy was in board shorts anyway. It was cool enough to be refreshing, but not cold. When they got back to the hut, she disappeared into the shower. He thought for a second about going in to join her, but then decided that she mightn't like that. He was supposed to be 'nice', whatever that meant. He decided to play it safe. He went in when she was done and by the time he came out she had the table set for four. There was a knock on the door and a beaming Prem walked in with a trolley. Jimmy didn't even recognise half of the fruits on the platter, but he was more interested anyway in the fried bacon, sausages and scrambled eggs that Prem produced from beneath silver covers before he gave Susan a small purple orchid, bowed and then left.

Aesop's bedroom door opened and Amanda stumbled into the shower with a small wave at the two of them.

'Jaysis. What time is it?' said Aesop. He was standing in the doorway with a white sheet wrapped around his middle.

'Lunchtime.'

'So why are we up?'

He looked around at the set table and all the food and blinked.

'What's going on?'

'Breakfast.'

Aesop looked at Jimmy. Susan was at the sink, getting a towel to hold the hot coffee pot.

'What the fuck are you doing?' Aesop mouthed.

'What?' Jimmy mouthed back, shrugging.

'Breakfast!' He nodded towards the sink and the shower. 'These two!' He shook a thumb over his shoulder. 'Tell them to fuck off!'

Jimmy just gave him the finger and got back to buttering his toast. Amanda came out of the shower and Aesop went in, glowering at Jimmy as he walked past. He came out and went into the room to get dressed and then joined them at the table.

'Jimmy was saying that we should visit the Namuang Waterfalls this afternoon, Aesop,' said Amanda. 'What do you think?'

Aesop's hand slowed as it approached his mouth with half a sausage on a fork.

'Eh ... but Jimmy, I thought you said you had to work this afternoon?'

'Ah, sure it's nothing important. I can skip a day or two, right? Anyway, who works on their holidays Aesop, I mean, c'mon.'

'Okay ... I just thought ...'

'It'll be great,' said Susan. 'I've heard they're beautiful. We can get a taxi there and then there's the Butterfly Farm we read about. We can go there on the way back before dinner.'

Aesop was rubbing his head.

'Butterflies?'

'It's not just butterflies, Aesop,' said Jimmy, pointing it out on the pamphlet. 'They have bees too, look.'

Aesop stuck the sausage in his mouth.

'There's a bit of luck.'

'Listen to grumpy-arse here,' said Jimmy to the girls, laughing. 'Not a morning person, are we Aesop?'

'I'm a delight to be around. But I can't be around bees. I'm allergic to the stings. Remember that time I nearly died, Jimmy?'

'But you can bring one of your injections with you, can't you? You must have one in your doctor's bag. And it's not like they'll be stinging you anyway. They're tame.'

'Oh right. And how do you tame a bee, Jimmy?'

'We can ask them when we get there.'

Aesop nodded slowly and took up his coffee cup, looking around at everyone.

'Well, isn't this lovely?'

AESOP WAS standing over Jimmy's hammock, hands on his hips. The girls were back at their hotel. They'd pick them up in the taxi later. Jimmy looked up and shielded his eyes from the sun.

'What?'

'What are you trying to do to me, Jimmy?'

'What are you on about?'

'Breakfast? Butterfly farms? Is this what happens when I leave you alone with a woman for five minutes?'

'Ah relax Aesop. They're nice.'

'Beer is nice, Jimmy. French knickers are nice. Spending two weeks in a place like this with the same two birds dragging out of you for the whole thing is a fuckin disaster.'

'I thought you were all on for me having a good time! I'm delighted that we met them. Susan's great. We got on really well and I want to see more of her. And Amanda is with Susan, so you'll just have to grin and bear it. Anyway, Amanda is lovely. I don't know what your problem is. Judging by the way she limped into the shower this morning, you didn't find her too objectionable last night. I thought you'd be happy.'

'Happy? Jimmy, is your head full of piss? I was gearing myself up for two weeks of razzle and now that pair will have their suitcases in the hall and their knickers drying over the shower rail before the day is out.'

'Don't be stupid. Anyway, it was your idea.'

'How was it my idea?!'

'You were the one who wanted me to meet women.'

'Women, Jimmy. Plural. Jesus, I fuckin knew this would happen. I told meself it wouldn't, but in the back of my mind I was saying, "Keep an eye on Jimmy, Aesop. You know what he's like. He'll meet some bird, fall in love, and the next thing you know he'll be bringing us all to look at fuckin waterfalls." Why couldn't you just be cool?'

'I am cool, Aesop. I can't remember the last time I was this relaxed. You're the one standing under a coconut tree in your jocks with spit flying out of your mouth.'

Aesop sat back on the table behind him, exasperated. He felt the laptop under him.

'What's that doing out here? You were probably talking about work, were you? It's a wonder you got your hole at all.'

'I was just playing her a couple of songs.'

'Caillte?'

'Yeah. Why not?'

'What did you tell her it was about?'

'I told her exactly what it was about.'

'About you and Kayleigh and all that?'

'Yeah.'

'Did it work?'

'Did what work?'

'Jesus, it's like talking to the only gay in the village.'

'She liked it Aesop, if that's what you mean. We chatted, lay here in the hammock and then we got up and watched the sunrise.'

'So you did her in the hammock? Nice.'

'I didn't do her anywhere, Aesop. We just got to know each other, had a cuddle, kissed a bit. She's a great girl.'

Aesop stood up again with his mouth open.

'You didn't even …'

'Nope. It just didn't seem like the right time.'

141

'The right time? Are you taking the ...? You're lying there with a gorgeous bird in a hammock in a place like this. The sea is gurgling away in the distance, there's a big sky up there with stars fuckin twinkling all over it and a sappy song is playing softly in the darkness. Meanwhile I've just kicked the gates open with a masterful story about Orla the Comet and your bird's got half a bottle of gin and four fuckin beers in her! My old man could've rode Susan last night! Jesus, I can't believe I let you have her instead of Amanda. What a fuckin waste.'

'I'm not you, Aesop.'

'You're not even you anymore, Jimmy. Why didn't you just ... and watching the sunrise? Please don't tell me that was your idea.'

'Actually, it was Susan's. The sun was coming up and we just went down there to look at it.'

Aesop looked out over the wall.

'So what are you telling me? She led you down the garden path? To look at the sun? Well, I've fuckin heard it all now.'

'It wasn't like that. Look, will you shut up. We should get ready to go. We're picking them up in twenty minutes. God, look at the face on you.'

'Ah Jesus, it's butterflies, Jimmy.' Aesop pouted like a little child. 'Stupid fuckin colourdy butterflies. For a whole afternoon. With the same two birds I was with last night! I might as well be on holidays with Norman.'

'They're gone at the weekend, Aesop. It won't kill you. Did you have a good time with Amanda anyway?'

'Yeah, I s'pose. Ah no, to be fair, I did. She's just broken up with some bloke so it was like bringing your mickey to the circus.'

'So at least you talked to her.'

'Talk to her? Nah. You can tell by riding them. They have that look in their eye, y'know? They're a bit nervous about being with someone new, so they start to focus on doing a good job. They think they'll feel better about themselves that way. Then they think they're concentrating too hard and you'll notice. So they let go a bit and start acting the trollop. But then they get worried cos they think they're coming across as some dirty slapper, so they get nervous and the whole thing starts up again.'

'Have you ever thought about writing self-help books, Aesop?'

'Yeah. Actually, I was going to do one on procrastination, but I couldn't be arsed.'

'Look, just be nice to her, okay? It's only a few days. I like Susan. Don't fuck it up.'

'Fuck what up? She'll be out of here by next Monday and you'll never see her again. What's to fuck up? Sorry for pissing on your chips Jimmy, but this isn't going to turn into a relationship. Even you and your twisted way of looking at things couldn't turn this into happily ever after. God. You'd fuckin cross the road to fall down a hole, you would.'

'What do you mean?'

'This! You're just fizzing at the bunghole to fall in love with someone, aren't you? You meet Susan, eventually ride her – probably the night before she leaves to go back to England, because that'll make it all the more special – and then I'm the one that has to look at the mopey fuckin head on you for the next six months while you get over it.'

'Don't be stupid. She's just nice. We had a laugh. That's all.'

'I know you, Jimmy.'

'Ask me bollocks, Aesop. Just try and be the bloke you pretended to be last night, okay? Consider it a challenge to your powers of deception. See if you can keep it up for more than five minutes at a time.'

'Do you realise the sacrifice I'm making for you?'

'Yeah, poor Aesop. We'll do whatever you want next week, right?'

'Anything?'

'Yeah. But c'mere. Listen to me, I'm not interested in trying to pull some brazzer every night of the week just so that you can put notches in your belt, so you'll have to come up with something else.'

'Maybe I already have.'

'What?'

'Well, it won't be anything to do with farms or fuckin waterfalls, I can tell you that for nothing.'

THE FOUR of them were sitting in a restaurant having breakfast. In the previous couple of days they'd pretty much done everything that the book said there was to do. They'd gone to see the Big Buddha, which was essentially a big Buddha, the magic Buddha garden, which was more interesting but not really worth the afternoon they'd spent getting there, and the Ancient House … which was an old wooden house. The girls were enthusiastic about absolutely everything, reading up on the backgrounds and details in the taxi and explaining to the lads what they were about to see. The four kilometre trek it took to reach the Hin Lad Waterfall, which wasn't even as good as the one they'd driven to the previous day, was the end of the line for Aesop.

'I've just about had enough of this shit,' he'd said to Jimmy that night. 'And now I've got a blister on my foot to go with the pain in my arse. It's only Wednesday! I can't do this for another four days. I don't care if you're living out your teenage girl's romantic fantasy life here, it's not worth it.'

'Come on Aesop. It's interesting.'

'And that shrine? I hadn't a clue what yer woman was talking about. Shiva this and Vishnu that and that Brahma bloke with all the arms and heads and Amanda pulling at me to take pictures of everything. It's not me. I'm struggling, Jimmy. I'm not good at this. I'm all upset.'

Jimmy laughed at him.

'You'll be grand. We'll head into the Reggae Bar tonight. You'll like that. Live music.'

144

'Yeah. Will they do any Peter Tosh do you think, or will it just be bleedin Buffalo Solider all night?'

'We'll find out. Will you cheer up, man? You were the one telling me to cop on a few days ago.'

'Can we go Go Kart racing? We've driven straight past it three times now only to end up at some crap statue where I have to smile and nod and pretend it's not all a pile of shite.'

'We've all next week for that. You can plan a whole week of Aesop-fun.'

Amanda and Susan had their own plan at breakfast.

'So what do you think?' said Susan.

'Could be a laugh,' said Jimmy. 'What do you reckon Aesop?'

'What is it exactly?' said Aesop.

'It's kind of a health farm,' said Amanda.

'A health farm? God, they're mad for farms in this place, aren't they? Snake farms and bee farms and butterfly farms. Do they have a beer farm by any chance?'

'Yeah. It's called the Green Mango. You liked that one,' said Jimmy.

'It says here,' said Susan, 'that they have three-day retreats where you just go and chill and detox.'

'Retreat?' said Aesop. 'I don't have a good history with that stuff. I was sent home from the last one I was at. Remember that Jimmy? The nun said there was an evil spirit in me. Imagine that now, Amanda.'

'A bit of detox wouldn't be bad,' said Jimmy.

'It would be great,' said Amanda. 'Quiet and peaceful. It's on the other side of the island, away from the crowds. Look at the photos. It looks beautiful. The perfect way to end the holiday.'

This seemed to perk Aesop up a bit. The girls would be packing up at the end of it.

'Okay. Let's do it. Three days. God, and then you'll be off, won't you? So soon!' He smiled sadly and then looked up. 'Right. We'll do it.'

'Great!' said Susan, clapping her hands together. 'I'll call them now and see if we can start tomorrow.'

Once they were booked in they had the rest of the day free.

'What'll we do?' said Susan. 'Why don't we have a nice big meal tonight if we're going to be doing the health thing from tomorrow?'

'Sounds good to me,' said Aesop.

'And we could spend the afternoon on the beach.'

'Or we could go Go Kart racing.'

'Did you see that crocodile farm in the brochure?' said Amanda.

'Is that the one next to the Go Kart track?'

'I think it's near the airport.'

'Right. Past the Go Kart track, so?'

'Would you like to go on the Go Karts, Aesop?'

Aesop nodded.

'Okay. Shall we do that then?'

He nodded again. He was smiling and looked around. The others all shrugged.

'Hurray for Aesop!' said Aesop, throwing his hands in the air. It was the first time Jimmy had seen him grin properly since he'd led Amanda into the bedroom on Monday night.

THEY WALKED to the Reggae Bar later after dinner, which was a bit away from the main drag; the two couples hand in hand and Aesop not even seeming to notice. At least he was keeping his end of the bargain about behaving himself. It was another gorgeous night, warm and clear and the road to the bar was dark and quiet. They'd had a pretty big feed in anticipation of going to the health farm, and this walk afterwards was perfect. It would've been even more perfect if Aesop hadn't insisted on telling the girls that Jimmy was a past winner of the North Dublin Fleadh and quite the handy Irish dancer.

'Shut up Aesop. Don't mind him Susan. I don't dance.'

'Under Twelve's, wasn't it Jimmy?' said Aesop. 'He has pictures of him in his little skirt and everything.'

'I'd love to see you dance,' said Susan, laughing.

'Really, I can't. I was only a kid.'

'We'll get him drunk in the Reggae Bar girls, watch, and you won't be able to stop him. Big kicks in the air and everything. He's like a puppet the way he can get off the ground.'

'Aesop, will you give over? Come on, the band will be starting soon down the road.'

But Aesop couldn't help himself and soon had the girls in stitches, doing the *haon-dó-trí* every few metres and laughing his head off. Eventually Susan and Amanda got the hang of it and then the three of them were at it.

'Look at sulky-bollocks behind us!' yelled Aesop.

They all laughed at him.

'All right, fuck it,' said Jimmy. 'If you're going to do it, you might as well do it properly.'

He kicked off his flip flops and hopped up into a jump, coming down and skipping across the road. The girls screamed and started clapping.

'I need music, Aesop,' shouted Jimmy.

'I'm with you, Jimmy!'

Aesop started to bounce and clap his hands, singing.

'Diddely diddely die dee die, dee diddley diddley die. Oh, diddely doodely diddely doo, dee diddely diddely die …'

They ended up roaring laughing and stumbling into the Reggae Bar holding each other up. It was the best night of the holiday so far. They were like old mates, all four of them. Aesop didn't even seem to mind that Amanda kept gazing at him and kissing him.

'So, are you having fun, then?' said Jimmy, when the two girls were in the toilet.

'Yeah, it's brilliant!'

'See? I told you we'd have a laugh. You just needed to get into it.'

'Yeah. And the cider we had at dinner didn't hurt either. Man, I love cider when I'm on me holliers. I love it.'

'I know. You keep telling me.'

'It's all cold and lovely.'

'Yeah. Listen …'

'Apples, Jimmy. Did you know it was made out of apples?'

'I did. C'mere Aesop …'

'Apples are brilliant, aren't they?'

'Will you fucking shut up a minute, Aesop? Listen, I'm going to head off with Susan. Do you want to entertain Amanda here for another hour or two?'

'Oooh, Jimmy! So you're going to, y'know …' Aesop started nodding and winking and punching Jimmy on the arm.

'Shush. We just thought we'd have an early night.'

'It's about bleedin time! Excellent. Well, listen, just relax okay? I know it's been a while, but there's no need to be nervous.'

'What? Will you stop messing? I'm grand.'

'Course you are. And you'll be a legend. I'm just saying, though, just be cool.' Aesop put a hand on Jimmy's shoulder. 'Okay? Just be cool. It'll be grand.'

Jimmy twisted away from Aesop's hand.

'Shut up for fuck sake! What are you trying to do to me?'

Aesop's hands went up in the air.

'Nothing! I just don't want you to feel like there's all this pressure on you to do a brilliant job, just because Amanda's probably been talking to Susan.'

'Aesop …'

'It's okay Jimmy. You've been out of the game a long time now. Don't go in there all worried that Susan's been hearing stories or anything, that's all I'm saying.'

'You're a fuckin eejit, Aesop.'

'I'm only trying to look out for you, man.'

'I don't need …'

'Here you are,' said Amanda behind them, moving in to link

148

Aesop's arm. 'Will we dance?'

'Sure,' he said, winking at Jimmy. 'Why not? Aren't we all warmed up now and everything after our little Riverdance performance earlier.'

Jimmy and Susan formally announced their departure before the other two disappeared into the crowd and then they walked slowly back to the hotel. He was fairly planking it at this stage, no thanks to bloody Aesop, and he could tell that Susan was nervous too. She was very quiet. If they'd just done it that first night then it would've been fine, but the longer they left it before something happened – and it was pretty obvious that something was going to happen at some stage – then the bigger the deal it all seemed to be for some reason. Maybe Aesop was right, thought Jimmy. At least partly right. Sometimes it's best not to think too much. Yeah, Aesop wasn't guilty of that.

Later on, it really didn't seem like such a big deal. They worked their way up to it gradually, and when they finally ended up together in Jimmy's bed it seemed like the right place to be. They fell asleep afterwards and didn't budge until eight the next morning.

Fourteen

'FASTING?' SAID Aesop. 'Like Lent?'

'Lent?' said Lars, the owner of the health farm. 'Well, the idea is that you don't eat anything while you're here.'

'Right,' said Aesop, nodding slowly. 'And what do you mean by that, exactly?'

'We've got a juice mixture that you'll be drinking. It's a special blend of melons, ginger and garlic. With fresh spring water.'

'Listen Lars, I like melons as much as the next man, but can we just back up a bit here to the part about …'

'Aesop,' said Jimmy. 'We're going to detox. That's the idea. Clean out the system.'

'If I want to clean out me system, Jimmy, I'll drink ten pints of stout and eat a kebab.'

'Well, I'll leave you to sort yourselves out,' said Lars, looking at the girls. 'I'll see you all in the Peace Room at one for our first session? I'll be demonstrating acupuncture as a means of purification.'

Aesop leaned in to Jimmy and whispered.

'Is the taxi still out there do you think? We can probably escape if we leg it.'

'Shush.'

'Really, Jimmy. What the fuck are we doing here? That one over there looks like a Turkish weightlifter.'

'Shut up. She'll hear you.'

'Not with all that hair growing out of her ears she won't. Jesus. I've seen better-looking darts players.'

Lars went on.

'This particular type of acupuncture is just a subset of the vast discipline that's been handed down from Chinese antiquity. Its specific purpose is to aid the body in detoxification. It channels *chi* in such a way as to expel toxins and speed healing.'

Aesop closed his eyes and shook his head.

'What a load of me bollocks.'

THE DETOX potions that they'd had to take all day kicked in that night and they spent most of it running to the toilet. By the time they met up the next morning they were all tired and a bit quiet. The verb 'to purge' had taken on a new and very vivid meaning for them. They felt empty.

'But I'm not hungry this morning,' said Jimmy. 'Isn't that mad? I thought I'd be getting a taxi on the sly back to town for some pancakes. But I don't even want to eat now.'

'I think they're brainwashing us,' said Aesop. 'I got up this morning and I actually wanted to go for a walk on the beach. They're after putting something in the water, the bastards. Hey Lars …'

Lars was walking past.

'Morning guys. How do you feel?'

They all looked at each other.

'Pretty good,' said Jimmy.

'Great. Did you have a good night?'

'Eh, well, I spent most of it in the toilet.'

'That's okay. Your first night. You'll sleep well tonight, I prom-ise. But I bet you don't feel hungry, right? And you're probably experiencing the beginnings of a heightened awareness. Your senses are starting to tune into the Earth's energies.'

'Well, I'm not sure that's how I'd put it …'

Lars laughed.

'It's not my job to convince you of things you don't believe. But you believe your bodies, right? Listen to your bodies. We pack so much rubbish into them that they're usually flat out trying to deal with it. We effectively poison ourselves from day to day. This could well be the longest you've ever gone without putting some-thing into yourselves that your bodies have to fight against. Wait till tomorrow and the next day. I think you'll enjoy the experience of being clean.'

'Yeah, right. So what did *you* have for breakfast then?' said Aesop.

Lars laughed.

'Actually, I'm a breatharian.'

They blinked at him.

'I don't eat.'

'You don't eat what?'

'I don't eat at all. Well, I have a bowl of rice every few days. But I actually get all the sustenance I need from prana. It's the vital life force of Hinduism.'

They all looked at each other.

'See you later,' he smiled, and walked off with his hands behind his back.

They sat for a while around the round table.

'This place is starting to scare the bejaysis out of me,' said Aesop eventually.

'But you feel okay, right?' said Jimmy.

Aesop nodded.

'So maybe there's something in it. What's to be scared of?'

'See that tree out there? The big bendy one?'

'Yeah.'

'What colour are the palm leaves?'

'Green.'

'Just green?'

'Well, a few different greens. And there's kind of a blue tinge at the edges. And grey and purple where the shadows move across it.'

'Exactly. And that doesn't scare you?'

Jimmy looked at the tree again. Actually, it was a bit unsettling. The sea wasn't just blue, the sand wasn't just sandy and Susan's hair wasn't just blonde; it was too many colours to name. The sounds of the breeze and waves and everything else were distinct and bright.

'Jimmy,' Aesop went on. 'Yesterday I didn't even notice the

bleedin tree. I spend one night shitting my brains out and now I can tell you how many times it bends on the way up. That's not normal.'

He shifted in his seat.

'What are they fuckin doing to us?'

'Guys,' said Amanda. 'Relax! This is exactly what we came here for. We're going through a cleansing process. There wouldn't be much point if we felt the same way afterwards as before.'

Jimmy nodded. He didn't want to stop, but he was aware that something was happening and he wasn't really in control of it. Christ, this was why he didn't do drugs! He liked control. Control was what he was all about. Doing stuff and making stuff happen. Now he didn't want to do anything. Not eat, not work, not make love to Susan. He didn't even want to talk. They'd only been here one day and all they'd really done was not eat anything and then crap like a buffalo.

They all had Thai massages that evening in a smaller hut lit with candles and smelling of incense. They played cards afterwards and were in bed by nine, pretty tired despite having done practically nothing all day.

JIMMY WOKE up the next morning, just before dawn. He left Susan asleep and walked out to the beach. He couldn't just lie in bed and there was something gnawing at him. He felt restless. The sun came up over at the other side of the island, so he didn't have the spectacular view of the other morning to look at as he sat cross-legged on the beach, but the brightening sky and relentlessly lapping waves held his gaze and soon the most overwhelming sense of calm started to seep into him.

He started thinking about stuff. Work. Music. But he wasn't really thinking. It was more like things were occurring to him in pulses and he was just casually observing them. A picture of his grandmother floated into his head then, surprising him. She'd died when he was in college. She was smiling. She was always smiling. Jimmy felt something on his hand, down in his lap. He looked down and saw a small, confusing splash. He was crying. What the fuck? Once he knew it, it was as though nothing in the world could stop it. He'd been doing exams when she got sick. He saw her a few times before she took that last bad turn, but even at the funeral his head had been full of maths and formulae and which bits of which notes he could safely forget about if he wanted to pass. A month later, when the term was finished and he was working for the summer in the States, she was cold in the ground. He'd never been back to her grave to say goodbye properly. He never even thought about her much. But the tears were falling down his face now and he didn't bother wiping them away.

The pressure he'd been under for the last few months bubbled up too. Always feeling like he was kicking like crazy to keep his head above water. Even the good things that had happened seemed to pile up in front of him, like they only added to the mountain that his life was turning into. The opportunities, the chances, each one like a little ball in his chest that he had to push down into him while he figured out how to make it all work. The song, 'Caillte'. He'd given something of himself to that song. The fact that it was for a girl didn't even matter now. 'Caillte' ... 'Lost' ... it said a lot more than the lyrics did. He was struggling when he wrote it and now, months later, nothing had changed. But now the song belonged to everyone. It was diluted. The part of him that was in it was now spread out across everyone who heard it. That part of him was lost too.

It was almost bright now and Jimmy's chest and throat were sore, and his shorts damp from crying. He was drained. Empty of everything; food, thoughts, tears. He stood up and stretched and then took off his t-shirt and walked into the sea, the cold water washing the stickiness and echoing pain away. He dunked himself again and again and looked up into the pale empty sky and then came out of the sea and back up the sand to the huts, where he spotted Lars sitting in the sand about twenty metres from where he'd been himself, his eyes closed. He tried to sneak past him, but Lars turned to him at the last minute.

'Jimmy.'

'Morning.'

'Sit with me.'

Jimmy walked over and sat down, his t-shirt in his hand and his skin tingling with cold.

'Eh, how long have you been there?' said Jimmy.

'I usually get up at around three.'

Shite. This fucker had been there all through Jimmy's little emotional collapse. Had he been blubbing like a little girl or had he kept it quiet. Jimmy didn't know. He faced out to sea again and said nothing.

'In the West, we tend to separate mind and body,' said Lars. 'It's ridiculous, but that's what we do. We don't even notice that we do it. Do we? We live, go through our time here only barely tripping along the fringes of our existence and never try to go deeper.'

Jimmy shrugged.

'When you purge your body of the poisons you've inflicted on it, your mind is free to purge too. It's part of you, Jimmy.'

Jimmy put his head down.

'You're healing. Do you feel it?'

'I … I'm not … really … eh …'

'Jimmy, you can't come here for three days, not from the place you've come, and suddenly find yourself able to embrace your spirituality.'

'To be honest, Lars, I'm not really a very spiritual person.'

Lars smiled.

'You are. We all are. You're a musician, Jimmy. Are you telling me that you don't catch glimpses of deeper truths when you play or write your music? You must do. Whether or not, or how much, you recognise it, however, is up to you. It's there one way or the other. Or do you think that's only a pile of oul hippy bollocks?'

He said it with a laugh and in an Irish accent. Jimmy laughed.

'Aesop's words?'

'He doesn't have a quiet voice.'

'No.'

'I live my life this way, Jimmy. You don't and probably never will. I would be astonished if Aesop ever does. But I think you'll benefit from your time here. Just try and remember it when you leave.'

Jimmy nodded.

'I do feel different.'

'Of course you do.'

'But I can't live like this. My life is … well, there aren't too many bloody palm trees in Dublin, let's put it that way.'

'I know. But even in your life, you can take the time to look inwards as well as react to everything that's going on around you.'

'I s'pose.'

'You'll be fine, Jimmy. You're fine already. I can see it. When you sat there earlier, I could see you. You let go.'

'You could see me?'

'More than you saw yourself, probably.'

'Christ, that makes me feel a bit stupid.'

'Crying for things you've lost is not stupid. But do it and be content.'

'How do you know that I've lost things?'

'Your aura told me. It changed as you meditated.'

'My aura?'

Lars winked at him.

'Only joking. We've all lost things, Jimmy. But if they're gone, they're gone. Aesop is also troubled. Did you know that?'

'Is he?'

'Very much so.'

'He hides it well.'

'He has suffered a great loss. I can see it.'

'His Mam.'

Lars nodded slowly.

'That's not all that troubles him.'

'What do you mean?'

'That's for Aesop to say.'

'Jesus, he's not gay or something is he?'

Lars laughed out loud.

'Perhaps! But I don't think so. It's time to start the day, Jimmy. I'll see you later.'

They both stood up and Jimmy walked back to the hut. Around him the resort was beginning to stir. He got back into bed beside Susan and looked at the ceiling. He felt good. He didn't even think it was the talk he'd had with Lars. It was what had happened earlier. Crying his tits off seemed to have lifted something from him, something he didn't need. Christ, he was turning into a right fucking girl in this place.

He woke up an hour later and wondered if it had all been a dream, but he didn't think so. He still felt good.

THEY WERE all in good spirits. They were still talking about food the whole time, but weren't actually hungry. It was mad. They hadn't eaten anything except for the juice and, three times a day, some volcanic ash thing mixed with water which was supposed to act as a kind of colonic plunger, collecting all the accumulated gunk that was clogging up their pipes as it went from one end to the other. Even Aesop seemed genuinely amazed by what was happening.

'It's been three days!' he said. 'I thought I'd be chewing on me arm at this stage. Hey, who's up for a swim?'

Aesop was now volunteering for physical activity. Bloody hell. Jimmy didn't get what was going on here either, but he couldn't deny that something was.

Lars found them reading magazines and listening to Jimmy's iPod later that afternoon. The girls were still showering after their swim.

'So, you guys are nearly done. Feel good?'

'Yeah. Great,' said Jimmy.

'Ready for your colonic?'

'I just had one,' said Aesop.

Lars looked at him. 'I don't think so.'

'I did. Look, there's the glass.'

'Aesop, that's not the colonic. That's just a bulking agent.'

'I'm not with you, chief.'

'The colonic is where we flush out your colon with an enema.'

Jimmy sat back in the chair. This was fucking news to him. Aesop glanced up from his *FHM*.

'Ah, no thanks. I'm fine Lars, really,' he said.

'Well how about I get them set up and then we can talk about it?'

Aesop shrugged and Lars walked off and started giving instructions to a few of his Thai staff.

'Aesop,' said Jimmy, slowly. 'Do you know what an enema is?'

'It's like a little gloopy starfish, Jimmy. I suppose I could just chop it up if he's going to have a pus on him over it.'

'Aesop, an enema is when they shoot water up your arse.'

Aesop looked up and turned down the iPod speakers.

'Sorry, Jimmy. I missed that.'

'They shoot water up your arse.'

Aesop stood and pointed at him.

'They sh … Jimmy, I've been more than patient with you, you fucker. I've let Lars there stick pins in me, I haven't cheated on the food thing and I've ponced around this place, looking at trees and marvelling at how wobbly and nice the sea is. I've even done Yoga for Wankers every day and made a tool of meself in front of the girls and I've been sucking on volcano mud like it's a mango smoothie but if you think I'm going to let that Swedish psycho come near me with a hose, you can hang your bollocks on it.'

'I'm not mad on the idea either.'

'Well whoopie for you. I don't care what you say, I'm out of here. Are you coming?'

'Eh … yeah. I s'pose so. It's a bit much, isn't it? We could just head off early. I mean ,…'

'A bit much?! Come on, quick. Before he comes back with his heavies. Listen Jimmy, being relaxed is one thing, but I didn't fuckin come here to lose me cherry.'

He stood up.

'I don't mind kissing, but I hate that.'

Fifteen

IT DIDN'T take Aesop too long to get back into the swing of things.

'We'll have four Singhas please, Prem,' he said, as they were strolling through the lobby. 'Out in the hammocks. Good man.'

'Ah, Dr Aesop. Welcome back. How was the health farm?'

'Far too bleedin healthy, Prem. And we're going to be needing food too, so bring your notebook with you.'

They sat around the hut later, surrounded by sandwiches and half-full cans of beer. They couldn't eat. A few nibbles and they were done. The beer tasted bitter and so fizzy that they could barely swallow it.

'It might take a while to adjust,' said Amanda.

'Yeah,' said Jimmy. 'Maybe we should take it easy for a day or two.'

'This isn't fair,' said Aesop. 'I've been having dreams about beer and now I can't drink it. I'll bleedin sue Lars, so I will.'

Jimmy plugged in his laptop to check his email, ignoring the look he got from Aesop. There were six messages from Simon. By the last one he seemed frantic. *Jimmy, where the hell are you? You need to get on this straight away. Hyderabad are going ape.* Apparently there was some kind of mis-communication with Kyotosei. One of the main issues they'd been dealing with in India, something Jimmy thought was already agreed upon, turned out to be a real sticking point. Kyotosei thought that it was to be handled by Eirotech. Jimmy thought they were doing it. Meanwhile, India thought they were being fucked around. It was a mess. He spent the next two hours on the phone, first calling Tokyo, then his contact in India, then Tokyo again. He marched up and down the garden, cupping the phone to his head and dashing back to the table to check his notes every few minutes. By the time he was done, he was shaking and soaked with sweat, his heart thumping. But it was fixed. Just.

He went back into the hut to mail Simon and Susan looked up from the couch.

'God Jimmy, what happened?'

'What? Nothing. It's fine. Just a problem at work.'

'Look at your face!'

Jimmy went into the bathroom to see. There was a roaring red rash crawling up the left side of his neck and across his cheeks and chin.

'Fuckin hell …'

'Aesop!' Susan called in to the room where Amanda and Aesop were having a lie-down. 'Aesop, Jimmy's sick!'

'What?' Jimmy said. 'I'm grand. It's okay.'

'It is not. Aesop!'

Aesop ran out of the room in a pair of shorts.

'What's wrong? What's all the shouting?'

'Look at Jimmy!'

Aesop looked in through the open bathroom door and back at Susan.

'What about him?'

'His face. It's gone all red.'

Aesop walked into the bathroom and laughed.

'The fucking state of you!'

Jimmy was touching his face gingerly. It felt tingly.

'It's not fuckin funny.'

'It is! You look like something out of *Star Trek*.'

'Aesop, I think Susan called you out here cos you're supposed to be a fuckin doctor, not cos she thought I needed someone to laugh their bollocks off at me.'

'Ah. Right.' Aesop stuck his head out the door. 'Just a minute Susan. It's fine. I think it's just, eh, heat rash. I'll take a closer look.'

He closed the door.

'Right. Now what?'

'Well, what's your diagnosis then, doctor?'

'Hang on a minute, Jimmy,' said Aesop.

He unzipped and went over to the toilet.

'Do you fucking mind?' said Jimmy, looking at the back of Aesop's head in the mirror.

'Sorry Jimmy,' said Aesop, half turning around. 'I was bursting, but I was in the middle of throwing a length into Amanda so I couldn't stop. Nearly done … ah, Jaysis … ah, that's lovely …'

'Fuck sake.'

'Right. Move over there, let me at the sink.'

'What is it?'

'What's what?'

'This!' said Jimmy, pointing.

'Who am I, Florence Nightingale? I don't know. Heat rash?'

'You're a useless fu … I'm having a cold shower. Get out and tell Susan I'll be out in a minute.'

Jimmy stepped into the shower. It wasn't cold like a cold shower in Ireland would be cold, but it was nice. When he came out and looked in the mirror the rash seemed to be fading slightly. He sat on the toilet seat and put his head in hands. He knew what it was. It was fucking work. He'd come back down to earth far faster than his chilled out melon-juice-filled head could cope with. Christ, but that had been a close one. Kyotosei were playing it cagey, but the head bloke in Hyderabad was yelling at him and everything. On a shite line and him with his big Indian accent. Yeah, he was nicely stressed up again all right.

'Jimmy?'

It was Susan.

'Yeah. I'm okay. Be out in a minute.'

He stood up and looked in the mirror again. It was fine. It was just that it had caught him off guard, when he was on his holidays and just back from the health place. He wasn't expecting it. It was cool. He went out and spent the next hour writing an email to Simon to tell him what had gone on. By the time he was done with that, the mark on his face was gone and just its shadow was left on his neck.

THEY ENDED up eating just salads that night in The Islander. It was all they could manage. Later on the girls were starting to look a bit down and Aesop and Jimmy couldn't seem to drum up the energy for a mad night of partying and dancing. It was like Lars had said – eating seemed to put a strain on the body that they'd never noticed before. They headed to The Club, which was a much more mellow venue than most of the other places around the Green Mango. The lads ordered cider but it was too sweet so they ended up on Pina Coladas, the same as the girls. There was a guy playing guitar and singing Everly Brothers and Beatles songs and they sat quietly listening and chatting. Then Amanda went to the loo and Aesop got up to go to the bar.

'Would you play us a song?' said Susan to Jimmy. She was grinning.

Jimmy looked at her.

'Ah, I don't know. He hasn't asked anyone up or anything.'

'I'll ask him can you play.'

'Ah … I'm not sure …'

'You can't, can you?'

'What?'

She smiled at him and put her hand on his arm.

'Well, you talked about your band and all and I heard your Irish song. But sometimes guys just say things to impress a girl. You were telling fibs, weren't you?' She laughed. 'It's okay, Jimmy. Really, I don't mind. It's not the first time I had to listen to a story from a guy.'

'You think I was bullshitting you? Are you serious?'

'Well, maybe. It was a bit far-fetched, wasn't it? Top ten in Ireland and all that. And when we were in the health farm, Aesop told me how you let your imagination get the better of you some-times.'

'Aesop? That cheeky bastard told you that, did he? Did he tell you I can't play?'

163

'Not exactly. But he told Amanda that he wrote Caillte for his sister as a wedding present and …'

Jimmy laughed now. Aesop writing Caillte. In Irish. That 'soft-cock, whingy poofter's song'. The more Jimmy thought about it, the more he laughed. He could hear himself laughing in the quiet pub and that made him laugh all the more. By the time Aesop came back from the bar, there were tears streaming down his face and he sat there pointing at Aesop and howling.

'Jaysis, what's up with the laughing policeman here?' he said to Susan, putting down the drinks.

Jimmy couldn't talk.

'I just told him that you said you wrote that Irish song and he started laughing,' said Susan, bemused.

'Ah right. That'll be nervous laughter, cos you caught him out lying his arse off.'

'Can he play?'

'Well, he's no Aesop …'

Jimmy was starting to calm down.

'Get up there Aesop, and sing Caillte for us,' he said. 'Go on. I'd really, really love to see that.'

'It's not me that's been snared rapid Jimmy. You get up.'

'I don't know what to believe now,' said Susan, looking between them. 'Is there really a band?'

'Yes, there's a band Susan,' said Jimmy. 'And we're brilliant. Aren't we Aesop, you big gobshite?'

'The best.'

'Right, well play us a song then! I'll go up … hang on …'

She jumped up and spoke to the guy with the guitar, who then announced that they had a guest singer and the sparse crowd started to clap. Jimmy smiled and shook his head at Aesop.

'One day, Aesop, you'll dig yourself a hole that they won't be able to pull you out of with a helicopter.'

He made his way to the small stage, took the guitar off the guy and sat on the tall stool, strumming it to check the tuning.

It was only then he realised that he didn't have a fucking clue what to play. He didn't want to do 'Caillte'. He was afraid he'd start laughing if he did. Something fun. He had it. He unplugged the guitar and got off the stool. The place was small enough for this to work if people shut up for a bit. He started to play. Sexual Healing. Perfect.

He strolled around the bar with the guitar, walking up to tables and singing to all the girls in the place and giving it a fridge-load of cheese. He ended up in front of Susan and Amanda who were now standing up and moving their hips, their hands in the air, and cheering. Aesop was hiding behind his huge cocktail glass. Whistles and shouts were coming from all over the place. He swaggered back up to the stage and finished the song with a bow. The girls in the bar all started roaring straight away for another one. He smiled and plugged the guitar back in, asking the guy if it was okay to do another one. The guy smiled and nodded. As far as he was concerned, this prick could play for the rest of the night. He'd already fucked him up with that smarmy display, the bollocks. This crowd wouldn't be too interested in Wake Up Little Suzie after that. He'd have to up his game or look like a right plonker.

Jimmy leaned into the mike: 'I'd like to sing this for Susan.'

Big cheer and clapping from Amanda. Jimmy looked down.

'And Amanda! The two coolest girls in Koh Samui and we're going to miss them ...'

He sang You're Beautiful. A bit sappy, but the pub was about seventy per cent women who were having a quiet one before heading out for another night of island partying and if there was one thing Jimmy was good at, it was nailing a set-list. When he wrapped it up and went back down to the table, Susan's eyes were huge and shining and her bottom lip was caught in her teeth. They kissed and he sat down, that old familiar buzz in his belly.

'Unbelievable Jimmy,' said Aesop, pushing another frothy white drink across the table to him. 'Is there an arsebandit song in the world that you don't know?' He tapped his camcorder. 'The lads at home are going to have a thing or two to say about what you just did, you big panty liner. I'll be running out of tape with you making a show of yourself out here.'

'Don't listen to him Jimmy,' said Amanda. 'That was fantastic.'

Jimmy smiled and leaned into Susan.

'Now do you believe me?'

She laughed. 'God, yes. I can't believe I didn't before. You're so talented! That was amazing.'

'Ah now. Don't be giving me a big head.'

But he was beaming. That felt good.

'Remember what you said before, about giving it up so you can work?'

'Yeah.'

'Are you really going to do that?'

'I have to Susan. I'll still play and all, but I have this job and … y'know.'

Susan looked down for a second.

'I think that would be a shame,' she said.

'Yeah, but I really have to do it. A lot of people can do that,' he pointed back at the stage. 'Not many people can actually pay the rent with it.'

She nodded and took up her drink.

'Jimmy, we've only really met. I don't want to start telling you what you should do or anything …'

'What?'

'See that guy up there?'

'Yeah.'

'A lot of people can do that. Not a lot of people can do what you just did.'

He didn't know what to say.

'Look, I'm no expert,' she went on. 'You do whatever you have to do. I know you'll be a success.'

She kissed him again.

'I got my song, that's good enough for me. And I got the best holiday I've ever had while I was at it. You're beautiful as well, mister.'

'I meant what I said up there,' said Jimmy. 'Meeting you was …'

He shook his head and smiled at her.

'I'm glad I came to Thailand for my holidays,' he went on.

'Me too.'

'Jaysis, what's this?' said Aesop, leaning into them. 'A fuckin love-in? Come on, let's move out before James Bluntybollocks here has the place in floods. I'm getting me second wind.'

'You said you wrote the song, Aesop,' said Amanda. 'You lied to us!'

'Ladies, I'm sorry. I was just nervous cos I liked you so much. I swear to God, that was the first time I've ever been dishonest with a woman in my life. Jimmy, tell them.'

'It's true,' said Jimmy. 'God, Aesop, you should be ashamed of yourself.'

'I am Jimmy, I am.' He put his hand across his chest. 'I promise I'll never tell a lie again, or my name isn't Doctor Aesop O'Shaughnessy.'

They went out and did the party thing, dancing like crazy to fast bass-driven electronic music and only drinking drinks that came in coconut shells or cored pineapples. It was great. At one stage they bumped into Linda, the girl Jimmy had met in the airport. She came up to him and grinned.

'Much better!' she shouted, nodding down at his clothes with a big smile.

'Thanks. I ran out of starch and this was all I had left in the suitcase.'

'Suits you. Shows off your snowy Irish legs. Very sexy.'

She danced off again with a wave and Jimmy turned back to the others. That was nice. He felt like he'd made a friend. It was a friendly place, Thailand. Even the Thais themselves. Every one of them he saw seemed to have a big happy smile for him. White teeth and cheerful eyes. A whole country of it. It was a long way from the hard what-are-you-fuckin-looking-at stares you got back home if you were in town on a Saturday night and weren't careful. And these people had fuck all, really, bar coconuts. Well, they had good weather. Maybe that was it.

They finished the night with a walk back along the beach to the hut. It was still early enough and they had another go at the hammocks for an hour or so before they all started to get drowsy and adjourned.

Susan and Jimmy stood kissing at the side of the bed until he moved them off balance and they both fell back onto the mattress and started pulling at each other's clothes. He was lying on top of her then and they both slowed down. Jimmy pushed himself up to look at her.

'Will you miss me?'

'Yep.'

'Good.'

'Can you do something for me, Jimmy?'

'Sure. Although, hang on … it's not weird, is it? Me Mam warned me about English girls. Very forward, so you are.'

'No, it's not weird,' she laughed. 'Will you write a song for me?'

'A song?'

Jimmy frowned at her, but he was still smiling too.

'Yeah,' she said. 'Sorry. I know it's a big thing and all. But I'd like a song.'

'Eh … okay. I could write you a song. I wasn't expecting that.'

'Why? Is it bad?'

'No no. It's not bad. But no one's ever asked me to do that before.'

'Good! We've got the photos and all, and Aesop said he'd

make a copy of the video for us, but something like that would be amazing. To remember you properly. When you sang to us tonight, I kind of started to wonder what it would be like if I wasn't going back to England and you weren't going to Tokyo. What might happen. What would happen … if … if I visited you in Ireland when you got back.' She said the last bit quickly.

Jimmy just looked at her, blinking, and she laughed.

'Oh man, look at your face! Sorry. I was just thinking out loud. I didn't mean I expect anything from you or …'

'No, it's not that. God, I'm just … I never really thought about afterwards. I'm not happy you're leaving or anything, but I didn't think you felt … eh …'

'What do you feel?'

Jimmy took a minute to think about it.

'I think maybe we'd do okay.'

'Tell you what.' She touched his face. 'Send me an email.'

'I will.'

She pulled his face down to hers and kissed him again, moving beneath him so he could put a hand under her. He did that, but then found himself not quite ready for the next bit. He wasn't used to all that talking when he was about to slot one home, and now he needed another run at it. When he was warmed up again he moved closer to her and she locked her ankles behind his back. He went for the top corner and was just waiting for the crowd to go wild when there was a knock on the door.

'Jimmy?'

It was Aesop.

'Jimmy? Sorry. Are you awake?'

Jimmy stopped dead inside her and he and Susan just looked at each other, their faces inches apart.

'What do you want?'

'Eh, sorry. Is Susan awake? Are you decent?'

'No. What do you want?'

'It's Amanda. She's upset and she went out to the beach on her

169

own. She won't let me near her and it's a bit late to be wandering around on her own out there.'

Jimmy looked back at Susan.

'I'd better go,' she said.

Jimmy nodded and pulled it back to the keeper, getting off her. She got dressed in a hurry and came back to the bed to kiss him.

'Won't be long.'

'Jimmy?' called Aesop.

'Jesus, we're fuckin coming Aesop. Wait a minute, will ye?'

He put on his shorts and they both went to the door. On the other side of it, Aesop was looking sheepish.

'What happened?' said Jimmy.

'Nothing. We were just talking. I think she was upset about leaving tomorrow. She won't talk to me. I thought she'd come back in, but she started walking off down the beach and when I tried to go after her she wasn't having any of it.'

'I'll go after her,' said Susan. 'Which way did she go?'

Aesop pointed.

Susan went to the sliding doors.

'I can see her. I'll be back in a minute.'

An hour later Jimmy and Aesop were in the hammocks, Aesop humming to himself softly. They could see Amanda and Susan about a hundred metres down the beach, sitting just in front of the waves.

'Well, thanks for that Aesop. My last night with Susan and here I am instead listening to you singing Metallica songs in the dark.'

'Wasn't my fault Jimmy.'

'I was ... right in the middle of it.'

'Yeah. Sorry about that. Anyway, you interrupted me earlier, remember, when you had that yoke on your face. We're quits.'

'My arse we're quits. Why did you have to upset the girl anyway? It's her last night.'

170

'I said fuck all! She was the one going on about how sad she was about leaving. I fucking love you Aesop this and my ex-fucking boyfriend Aesop that. Blah, blah, blah. Out it all came. The full fuckin life story I was getting Jimmy, and me kneeling there with two handfuls of arse and the Horn of Plenty on final approach. That's terrible distracting, so it is. I thought that if I just talked to her a bit then she'd get it out of her system and we could get back to it. No chance. She wouldn't shut up. So then we're lying there and I'm telling her she's great and she'll meet someone and all that bollocks. But she keeps whinging about this fucker that dumped her after they were engaged and then robbed money off her or some shit. Fuck sake, Jimmy. I'm there stroking her hair and telling her it's okay and just when I think we're back on, she's out the door and down the beach, telling me to leave her alone.'

Jimmy sighed.

'Fuck, that's terrible.'

'Who are you telling?'

'I mean it's terrible for her. He must have really fucked her up.'

'Who?'

'The fucking bloke that … the … do you know something Aesop …?'

'They're not coming back any time soon, are they?'

'Doesn't look like it.'

'Beer?'

'Yeah, fuck it. Why not.'

It was four in the morning before they all got to bed.

The next day the girls had to shop so Jimmy and Aesop stayed in the hut and chilled out all afternoon. They went to the airport together and this time Susan and Amanda were both crying a little. After lots of hugs and promises, the lads saw them disappear behind the barrier. They walked back out to get a taxi. Jimmy was quiet. It had only been a week – less, even – but he liked Susan. They got into the taxi and he saw Aesop smiling.

'I suppose you're all happy now that they're gone,' he said.

'Well I won't be writing any sonnets Jimmy, if that's what you mean. No, I'm smiling because now it's my turn. My week, remember?'

'God, yeah. So what's first on the agenda?'

Aesop winked and leaned forward to the taximan.

'Can you take us to the Go Kart track please, pal?'

Sixteen

THE NEXT week was spent on the beach, in the hammocks and getting pissed up in every bar Aesop could squeeze into an evening. It was as if they'd never even met Lars, and all Jimmy's ponderings on the dangers of polluting his body with alcohol, caffeine, meat and tobacco were out the door and hailing a taxi. But it was good fun. Aesop knew how to enjoy himself and Jimmy was caught up in it. By Tuesday night, he'd even stopped thinking about Susan non-stop. He'd already had one email from her and had felt a double thump in his chest when it popped up in his inbox, but Aesop had noticed him sitting at the laptop, grinning like a fool, and now wasn't giving him a chance to ponder very much of anything. Daylight had become just an opportunity to recover from the last night's excesses and prepare for the next. It was a laugh.

And then came the phone call from Dónal.

Sultan were releasing 'Caillte' in the UK. They wanted a CD single – four songs. And if it made the top twenty, Senturion would take over and an album deal would be on the table.

'Calm down Jimmy.'

'No! Dónal, this is going to fuck me up.'

'It won't. Listen. I know what you can and can't commit to. I promised that nothing I put together would affect your work, and I meant it. This was just an opportunity to throw something out there and see what happens. I was on the phone all last week with Sultan and explained the situation. To be honest, I thought they were just going to tell me it wouldn't work out, but they said they'd take a punt.'

'But what about all the promotion it'll take?'

'I'll take care of it Jimmy. We'll work around you.'

'And what happens if it all works out?'

'Well, that'd be great, wouldn't it?'

'Did you tell Sultan that I was getting out?'

'I told them you were considering your options.'

'That's not what I said. I already considered my options Dónal. I'm gone.'

'But don't you see it Jimmy? The fact that we're not crawling all over them is making our bargaining position even better.'

'I'm not bleedin trying to bargain with the fuckers! Jesus, why can't anyone … am I talking to the fuckin wall?'

'Jimmy, they're putting up the money to release the single. They'll pay for a video. They'll make sure it gets airplay. They know that you're not a hundred per cent on board, that you might just pack it in … and they're *still* firing dosh at it. These people don't do this. They're pissing their pants they're so excited. And for the promotional stuff, we could always use Aesop for some of it, right?'

Jimmy turned and looked out the window of the hut into the garden. Aesop was standing up against the door, his mouth against the glass and his cheeks blown up. He was licking the window, his eyes crossed, and pretending to wank at Jimmy.

'For fuck sake …'

Jimmy turned around again.

'Dónal …'

'Jimmy, listen. Trust me on this. I promise that your schedule takes full priority. I swear to God. I'll never ask you to do anything that means you can't do your job. Please. Trust me. You won't be sorry.'

'Will I not? Oh, that's grand so.'

'Jimmy, I'll pull the plug on it if that's what you really want. I'm just asking you to think about it. Okay?'

'God. Why can't …'

'Just think about it, Jimmy.'

'I … oh, fucking all right. I'll think about it. I'll talk to you when I get to Tokyo, right?'

'Thanks Jimmy. You're doing the right thing.'

'Not yet I amn't. Seeya Dónal, right?'

'Yeah, good luck. Enjoy the rest of your holiday.'

'I will. Seeya Dónal.'

THE TWO of them were pretty wrecked with all the partying at this stage, so they just hung around the beach and bars and didn't go too mad. They rented jet-skis one afternoon and buzzed about in the bay, having races and playing chicken and laughing about how they used to do this on bikes when they were kids. It was all nice and chilled and before they knew it, they were checking to see where they'd put their passports and tickets and rushing off postcards and buying presents.

They were up early the next morning and suffering pretty badly again from the drink. They had to be at the airport by midday to get back to Bangkok in time for their connection to Tokyo.

'What was that blue thing we were drinking?' said Aesop. He had one hand on his face. 'I can't see out of me left eye.'

'Don't know,' said Jimmy. His eyes were red and weeping and he couldn't focus on the switch to put the kettle on.

'You're not supposed to drink blue things,' said Aesop. 'Blue isn't a good colour for drink.'

'Or green,' said Jimmy.

'Oh God, yeah. What was that one?'

'Don't know.'

'Fucking cocktails. Whose idea was that?'

'Yours, you fucker,' said Jimmy. 'You wanted the t-shirt.'

'Oh yeah. Where is it?'

'You gave it to that Spanish bird.'

'Right. Elisa?'

Jimmy nodded.

'What happened her?' said Aesop.

'She disappeared after you told her your dick was so big that clowns cartwheel out of it when you come.'

'Oh. Right. Jimmy, I've an awful headache so I do.'

175

'We should jump in the sea. The taxi will be here in an hour and I need to eat something so I'll have something to puke up later on.

Prem delivered their bacon and eggs after their swim and they sat around the table drinking coffee and staring into space.

'Well, that was a laugh,' said Aesop eventually, looking around.

'What was?' said Jimmy.

'Thailand.'

'Yeah.'

'I like Thailand.'

Japan

Seventeen

JIMMY'S MORNING was turning to shite on him.

He looked around. He didn't have his own office here, just a big desk in the corner of the huge open plan space. As a visiting dignitary of sorts, his desk was one of four that was at ninety degrees to the thirty or so others occupied by engineers. The three desks to his right were where the various group managers sat, but he hadn't quite worked out yet what they managed. There were a lot of projects going on and Jimmy's responsibilities spanned more than a few of them. He spent most of his time in meetings that seemed to last all day and stumbled out of them and back to his desk only to discover that it was only bloody eleven o'clock. And just now Shiggy had informed him that he was scheduled to give a presentation to all of the IT managers in this division at three in the afternoon. A Friday afternoon. There would be over a dozen of them in attendance and Jimmy's job was to outline Eirotech's strategy for the next three years. Not just their strategy for the India project – their actual vision for the company as a whole. And Jimmy was supposed to fucking know this how?

Since they'd arrived in Narita airport on Sunday night, Jimmy had felt like he was watching a programme on the Discovery Channel. Shiggy had met them and they took a train into the city; Jimmy and Aesop gawking out the window like they were on a guided tour of some futuristic movie set. Shiggy was all excited, chattering away and asking them all about Thailand and how the band had been going and how Norman and Marco and everyone was getting on. The lads were delighted that he was there to bring them to their apartment, but found it hard not to just stare and point at things.

Not that it was a pretty city. Jimmy was kind of expecting pagodas and temples and people wearing traditional garb and the whole place to look a bit like something from *Shogun*, but it didn't. It looked like slabs of concrete, dropped with great precision into place from above with no regard whatsoever to how they looked or what was next to them when they hit the ground. The slightest irregular gap between two buildings was game for development and if the result was an office or apartment block that looked like it had been designed in a very dark room, so be it. Space wasn't something that was wasted here. Every now and again, a flash of green from the corner of his eye would reveal itself to be a golf driving range, or possibly a big green building, but there wasn't much in the way of open spaces, especially as they got closer to the city. At that stage they were in tunnels most of the time anyway and able to give Shiggy their full attention. When they were standing up to get off the train in Tokyo station, Aesop looked around at all the other passengers and leaned into Jimmy.

'Hey Jimmy, do you feel very tall all of a sudden?'

Jimmy glanced around. He did actually. He was about six foot anyway, but towered above almost everyone else.

'This is bleedin deadly,' said Aesop. 'It's like standing on a box. Except for the box.'

That first week for Jimmy had been very tough. He had to smile and bow and be polite to everyone, exchanging business cards and looking sincere. He was in the office by eight every morning and hadn't left before seven in the evening. A lot of the time he was just left on his own at his desk, poring over his notes and checking his calendar to see when the next meeting was and when he wasn't scratching his head and wondering what the fuck he was doing there, he was being introduced to yet another manager and wondering if this was one of the ones whose name he'd have to try and remember. He hardly saw anything of Aesop. He'd get home and find him watching the telly with his feet on the coffee table and eating pizza.

'Did you go out today?'

'Nah. Well, I was down in Starbucks for an hour, but they were showing *Lord of the Rings* on the telly, so I came back up to watch it.'

'You're in Tokyo, Aesop. Why don't you do some exploring or something?'

'Ah I will. I'm just resting up a bit after Thailand.'

'Yeah, you must be bollixed, getting up at lunchtime every day like that.'

'You'd be amazed. What did you do today?'

'I worked. Aesop, there's a gym and pool downstairs in this place and everything. Why don't you have a look around?'

'I did. I was in the gym this afternoon. It's lovely.'

'Did you do anything?'

'Nah. Well, I had a quick go on one of the bikes, but the bloke who looks after the place started annoying me.'

'What? How, for fuck sake?'

'Ah, he kept standing there looking at me, y'know? Telling me to stop smoking and all. I got a pain in me hole with him. How's Shiggy?'

Jimmy shook his head.

'He's grand.'

'Are we going on the piss?'

'Friday night.'

'Brilliant. Do you think Liv Tyler's a bigger ride than Hilary Swank?'

'Yeah. Who's Hilary Swank?'

'Who's Hilary Swank? Jimmy, she's won Oscars for being a ride.'

'Has she? Who's Liv Tyler?'

'I worry about you, Jimmy, so I do.'

Shiggy was helping him with his presentation. Actually, only for Shiggy, Jimmy would've been completely fucked. He was a bigger fish here than Jimmy had realised. His time in Ireland was seen as a big step up for him and he was Jimmy's main point of contact with Kyotosei. He sat in on all the meetings and dropped down to see Jimmy at least three times a day, making sure that everything was okay and offering pointers on what was expected of him. This latter was the most important thing for Jimmy. He was starting to realise that his brief from Simon had been laughably so and if he was going to get anything out of this trip then he'd have to be the one to push things. He spent an hour every night on the phone with Simon and woke up every morning with dry heavy eyes and a feeling in his belly that it was going to be a long two months.

The presentation lasted two hours. It was hell. All the Japanese guys just sat and watched and listened and no one said a fucking word. Occasionally they'd flick through the Eirotech folders that Jimmy had prepared when he mentioned that something was elaborated on therein, but only Shiggy actually seemed to be following him. He stood and pointed at the overhead slides and tried to throw in the odd light-hearted remark about some aspect of Ireland or Japan, but was met by stony stares. One guy at the table was actually asleep. He was sitting up straight and his eyes were closed as though in concentration. But he jerked at one stage and looked around, puzzled, before settling back again. At the end they all stood and nodded and thanked him, but by that stage he was just fit to get out of there and go for a pint. It had all seemed like a big waste of time and worry. His back was killing him from standing and he was hoarse. Shiggy gave him a big smile.

'Great job, Jimmy.'

'It was shite, Shiggy.'

'No no. You exprain everysing berry well.'

'They were asleep!'

'Ha ha. Maybe one or two. But they are not important sing. Important sing is that we had meeting.'

'But what's the point of that if no one was bleedin listening? One bloke nearly shat himself when I asked him what he thought of the timing being proposed by Hyderabad. You'd swear

I was after asking him to get up and sing us a song.'

Shiggy patted him on the arm.

'Don't worry Jimmy. Japan is not rike Ireland. You will understand more before you go home.'

'Yeah. But, man, it's hard going. Being off your home turf like this.'

Shiggy smiled.

'Who you fuckin terring, Jimmy?'

Jimmy laughed. That was true. He hadn't exactly been falling over himself trying to make Shiggy welcome when he arrived in Dublin the previous year. If anything he'd done his best to ignore him at first, only taking a close look at him eventually because he played the bass and Jimmy was stuck for a bass player. It was Marco who had looked after Shiggy, making sure he knew who everyone was in the office and what was going on. Come to think of it, Jimmy had been pretty dismissive of Marco too, when he'd arrived from Italy. A bit rude even.

'Hmm. The shoe's on the other foot now, isn't it?'

'Shoe?'

'I mean what goes around … eh … I mean I know what it's like now. What it was like for you in Ireland. I was a bit of a prick, wasn't I?'

Shiggy laughed now.

'A bit. But that's okay Jimmy. Next time you won't be.'

'Do you really think the meeting went okay?'

'Sure. But, *ne*, you should talk a bit more srowry I sink.'

'Was I hard to understand?'

'Well, you speak with Dublin accent, Jimmy. *De mayne probarem a' dis stayage wi' de ting wor taw-kin abou' is de rack of im-puh wor geh'in from de cunts in markehding.* Not easy to forrow for Japanese.'

'I didn't say cunts!'

'Yes, but I keep waiting for you to say it! Japanese learn American Engrish. Try to speak rike zem.'

Jimmy frowned.

'Okay. Okay. I can do that. But I'd never say … hey, how do you say cunt in Japanese anyway?'

Shiggy laughed again.

'We don't curse rike Irish.'

'But what do you say? If you really want to tell someone what you think of them.'

Shiggy thought about it for a minute. Then he looked around and whispered: '*Onara atama.*'

'Right. And that's a bad one?'

'Oh yes,' he said. 'Berry, berry bad word.'

'What does it mean?'

'Fart head.'

'Fart head. Right. Eh … I'm beginning to think that being in Ireland must have been difficult for you, Shiggy.'

Shiggy nodded.

'When Aesop and Sparky argue …' He put his hands over his ears and shook his head. 'Berry berry difficult.'

'Yeah, I'd say,' laughed Jimmy. 'So where are we going tonight?'

'Ah. Where you want to go?'

'Well, Aesop hasn't gone further than the coffee shop since we got here. I think he's in Guinness withdrawl. Can we get a pint somewhere?'

'Sure. How about steak and pint? Poor Aesop. He not rike Japan?'

'To be honest, he's afraid to walk around on his own. He can't understand why everything has to be in Japanese, the dopey bastard. He's afraid he'll get lost.'

'Easy in Tokyo. Even for me sometimes.'

'So where are we going? Is there anywhere like, y'know, a party area? Like Temple Bar?'

Shiggy laughed.

'Yes, we have. But maybe not rike Temple Bar.'

'Where is it?'

'For you? Roppongi.'

'Roppongi? Will Aesop like it?'

'Oh yes. Aesop will rike berry much.'

'Because he keeps going on about Japanese women like his whole life has been leading up to this. What have you been telling him? Anyway, he said he's waiting for you to show us around so he'll know how to get home in a hurry if he needs to. Will there be women in this Roppongi place for him to pester?'

Shiggy nodded, smiling.

'I sink so.'

AS IT turned out, Roppongi was only a fifteen-minute walk from the apartment. They were practically living there. Shiggy collected them at about eight and they headed out, Jimmy and Aesop all excited that they were finally getting to see something of Tokyo.

'How do you say hello to a bird in Japan, Shiggy?' said Aesop.

'Many ways to say.'

'But just to say hello. Y'know, "howarya love", that kind of thing?'

'Just say harro.'

'In English?'

'Sure.'

'They speak English?'

'A rittle, probabry. Enough for you.'

'God, that'll make things easier, won't it?'

Aesop kept looking down at himself, straightening his shirt and jeans and flapping his arms nervously.

'Is there anything I shouldn't say?'

'Jesus, Aesop,' said Jimmy. 'Look at you. You're going for a pint, not joining the bleedin Freemasons.'

'I'm just a bit nervous.'

'Why? Shiggy, do you know what this eejit is going on about?'

Shiggy just laughed. 'No.'

'But Japanese women, Jimmy,' said Aesop. 'Do you not get it? Do they not make you all … y'know … what's the word?'

'The word is horny, Aesop. All women do that to you.'

'No, no. This is different. I've read about it. It's called the Asian Cravin'. Very common, so it is.'

'Yeah. Among magazine readers.'

'I'm serious. I don't know what it is. I've built it up in me head now and everything. It's all I've been thinking about since I heard we were coming here. It consumes me.'

'It consumes you?'

'Isn't it funny?'

'Hilarious. Well I hope you won't be disappointed.'

'He won't be disappointed Jimmy,' said Shiggy, giving Aesop a wink. 'It will be the best sing in his rife.'

Aesop blinked at him and flapped his arms again, picking up the pace.

AFTER A huge feed in Tony Romas, they went around the corner to the pub.

'Irish pub,' said Shiggy, leading the way.

'They have Irish pubs here?' said Aesop. 'Does that mean …?'

'Yes. Guinness too.'

'Ooh, lovely.'

They went down the steps into the basement of a huge tower block and stopped dead, looking at the sign. Paddy Foley's Irish Pub. It looked real enough, but a bit mad, considering the setting. They went through the double-doors and stopped again.

'Is it real Irish?' said Shiggy.

'It's as Irish as scattered showers Shiggy!' said Aesop. 'Brilliant!'

He went up to the bar and ordered three pints of Guinness from the barman, who was from Dublin. It looked just like an

Irish pub. Dark woods and high stools and people standing around drinking and laughing and talking shite in Irish accents.

'There yiz go lads,' the barman said, putting the pints up on the counter.

Aesop beamed at him and turned around to the lads.

'Where we're living is only fifteen minutes away from this place! We're set up, Jimmy. Home away from home!'

'Yeah,' said Jimmy. 'Jesus, get a taxi door to door Aesop and you'll never have to deal with being in Japan, will you?'

'That's what I was thinking!'

'A regular bleedin citizen of the world, aren't you?'

'It's nice to have a base where you feel comfortable, that's all I'm saying.'

'Yeah, right. If they had somewhere for you to put a sleeping bag down, you'd never leave.'

But Aesop wasn't listening anymore. He was looking at his change from the three pints and trying to do the maths in his head. Something wasn't right.

'Shiggy, how much is the pint?'

Shiggy looked at the money in Aesop's hand.

'Ah … about seven euro.'

'Each?! Are you fucking taking the piss?'

'Berry expensive, *ne*, to live in Tokyo.'

Aesop looked at him and back at his money.

'Having second thoughts about moving in?' said Jimmy.

'No. But there might be some budgeting to be done at meal-times.'

'Pint okay?' said Shiggy.

'I haven't tasted it yet. But if I'm not running me fingers through its hair in about two minutes and asking it to marry me, I'm going to be very disappointed so I am. Seven fuckin euro …'

There were lots of Irish around and the lads started getting into it. Jimmy met a guy from Galway about his own age who was doing pretty much the same job as he did himself. He looked around after a while and saw Aesop and Shiggy talking to two girls at the end of the bar, so he wandered over. They were Canadian and the two lads were giving it loads. Aesop was talking about Brian O'Driscoll for some reason. Jimmy listened for a second before realising that Brian O'Driscoll was probably the only rugby player Aesop had actually heard of.

'Jimmy!' said Aesop. 'This is Marsha and this is Tara. They're over here playing rugby for their college in Canada. Isn't that great?'

'Hello,' said Jimmy, sitting down.

'Hi,' said the girls.

'Jimmy Collins,' he said to the nearest one.

'Tara Towers,' she said.

Jimmy stifled a giggle and she looked at him.

'What?'

'Oh, eh … nothing. Sorry. I just … I know a Tara Towers … at home.'

'Tara's grandparents are from Donegal, Jimmy,' said Aesop. He turned back to her. 'Do you know the story of Tara in Ireland?'

'No. What story?'

'Ah,' said Aesop. 'You see, there's a place called Tara in County Laois, over there in the west. It's the most magical place in the whole country. The high kings of Ireland used to have their castle there, y'see? But the problem was, that's where the Little People used to live as well. The fairies. So anyway, wasn't there this one king who had a queen, and her name was *Eimear Mac an Peann Luaidhe*, which means Emer of the Beguiling Fragrance …'

Jimmy shook his head and left him to it. He tried talking to Shiggy and Marsha, but they seemed to be getting a bit cosy, even though the girl was pretty hefty and Shiggy looked like a little kid next to her. He stood up again and went up to the bar to get another pint. The plan was supposed to be that they just have a few in here and then go off and explore a bit, but now

Aesop was in full swing and they wouldn't be going anywhere for an hour or two anyway. That was fine actually. It was a cool pub. Decent music over the house system and a good buzz among the after-work crowd. He didn't want to spend his whole trip in a bloody Irish bar, but Aesop was right about one thing. It would be cool to have a base like this so far away from home.

Just before twelve, he decided that he wanted to see what else Roppongi had to offer and went back to the lads.

'And do you eat beaver in Canada?' Aesop was saying.

'Oh no,' said Tara. 'You don't eat it.'

'But there's lots of beaver over there, yeah?'

'Lots.'

'And you've never eaten beaver yourself.'

'No. Really, I'm not sure it would taste very good.'

'Ah, you might be surprised …'

'Some people make things out of the skins.'

'Like what?'

'I don't know … hats and things …'

'Do you hear this Jimmy?' said Aesop, looking around. 'If it gets cold in Canada, you just slip yourself into some beaver to keep you warm.'

Jimmy was trying not to laugh.

'Really?'

'Yeah. And Tara, tell me this now, did you ever stroke a beaver? What's it feel like?'

Aesop got another five minutes out of it before even Shiggy, who wasn't part of the conversation, was starting to laugh. They decided to move on and try somewhere else. The girls said they might catch up with them later. They were flying back to Toronto the next evening and were up for some partying before they left. Jimmy, Shiggy and Aesop finished their pints and went back up the stairs to the main drag. Jimmy could see why Shiggy had laughed when he mentioned Temple Bar. This place was like fifty Temple Bars and stretched up into the skyscrapers as well as along the length of the road. There were pubs and clubs everywhere. Thousands of them, it seemed, and the whole place was heaving. And there were Japanese girls everywhere. They were stunning.

Now that he wasn't being distracted by the fact that it was possible to drink Guinness in Tokyo, Aesop was looking around the street with his mouth hanging open.

'They all look about seventeen!' he said. 'Look at what they're wearing. If that skirt was any shorter, it'd be a belt.'

Jimmy was pretty impressed as well. They were gorgeous. A bit mental-looking with mad make-up and some outrageous clothes, but they stood around in twos and threes like something out of a pop video, all pink and girly.

They went up to two girls who were handing out flyers.

'*Konnichiwa*,' said Aesop, with a wry grin at Jimmy.

The girls giggled.

'What have you got there?' Aesop went on, holding his hand out for a flyer. He took one and read it. 'Sexy Dance Girls?' He looked around at the others. 'Sounds like the very place, doesn't it? Where is it?'

The girls just giggled again and Aesop turned to Shiggy.

'Eh Shiggy, can you get the story here? I don't think they understand me.'

Shiggy talked to them for a minute and then nodded and led the others a little bit down the road and into a skyscraper.

'We're going up there?' said Aesop, looking up the huge face of the building.

'Yes. Up to top.'

They got in the elevator and whooshed up the side of the building, Jimmy closing his eyes rather than look out the glass wall where Tokyo suddenly appeared before them, vast and bright with neon. The doors slid open and they found themselves looking at an enormous black man. He must have been at least seven foot tall and was wearing a very sharp suit. He smiled at

188

them and his big teeth shone.

'Welcome to Sexy Dance Girls,' he said. He sounded like Barry White.

He moved to one side, revealing a door behind him. A thudding bass sound was coming from the other side of it. The bouncer pushed open the door with an arm the size of Jimmy's leg and gestured them inside. Aesop went in first and got about six feet inside before he stopped dead. Jimmy and Shiggy fanned out either side of him and the three of them stood in a line and fairly shat themselves. They were the only guys in the place who weren't black.

'I don't feel very tall all of a sudden,' said Aesop.

'I think we're in the wrong place,' said Jimmy.

They turned around and found that the bouncer was standing inside the door now grinning at them.

'Please. Go inside. Relax. Enjoy yourselves.'

Jimmy swallowed.

'Right. Are you sure we're … eh … y'know … eh …'

'Enjoy,' said the bouncer again, going back outside. Jimmy felt inclined to take it as an instruction rather than a suggestion.

'Let's just have a quick beer and fuck off.'

The others nodded.

'Why did you fuckin bring us here, Shiggy?' said Aesop.

'You wanted to come here.'

'Yeah, but there must be a reason it's full of black people.'

'Irish pub full of white people.'

'Yeah, but …'

'Can't be racist in Tokyo, Aesop.'

'I'm not fuckin racist! Believe me, right now I think black people are the coolest people in the world and I'll stand up on the bar there and yell it to the fuckin world, no problem.'

'Everyone rook happy. Friendry.'

'They're all looking at us though.'

'Everyone rook at me in Dublin.'

'Jaysis. It's always about you, isn't it Shiggy? Fuck. I wish I'd worn me Jimi Hendrix t-shirt.'

'Come on. Let's get a beer.'

On the way to the bar they noticed that all the guys were black but all the girls were Japanese. It was a funky place, all leather sofas and glass, and most of the space was taken up by a dance floor that spread across three levels. They got their beers and stood with their backs to the bar, watching the action. This place was about dancing. Most people seemed to be drinking water and just a few were sitting and chatting. The rest were all on the floor in groups and couples. The music was loud and hip-hop and the guys were all either in suits or basketball tops. Either way, they looked huge. They looked after themselves, this lot. No pencil necks or fat bastards.

Halfway through their beer, and before they even had a chance to say anything to each other, two enormous guys started walking up to the bar towards them, smiling.

'Right lads,' said Aesop, quietly. 'Keep cool … don't say anything … keep cool … here they come … we're grand … no problem … they're just getting a beer … we're all right lads … don't panic … nothing to worry about … oh Jesus, yer man's looking at me … oh holy fuck … Ah, howarya lads. What's the story? Nice club you have here isn't it?'

The guys stopped in front of him. One of them held out a hand.

'Robert,' he said.

'Howarya Robert. I'm Aesop. This is Jimmy and Shiggy. How are ye doing?'

'Really good. I notice that you guys aren't dancing.'

He had a funny accent.

'Well, to be honest, we've just had a big feed and … eh … Jimmy's got a bad back …'

'But this is a dance club. Please, come and join us. Jimmy? Dancing is good for the back.'

'Is it? It's just that, eh … the doctor said I should be careful … and…'

'Oh well. And Aesop? Shiggy? Please? Everyone dances here. And we have the most beautiful girls.'

'Right. Well, y'see, Robert, eh … this music is kind of … eh, I don't really know black music … oh, sorry, shite, I meant African American … sorry … eh … I didn't mean …'

Robert laughed. 'We are not African American. We are just African, mostly. I think. Anyway, it doesn't matter. Music is for everyone. Please. Come on over and enjoy yourselves. When you finish your drinks. No hurry. This is my club and I would be delighted if you would stay for a while.'

He left them with a smile and walked off again with his mate.

'What are we going to do?'

'I'll tell you what we're going to do, Jimmy. We're going to dance our holes off and love every minute of it.'

'But look!'

'Look at what?'

'Look at the fucking dance floor!'

'What about it?'

'Aesop, in case you hadn't noticed, black people can fucking dance. They'll think we're taking the piss if we get up there.'

'Keep smiling for Jaysis sake. Robert's looking at us.'

'I am fucking smiling! Shiggy?'

'Me tsoo. Happy Shiggy … happy Shiggy …'

'We have to give it a go. The beer's nearly gone.'

'Fuck. Okay. Okay. Right. Go on. You first.'

'Me? Fuck off. Do I look like Snoopy Doggy Doggy? Maybe we'll know the next one.'

'Yeah, right. They have a stash of Dexy's Midnight Runners albums, do they? In case two fucking honkies walk in off the street and feel like a bit of line dancing? Get up and dance you fucker. We're only here because you wanted to nail a Japanese bird. Well there you go. There's about a hundred of them in here.'

'Fuck that! I'm not going near anyone's bird in this place.'

'You two such babies,' said Shiggy. He put down his bottle and walked over to the dance floor. He smiled at two Japanese girls who were right at the edge and said something. They smiled back and he started dancing. Jimmy and Aesop looked at each other.

'He's the bravest man I know,' said Aesop.

'We have to go over. We can't leave him there.'

'Well … fuck it anyway.'

'Come on.'

They went over and started dancing next to Shiggy and the girls. It was horrible. When they did their normal dancing, they felt like a couple of poncy geeks. Then they tried to dance like the black guys around them, but that was even worse. The black guys danced like they were having sex with an invisible partner, but when Jimmy tried it he just felt himself going red and thanking Christ that no one he knew could see him. There was nothing he could do that fit in with what everyone else was doing. A couple of songs later, Robert and a couple of his mates joined them with a few more girls and soon there was a group of about a dozen people twisting and thrusting around them. Every now and again they'd all go 'Yo Yo Yo!' in time to the record with their hands in the air, but Jimmy kept coming in late and felt like an even bigger lemon. Aesop leaned in to him.

'I think I'm getting the hang of this,' he shouted.

Jimmy looked at him. Aesop had decided to try and be 50 Cent. He was moving from side to side and going up on one leg as his skinny arse moved back and forth like he was trying to shag a moving target.

'You're fucking not, you know.'

'Well at least I'm not doing the fuckin hokie kokie.'

Robert and his mates seemed to be really enjoying having them there. They kept laughing and mimicking their dancing.

After a bit the lads finally relaxed and started to enjoy themselves. They felt so fucking ridiculous that it was funny. They tried to get Robert to teach them how to dance properly, but if there was a school for cool dancing, then Jimmy and Aesop would have been in the special class. Robert kept laughing at them and calling his mates around to watch and before they knew it an hour had passed and they figured they'd head off again and try somewhere else. Robert walked them to the door and shook their hands. He was still grinning.

'Guys, that was some of the worst dancing we've ever had in here. Where you guys from?'

'Ireland,' said Jimmy.

'Ireland? You don't dance in Ireland?'

'Well, not like this. Our dancing is a bit more … eh … well … crap.'

'Come back any time guys. Ask for me.'

He tried to give them a pretty involved high-five style hand-shake, but they made a balls of that too and he laughed again and walked off, shaking his head. The bouncer, Timothy, showed them to the lift and then they were down in the street again.

'Well, that was a bit of an adventure on our first night out.'

'Yeah. And we only had one beer.'

'That must be why all those black fellas looked like boxers. Everyone in the Irish pub was skulling pints and eating fuckin burgers and chips. Everyone up there was dancing non-stop and drinking water. Probably explains why the Irish have such an impressive record in the Olympics.'

'What now?'

'What time is it?'

'Half two.'

'What time is last orders, Shiggy?'

'Depends. When sun comes up?'

'Really? Excellent. Where to?'

'Can we just go to a normal pub, Aesop? Or had you got your

heart set on a lesbian drawrf club, or some other place where we'd fit right in?'

'Normal pub is grand.'

'Okay. Shiggy? Lead the way. And Aesop, stop singing.'

'What? It's stuck in me head now.'

'I don't care. *Niggas don't give a fuck, nigga, all my bitches and my niggas put your motherfuckin hands in the air* … you don't go around the place singing lyrics like that in a new city.'

'I think I could get into it, Jimmy. I'd say it's great ridin' music.'

'Yeah. Well save it for the bedroom, Romeo, and there'll be less chance of someone beating the fuck out of you.'

'Robert was singing along to it.'

'When you grow up to be the same size as Robert you can sing whatever you fucking like. Anyway, you're not from some ghetto in LA, Aesop.'

'But it's not where you're from Jimmy, it's where you're at.'

Eighteen

'WHY ARE you wearing sunglasses, you spa?' said Jimmy, nodding at Aesop's head.

They were sitting in a café close to the apartment the next day. Shiggy had called at about two and arranged to meet them. After Shiggy had gone home the previous night, Aesop had followed a couple of models into a bar. Jimmy was too knackered after his week's work, so he left him to it. Next morning, Aesop still hadn't come home, so Jimmy left him a note and a map based on Shiggy's instructions so he could meet them when he got in. He turned up just as Jimmy's breakfast arrived and wobbled over to plonk himself next to Shiggy, shades on and a baseball cap pulled tightly down on his head.

'It's bright out.'

'It's not bright in here.'

'It is. Shut up. Shiggy, will you order coffee for me? I can't do it. I'm not well.'

'Sure. You want food tsoo?'

Aesop leaned over and grabbed a slice of toast off Jimmy's plate.

'You might want to get more toast for Jimmy.'

Shiggy went up to the counter and Aesop sat there, his hands folded over the top of his head and his elbows on the table.

'So?' said Jimmy.

'So what?'

'Did the evening live up to your expectations?'

'Not exactly.'

'Why? What happened?'

Shiggy arrived back with Aesop's coffee and toast and sat back down.

'Good night Aesop?' he said.

Aesop just grunted.

'Are you going to tell us what happened Aesop?' said Jimmy.

'It's not like you to keep it all to yourself.'

'Gimme a minute Jimmy, will ye? I need to collect me thoughts.'

'Jaysis. She must have been good.'

'Shush now. Let me have me coffee. Can you smoke in here?'

Shiggy nodded and Aesop lit up. He drank half his coffee and smoked his cigarette while the other two watched him, bemused. Eventually he pushed the cup away and leaned back.

'Right. It's easier if I just show you.'

He took off his baseball cap and then his shades. His left eye was a mess. There were some stitches in the eyebrow and the whole socket was swollen and red. Even the top of his nose looked bumpy and out of whack.

'Fucking hell!' said Jimmy. 'What the fuck happened to you? Did you get mugged?'

'No. Tara fucking Towers happened to me.'

'What?!'

'She was in the pub after.'

'What happened?'

'It's a long story.'

'We're not going anywhere. I want to fucking hear this!'

'Okay, well we were in her bed, right? In the hotel. I'm a bit tired and all, so I'm not in the mood for the fifteen hundred metres, y'know? But she's not wasting any time either. I mean, there was no fuckin about with her. She just grabbed me and pulled me on top of her, right? I even went to diddle her bean for her but she was having none of it. She just slapped me away like I was wasting her time.'

'I hope you're taking this down, Shiggy,' said Jimmy.

'Will you shut up? I'm not telling this twice. Where was I? Right, so I'm going, grand, we're on the same page, me and this bird. Anyway, I'm baytin' away into her and everything's going grand. The next thing she starts moaning and groaning, right? Lovely, says me to meself, cos I'm already looking forward to a bit of kip afterwards and this one didn't sound like she'd be taking all day about it. So she starts to wiggle and give it loads of verbal. I'm there, okay, whatever butters your muffin, love. But she starts to get a bit louder and then another bit louder and I'm going, fuck, she's one of them. I mean, we're in a hotel right? There's probably poor bastards next door with pillows over their heads. And then she grabs me by the arms and goes "Talk to me, Aesop". Ah Jaysis, I'm thinking. And I couldn't be arsed, but what am I supposed to do? So I say something like, "Come on Tara. You're so beautiful, you're so sexy" and all that shite, right? I mean, it's fuckin half six in the morning, y'know? If it's all the extras she was after, she should have fuckin said something in the Irish pub, shouldn't she, when I wasn't full of kebab and me head ringing with the drink.

'Anyway, of course she wasn't happy with that. "No no," she says. "Dirty. I want you to be dirty." For fuck sake, I'm thinking. At this hour? And it's not like she even needs it, the greedy fucker. She's already pulling the bullets off herself as it is. But she's giving me the hairy eyeball now and I'm thinking I better come up with something. "Say it Aesop," she's going. "Come on, say it, say it, say it, say it …" like she thinks I've got a list of things I want to get off me chest now. But what are you supposed to say? She won't shut up. She's shouting now, screeching at me to talk dirty and curse at her. It's doing me head in. I'm waiting for the phone to ring with complaints and she's still going "Say it, Aesop! Talk to me, curse at me, Irish, say it, go on, say it …" So anyway the next thing there's a bang on the wall over the bed and I'm going, I bleedin knew it. Now we're in trouble. But she *still* won't shut up. She probably didn't even hear it with the racket she was making. "Aesop! Come on, Irish. Talk dirty to me, Irish! Curse at me, Aesop! Tell me I'm naughty. Tell me I'm silly. Call me names!" I can't take any more of this bollocks. She's pulling me hair and everything, demanding it, y'know, wreckin' me buzz, and I still don't know what she wants from me. So I thought I'd give it a go and I lean down into her face and go "You're a nasty girl. And you're very fuckin dirty." She goes "Yes, yes I am!" So I think, right, so now I know the story. "You're silly," I say. "Yes. I'm silly. I'm fucking silly. How silly am I, Irish? Come on, tell me!" Now this is all new to me, right? I'm just playing along. "Tell me how silly I am!" she shouts again. She's got four fingers in me gob at this stage for fuck sake. "Tell me! How silly?" Bang goes the wall again and someone roars at us. "How fucking silly am I?" And I've had enough of this shit, so I spit out her hand and go, "You're a fuckin dopey cunt."'

Jimmy and Shiggy stared at him in shock.

Aesop took a sip of his coffee.

'Which, apparently, wasn't what she had in mind at all,' he said.

'She hit you?'

'Jimmy, it was like it happened in slow motion and I still couldn't get out of the way. She just stopped all the jiggling about she was doing and her eyes went all funny. Then she twisted around under me. I mean, she really revved up. I was looking at the back of her head there for a minute she was putting so much into it. The next thing there was a blur of movement somewhere off to me left and then I was lying on the bedroom floor about six feet from the bed with the ceiling spinning over me and blood running into me eyes. I'm telling you Jimmy, that punch would have floored Norman.'

'Jesus.'

'Yeah. But she wasn't finished yet. That was only to get me on the ground. I couldn't see properly with the blood and the fuckin concussion, but she hopped out of the bed and started kicking me in the guts. Four big boots I got. Remember she said she's the one that kicks the ball over the bar after they score a goal? I believe her. It was like falling off four sheds.'

'What happened then?'

'She ran into the jacks and locked the door. I don't know why she locked the fuckin door. I was the one getting a hiding. I tried to say sorry but she told me to get the fuck out. But how could I? There was blood all over me face and I was still wobbly from the dig she gave me. I sat on the bed and got dressed, but the blood was running down onto me shirt now. So, fuck her, I grabbed her t-shirt and used that to clean meself. Then I found a towel on the shelf and took it and got out of there.'

'Did you say anything else to her?'

'Did I fuck! You've to watch your mouth around that one. I just went down and got a taxi. I told him to bring me to Roppongi cos I knew the way home from there, but he drove me to a hospital instead. That was nice, wasn't it? But it took about six hours to get it all sorted. Five stitches. And the doctor said I probably had a cracked rib as well.'

'Fuck sake.'

'Yeah.'

'What are you going to do?'

'What do you mean?'

'I don't know. Tell the police or something?'

'Get fucked! What am I supposed to say to them? I got beaten up by a girl? Anyway, she's leaving for Canada tonight.'

'But look at your face.'

'I know. But life is about learning lessons, Jimmy. I've learned mine.'

'What lesson did you learn?'

'Be careful about riding rugby players.'

'I suppose that's not a bad one. You know, Aesop, it was kind of your fault though, wasn't it?'

'What?' Aesop looked at him. 'How the fuck was it my fault?'

'That was a terrible thing you said. You can't say that to a girl. What did you expect her to do?'

'I expected her to calm the fuck down and let me get on with it!'

'But you can't say …'

'I know! It's not like it's part of me regular repertoire Jimmy, for fuck sake. She was screaming the place down and grabbing me and roaring for me to curse at her. You can't carry on like that and then thump the shite out of the bloke just because you don't approve of what he comes out with. That's not fair! How was I supposed to know what she wanted me to say? Is there classes now on this stuff we can take?'

'But you called her a cunt!'

'It just came out! And look what she did to me. They had to x-ray me fuckin head! I don't care what you say, Jimmy. That wasn't called for. Jesus, your average Irish bird just wants you to do your best for fuck sake. Maybe make her a nice cup of tea afterwards before you fuck off. There's none of this roaring and yelling and acting the knacker. What the fuck is that? And anyway, I'd never say that to a girl normally. What do you take me for? It was her fault, Jimmy. I'm never going near a Canadian bird again, I'll fucking tell you that for nothing. Them beaver hats must give them all rabies or something.'

They all just sat for a minute and stared into space. Then Shiggy started laughing.

'What's so bleedin funny?' said Aesop. He had his glasses and hat on again now.

'Just thinking,' said Shiggy, still giggling. 'So happy I went home rast night. Tara's friend Marsha rike me, I sink. And me in same situation? I would be dead now …'

The lads laughed. It was true. Marsha looked like she could have easily pulled Shiggy limb from limb and hidden the pieces under one of her chins.

'But you wouldn't have said something like that,' said Jimmy.

'What would you have said to Tara then, Shiggy?' said Aesop.

'Don't know. "Nice tits"?'

'Right. Yeah. Maybe that's all she was after.'

THE LADS were starting to fade and couldn't face another night on the rip, so they just decided to head home. Shiggy went home too. He was meeting some bird later and wanted to get cleaned up. Back in the apartment Jimmy and Aesop ordered a pizza with the help of the guy in the foyer and then stuck on the telly to see if anything was on. Luckily the place they were staying had cable, because they couldn't follow anything that was on Japanese television. It was all zany game shows and talk shows and was way too high-energy even if they'd been able to understand a word of it. There wasn't much on cable either, though, so they munched on the pizza and had a couple of cans and flicked through the channels until they decided that the Antiques Roadshow was better than fuck all. They started betting a hundred yen on who got closest to the value of whatever the gimp on the telly had brought to be appraised. Aesop ended up winning by six hundred yen, and sat there with his hand out until Jimmy found the money and gave it to him.

'It's a bit sad though, isn't it?' he said.

'What is?' said Jimmy.

'This. It's Saturday night in Tokyo and we're sitting in watching the Antiques bleedin Roadshow. I wonder what Norman's doing? He's probably out with Marco.'

'I doubt it. It's only eleven o'clock in the morning at home. He's probably bringing his Ma to the shops.'

'Is she still sick?'

'Yeah, I think so.'

'Jaysis, I thought that woman would be around forever, scaring the shite out of the kids on the street and picking his clothes out for him.'

'She's not bleedin dying. She's just got something wrong with her blood and she can't get about sometimes.'

'What do you think of him being a gardener?' asked Aesop.

'I think it's great. He hated the bank. It'll be good for him to be out of that and doing what he wants.'

'Yeah, but cutting grass? There must be more to life than that.'

'That's not what he's doing, ye fuckin eejit. He'll be taking on big jobs, looking after apartment blocks and companies and all that. There's a lot of work in it. All the flowers and plants and trees and all as well as the lawns. Keeping them all nice and everything. He's been going on about it for years and now he's doing it, so fair fucks to him.'

'It's a bit like you, isn't it?'

'Me? How is it like me?'

'Well, except you want to go the other way. You're sticking with the job you hate instead of doing what you want.'

'Aesop, that's not what's happening. And anyway, I don't hate my job.'

'What's better then, doing a gig or sitting in your office? Which one do you enjoy more?'

'Ah Aesop, that's like saying do you prefer being on holidays or being in work. They're completely different.'

'Yeah, right. Well anyway, what about the song going out in the UK? Did you talk to Dónal yet?'

'No. Not yet. I'll probably give him a call at home tomorrow evening.'

'It'll be brilliant, won't it?'

'Aesop, I didn't say I was going to do it. I told him I'd think about it. And I have been thinking about it. It's not going to work, man. I knew I'd be busy, but this week has been insane. I'm up to my goolies with it. There's no way I can get involved in a UK release or any of that shite now. No way. I didn't realise just how hard it was going to be over here.'

'Come on, Jimmy. You can't walk away from it. For fuck sake, it's the biggest thing that's ever happened to us! You're not seriously thinking …'

'I am, Aesop. And if it wasn't for the fact that you're already bleedin out here, I'd be telling him that I can't do a gig either. I just don't want to get caught up in it all at this stage. It's better if I just put a lid on it and move on. If you saw me in the office this week you'd see what I mean. It's really fucking tough going, so it is.'

'So that's it.'

'Yeah.'

'Nothing's going to change your mind?'

'Nothing I can think of. I'd only be digging a hole for Dónal if I said I was on board with the whole thing.'

'Well if that's your concern, then it's a bit bleedin late.'

'How is it late?'

Aesop put down his can of beer and sighed.

'Look, I told him I wouldn't say anything to you, but I might as well now if you're packing it all in anyway.'

'What's the story?'

'He's fuckin broke, Jimmy.'

'Who? Dónal?'

'Yeah, Dónal.'

'What do you mean he's broke?'

'I mean Sin Bin is going down the tubes. Sparky told me. Well, Sparky started telling me and then Dónal came in and caught him, so then he had to tell me.'

'But they've only just started. How can they be broke?'

'It's a few things. A bunch of the other partners wanted out. They decided to put their money into property in Europe or something. He had the choice of selling the place or buying them out and keeping it going. So he kept it going, but he had to put his bollocks on it. Sparky too. Then, remember when there was bands coming over from England to record there? Well they're not now since that whole artist tax thing. So he says anyway. I couldn't really follow a lot of what he was going on about.'

'And what's the story now?'

'He says nothing's happening. They've got a few little things going on, but that place is set up for a proper studio, not kids coming in for a couple of hours' rehearsal. He says he can't keep it going. When Caillte did well in Ireland he thought it would work out, and then when that crowd came over from England to see us in McGuigans it looked like we were all laughing. An Irish single isn't worth a wank, but getting into the English charts ... and then an album ... that would've, y'know ...'

'Fuck.'

'Yeah. So anyway, he was hoping it would work out with The Grove. He told me he was an awful fuckin eejit for putting all his eggs in one basket, but that wasn't the way he planned it. It was supposed to only be the start of it all, but then shit just started happening on him and suddenly we were all that was left. Until now I s'pose.'

'But he gave you two grand to come out here! Why would he do that if he's got no money left?'

'Yeah. I asked him about that. He just laughed and said it was a long shot, but if something happened out here with that mate of his, then maybe you'd come around and give it another lash. Whoever this bloke is, Dónal seems to think a lot of him.'

'Why didn't you fucking tell me all this?'

'What do you think I'm doing?'

'Why didn't you tell me before, but?'

'He said not to. He said that you had enough on your plate and this was a very big decision you had to make on your own, without him or anyone else fucking with your head.'

'Fuck sake.'

Jimmy stood up and walked over to the kitchen. He turned around.

'How bad is it? I mean, how long before Sin Bin is in the shit.'

'It's pretty much in the shit now. He said if the single did well in the UK, he'd be able to keep going till Christmas. Maybe. If Senturian come in with an album offer by then, then everything's sweet and he's right back on track. Money in the bank. But if there's no single, then he'll probably be shutting up shop in a few weeks. He has to. He gets an advance for the single that'll keep things ticking over, but without that he's just flushing his own money down the jacks. And he's got Mags and the kids to think of and all, right? I mean, he won't be out on the street but all he'll have left is his gaff and his name he says.'

Jimmy said nothing for a bit. He just looked down at the beer can in his hand. It was Kirin beer. The one Shiggy had introduced them to when he'd first arrived in Ireland. The one that gave him the idea for 'Caillte'.

'Fuck.'

'Well anyway, that's the story Jimmy. You asked.'

'Fuck.' Jimmy got two more beers out of the fridge and sat down again. 'Now what?'

'Up to you, pal.'

'Jesus, I can't be … this can't be up to me … I've got other …'

'Jimmy, I told you all that because I knew you'd want to know. I promised Dónal I wouldn't, but I was hoping you'd be cool with everything and just keep going. I thought the album and all would come through and you'd never need to know that things were close there for a while. I really didn't think you'd bail on the band. Sorry, man, but after everything that's happened I thought you'd be grand to keep at it and see if it took off.'

'I would have been Aesop, but all this stuff happened at work and the next thing I'm being dragged this way and that way and then I'm puking up me beer in the middle of the night cos I'm so worried about everything. I had to just …'

He put his can on the table in front of him and sat back with his hands over his face.

'I didn't think anything like this was going on.'

'That's cos Dónal made sure you didn't know. He said it wasn't fair.'

'The poor cunt. He put everything into Sin Bin. He worked his bollocks off at it. Said it was payback for every crap fucking

205

job he's ever had. This was the big dream. Christ, how could it go tits up so soon?'

'Shit happens Jimmy.'

'Well, I have to do it now, don't I? The single in England.'

'Jimmy, you know that's what I want. But … ?'

Aesop shrugged and Jimmy stood up again.

'I have to. Dónal gave us a chance when we had fuck all. Sparky spent the last six months with me in the studio to make sure I could do anything I wanted to with the gear. All that time … and they could've been out getting other bands or looking for business for Sin Bin. I can't just leave them in the shit.'

'But what about work?'

'I know. But fuck it. I'll just have to do what I can, won't I? Hope no fucker notices if I'm a bit stretched. It's just one single. I'll call Dónal now. He'll be at home.'

'Okay. Jimmy, it's going to be grand,' said Aesop. 'And, c'mere, I'll help, right?'

Jimmy sighed at him.

'Yeah, right. What the fuck are you going to do?'

'Whatever you want! I promise. This is a big thing for me too, y'know? I know I'm a bit of a dosser and all, but if I can do anything to make it easier then just tell me and it's done.'

'We'll see how long that lasts.'

'I swear. I've got time, right? I'll do interviews or whatever Dónal wants, and I won't make a joke of everything. I'll do it properly.'

'Yeah. Well anyway, I'll give him a bell.'

'C'mere, don't say anything about all this, right?'

'Why not?'

'Because I promised I wouldn't say anything. He'll go mad. Anyway, it would look like you're only doing it out of charity. Have a bit of respect for the bloke Jimmy, y'know? He made sure you got to do things your way and didn't try and mess around with you. Just tell him you'll do the single and he'll be chuffed. If you tell him you know all this shit about Sin Bin, he'll probably tell you to forget about it. He can be a stubborn fucker as well, like someone else who we won't talk about.'

'I'm not stubborn.'

'Would you fuck off, Jimmy. You're like a child, sure.'

Nineteen

DÓNAL WAS beside himself.

'That's brilliant Jimmy! I knew you'd be up for it. And, remember, we'll be working around you and work all the time.'

'Yeah, no problem Dónal. It'll be great. And thanks for putting it all together.'

'Ah stop it. We're in this together Jimmy. Is Aesop there?'

'Yeah, he's trying to work the toaster. Do you want to talk to him?'

'Put him on a minute, sure.'

'This yoke has a hands-free setting. Hang on …'

Jimmy pressed the button and took the receiver away from his ear.

'Can you hear me?'

'I can, yeah.'

'Grand.'

Jimmy put the phone down altogether.

'Still there?'

'Yep.'

'Hey Aesop, Dónal wants to say hello.'

'Howarya Dónal,' shouted Aesop from the kitchen.

'How's Aesop?'

'Grand. I'm fuckin loving this holiday you're after sending me on.'

'It's not a bloody holiday you lazy shite. Have you been getting under Jimmy's feet?'

'Only a little bit, Dónal. I got a box off some bird last night so I'll be keeping a low profile until the stitches come out.'

'Stitches? Jesus, what did you do?'

'It'll only sound bad if I say it out loud.'

'Come on. Tell me.'

'Eh, well I kind of called her a bad word.'

'Well it feckin serves you right so. I hope she gave you a good slap.'

'She battered the shite out of me.'

'Excellent. Sounds like you deserved it.'

'Why does everyone keep saying that?'

'Hey Jimmy,' said Dónal. 'I've to talk to you about something.'

'What's that?'

'Well, it's about Caillte.'

'What about it?'

'It's in Irish, Jimmy.'

'Yeah.'

'Jimmy, we're releasing it into England, y'know?'

'I know.'

'Well, Sultan are a bit worried about the lyrics. No one will know what they're about.'

'Sure most lyrics in the charts are only bollocks, Dónal.'

'Yeah I know. But at least it's bollocks that people can sing along to.'

Jimmy knew what was coming and he didn't know how he felt about it.

'You want it in English.'

'Sultan do. And I can see their point.'

'Yeah … but …'

'Come on Jimmy,' said Aesop. 'Don't be an arsehole. I know you're into your bogger and all, but those dopey English fuckers over there won't have a clue what it means.'

'The dopey Irish fucker looking at me doesn't know what it means either.'

'We're not talking about me. I won't be buying it.'

'Jimmy,' said Dónal. 'What do you think?'

'Eh …'

'Jimmy, I'm not going to try and make you. I'm just saying it makes sense.'

'"Harry's Game" was in Irish …'

'Jimmy, Clannad are about soundscapes and mood. You wrote a pop song. People need to know what they're buying in that market. It's not background music for dinner parties and movie scores.'

'Yeah. But … it's just that …'

'Don't mind this fucking nancy, Dónal,' said Aesop. 'He'll do it. Won't you Jimmy?'

'Shush you. I'm thinking …'

'Jaysis. What's the big deal? Hey Dónal, how many songs on the disc?'

'Four.'

'Right. What are you putting on it?'

'"Caillte", "Alibi", "Bush Whacked" and one of the others. Haven't decided yet.'

'What about "Meatloaf's"?'

'Not this time pal. "Meatloaf's Underpants" and "Caillte" on the same single? They'll think we're a bloody joke band.'

'Well, how about the bogger version of "Caillte" as well as the English version?'

'Actually, Aesop, that's a pretty good idea. What do you think Jimmy?'

'Eh, yeah … I s'pose …'

'See?' said Aesop. 'I'm making meself useful already! Jaysis, I'm brilliant. If anyone needs me to sort something else out, I'll be out having a smoke on the balcony.'

He wandered off.

'Jimmy?'

'Yeah, Dónal. Okay, we could do that.'

'Great.'

'How do we do it, but? I never recorded an English version. And I'd have to look at the lyrics again.'

'Johnnie will sort that out. He'll record it for me over there.'

'Who's Johnnie?'

'He's my mate out there who I told you about. I've already talked to him about what we're all trying to do.'

'Jaysis, he has a name. I didn't think we'd ever get to meet him. I thought you were after making him up.'

'No, Johnnie's there all right. Take down his number there and give him a bell during the week.'

Jimmy grabbed a pen and wrote it down.

'What's he like?'

'Johnnie? Johnnie's a great bloke. You'll like him.'

'He's not like Sparky is he? That'd be hard to handle from scratch all over again out here!'

Dónal laughed.

'No. He's nothing like Sparky. They do know each other though. He'll be able to tell you some stories.'

He laughed again. There was definitely something going on with this Johnnie bloke.

'Right. Okay, well anyway, I'll give him a shout when I get a minute. Any other news?'

'Ah not much. It's a bit quiet round here at the moment, so I'm catching up on paperwork and all that.'

'Okay. Well take it easy. I'll be onto you on email.'

'Cheers Jimmy.'

'Seeya.'

THE NEXT night was Jimmy's official welcome party in work.

'So, where are we going tonight?' he asked Shiggy.

'Nice restaurant. I pick. Berry dericious food.'

'Grand.'

They all met downstairs in the lobby, about a dozen of them, including the head of the department, Sakamoto-san. He was a bigwig all right. The Japanese lads nearly fell over themselves bowing at him whenever he opened his gob. To Jimmy he didn't seem like much. He was in charge, but he wasn't technical. He didn't even seem too concerned about Jimmy's work and just nodded every now and again in the few meetings he bothered his arse going to. Maybe he was a regular busy bee behind the scenes, but to Jimmy he just seemed to be the bloke that said yes or no – and even then he seemed to do it on the spur of the moment, rather than after careful and considered deliberation. Anyway, Jimmy didn't give a fuck. He just smiled and tried to be polite and let them get on with their end of things their way.

They caught a subway into Shinjuku, the part of town Shiggy had said he'd bring himself and Aesop to one day. It was like its own little city, full of skyscrapers and restaurants and the usual flashing neon and traffic noises. Tokyo had a mad mix of traditional and modern going on: outside the most sophisticated-looking buildings, all steel and mirrored walls, you might easily see a little old fart selling baked sweet potatoes out of the back of his rickety van. Or right next to a ludicrously complicated fountain sculpture, you might see a wooden restaurant with red lanterns hanging outside. The oul biddy in the kimono would be sitting next to the punk rocker on the train. Jimmy loved it. It was cool. Mad but cool.

They all congregated outside the restaurant and Jimmy looked up at the sign: *Unagi*, it said.

'What's that mean?' he asked Shiggy, pointing.

'Means "eel",' said Shiggy. 'In Japan, berry important fish.'

'Is it? That's nice. What kind of food do they have?'

'*Unagi*,' said Shiggy.

'Eel? What else?'

'Just eel.'

'Shiggy,' Jimmy whispered now, his face stuck in a polite smile for the others. 'Are you telling me I'll be eating fucking eels tonight?'

'Yep. Well, you have choice of course.'

'What's the choice?'

'Hungry or eat eel.'

'You fucking gee-bag. You said you picked this place.'

212

Shiggy smiled.

'You said you want to learn about Japan.'

'You know that's not what I meant!'

'Eel berry good. Try.'

'You fucker …' said Jimmy, under his breath as the others herded him inside.

He bent low to avoid smacking his head off the doorframe and immediately saw that his shoes would have to come off. He was getting used to this. Any place that had the slightest bit of tradition to it – a restaurant like this for instance – was a no-shoe zone. The floors were made of straw mats and you sat on your arse on a cushion and tried to find somewhere to fit your legs. Jimmy sat between Shiggy and Sakamoto-san and tried to get comfortable, but he knew it was pointless. In half an hour the cramps would set in and then he'd spend the next two hours shifting around on his bum and changing his position and trying to ignore the ache in his lower back. For a change, though, that wasn't the worst part of the ordeal.

There were gas burners at intervals down the long table and small pans were placed on each one to heat up. Two bowing waiters arrived with ten tall bottles of beer and shared them out as Jimmy looked longingly at the nearest one. There was a bit of a ritual to the beer pouring. Shiggy picked up a bottle and filled Jimmy's glass, a small thing about the size of two eggcups.

'Good man Shiggy.'

'Ah, Jimmy, you must now pour beer for me.'

'Really? But you have the bottle in your hand sure.'

'Yes. But … is porite.'

'All right. Here you go.'

He filled Shiggy's glass.

'Now Sakamoto-san,' whispered Shiggy.

'Oh right. Here you go Sakamoto-san.'

Sakamoto-san gave a little bow and smiled.

'Ah! *Domo*.'

'Right. Can I drink mine now Shiggy?'

'Yes … but …'

But it was too late. Jimmy's glass was empty.

He went to fill it again, but Sakamoto-san immediately took the bottle out of his hand and did it himself.

Jimmy was starting to feel uncomfortable.

'Shiggy, what the fuck is going on?' he said out of the corner of his mouth.

'Don't drink all in one go. And don't pour own beer. Not yet anyway.'

'But the size of the glass!'

'I know. Different from Ireland.'

'Sakamoto-san will get a pain in his hole doing that every two minutes.'

'I will do it.'

Sakamoto-san knew something was up. He leaned forward and said something to Shiggy. Shiggy laughed a little and said something back. Jimmy leaned back out of the way and felt like a bit of a spare prick. The two of them did some more back-and-forth and then Sakamoto-san called to the waiter and started to talk to him.

'What's the story, Shiggy?'

Shiggy was starting to look a bit flustered.

'Eh, Sakamoto-san wants you be comfortable.'

'I'm grand.'

'Too rate.'

The waiter nodded and bowed and scurried off.

'What's happening?'

'You getting bigger grass. I tell him about beer in Ireland.'

'Ah no. I'm grand. Tell him. I'm grand.'

Shiggy was already a bit red. He always went red when he drank beer, but he hadn't even had a chance to taste his yet.

'Eh, Jimmy, you are guest. You can have anysing you want.'

'But I'm grand!'

The waiter arrived back. He looked embarrassed and said something to Sakamoto-san, who just waved him away.

'Oh fuck,' said Shiggy.

'What? Jesus, what did I do now?'

'You will see.'

The waiter appeared again. He was carrying a large glass vase that he'd obviously just washed out and gave it to Sakamoto-san with a very low bow. Sakamoto-san nodded at him and presented the glass to Jimmy with both hands. Jimmy took it. He was mortified. The vase would hold about a litre and a half when full. Jimmy put it down and looked at it. Sakamoto-san picked up the half empty bottle of beer in front of him and poured it into the vase. Then he got a fresh bottle from the middle of the table and poured that in too. It still wasn't full and he asked one of his lads to pass him down another one. Jimmy looked as the level in the vase slowly went up the side of the glass. Everyone else was looking at it too, in total silence. The vase full, Sakamoto-san bowed and smiled and picked up his own drink.

Jimmy glanced around the table. Everyone was looking between him, Sakamoto-san and the enormous pail of beer on the table.

'Oh God,' he whispered to Shiggy, his lips not moving. 'I feel like a right arsehole now.'

'Good,' said Shiggy, his shoulders slumped. 'Me tsoo.'

'What do I do now?'

'Drink your beer, Jimmy, you gobshite.'

Jimmy took a long pull on it and smiled at everyone. They were sniggering between themselves now, but the moment had passed. He was just another stupid *gaijin* with no fucking manners, but that was okay with them because it was okay with Sakamoto-san.

Jimmy got into a conversation with Sakamoto-san, whose English was actually pretty good. He'd spent a couple of years in Germany for the company. They chatted about Europe and the weather and Roy Keane and Jimmy gradually began to relax. The only problem was that the cold beer had made the sides of the huge vase all wet and slippery and he had to use two hands to drink it for fear it would go flying all over everyone. The Japanese were all small and neat and elegant and here he was, his knees sticking up in front of him and sucking on his beer like a pig at a trough. So much for the growing possibilities of being out of your fucking comfort zone. He felt like a total prat. And now his back was starting to throb.

The waiter suddenly appeared at his shoulder and thrust a plate of squirming eels out towards the now-sizzling pan in front of Jimmy. It happened so fast that he jumped backwards in fright, almost taking the waiter's knees with him, but then just watched in horror when, with a deft flick of the wrist, the guy poured the contents of the plate into the pan. A whosh of steam bellowed up from the table and Jimmy's stomach lurched as what looked like a couple of hundred fat wriggling worms briefly protested their fate. He felt someone staring at him and realised that he had grabbed Shiggy's leg with the shock and was squeezing hard.

'Jimmy ... prease ...'

He let go, but the room was starting to swim. He couldn't take his eyes off the mess of writhing slop in front of him. It was like something from a sixties movie, the plate moving in a kaleidoscope of colour and shape. One of the eels, about four inches long, flopped off the side of the pan and wriggled once or twice on the table before becoming still. Jimmy watched it and it seemed to be watching him back. There were more sizzles of steam and he knew more plates of live eels were meeting their maker up and down the table. His eyes suddenly found them-selves focusing on a small beaker of some brown sauce on the table ... and then he was gone ... on his holidays in the Isle of Man, aged eight. He was watching a horse-drawn tram coming towards him along the promenade in Douglas and his Dad pulled him out of the way. He could hear the sea and his Mam yelling at him to watch himself.

'Jimmy!'

'I'm grand Mam. I'm grand.'

'Jimmy, you okay?'

'Did you see the horse, Mammy?'

He got a little slap on the face and opened his eyes.

'What the fuck?'

'Jimmy. Are you okay?'

Shiggy was looking down at him. Past his face was a ceiling fan going around and around.

'What happened?'

'I sink you faint.'

'What?'

'Can you sit up?'

'Eh … yeah, I sink so … or, I think so.'

He sat up and looked around.

This time the entire restaurant was looking at him. The by-now-distraught waiter was standing there, flapping his arms and rubbing his head. He handed Jimmy a steaming hot towel and Jimmy cleaned his face with it.

'You okay?' said Shiggy again.

'Yeah. I'm fine. Jesus, that was weird.'

Sakamoto-san was still there. Everyone was still there. He hadn't fallen very far. He was already sitting down, so he just fell backwards and smacked his head off the floor, which he was now extremely happy to see was still made of straw mats.

'Okay Corrins-san?' said Sakamoto-san.

'Yes. Thank you. I'm very sorry.'

'It is okay. You don't have eel in Ireland?'

'Eh, I don't think so. Maybe. We never ate it in my house.'

'Ah. I see. Would you like to try?'

Jimmy cast a wary eye in the direction of the bubbling pan. You'd only be able to make the eels out now if you knew they were in there. It was like a small pool of bubbling brown jelly. With thousands of black dots. The eyes.

'Eh …'

'Maybe just one?'

I just fainted from the sight of the slimy bastards. You think I want to eat one now, you funny fucker?

'Eh …'

'Try? Berry good. Famous restaurant.'

This bastard is just getting me back now for the beer. I'll fucking show him.

'Okay. Maybe one.'

He took up his chopsticks. The first one he grabbed at didn't even make it halfway to his mouth before it slid off and landed on the table. He went for another one and this time it fell onto the small saucer in front of him. The Japanese lads were loving it. The younger ones were fit to piss themselves with the laughing but Sakamoto-san glanced around the table and everyone shut up. Jimmy had another stab at the one on his saucer and managed to flick it into his mouth before it, too, absconded. The texture was gross, but the taste was actually fine. A bit sweet. It tasted pretty much like teriyaki, which he'd had before. He took another one and ate it. That was his lot. Putting this string of congealed snot in his mouth was just too disgusting and he'd made his point. He looked up at Sakamoto-san.

'Hmm. Interesting. Reminds me of *teriyaki*. I think I prefer *yaki-niku*.' Shiggy had brought them to a *yaki-niku* restaurant in Dublin for their Christmas presents. It was fried meat. No problems there.

'Ah yes. I see. Next time we will go to *yaki-niku*.'

Sakamoto-san was smiling at him now. A real smile, not the little tugs at the side of his mouth that everyone else got. Jimmy smiled back. Sakamoto-san bowed. Jimmy bowed. He was feeling better. He washed the last of the slime down his throat with a big mouthful of beer and wondered what he was supposed to do now. Sakamoto-san had it covered though. Five minutes later a steaming bowl of *miso* soup and a bowl of rice was placed in front of him. A bit later he was presented with chicken satays on sticks. All of it was lovely.

Near the end of the meal Sakamoto-san made a welcome speech to Jimmy in English, at which everyone clapped, and then Jimmy was invited to give a speech of his own. He thanked everyone for the welcome and the meal and made a little joke about the beer, the eels and the fact that he had fainted. They all laughed, even though at least a few of them didn't understand what he was saying. By the time they left the restaurant he was a little pissed and happy that he hadn't completely fucked up the evening.

'Jesus, Shiggy. That was all your fault.'

'Why?'

'Bringing me to a place like that! Fucking eel!'

'I didn't sink you faint, big girl.'

'Piss off! I didn't think the fuckers would be alive. What kind of country is this?'

'Anyway, it okay. You eat a few. All okay.'

'But they all think I'm a fuckin eejit. They'll be laughing their holes off at me from now on.'

'No. Tomorrow nobody say anysing. All forgotten.'

'Get fucked.'

'Reary. Tonight it finish. That is Japanese way.'

'Are you serious?'

'Yep. And Sakamoto-san rike you.'

'He does not. He must think I'm a terrible plonker.'

'No. He rike you. You faint and then try eel anyway. He rike zat.'

'Sadistic fucker. Anyway, I only had two.'

'No no, Jimmy. You try. That's important. Berry good. When I saw zat I was berry happy.'

'Are you sure he likes me?'

219

'Yes. Send waiter out to get you *yaki-tori*. Chicken sticks? *Unagi* restaurant not make *yaki-tori*. Come from other restaurant.'

'Are you taking the piss? He did that?'

'Yeah. He rike you.'

'This country is fucked up. Who eats eels for fuck sake?'

'Who eat brack pudding?'

'What? That's not the same. Sure that's only … eh … blood and … eh … ah, ask me bollix …'

'Show me that Goolies thing again,' said Aesop, later.

'It's called Google.'

'How does it work?'

'How does it work or how do you use it?'

'I want to use it for fuck sake, don't I? I don't give a wank how it works.'

'You just type in whatever you want to know about.'

'Black Sabbath.'

'Right. Well just type it in there. Like this look …'

Jimmy typed it in and clicked on Search.

'See? You get a list of all the websites that have something about Black Sabbath. Look, there's about four million websites.'

'Four million! Jesus. What happens then?'

'You just click on the one you want to look at. Watch …'

Jimmy clicked on the link for the Black Sabbath Wiki site.

'There you go. Everything you wanted to know about the band.'

Aesop took the mouse and scrolled down the page the way Jimmy had shown him.

'That's brilliant! They have the whole thing here.'

'I know.'

'How did that get into your computer?'

'It's not in my computer. It's on the Internet. The computer just connected to the Internet and downloaded it. Now listen,

Kyotosei are after giving me a new laptop to use. One of their newest models so I can try it out. So I'll leave this one here in the apartment and you can use it to do your email and learn all about heavy metal bands that you already know about.'

'Ah that's cool, Jimmy, thanks. What else does it do?'

'Whatever you want.'

Jimmy was getting tired. It had taken him two hours to get Aesop to the point where he could use his Hotmail account and now Google.

'Well, what happens if I type in "Halle Berry"?'

'Type it in and see. Press this button up here, see it? It looks like a house. That'll bring you back to Google.'

Aesop typed it in slowly using one finger and then clicked on Search. A list popped up straight away.

'Look! Jimmy, I did it! See what I did?'

He turned around to Jimmy like he was after pulling a rabbit from his trousers.

'Good man. Now click on one of the links.'

Aesop did it and looked up, frowning.

'Computer says no.'

'You pressed the wrong button that time. Use the one on the left, under your index finger.'

Aesop tried again and a Halle Berry fan site came up.

'There she is! Look at her! Isn't she a ride?'

'Yeah, she's gorgeous.'

'But there's only a few pictures. How do I get more pictures?'

'Well, go back to Google. Right. Now see where it says Images? Click that.'

Aesop did it.

'Now type in Halle Berry again … yeah … that's it …'

'Jimmy! Look! You can see her baps! And see that? There's Billy Bob giving her one in that movie! Bleedin hell …'

'Oh Jesus. Listen Aesop, there's other things on the Internet besides pictures of Billy Bob Thornton's arse, right? Get a fucking life and see if you can learn something useful. Next week I'll show you the band's site and you can help me on that. Maybe you could write a diary or something on it for people back home.'

'Write? You mean I can have one of these sites?'

'Eh … yeah.'

'Will you show me how to do it?'

'What are you going to put on there?'

'I don't know Jimmy. But, Jesus, don't you think it's about time the world heard what I have to say?'

'No I fucking don't actually. Anyway, I'm going asleep. You all right? You can play music, do your email and use the Internet now. It's been a big day for you.'

'Yeah, thanks Jimmy. Seeya tomorrow. Ooh, look! Catwoman … God, the Interweb has everything, doesn't it?'

Jimmy left him grinning at the screen and went to bed, shaking his head.

Twenty

'IT'S A bit packed,' said Aesop. 'How are we going to recognise him?'

'Well, for starters, he's from Dublin. So there's a fairly good chance he won't be Japanese-looking, isn't there?'

'There's other *gaijin* here as well but.'

'*Gaijin*? Jaysis, getting into the swing of things, are we Aesop?'

'I'm not a fuckin dope Jimmy. I can remember the odd word here and there.'

They looked around the place from their stools at the bar. They were in Shibuya, the *Bladerunner* area in Tokyo, and the bar was getting a bit full with people coming in after work.

'The Guinness is a bit shite, isn't it?'

'Yeah. They probably don't sell much of it.'

'It was nicer in Foley's.'

He held up the pint and looked over at the barman.

'Look at the state of that head. Who does he think he is, Mister fuckin Whippy? I should have asked him for a Flake to stick in it.'

'God. Will you stop whinging Aesop?'

'Jimmy, it took me a bleedin hour to find this place. That map you gave me was missing two streets. And it pissing down outside …'

'Well you're here now. Shut up and drink your pint.'

'What's a bloke from Dublin doing out here anyway?'

'You're here, aren't you?'

'Yeah, but I'm not … hey, that bloke is waving at us.'

Jimmy looked around. A guy about Dónal's age had just come in the door and was looking at them. He waved again.

'That must be him. Actually … Aesop … y'know something … I think I've seen him somewhere. He looks familiar, doesn't he?'

'Does he?' Aesop was still frowning at his pint.

'Ah. I know what it is. Look at him. He looks like Johnnie Fin …'

Jimmy stopped talking and his mouth dropped open.

'Johnnie. That's him! Jesus Christ, Aesop!'

'What?'

'Do you know who the fuck that bloke is?'

The guy was putting his umbrella in a plastic cover. Aesop turned around and looked again. He was coming over. Aesop blinked a couple of times and then his mouth dropped open as well.

'That's Johnnie … Johnnie Fing … oh holy fuck. Jimmy, he's coming over!'

'It's him, isn't it?'

'Yeah. Definitely! I had a Rats poster on me wall for years. That's him.'

'He's here to fucking see us! That's Johnnie. Dónal's Johnnie.'

'Get fucked.'

'It is! Shut up … here he is now. Be cool … just be fucking cool Aesop … oh Jesus … here he is …'

They both stood up and turned towards him. He got there and stuck out his hand.

'Johnnie Fingers. How are you doing lads? I take it you're the two Dublin rockstars I'm here to see. Not too many other people sitting at the bar drinking Guinness in this place. You might as well be waving a tricolour in the air.'

Aesop was the first to find his tongue.

'Eh …' he said.

'Jimmy?' said Johnnie.

Aesop nodded and Johnnie shook his hand.

'And you must be Aesop.'

'I'm Jimmy,' said Jimmy, shaking his hand.

'You're both Jimmy?' said Johnnie.

'He's Aesop,' said Jimmy.

Johnnie looked back and forth between them.

'Right,' he said eventually. 'Okay. You want a drink?'

They both nodded and he ordered three drinks in Japanese.

'Johnnie Fingers speaks Japanese, Jimmy,' whispered Aesop.

'I heard him. Shut up will ye?'

'So, lads,' said Johnnie, turning around from the bar. 'I heard your song. Dónal sent it over. Very good. I believe it's gone down well at home?'

Jimmy nodded. Johnnie Fingers had just said he liked his song.

'Yeah,' Johnnie went on. 'Actually, the production has Sparky all over it. Was that the first time you worked with him?'

Jimmy nodded again.

'What did you think? He's a mad bastard, isn't he?'

Nod.

'Lads, you're not very talkative, are you?'

'Sorry. It's just … eh … Dónal didn't say you were Johnnie Fingers. He just said Johnnie.'

'Ah right. Well there you go. Here, grab your beers there. *Kampai*,' he said, holding up his own. They clinked glasses and took a sip. 'Welcome to Japan.'

Jimmy looked at Aesop, but Aesop was just staring at Johnnie, his eyes huge. He looked like a man about to cry.

'Anyway, Dónal asked me to put a few things together for you. You want to do a gig in Tokyo, right? Well that shouldn't be a problem. I can get a club or something. Nothing fancy, but you'll get a feel for the place. But I heard that the song is going on for UK release too? So Dónal asked me about getting you guys on film for a video. There's a good bit more involved in that. I was thinking we'd shoot some of the gig and then location shots around Tokyo. That okay with you? I don't think Dónal was after something mad. It's a pretty mellow song. Maybe we'll get you into some Japanese gardens or that? And then he told me the other day that you want to re-record the song in English as well.

Well I can do that myself. No problem. So how does that sound? When are you ready to get started? Jimmy?'

'Eh, whenever … I mean … I'm working over here, but …'

'Yeah, Dónal mentioned that. Sorry, Aesop, are you okay?'

Aesop was now fixed on Johnnie's beer, following it with his head as it went from the bar to his mouth and back.

'Sorry?'

'Are you okay? You're looking at my beer. Is there something wrong with it?'

'I was looking at your hand.'

Johnnie put down the beer and lifted his hand up, looking at it.

'This one?'

'Yeah.'

'What about it?'

'That hand played the piano on "I Don't Like Mondays", didn't it?'

Johnnie smiled.

'Yeah. This one too.' He held up his other hand and winked at Jimmy. 'It's a real bugger trying to play it on one hand, let me tell you.'

'That's just so … fucking … cool,' said Aesop. He looked around the bar. 'I'll be back in a minute.' He scampered off.

'Eh, okay,' said Johnnie, watching Aesop disappear towards a group of Japanese people. 'Anyway Jimmy, I told Dónal I'd help any way I can. Dónal's a great bloke. Sparky too. We had some good times back in the Rats days. I haven't seen him in ages now. And it must be going on ten years since I've seen Sparky. Did they tell you about the row he had with Geldof?'

'Yeah,' said Jimmy.

'God, we had a laugh over that. Well, eventually we did. Sparky's got some temper on him, doesn't he? Scared the shite out of me the first time I met him. Afterwards, though, me, Simon, Garry, Gerry, Sparky …'

He trailed off and gazed away to the side, a small smile on his face.

'Anyway,' he went on. 'Enough of all that. You're good to go on all this stuff? The gig will have to be first. I'll get you in somewhere on Saturday week. Get some people there. How does that sound? You've got your bass player here as well, right? A Japanese guy, Dónal says.'

'Yeah. Saturday week would be brilliant. Shiggy's the bass player. He had to work late tonight, but he said he's grand with whatever you come up with.'

'Grand so. I'll give you the details in the next few …'

Aesop arrived back. He had a sheet of paper and a pen.

'Sorry, Johnnie, but do you mind?' He held them out.

'Autograph?'

'Yeah. But can I draw your hand too?'

'My hand?'

'Yeah. Just put it on the bar there and I'll draw around it.'

'Eh …'

Aesop put the sheet of paper down on the bar top and nodded at Johnnie. Johnnie put his hand on the page and looked up at Jimmy, bemused. Aesop took the pen and traced around Johnnie's right hand. Then he turned the page around and took Johnnie's left hand without saying anything. Around the hand went the pen again.

'Right. Now will you sign them?'

'Sure, if you want.'

He took the pen and autographed both sides of the page in the middle of the outline of his hands.

Aesop grinned at him and took the page and the pen back. He ran off to return the pen and then came back to the bar.

'Sorry, Johnnie. I suppose that happens to you all the time, doesn't it?'

'I can't say it does, Aesop, to be honest,' said Johnnie, glancing again at Jimmy. 'The odd autograph maybe, but …'

'Can I tell you something, Johnnie? You were the only cool keyboard player. Ever.'

'Well, thanks Aesop, but …'

'No, I'm serious. Everyone else was shite. You were brilliant.'

Johnnie laughed.

'Stevie Wonder was shite? Ray Charles was shite?'

'Ah Johnnie, it's not the same. You had the cool head on you. And the pyjamas!'

'I haven't done that in a long time now, Aesop.'

'Still. I wore stripey pyjamas in bed till I was sixteen. Didn't I Jimmy?'

Jimmy nodded.

'That was you, Johnnie,' said Aesop.

'Good. Well I'm glad, Aesop. It was just a stage thing though. Something to get noticed.'

'Where did you get them?'

'What? The pyjamas?'

'Yeah.'

'Eh, Dunnes I think.'

'Me too! Jimmy, did you hear that?'

'Aesop, will you leave Johnnie alone? He's not here to talk about his pyjamas for fuck sake. Sorry Johnnie.'

'It's okay Jimmy. I don't mind. They were good days. Anyway, Dónal mentioned that Aesop could get a little … em … excitable.'

'That's not what he said, is it?'

'Well, no. Not quite. Sparky had a few things to say about you too, Aesop. Are you always like this?'

Aesop nodded.

'Jimmy's Mam says I'm a tonic.'

'Does she?'

'C'mere, what's Simon Crowe like? He's a fuckin great drummer. I used to play along with "Rat Trap" when I was learning. I bleedin loved it. It was like he was really playing the song, not just keeping time, y'know? He plays something different every couple of bars. It's almost like a separate set of lyrics going through it except being played on the drums instead of being sung. It took me six months to learn it, and then I had to start all over again when I got real toms. And then I did me own version later on. Didn't I Jimmy? That song taught me more about how to play the drums than the six months of lessons I took. Especially cos we're a three-piece. You know what I mean Johnnie? Cos you have to fill out the sound. Simon was the one who showed me how to add to the song, not just play along with it. Him and Bonzo Bonham. Simon's not here too is he? In Tokyo? Oh Jesus, I'd love to meet him. Oh Christ, that'd be brilliant, that would. Is he here Johnnie? Is Simon Crowe here, is he?'

Aesop stopped talking. He was panting and had one hand on Johnnie's arm, staring at him almost beseechingly.

'Sorry, no. But I'll tell him you were asking for him.'

'Do! And tell him that I said …'

'Aesop, that's enough,' said Jimmy. 'Will you relax for fuck sake? You're going to freak Johnnie out. Just calm down.'

'Okay. Okay. Listen I have to go for a squirt. All this excitement. Don't go till I come back, Johnnie, will you?'

'I'm not going anywhere Aesop.'

'Good, good. Grand.'

He went off to the toilet.

Johnnie watched him go.

'He must be a good drummer,' he said.

'Why do you say that?'

'The good ones are always a bit …' He made his eyes go around in circles. 'Y'know …'

They spent about an hour talking about stuff. Music at home, how Johnnie ended up in Japan, what he did these days and, of course, the Boomtown Rats. Aesop wouldn't stop asking questions about what it was like being in a real, big, fuck-off rock band. This guy had played Live Aid for fuck sake! He wanted to know about everything. Playing on Top of the Pops, the tours, the women, the parties. Johnnie was cool about it, though, and didn't mind being pestered.

'I can't remember a lot of it, though.'

'You were out of your face the whole time? Brilliant!'

'No,' Johnnie laughed. 'It's not that. It was twenty years ago. More! Do you remember what you were doing twenty years ago?'

'Actually,' said Jimmy, 'it's pretty much the same as what he's doing now, except that now he can get into pubs.'

Eventually Johnnie had to go. He said goodbye to the lads and walked off, grabbing his umbrella on the way out and giving them a small wave.

'Well?' said Jimmy.

'I can't believe I just spent the last hour having a beer with Johnnie Fingers.'

'I know. It's mad, isn't it?'

'This is what it'll be like when we're famous. We'll get to meet all our idols.'

'He didn't really behave like an idol, though, did he?'

'That's the cool fuckin part! He's just like me!'

'He's nothing like you, Aesop. He's articulate and interesting and cool and he doesn't say "fuck" every two words.'

'You thought he was brilliant as well, but, didn't you?'

'Yeah. Jaysis, I'll kill Dónal for not saying anything. He knows we were huge Rats fans.'

'That's probably why he didn't say it. To surprise us.'

'Well it worked, didn't it?'

'Jesus, yeah.'

They both looked towards the door, grinning.

'What does articulate mean?'

'Eloquent.'

'Right. And what does eloquen … ?'

'He expresses himself well.'

THE ARGUMENTS over the laptop started on Tuesday night. Aesop was bent on reinventing himself as an Internet wizard and was never off the thing. The problem was that Jimmy had no amp for the new guitar he'd just bought the previous Saturday. There was no point in buying an amp in Tokyo because the voltage was different from home. Instead, he was able to plug the guitar into the external soundcard for his laptop. All the software he needed to play and even record it were installed there and he could then listen to himself on his headphones or the portable speakers. It wasn't the same thing, but there was no way he could just leave his new guitar sitting there without playing it.

'Get off it Aesop,' he said.

'I'm busy Jimmy.'

'It's my fucking computer. You had it all day, now I want a go.'

'But I'm doing research.'

'I don't give a shite.'

'Use your new one.'

'Nothing's installed on that. I can't play properly through it. It's only for work.'

'Why didn't you buy an amp?'

'Because I just spent a bleedin fortune on a guitar!'

'Ah Jimmy.'

'What the fuck could you possibly be doing research on anyway?'

'I'm writing a song.'

'About what?'

'About Halle Berry.'

'Jesus …'

'Shut up. I don't slag you about your songs.'

'Yes you fucking do!'

'Well. Maybe the gay ones …'

'Why are you writing a song about her anyway?'

'It's kind of a thank-you song.'

'How?'

'Well, it's called Hallewood.'

'Hallewood?'

'Yeah. Because, y'know, her name is Halle. And she gives me wood.'

'Oh for fu … how old are you?'

'Thirty-two and a half. So Halle lives in Hollywood, right? Eh, probably. That's why I'm doing research, y'see? To get the details right. I was hoping to get it finished for the gig on Saturday.'

'Aesop, we only have one rehearsal. We can't spend it trying to learn new stuff at this stage. We've got three hours in a studio tomorrow night and that's it. Hallewood will just have to wait till another time. Shiggy hasn't played with us in ages.'

'But it's nearly finished!'

'Well, here then. Play it.'

He handed Aesop the guitar.

'Eh, well, I haven't got a tune yet. I'm working on the lyrics.'

'Well then forget about it. We're not playing it on Saturday.'

'But listen, it has a local influence and everything. It sounds like Shiggy. I'm really getting into it …'

> *I rike you berry much,*
> *In Japan I'm za man,*
> *I get you in my crutch,*
> *I dig you Halle Berry much.*

Jimmy looked at him.

'You had to research that?'

'That's only the first verse. It gets better.'

'Aesop, I'm going in for a shower. When I come out I want the laptop back.'

He went into the bathroom and stepped under the hot jet of water. As he was washing his hair he thought of Aesop's lyrics and smiled. They were actually the most sophisticated words he'd ever put to a song. Double meanings and everything. Christ, what next? He was starting to get a bit nervous about the gig. Johnnie had called on Sunday afternoon to tell them they were all set for a gig in a pub called What the Dickens.

'It's not the Albert Hall, Jimmy, but it's a good local venue. I've been there a few times. Good atmosphere and it really fires up on Saturday nights if the band is hot. Anyway, the main thing is that it's a bit unusual-looking and we can make use of that in the video. I'll have a few people there and I cleared it with the manager that we can do our own lights and sound and all that. You need to get some people there if you can. People who know the song. Do you know anyone out here?'

'Well, we've been hanging around Paddy Foley's a bit in Roppongi so I know a few of that crowd. And Mick Shannon, the manager in there, has been playing "Caillte" a lot. I gave him a CD.'

'Right. Any posters?'

'I have some stuff on the computer that we used for McGuigans back in Dublin. I can just mess with that a bit. Maybe Aesop can do it. I've been showing him how to use the computer.'

'Perfect. Email it to me and I'll get it translated and send them around. You get them up around Roppongi. We only have a week. The place will have a crowd in anyway, but it's important that we have friendly faces. Make sure everyone you talk to knows that they'll get to be in a music video if they turn up. And girls. Get girls there. Pretty ones.'

'Ah. That definitely sounds like a job for Aesop. He's been pestering me to help.'

'Grand. Talk to you during the week. Are you set up for a rehearsal?'

'Yeah. Shiggy sorted something out for Wednesday.'

'Cool. Seeya.'

Jimmy dried himself and wrapped a towel around his waist.

He was thinking of his new *Les Paul* again now, smiling to himself.

'Are you done yet?' he said to Aesop, who was hunched over the computer, taking notes.

'Not really. But I think I have the chorus, listen …'

> *I'd gib Halle wood, I would*
> *Cos she gib it tsoo me.*
> *Not just any wood, bud,*
> *She gib me Hallewood.*

'Sheer fucking poetry, Aesop.'

'Thanks Jimmy.'

'As soon as the skin on my fingers dries out properly I'm taking the laptop, right?'

'Ah Jimmy …'

'If you're only using the Internet, you can use the new one. And don't be dropping fucking pizza on it, you hear? It's not mine. I'll copy all the music over for you as well.'

'Does it work like this one?'

'Yeah. It's easy. Same as that one.'

'Okay then. You can have this.'

'Very generous. And what happened the toaster, by the way?'

'Eh, it broke.'

'How?'

'I kind of dropped it.'

'Dropped it?'

'Well … drop-kicked it.'

'Aesop, I showed you how it worked. It's not that fucking hard.'

'It burned me toast!'

'Look at the state of it. The side's hanging off it.'

'It was asking for it, Jimmy. That's twice now. The fire alarm went off and everything. Scared the shite out of me.'

'Well what are we going to do now?'

'I was reading on the Interweb about this low-carb diet thing. It says you shouldn't be eating toast anyway. It's fried bacon you should be having for your breakfast.'

'And what happens when you burn that? Are you going to kick the fuck out of the cooker as well?'

'If it starts annoying me I will. Oh, you might want to be careful with the washing machine by the way. The lid is a bit loose. I couldn't get it to use hot water and …'

'I don't want to fucking hear it Aesop. Just don't break that computer or you'll be the one getting drop-kicked, so you will. I only have a lend of it.'

'I'll treat it like me very own.'

'That's what I'm afraid of.'

Twenty-one

JIMMY FINALLY got through to Simon back in Ireland. He didn't know what was going on, but every time he called, Simon was in a meeting and he hadn't called back in about a week. Email was fine, but Jimmy wanted to talk to him properly to let him know how things were going. He tried calling Marco, but Marco didn't know where he was either. He was around the office somewhere, he said. Jimmy asked Marco to get Simon to call him, but he still hadn't rung. As Jimmy was running out the door to get to the rehearsal he gave it another go and Simon picked up the phone himself.

'Simon! Jesus, you're a hard man to get a hold of these days.'

'Ah, Jimmy. Yeah, sorry about that. It's been a bit crazy in here the last few days.'

'Okay. Well, I thought we should have a quick chat about a meeting I had with the Compliance team here. They're keen that the whole thing should be completely tri-lingual, even though the Japanese side of the development won't be …'

'Yeah, Jimmy, I'm a bit short of time now. Can you put it in an email for me?'

'I did Simon. I sent it to you on Monday.'

'Oh right. God, it's just been hectic, y'know? I'll take a look at it tomorrow and get back to you then.'

'Eh, okay. It's a bit of a priority though, Simon. If we're going to …'

'I know Jimmy. Listen, I'm sorry, but I have to head. I'm meeting with Accounts five minutes ago.'

'Oh. All right.'

'How's it going out there anyway?'

'Hmm? Oh, it's grand. Pretty busy, y'know?'

'Yeah. You like Japan?'

'Well, it takes a bit of getting used to, but yeah. It's a cool place. I'd like to see a bit more of it. But listen, Simon, about this …'

'Well I'm glad you're enjoying it. Could you get into the Asian thing?'

'What? I suppose it's grand. What do you mean?'

'Nothing. I just wanted to make sure you're all right. You know, you're not homesick or anything.'

'Simon, I don't have time to be homesick. I'm doing twelve-hour days. The head honcho over here, Sakamoto-san, is starting to get very interested in the project this week all of a sudden and …'

'Is he? That's good. Look, Jimmy, my phone is ringing here. I better go.'

'Oh. Right then. Will you give me a call when you read the report?'

'Will do. Seeya Jimmy.'

'Yeah. Seeya.'

Well that was a bit fucking weird. Since when was a meeting with Accounts more important than being updated on the biggest project Eirotech had ever tried to put together? Jimmy checked the clock on the far wall and tried to put it out of his mind. He was meeting the lads in the studio at eight and he had to find the place yet.

SHIGGY WAS waiting for him, tuning up his bass. He'd been on site, so wasn't in the office to show Jimmy the way. That was okay. Jimmy was getting the hang of the subway system now. It looked huge and complicated, but if you just used the maps that were up everywhere to find the station you were in and the one you wanted to get to, it was fine. All you had to do was join the dots and follow the colour-coded lines until you arrived. It was quick and cheap and the trains themselves were spotless. Some of them were a bit crowded though, especially at this hour of the day, and by the time Jimmy pushed open the heavy sound-proofed door of the room they'd rented, he was a bit hot and bothered.

'No sign of Aesop?' he asked Shiggy.

'No, Jimmy.'

Jimmy looked at his watch.

'Well he'd better get a move on. We've only got a few hours.'

Aesop arrived half an hour later and threw down his bag.

'This fuckin city.'

'What happened?'

'I thought this place was in Shinjuku, not Shibuya. I was walking around like a fuckin eejit looking for it. I asked a few people, but they kept directing me back to the train station. I thought they were fuckin winding me up. Eventually I asked a copper, and he told me I was in the wrong place. So then I get on a bleedin subway train instead of the green one that goes around and around and ended up in Akasaka Mickey-take or some place where I had to change. That was a two-mile fuckin walk. And then when I get to Shibuya, I got lost again because the poxy map was all mangled at this stage. It's too big here Jimmy. There must be a million people in Tokyo.'

'Do you reckon?'

'Yeah. Anyway, c'mon. Let's play something loud. I need to calm me nerves.'

The rehearsal went really well. Shiggy had obviously been practising on his own since he'd gotten back to Japan and all they had to do was tighten things up a bit. They'd be playing from about nine till midnight on Saturday. A three hour set – pretty long, but they had plenty of songs so it wasn't a problem. The important thing was to get Caillte right. Johnnie would be using the gig to record for the video that would go with the song on the UK release. Just the visual – they'd do the new vocals properly in the studio later – but it meant that they had to work on their timing now in rehearsal so that when they mimed on Saturday night, they wouldn't be all over the gaff. Jimmy hadn't even put the new English vocal track down yet, so he'd essentially be singing the English words over the original Irish backing track.

'So, Aesop, did you go into Foley's?'

'Yeah, I was in there this evening. Talked to Mick. He put the flyers up and promised to spread the word about Saturday.'

'Grand. Who else do we have coming?'

'Ishihara-san said he will come,' said Shiggy. 'From music shop where you buy guitar. He say he bring his band and some friends tsoo.'

'Great.'

'Anyone coming from work Jimmy?' said Aesop.

'Jesus, no. I'm trying to keep all this shit quiet in there. Simon doesn't even know that I'm doing it. He'll have twins if he finds out I'm playing gigs out here.'

'Right. Oh, Yuki is coming too. And a gaggle of her mates.'

'Who's Yuki?'

'You know her. The young one in Starbucks downstairs.'

'Ah right. That explains all the paper cups I keep finding in the apartment. Drinking a lot of coffee these days, are you Aesop?'

'Yeah. A good bit. She's nice though, isn't she?'

'I suppose. She's awful young, but.'

'Twenty-two. She's a student.'

'And she's the girl you want to get your Asian wings with, is she?'

'Well I'm trying. But I'm telling you, the force is strong with that one Jimmy. I've asked her out twice, but she just giggles. She doesn't say no or anything. Just gets all embarrassed and giggles at me. I even told her we could nip upstairs – eh, sorry Shiggy, pop upstairs – and I'd make her lunch, but she's not having any of it. Actually, that's probably a good thing now that the toaster is fucked. Anyway, she'll be there. I told her I'm on tour here with me band. I'm telling everyone now Jimmy. It's brilliant. She giggled again, but I think I'm wearing her down. She gave me a free brownie.'

'A brownie? Oh you're in there so.'

'Yeah. I think they were after making too many in the shop or something. And guess what I did then?'

'I don't know, Aesop,' said Jimmy with a sigh. 'You diddled her bean?'

'No. I told her I wouldn't eat it until she agreed to go out with me.'

'And what did she do?'

'Eh, well, she giggled.'

'Yeah, sounds like she's gagging for you.'

'That's what I'm thinking.'

'Anyway, she's going to the gig. That's grand. Is that it?'

'Nope. Robert is coming in with a couple of his lads.'

'Robert? From Sexy Dance Girls?'

'Yeah. I ran in after Foley's. It wasn't open, but Timothy was there and he let me in. Robert was setting up for tonight.'

'We don't really play Robert's kind of music though.'

'That's what he said. But then I told him that he made us dance to his music and it was only fair that he try and dance to ours. Anyway, rock music all came from the blues, right? And who invented the blues? You might be surprised. I was on the Interweb Jimmy. You wouldn't believe what they have on there. Y'see, the black people were all hanging around Mississippi and Tennessee and they had all their own folk and trad music from Africa, and their hymns. They were pretty down though, after the slavery thing and all, right? But they still had their music and that. The next thing, all these Irish arrived on boats cos they were fucked with the spuds going bad at home. But *they* had their music as well! So the black people listened to the Irish people singing and playing Irish trad and realised that they were after stumbling across an absolute goldmine of misery. I mean, think about it Jimmy. If it's utter fucking desolation you're trying to inject into your songs, you can't go past an Irish ballad, can you? So then the black musicians took some of those ideas and invented the blues. Y'see? It was all because the Irish came along and depressed the fuck out of them. So, really, me and Robert have a lot in common, Jimmy. We both have this cultural link …'

'Okay Aesop, for fuck sake I get it, I get it. What did Robert say?'

'He said I was very funny. Then he rubbed me head. You should see his hands, Jimmy. They're like manhole covers.'

'But he's coming?'

'Yeah. He'll have to get back to the club, but he said he'd try and catch as much as he can and that he'd bring a few of his mates with him. Didn't Johnnie say he'd have some people there as well?'

'Yeah, but I'm sure that's just the lads that'll be doing the shoot and all. That's probably grand. If we get some heads in from Foley's plus the usual gang that goes in, it should be fairly full. But we haven't seen the place yet. Will we head in on Friday night and check it out?'

'Yeah, cool.'

'Shiggy?'

'Yep. No plobrem. Food is supposed to be good tsoo.'

'Oh is it? And what kind of food do they do?'

Jimmy was reluctant to take Shiggy's word anymore when it came to cuisine.

'Western food! You will rike.'

'Yeah. We'll see about that. Oh and by the way Aesop, just so you know, not everything you read on the Internet is true, okay? I'm sure the blues had a lot of influences on it.'

'Me bollocks Jimmy. It was all us.'

'Whatever …'

JIMMY HADN'T heard back from Simon since he'd talked to him on Wednesday and he was getting a bit of a pain in his arse. It was hard enough being out here on his own without being unable to discuss all the developments with the guy who'd actually be calling the shots. Maybe this was part of Simon's idea for throwing Jimmy in at the deep end and seeing how he got on. A test for the big Board decision that would determine whether or not Jimmy was director material. Well, he'd fucking show them. He was already starting to get along well with Sakamoto-san. Ever since he'd made a gobshite of himself at the restaurant, Sakamoto-san had started to really get into the project and insisted on going to all the meetings. It was great. Fuck Simon. He'd find out soon enough that Jimmy was on fire out here and that Eirotech looked like chocolate because of him.

They got to What the Dickens at around eight on Friday night and Aesop made a beeline for the food service area. He'd been eating noodles and pizza pretty much since he got to Tokyo and was anxious to try anything that looked like it might be real food. But Shiggy was right. The nosh was brilliant. Big shepherd's pies and chicken pies and steak pies were laid out under the heating lamps and they all ordered and sat with their pints to look around while the place filled up. It was mad. Dark and cavernous with lots of nooks and angles around which people sat eating by candlelight. The roof was way up in the shadows and huge sombre portraits and other pictures hung on the walls. The stage was pretty small, but the sound system looked fine. There was plenty of space for dancing too. The whole effect was of someone having turned the Bat Cave into a bar.

Jimmy talked to John, the manager of the place, and told him they were the band that was doing the video the next evening. John was cool about it.

'What kindae of music is it?' he said. He wasn't from around there either. 'Yir manager said it wis rock?'

'Yeah, that's it. Pretty loud, most of it. We'll do some covers too.'

Jimmy grinned. Johnnie Fingers was calling himself their manager!

'Aye, that's fine Jimmy,' said John. 'That gits the pint-drinkers in. Sometimes we git bands playin' some experimental shite ain the next thing ah'm up here mixin' fuckin cocktails fir the punthers who wantae listen tae it. Fuck that. It's better fir me if the guy jist comes up and ordhers four pints o' heavy, y'ken? Thanks very much pal, who's next? None o' this choppin' fuckin pineapples ain lookin' fir the fuckin raspberry juice.'

'Yeah, well we don't usually get too many cocktail-drinkers at our gigs.'

'Great. Well, ah'll seeya t'morrow, Jimmy. About four, isn't it? Ah've goat aw the posters up fir the gig aftherwards.'

'Yeah, listen thanks for that. Seeya tomorrow.'

They were going in early to get everything set up and do a few video shoots before the actual gig started. The more footage they had to play with, the less chance of missing something. It was easier for close-ups too. Afterwards they'd pull it back and take in the whole band and the crowd and all that. Jimmy was really excited. So was Aesop.

'Come on. Let's go downstairs,' he said, when he was finished his dinner.

'What's the hurry? There's a band on in half an hour.'

'Yeah, but Shiggy says there's a famous nightclub downstairs. Milk.'

'Milk?'

'Here, look at the flyer.'

Jimmy read it and looked up.

'The World's Greatest Enjoy Space?'

'Sounds brilliant, doesn't it?'

'Well we can go in a bit. I want to hear what the house system is like. That's what we'll be using tomorrow.'

The band came on at nine and the singer introduced them as Yer Mot's a Dog.

'Yer Mot's a Dog?' laughed Aesop, looking around. 'They must be Irish!'

They watched for the best part of an hour. The band was okay. Well, the singer was obviously the one with all the talent, but he was able to cover for the other three when they slipped up. He had that kind of presence that drew attention to himself and away from whatever else was happening on the stage. Jimmy knew what that was like. He used to have Beano on the stage with him and that was always hard work. Anyway, this guy knew what he was doing and after only about fifteen minutes the floor was full of happy, in-the-mood-for-getting-shitfaced dancers. Jimmy turned his attention to the punters now that he was happy the sound system was up to scratch. He needed to know what kind of people came here. It was fine. Basically the same as a typical McGuigans crowd. Twenty-somethings on the piss. Perfect. Throw some beer into this lot and they'd be bouncing off the walls. Roll on tomorrow.

They headed down in the lift to the club, Jimmy looking again at the flyer for the place. Milk? What kind of name was that for a nightclub?

THE LADS lasted an hour before Aesop practically ran out of the place. It started off fine. They went in and down a flight of curling stairs. There was another stairs going even further down, but Aesop was nervous because of something he'd read on the Internet about earthquakes. Now that he was fast becoming an expert on geology, as well as everything else, he figured that being too far underground wasn't the best place to be if a big one hit.

'Why are you so interested in everything all of a sudden Aesop,' asked Jimmy.

'What do you mean?'

'Jesus, in school you wouldn't open a book except to see if it had dirty pictures in it. Now you're a regular fucking encyclopedia.'

'The Interweb isn't like school, Jimmy. Did you know that they haven't had a big quake in Tokyo since 1923? We're due man, I'm telling you. Every seventy years they're supposed to be.'

'I don't think they're that predictable.'

'Sure what do you know about earthquakes, Jimmy?'

'Piss off! A few days with a computer and now you're the fucking Oracle of the Ages all of a sudden.'

'Hang on Jimmy. Shush a minute,' said Aesop, holding up his hand and looking over Jimmy's shoulder. 'I'm just undressing that bird over there with me eyes. Jaysis. That's gorgeous, that is.'

Jimmy shook his head and sighed.

'I'm going to the bar. Shiggy, what do you want?'

'Kirin prease, Jimmy.'

'And you, fuckin', Benny Hill ... what do you want?'

'Yeah, Kirin's grand, Jimmy. Ooh Jaysis. Look at that ... oh that's lovely. That's it ... good girl ... you go ahead and dance love ...'

There was a long platform running through the middle of the seating area, which people were using as a kind of seat and to put their drinks down on. It was about a metre high. They sat on stools next to the platform and looked around. People were dancing but the place hadn't really gotten going yet.

'We dance?' said Shiggy. He was looking around and grinning. The place must have been three-quarters full of girls.

'Just a minute, Shiggy,' said Aesop. 'This is all just jungle and techno they're playing now. That's fuckin ancient. We'll see if they're going to give us a bit of neurofunk or clownstep. The flyer says there's supposed to be a wobble DJ in tonight and ... what's wrong?'

Jimmy was staring at him.

'What the fuck are you on about? Wobble?'

'It's a kind of drum 'n' bass dance music with wobbly basslines and lots of swingbeats. A bit like a sub-genre of clownstep. Will you ever get with the programme Jimmy, for fuck sake? You're living in the past.'

'Am I? What happened to Sabbath and System of a Down and Slipknot.'

'Apples and oranges Jimmy. One of them is for playing and

listening to, the other is for meeting women in places like this so you can ride them.'

'So you don't like the music then?'

'Well, it's not really music, is it? It's only all made with machines. Anyway who gives a wank? The chicks dig it. Robert's after opening me eyes, Jimmy. I've been neglecting a whole demographic.'

'Demographic? Aesop, what the fuck is going on with you?'

'Word of the Day, Jimmy, you big schmendrik. They email me a new word every day. That was today's one, by the way. It means a foolish, clueless and naïve person. Anyway, what I was saying was, techno makes me very somnific so I'm not dancing until they put something cool on.'

Jimmy turned to Shiggy.

'All I did was show him how to use Google. Now it's like he's picking it up by osmosis. It's like someone pissing on a thirsty tree.'

'Capillary action,' said Aesop, taking a sup of his beer and looking around at another group of girls.

'What?' said Jimmy.

Aesop put down his beer and made a tree out of his hands.

'Plants draw water in by capillary action, Jimmy. Not osmosis.'

Jimmy blinked at him and then looked at Shiggy again.

'Do you fucking hear this now?'

'Technorogy not suit some people, Jimmy,' said Shiggy.

They sat around and got another few beers in, but it was a bit boring if you weren't joining in. You had to be in a certain mood to enjoy a place like this and the lads weren't really prepared. Aesop got up and winked at them.

'Just putting up a few posters for tomorrow.'

'Wait, Aesop. You can't just …'

But he was gone.

When he came back ten minutes later, all the posters were gone.

'I put them on the back of the jacks' doors. And a young one over there promised to put them in the Ladies. I told her I was a rockstar. "Rockstar *desu*," I said. Isn't that right Shiggy? That's all of them, Jimmy. I'd say we're going to have a full house tomorrow. It's going to be deadly. I was thinking though … will I wear pyjamas for a laugh?'

'No you fucking will not! There's no way I'm having you slagging Johnnie off.'

'Who's slagging him? It's a tribute. I wonder how he stopped his mickey falling out, but. Hang on till I give him a call and …'

'We've only met him once Aesop, and he's doing us and Dónal a big favour helping us out like this. If you start annoying him I'll bleedin kill you.'

'Jaysis. It was only an idea.'

'It was a shite idea. Jeans and a t-shirt – and your fucking miner's lamp if you have to – but no pyjamas.'

It was just then that the floorshow started. The lights and music suddenly changed and people grabbed their drinks from the platform and got up off it to stand around the wall or sit at the low tables. The lads took their beers down too and shrugged at each other. What floorshow? At the end of the platform, which was now starting to look very like a catwalk, a curtain fluttered and dry ice started billowing from underneath it. Aesop smiled at the others.

'I think I know what's going to happen next,' he said. 'Jackpot. I didn't even know it *was* one of those places.'

A stockinged leg appeared from behind the curtain and Aesop led the whistling and cheering, looking around at the others like he was about to meet Santa Claus himself. He stopped mid-clap, however, when the crotch that was attached to the leg revealed itself. It looked like someone had stuffed half a kilo of walnuts into a pair of small red underpants.

'Is that a bloke?' whispered Aesop, horrified.

'As I recall, Aesop, you're the expert when it comes to this type of thing.'

'Shiggy … what's going on?'

'Ah, transvestite show I sink,' said Shiggy. He was scanning the flyer. 'Ah yes. This guy famous. Berry good singer.'

The guy behind the curtain finally came out, accompanied by the horns of 'The Lady is a Tramp', and started singing. He was a foreigner. European, judging by the accent, and he looked like a cross between something out of *Moulin Rouge* and *Rocky Horror*, all feathers and thrusting bust.

'Those fuckin Germans again!' said Aesop. 'Is there nothing the dirty bastards won't do?'

'No Aesop. He is French. Madame Tina.'

'French? That's worse! Sure they're filthy, so they are. Look what he's doing with the mike! Ah Jaysis … that's … look … that's pure against God that is …'

'You were complaining that the place hadn't gotten going. It's taken off now hasn't it?'

'He's coming down here. Why are we sitting next to the stage for fuck sake?'

'I didn't know it was a stage.'

'Ooh … Jimmy. He's looking at me.'

'We're the only foreigners in the place.'

'What's he doing? He's coming over here! Jesus, Jimmy … what's he doing?'

Aesop tried to move away from the platform, but there was nowhere to go. The Japanese crowd had all bunched forward to get a better look and they were stuck. The lights changed again and a blue spot followed Tina as he shuffled down towards Aesop with a big grin and started singing I Get a Kick Out of You in his husky baritone. He stopped right in front of him and bent over to put a finger under Aesop's chin as he sang. Aesop was paralysed with fear, his eyes enormous and staring. Everyone in the crowd roared laughing. Jimmy threw his head back and cackled until he thought he was going to throw up.

Tina stood up again and went into the second verse. He

turned around as if he was going to start singing to the Japanese guy on the other side of the platform, but instead he bent right over until his arse was in Aesop's face and leaned under to sing to him upside-down from between his legs.

'Aw Jesus …' moaned Aesop. He was nearly crying. 'He's got a bigger bollocks than I do.'

Tina wasn't finished yet though. He prostrated himself on the stage, curling one leg up and putting his head on his hand as the instrumental break took over, gazing into Aesop's eyes and walking two fingers up his arm to his neck where he tweaked his ear. He winked and stood up again to give it some kicks and wiggle his hips for the crowd before finishing out the song by draping a pink feather boa over Aesop, throwing the end of it around his neck and, before Aesop could get out of the way, pulling him in and planting a kiss right on his lips.

He waved at the applause and did 'Strangers in the Night' as his last song before gliding off behind the curtain blowing kisses to everyone and winking back at Aesop, who at this stage was sitting there and staring at his beer like he'd just found out his dog had died.

Jimmy was still laughing, wiping the tears off his face and holding his stomach.

'Oh Jesus,' he stuttered. 'Oh God, that was brilliant. I wouldn't give that back for anything in the world. Where's your camcorder Aesop?'

'Get fucked,' said Aesop, without looking up.

'Come on. It was only a bit of fun, Aesop.'

'Did I look like I was having fun?'

'I meant for me.'

'What the fuck did I do to deserve that? He could've picked anyone.'

'He probably saw you cheering your hole off when you thought you were going to see some slapper in the noddy and thought you were up for it.'

'Bastard.'

'Is that it Shiggy? Three songs?'

'No Jimmy. Every hour. Three songs. He come back later.'

'Well he won't find me fuckin sitting here waiting for him.'

'What? We can't go. You'll hurt his feelings Aesop,' said Jimmy.

'I'll hurt more than his feelings Jimmy. That's sexual assault, what he did.'

'Well, you could've said no.'

'When was I s'posed to say no? When his arse was in me face? Come on. I'm getting out of here.'

'You big baby.'

'You stay if you want Jimmy. I'm gone. I need a shower and a pint of Listerine. I'm very, very … disgruntled so I am.'

'All right. We should probably get some kip anyway. A big day tomorrow.'

'And listen, you two fuckers won't be telling anyone about this, will you?'

'Depends Aesop. You've got something on just about everyone. Some of it on that bloody camcorder as I recall. I'll keep it under wraps, just in case. Norman now, for instance, would love it …'

'No! Not him especially.'

Shiggy was looking at Aesop's face and smiling.

'What's so bleedin funny, you?'

Jimmy gave Shiggy a small kick to keep quiet. It would be much funnier if Aesop only found out about the lipstick on his mouth when he got home.

Twenty-two

WHEN THEY got to What the Dickens the next day at four, Johnnie and his crew were all ready to go. They'd been there since two and everything was set up to shoot the video. There was a fixed camera up on the balcony and various lights hoisted up over the stage. He'd also supplied them with a drumkit and amps and the other bits and pieces they needed and it was all sitting there just waiting for the lads to arrive and plug in. It was brilliant. They usually had to spend an hour before every gig doing this for themselves. One Japanese guy was going to do the sound for them, one was in charge of lights and the other two would be doing the filming itself. The second cameraman was walking back and forth across the dancefloor with his camera on his shoulder, making sure he'd be able to get them from all the angles he needed. There were only a few customers there at that time of the day, watching it all curiously.

'Jesus,' said Jimmy to Aesop. 'This must be costing Dónal a fortune. I hope it turns out well.'

'Look who's in charge of it Jimmy. How could it not turn out well?'

'Yeah. But if a pint costs seven euro in this country, what does it cost to have four professional technicians here for the whole day? Not to mention Johnnie's time.'

'Maybe Johnnie's doing Dónal a favour?'

'Even so. This gear all had to be rented as well …'

Jimmy was looking around nervously.

'Man, I wish to God Dónal wasn't putting his last few quid into all this,' he said. 'It's too much. And if nothing happens …'

'Jimmy, the whole point of having a manager is that he takes care of all this shit and we just do our jobs on the stage. Will you stop worrying about Dónal? He knows what he's doing.'

'Yeah I know. It's just …'

'Shush Jimmy. They won't play the video at all if you've got that head on you all night.'

They plugged in and did a quick sound check with the sound guy. Then they played the song. They did it six times and soon it was starting to feel like hard work instead of a laugh. The guy with the camera was on the small stage with them for some of the filming and it was very crowded up there. He stood on Jimmy's guitar lead at one stage and pulled it out.

'Keep going lads,' called Johnnie. 'Remember, this is just for the visual. Doesn't matter what you sound like, we're not recording it.'

Jimmy gave him a small nod and kept singing. He could hear Aesop singing out of tune behind him, taking the piss now that he knew they weren't recording the sound.

'All right lads, stay focused. We'll do one more after this and then you can get some food into you.'

They eventually got to the bar to order some shepherd's pie. It wasn't a moment too soon for Jimmy. 'Caillte', or 'Lost' as it was now, was starting to get on his nerves. Every time they did it, it was harder for Jimmy to find the same feeling as he had when he was writing it. It was so important to him then. Now it was just a piece of product. It was like hearing the same joke over and over. You just stopped giving a shit after a while and wished something new would come along. He sighed, pouring some brown sauce onto his dinner and tucking in. He told himself to just keep at it. It wasn't about what he wanted anymore. This single was for Dónal and then Jimmy was gone.

AT NINE o'clock the place was packed. The lads stood at the bar and looked around. John, the manager, and his staff were run off their feet trying to keep up with the punters. It was all pints too. There wasn't a pineapple in sight and even though he was sweating and going non-stop, John still had a grin on him.

'Lookin' forward tae this, lads,' he said on the way past. 'This is quite a followin' ye huv here tonight.'

252

He slapped three pints onto the counter in front of them and winked.

Jimmy thanked him and was about to grab his when someone tapped his shoulder. He looked around. There was a tiny Japanese girl standing there.

'Ah Jimmy,' said Aesop. 'This is Yumiko. It's Yuki's friend. Howarya Yumiko. Is Yuki here?'

'Hi Aesop. Yes, she is here. She rooking for you. Harro Jimmy.'

'Hiya Yumiko. Nice to meet you.'

She bowed and smiled up at him. She was gorgeous. Cute as a fucking button.

'Berry excited,' she said, pointing back at the stage. 'I sink you berry sexy.'

She giggled, putting a hand over her mouth.

'Oh. Eh, thanks very much. Have you met Shiggy?'

They bowed at each other and said some stuff in Japanese. Then she bowed at the three of them and went off to find Yuki.

'Jimmy. I sink she rike you.'

'What did she say?'

'She say can't wait to see your big Irish cock.'

'She what?!'

'Only joking Jimmy. She say she hear CD. Aesop give to Yuki-chan. Sink you hab great voice.'

'Oh. Well that's nice, isn't it? She was a bit ... she said I was sexy. To me face, like. Is that normal?'

'I sink she sink you expect this things. Big foreign rockstar, *ne*?'

'Ah Jaysis. Tell her I'm not like that, will you? I'm just ...'

'Tell her fuck all Shiggy,' said Aesop. 'And you, Jimmy. You don't start acting the knobjockey, you hear me? I'm planning on filling Yuki in like an application form tonight and if buying big fuck-off buckets of coffee doesn't impress her, then maybe this gig might. As far as they're concerned you're the next Bono, so start acting like it and maybe you can boff Yumiko as well.'

'I'm not touching her. She's about sixteen!'

'She's fucking twenty-four, Jimmy. So you've no excuse.'

'Whatever. Where's Johnnie? We should be going on soon.'

'He talking to Tanaka-san. Sound guy.'

'Okay. Howyis feeling?'

'Brilliant,' said Aesop.

'No sweat,' said Shiggy. 'You?'

'A bit nervous.'

'Come on Jimmy. We're playing Tokyo!'

'I know. I'm always nervous before a gig.'

'Right. Hey John?' called Aesop.

John looked over from one of the taps.

'What cannae git ye?'

'Can I have three shots of tequila, please?'

'Nae problem. Jist gimme a minute.'

'Aesop, I'm not drinking that piss before a gig. I'll puke.'

'One shot Jimmy. To focus the mind.'

'But Aesop …'

'Ah-ah! Shush. Here you go …'

John had put three small glasses down in front of them.

'One each,' said Aesop. 'Are you right? Lads … here's to our first tour of Asia …'

They all downed their shots and made the requisite faces at each other.

'Ugh …' said Jimmy, with a shudder. 'That's fucking horrible.'

'But you're not nervous anymore are you?'

'Only about gobbing me shepherd's pie onto the back of that fucker's head.'

There was some noise from the stage and they all looked up. Johnnie was standing at Jimmy's mike, tapping it and looking out into the crowd. The house system went down. Johnnie introduced himself and told them what would be happening tonight in English and Japanese. It was a regular Saturday night gig, but they'd be filming some of it for a video to accompany the release of 'Lost' in Britain. The punters all cheered, turning to each other in excitement. They knew about it anyway from the posters, but now that they were here it was like a big event. Johnnie told them just to act naturally. Not to look at the cameras, but it was perfectly okay for them to cheer and dance and whistle as much as they liked. They got a bit of practice in then as Johnnie introduced the band.

'And here they are, fresh from their recent tour of Europe. Will you please give a big Tokyo welcome to … The Grove!'

Aesop was so excited that he bolted away from the bar and ran through the squashed, applauding crowd up to the stage. Jimmy and Shiggy grinned at each other and followed him. They all waved out once they were in position. It was weird. This place wasn't much bigger than McGuigans, but they felt like they were staring out from the stage of the Point Depot. The McGuigans crowd were used to them at this stage, but this lot were hopping off the walls, waiting to see what was going to happen. Plus, of course, there were two big cameras trained on their every move and a big lightshow hanging from the ceiling. The four crew were all connected with headphones and wireless mikes, as was Johnnie, and the gear that they'd borrowed to play the gig was absolutely top shelf. They sure as shite weren't in Kansas anymore.

'Hello everyone,' said Jimmy, stepping to his mike. 'Thanks for coming and helping us out with this video we're making.'

The noise was deafening.

'Right,' he said turning away from the mike and nodding to Aesop. 'No point in dragging it out …'

Aesop counted them in and they kicked off with 'Alibi'. The whole bar seemed to be a dancefloor. As Jimmy started singing, he looked out. All he could see were heads bopping up and down. In front of him, right at the back, over towards the bar and up on the balcony. Wall to wall buzz. He smiled. Excellent. They didn't even know the song. He could see Shiggy beside him giving it loads and a quick glance back at Aesop revealed a man in his element. He'd already lost the t-shirt and was pummelling the drums like he was pissed off at them. The sound was great too. These Japanese guys knew what they were about. He was getting a huge stadium sound in a place like this. He was already starting to think that they needed a regular sound guy for gigs at home. Would Sparky do it? Maybe if … oh God, what was he doing thinking about stuff like this? That wasn't the plan at all. But he couldn't help it. Up here, on the stage … Jesus Christ he missed this. Playing for a crowd of mad fuckers, his best mates up here with him. He was only two minutes into their first song and he was already confusing himself again.

Johnnie had said that it was best to get 'Lost' out of the way sooner rather than later, while the crowd were still mad for it. They might start to calm down the longer they left it. It was roasting in here and the area in front of him was already a mass of wet, writhing bodies. They did three more fast ones and then Jimmy held up his hands.

'All right. Are yis ready to be on MTV? Okay then. We're going to be playing this one to a backing tape. That's the way they do it, okay? But we'll play it live later on.'

He was shouting to make himself heard and looked over at Shiggy.

'Jesus, this is mental!'

Shiggy grinned, all sweat and hair. 'See girls?'

He nodded down towards the front of the stage. There were about a dozen girls, mostly Japanese, all standing there gazing up at Jimmy like he was the Second Coming. Jimmy hadn't even noticed. They were too close, right down at his feet. He looked now and smiled at them. Yuki and Yumiko were there, along with a load of girls he didn't know. They all giggled behind their hands and pushed each other. He bent down and handed Yumiko his guitar pick with a wink. He'd never done that before. Jesus, if he tried that in McGuigans he'd have gotten some slagging. The whole place would have laughed their arses off at him. But here, tonight, it just happened and he didn't even feel like a wanker. Yumiko stopped smiling all of a sudden, her mouth in a big O as she took it. She stared at it and then back at Jimmy like she was ready to do him right there and then.

'Go on, ye dirty bastard!' he heard Aesop shouting from behind him. 'I saw that. Jesus, Eric Clapton now, is it?'

Jimmy gave him the finger behind his back and nodded up at Johnnie, who said something into his headphone mike. The song started slowly, lush and sounding brilliant through the house system and he leaned in to the mike and started singing. His voice was the only thing that wasn't pre-recorded because they still hadn't gotten around to doing an English vocal. His guitar and Shiggy's bass were turned off at the desk and Aesop was under instruction to go easy on the drums. The roving cameraman moved around the stage and the dancefloor taking in as much as he could as the crowd weaved slowly around and a few cigarette lighters popped up into the air. It was a bit distracting, singing live with a huge camera twelve inches from his face, but it was also pretty fucking cool. Jimmy closed his eyes and gave it some proper heartfelt welly. He suddenly loved his song again.

He could feel drips of sweat running down his face and imagined how it would look in the video under the single blue spotlight that added to the heat and the steaming, muggy atmosphere. He could feel himself playing with the camera a bit. Not looking at it, but clenching his jaw and doing these little shakes of the head and pulling away from the mike now and again so he could look properly bleak and thoughtful. He'd been practising all his life for this and it came to him now without even having to think about it. Near the end he opened his eyes nice and wide and looked straight into the smaller white spot that was hanging from the balcony. That'd make them all big and sparkly. As the guitar rang out he looked down at Yumiko and blinked, feeling his eyes getting moist from some long-forgotten pang that bubbled up and reminded him of the torment he was in when he wrote it. Then it was over and the crowd screamed and stamped on the floor, their hands clapping and punching the air.

He waved and called Aesop and Shiggy out to the middle with him. They stood and bowed together as the punters kept up the furore and called for more. They thought the gig was over already. Jimmy grinned and the other two went back to their spots.

'Jaysis!' he said into the mike. 'Well I don't mind telling you, that was pretty fucking brilliant. Great job! We'll all be on the telly in a couple of months.'

They were in his pocket now and he knew it. He checked his watch. It was only ten. Cool. They had at least two more hours and he wasn't going to waste a minute of it. He stepped on one of his pedals and started the intro to 'Where the Streets Have No Name'. They recognised it immediately and roared, waiting for it to start properly.

'We thought we'd play a few Irish songs for you, seeing as you've made us so welcome here tonight. I think you know this one. It's Aesop's new favourite song too. He's been getting lost a lot since we arrived in Tokyo. I was talking to Bono last week by the way … he told me to say hello … one, two … *I wanna run …*'

They all crashed in on the first line and the place suddenly looked like a riot was about to break out. All the lights came on over the stage and swung around to illuminate the bouncing masses. They played it much heavier than U2 did on the record and Jimmy noticed John away off to the right behind the bar with his hands over his ears. Cool. It was always a cool gig when the manager was shitting himself about the neighbours. Jimmy grabbed the cameraman as he was walking behind him and got him to aim the camera out into the crowd and take in the bedlam that was going on. He wanted to have this for later.

And anyway, a crowd that knew it was being filmed was a happy crowd. They preened and played air guitar as they bashed off each other.

Yumiko and Yuki were getting a bit knocked around so he nodded at them to get up onto the stage next to him. He moved over and sang into the side of his mike as they hopped up and started dancing around in the tiny space he'd left for them.

They played out the set with more Irish stuff. Stiff Little Fingers, Lizzy, Ash and The Undertones and then, before someone had a fucking heart attack, 'With or Without U'.

'Just five minutes, lads, okay?' said Jimmy to the others as they were getting off the stage for a break and the house system came up with Guns n' Roses. 'We want to keep them going like this. Don't give them a chance to cool down or anything.'

'Not likely, is it?' said Aesop. He was soaked. 'It's bleedin roasting in here.'

'You know what I mean. A quick squirt and then come on back.'

'It'll take ten minutes to get to the fuckin jacks!'

The stage was backed into a corner and Jimmy had to squeeze past the pulsing throng to get to where Johnnie was standing with Tanaka-san.

'Howya Johnnie. Hey, thanks Tanaka-san. The sound is brilliant. *Arigato* very much.'

Tanaka-san bowed and smiled.

'Jimmy, that was pretty impressive,' said Johnnie.

'Yeah? Thanks, man.'

'I mean it. You had them on a string. Very impressive indeed.'

'Cheers. It's a good laugh up there.'

'Yeah, I can see that.'

'How does it look?'

There was a feed from the cameras to a console over the sound desk. Tanaka-san played around with a few buttons and then Jimmy saw himself in close-up. He recognised the part of the song, even though they couldn't hear anything with the racket around him.

'Hey, that looks all right.'

'It's great,' said Johnnie. 'We'll have about two hours worth of footage by the time we're done. Then we'll send it all to Dónal. He can put the finishing touches to it.'

'Listen, Johnnie, thanks for doing all this for us.'

'No problem. I was doing it for Dónal. But now that I've seen you, I know why he's so keen to make it happen. He said you were thinking of packing it in?'

'Eh … well, it's a bit complicated … y'know … I've got this job and all, so … eh …'

'The lads are back on the stage, look. You ready to get going again?'

'Oh. Sure, yeah. Seeya afterwards.'

'*Gambatte.*'

'What?'

'Nothing. Go on. You're doing great. I doubt if this place has seen anything like you before.'

'Thanks Johnnie. Eh … what do you mean?'

Johnnie just looked at him with a small smile.

What the fuck did he mean by that?

Back at the stage Aesop was just sitting down at his drums.

'Jesus Jimmy, I swear I'm on three promises from young ones since the last time I saw you. Shiggy's on two. How are you doing?'

'I was talking to Johnnie.'

'Listen Jimmy, Johnnie's great and all, but he's not exactly the best-looking bird in the place is he? Will you spread yourself around a bit? I think Yumiko over there is going to have that pick you gave her mounted behind glass for fuck sake. Give her another wave and she'll probably have one on the spot. Yuki is after … oh holy fuck …'

260

'What?'

'Look what's after coming in.'

Jimmy looked over his shoulder. Madame Tina from Milk had arrived in with some girls from the club.

'Good Jaysis. What the fuck is he wearing now?' said Jimmy.

'It's called a gimp suit Jimmy. Look at him He's one snooker ball away from getting a hiding off Bruce Willis. Jesus, he better stay the fuck away from me. Come on, let's get started before he sees me.'

Jimmy started with 'Everlong' just to get the crowd moving again with something they knew. It was also a good workout for Aesop and he looked like he needed something to focus on the way he kept peering from around his crash symbol to see where Tina was. After that they played out the next hour with their own songs and the crowd kept it up. Christ, they were up for it tonight. Jimmy checked his watch near the end of the set and saw that they were running out of time.

'Right!' he called. 'Are there any Japanese people here tonight?'

He put his hands over his ears at the noise and smiled.

'Okay. This one's for you.'

He picked up the acoustic guitar that Johnnie had brought for him.

'You're going to have to help me out on the chorus now. My Japanese isn't very good.'

It was 'Teo Torriatte' by Queen. Only the real Queen fans would know it. Plus the Japanese of course. Jimmy had worked out a version that the others didn't need to play on since they never had a chance to practise it together. It was a weepy ballad and the girls in the audience screamed all through the English verses and then joined in with him on the Japanese bits. Aesop knew the song well enough to keep a gentle beat behind it and Shiggy improvised once he saw the chords Jimmy was playing. At the end of it, when the chorus repeated, he stopped playing and singing and raised his arms to conduct the Japanese in the audience through it as they belted it out *a cappella*. Then it was over and he gave them a big clap and bowed. High-pitched squeals rattled the windows. There wasn't a Japanese bird in the place who didn't want him. Even a few of the blokes were looking at him a bit funny.

He looked over to Johnnie and saw him holding his hand up over his head, like he was signalling something. Jimmy didn't know what he wanted, but it was time for another quick break anyway so he bowed again and the house system came back on. They'd have to cut the last set short unless John let them play later than midnight. Jimmy squeezed his way over to Johnnie again to see what he wanted, but Johnnie was on the phone. That's what he'd been doing. Holding the phone up so that whoever was on the other end could hear what was going on.

'Someone here to talk to you Jimmy,' he said, holding it out to him.

'Hello?'

'Jimmy?'

'Dónal!'

'Sounds like you have them wrapped around your finger there! Jesus, where the fuck did you pull "Teo Torriatte" out of? They must have loved that.'

'Ah sure, that song is ancient. I knew they'd know it. I've been messing with an acoustic version since I heard we were coming here.'

'You're a clever bastard Jimmy. Anyway, I hope you're enjoying the gig. What do you think of my mate Johnnie?'

'You're still a fucker for not telling me it was him. But yeah, he's great. You should see the setup he's after laying on for us tonight. Four crew and everything doing the sound and the lights and all. Must be costing a mint.'

'Don't worry about that. We're all behind you on this thing. Just blow them all away. Put him back on there.'

Jimmy handed the phone back to Johnnie and thanked Tanaka-san again for the great job he was doing. Then Johnnie hung up and looked at Jimmy.

'Listen Jimmy, that was fucking brilliant, that was. I called Dónal halfway through the Japanese song so he could hear it. Man, I think we should get a few more gigs together. Bigger venues than this one. How long exactly will you be in Tokyo?'

'Eh … well, another six weeks anyway. But …'

'We'll talk about it later. But I've got some people who'll want to hear you. I told the lads to keep shooting. We've loads for the video, but I want to get this out to a few heads while you're still available.'

Heads. That's what Dónal called them as well. Christ, where was this going?

'That's great Johnnie. There's the thing about work though …'

'Later, Jimmy.' He looked at his watch. 'You've about half an hour left. Go on up and bring them home. They won't forget this.'

What was he on about? It was a great gig and all, but it was just a gig. He looked around to see Aesop and Shiggy back on the stage and shook his head and started beating his way back there.

They opened with 'Meatloaf's Underpants', complete with Aesop's drum solo and the debut Tokyo appearance of his miner's lamp. It was a huge hit. The only problem was that there were so many gorgeous women in there that Aesop couldn't decide on who to land the beam on at the end. He eventually found Yuki and settled there, figuring that the groundwork was done anyway, so he might as well go in for the kill. By this stage, Jimmy's t-shirt had to go as well. It was soaked and clinging to him uncomfortably and he only had one spare for afterwards. He pulled it off as he stood in darkness waiting for Aesop to finish, and when the lights came on again the roars from the girls reached a new crescendo at the sight of his nipples. Straight away the roving cameraman was back in front of the stage, the camera at Jimmy's knees and pointing up along his body towards his face, which was launching into 'Lose Yourself' by Eminem. This one was a real bugger to do live. Luckily there wasn't much to the guitar, because getting the rap lyrics out properly was a full-time job. But as far as the people in front of him were concerned, he could do no wrong.

For the first time he saw Robert. He must have been at the back or something earlier. Or maybe he'd just come in. Either way, now he was in the middle of the floor with two mates and dancing like he had at his club. The Japanese girls out there loved it, crowding around them and clapping. During one of the choruses some muppet jumped onto the stage and put his arm around Jimmy, punching the air with the other one and trying to sing into the mike. Jimmy leaned back to give him a go, but the dopey bastard didn't even know the words. Jimmy moved behind him and pushed him off with a foot to the arse and he fell back into the crowd and hopped around like nothing had happened. There was only ten minutes left, so Jimmy announced their last song as 'Walk On'.

It was during 'Walk On' that Tina decided that she too wanted some of the spotlight. Jimmy watched her approach the stage as he sang, cursing to himself. Did he really want a six-foot-two man in a shiny black latex bodysuit up here with him? He didn't have much choice. Tina hopped up and started to gyrate against his leg and wave out at the crowd. For fuck sake. He looked out and could just see Johnnie laughing at him. Ha bloody ha. This never happened at home. It was a very brave gimp that walked around the centre of Dublin City dressed like that. Behind him, Aesop was practically sitting on the floor and out of sight. Shiggy was laughing his arse off as well though, and the punters seemed to be enjoying it. Fuck it, they were nearly done anyway.

Tina kissed him on the cheek when the song was over and

then reached around to plant one on Shiggy too. Then she looked behind the drumkit for Aesop, but Aesop was ready for her and had no difficulty indicating where his drumstick would be going if the dirty bastard came anywhere near him. Tina got the idea and blew him a kiss instead and then got off the stage with another wave at the cheering masses and an elaborate bow to the camera. No gobshite, Tina.

John was making gestures at Jimmy from behind the bar as the calls for 'One More Song' thundered from the floor. The main lights overhead flashed on and off. It was time to wrap it up. He held up his hands and got them to shut up. He introduced the lads. Shiggy bowed and Aesop stood up and pumped the air with two fists. They finished out with 'Caillte' and then the three of them stood at the front of the stage again and bowed, their arms around each other's shoulders. The punters wanted them to keep going, but a quick glance at John was enough to convince Jimmy that they'd shot their load. It had been great, but there was no point in getting him into trouble with the coppers just for an extra song or two. Anyway, always leave them shouting for more. That was part of the game.

When he straightened up after yet another bow to wave at them, he saw Yumiko, Yuki and some other Japanese girls standing just below them, beaming and clapping. Aesop shouted in his ear.

'Do you reckon I'll finally be able to eat that brownie tonight, Jimmy?'

Jimmy laughed.

'I hope you're talking about the cake.'

Twenty-three

JIMMY WANDERED out to the living-room in the apartment on Sunday morning in his boxers, rubbing his eyes. Aesop was on the couch with his legs stretched out before him and his hands over his face.

'Where's Yuki?'

'Is me face red?'

'Where is she?'

'She's down getting coffee.'

'Right.'

'Where's Yumiko?'

'She's … eh … she's tidying up the bedroom.'

'What? What were you up to in there, you dirty bastard?'

'Nothing. When she woke up she … well, first she … eh, anyway … then she got up and started folding clothes and all and putting them in drawers and hanging up shirts.'

'Why?' said Aesop.

'I don't know. I told her to stop but she wouldn't.'

'So how did you get on?'

'Grand. You?'

'Christ yeah. Even better than I was expecting. And I'm telling you, I had some high expectations after getting meself all worked up.'

'Hmm … I'm not sure Aesop. Yumiko seems very young.'

'I told you. She's twenty-four.'

'Are you sure?'

'Yeah. They're both in the same class in college. Anyway, did she act like a teenager in there?'

'Jesus, no.'

'Well then.'

'I feel a bit … are you absolutely fucking sure?'

'Yes! Look, there's her bag. Take a look in her wallet.'

'Get fucked! I can't do that.'

'Go on. I'll keep sketch.'

'No way. That's a terrible thing to do.'

'Stop being a blouse and just have a quick gander.'

'But … but … ah, fuck it. All right. Hold the door closed there.'

Jimmy opened her bag and took out her wallet. There was a photo id of some description behind a plastic window.

'Well?' said Aesop. He had one hand on the doorknob of Jimmy's bedroom.

'Eh …'

'How old is she?'

'I don't know. It's in fucking Japanese, isn't it.'

'Ah, just forget about it, you're grand. Shiggy was talking to them and everything.' Aesop walked back to the couch and Jimmy threw the bag back down in a hurry and sat beside him.

'Aesop, are you absolutely, one hundred per cent …'

'Jimmy, I don't know about that bird in there, but I'm telling you that Yuki has been around. They're old enough.'

'I can never tell with Japanese birds.'

'Sure Shiggy is nearly forty and he looks younger than us. I think it's the green tea.'

'Who was that other one he went off with?'

'Ayako. She's another mate. Wouldn't it have been gas if he'd brought her here? We could've had a race.'

'Yeah. So, Aesop, was Yuki, eh … kind of … y'know … noisy?'

'You as well? Yeah. I love that. No idea what she was on about, but it sounded filthy. Shiggy told me about that before. He was surprised with the few birds he rode in Ireland. He thought he was making a balls of it because they weren't in his ear and him lashing away. I told him not to worry about it. Irish birds make up for it the rest of the time. Anyway, I was playing Yuki like a tin-whistle last night. She's a cracking girl.'

The bedroom door opened and Yumiko walked out with a bundle of Jimmy's washing. She smiled at the two of them on the couch and disappeared into the laundry room. They smiled back.

'Ah, that's nice.'

'It is not, Aesop. She doesn't have to do that for fuck sake.'

'Well, the thing about Japanese culture, Jimmy …'

'Piss off. I don't care. That's not right.'

The intercom buzzed and Jimmy got up to let Yuki in. She had two huge coffees with her and a brown Starbucks paper bag filled with pastries, juice and cheese and ham croissants. She smiled at them and started to clear up the previous night's beer bottles and ashtrays. Then she set the table and put all the food out. Yumiko helped her when she was finished with the washing and then the two of them got their bags and came over to the couch to say goodbye.

'But … wait a minute,' said Jimmy, standing up in surprise. 'Are you not staying for breakfast?'

'No. Sank you. Not hungry,' said Yumiko. 'Prease. You eat.'

She kissed him as Yuki was doing the same to Aesop, and then they both walked out the door and closed it with a wave.

The lads looked at each other. The thump of the washing machine was the only noise in the apartment.

'Jimmy?'

'Yeah?'

'I was just thinking … you know the way I was supposed to be going home next week …'

JIMMY MADE himself comfortable. Feet up on the table, cup of tea on a coaster in front of him and a nice fat cushion behind his back. It had been eight days. He couldn't put it off any longer. He picked up the phone and dialled.

'Hello?'

'Hiya Ma.'

'Jimmy! Jimmy! My pet. How are you?'

'I'm grand. How are …'

'Hang on love till I turn down the radio. Hang on … hang on … there. Now. Can you hear me, love?'

'Yeah.'

'Grand. So tell me, how are you? How's everything over there? I was only telling your father this morning that we hadn't spoken to you in ages. Is everything okay? How's work?'

'Everything's great Ma. I've been busy, y'know, in work and …'

'Ah of course you have Jimmy. Sure that's why they sent you over, isn't it? God, imagine being all the way out in Japan. Isn't it great? They must think you're the bee's knees, mustn't they? And how are you finding the Japanese? I'd say you're towering over them. Are they looking after you? And what about the food? Is it really terrible? You must be starving. Did you cook up the pasta and tomatoes I gave you to bring out? I can send out some more tins if you like.'

'Thanks Ma, but I can get them here.'

'Ah but they're not the proper Irish ones.'

'Ma, the ones you gave me were from Italy. All three kilos of them.'

'Sure that's nearly as good. Because you need to have proper food in you if you're working hard like that. Gertie was telling me they eat like birds out there. And the size of you. Are you eating properly, love? She was in a Japanese restaurant in town there a few months ago. Her son brought her and Tommy out for their anniversary. You know her little fella Kevin? The pilot. Well he's after moving over to the States now. Some big job he's after getting with that crowd. What are they called? You know them, they have the red planes with the white wings. Well he trains them now. The young pilots. Anyway, she said it was only for picking at. And poor Tommy would only eat the rice. Afraid of his life he was, because he didn't know anything on the menu. He wouldn't even eat the steak because they put some kind of sauce on it on him. But anyway, are you eating well? Do they have proper stuff, you know, like cornflakes and meat and all that?'

'Yeah, everything's great. The office is just next door and Shiggy is …'

'Oh, how's Shiggy? Is he delighted to be back home? God, it seems like only yesterday that you brought him home here for his dinner the first time. Do you remember that? The size of him. Shiggy's gas. How's his Mam? Didn't she have that thing on her leg?'

'I think she's fine now.'

'Ah, that's great. Oh, c'mere till I tell you, your father's after booking us in for a weekend in Ashford Castle for my birthday! Can you believe it? Ashford Castle, Jimmy. That's where your man James Bond got married. It's supposed to be amazing. Oh here he is. Hang on. Seán … Seán … your son is on the phone. Hang on Jimmy … wait a minute now, here he is …'

'Hello?'

'Howarya Da.'

'How're things Jimmy?'

'Brilliant.'

'What's the weather like out there?'

'Roasting.'

'It's pissin' down here. August me arse.'

'I hear you're off to Ashford Castle. Very snazzy.'

'Yeah. Well the head on your Ma since you went off. I had to do something, didn't I?'

Jimmy could hear his Mam in the background.

'Tell him about the Irish coffees they do.'

'The what?'

'You know. They serve it in these huge Waterford Crystal goblets and it comes out on a big silver tray and everything.'

'It does in its arse. Sure everyone would be robbing the glasses.'

'They would not. Who do you think goes to Ashford Castle, Seán, in the name of God? Tell him.'

'Eh Jimmy, your Ma says they do a nice Irish coffee.'

'That's not what I said. Tell him properly.'

'I'm after telling him. Did you hear that, Jimmy?'

'Yeah, I can hear Ma. Waterford Crystal.'

'Now. He knows. So Jimmy, what are they like out there?'

'Ah they're grand.'

'Tell him Liz might be coming home for a weekend for Barbara's wedding.'

'Liz might be coming home for Barbara's wedding.'

'Yeah? That's great.'

'It's bleedin stupid is what it is.'

'Oh, right.'

'I told her they should be saving their money for their own wedding, but sure I might as well be talking to the wall.'

'Tell him her dress is nearly ready.'

'He doesn't give a shite about her dress, Peggy.'

'He does. Tell him.'

'Oh for fu ... Jimmy, Liz's dress is nearly ready.'

'The design, just.'

'The design, just.'

'And tell him ...'

'For Jaysis sake Peggy, what's the point in me talking to him at all?'

'Ah give over. You're not telling him anything. Here, give me the phone. You're hopeless.'

'Christ. Here's your Ma, Jimmy. I'll talk to you again. If I'm let.'

'Seeya Da.'

'Jimmy?'

'Howya Ma.'

'Sorry pet. He's watching one of his videos here. You know, when Dassaev took down Tony Galvin in Hanover and the ref did nothing? It's been twenty years nearly, and your father still gets himself into a state over it. Roaring at the dog he was a minute ago. Poor Horace doesn't know what he did. Anyway, Norman called around last week. He said you emailed him about some girl out in Thailand? So come on. Tell me all about her. She's English, isn't she? What's her name?'

'Susan.'

'Susan? Oh, that's very English. So tell me Jimmy, what's she like?'

'Sure we only hung around for a few days, Ma. It wasn't like ...'

'And will you be seeing her again when you get home? You can get to England now for a fiver just, on Ryanair. Doreen was over there last week with Billy. They went to one of those Andrew Lloyd Webber shows. *Evita* it was. God, do you remember I sang "Don't Cry For Me Argentina" at Shay's wedding? And then Frances sang Memory. Well anyway Doreen heard since that they might be bringing it to the Point. I've never seen one and I'm dying to go. She said she'd go again with me. There's no point in asking your father. The things he says about Andrew Lloyd Webber, God forgive him. I don't think that one is in it anymore, you know, his wife or whatever she is now. She was on the telly there the other day singing "Panis Angelicus". You know that one? Liz was thinking of it for her wedding. Honest to God Jimmy, she has the voice of an angel. But your father has no time for her at all. The face of him when she comes on. You'd swear she was only singing to get a rise out of him. So what does she do Jimmy?'

'What does ... Sarah Brightman?'

'No, you eejit. Susan. Who are we talking about, sure?'

'She works in London. In the City.'

'Well that's handy then, isn't it? A fiver on Ryanair. Well, you have to pay the taxes on top of that, but still. And how's Aesop getting on? Is he behaving himself?'

'Eh, well … you know Aesop. He's enjoying himself though.'

'That's great. So you've no other news for me?'

Jimmy sighed.

'No, Ma. That's about it.'

'Ah well. It sounds like everything's going well anyway. I might as well tell you what's been going on around here. Hang on till I get a chair … hang on … there. Now. Seán, will you put the kettle on? Seán? Oh God, can you hear him, Jimmy? That'll be Wim Kieft's header. Where was I? Oh yeah, so I met Jennifer for coffee in town last week. She said something about a goldfish? Anyway, herself and Marco are hoping to go to Palermo around Hallowe'en and …'

Jimmy rubbed the back of his neck and sunk a little lower into the couch. No fucking way would he be leaving it eight days before the next call.

WHEN HE finally got off the phone, he walked into Roppongi with Aesop for a quiet pint in Foley's. It was nice and subdued in there, just what the lads needed after spending Saturday night being rockstars. Shiggy was still off with Ayako and couldn't face any more beer anyway, so he said he'd see Jimmy in work the next day.

'How's your Ma?' said Aesop.

'She's grand. She was asking for you. By the way, I think you're fucked for killing Séamus. Jen told her she was going to murder you.'

'Jaysis, that girl can hold a grudge.'

'Ma said that Jen said you're a useless gobshite and that she'd be better off having a wheelbarrow than having you for a brother. At least she could put things in a wheelbarrow.'

'She said all that to Peggy? How do you know?'

'Because my mother related every single conversation she's had in the last week to me. Word for word. Christ, I thought I'd never get off the bleedin phone.'

'Would you give over, Jimmy? Jaysis, I don't understand you at all. That woman worships the ground you walk on, so fucking leave her alone. I was talking to her last week, and she didn't say anything because she probably doesn't want to upset anyone, but I'm telling you it's killing her that you're over here. Have a bit of respect for fuck sake.'

'Fuck off. I do have respect.'

'Well stop whinging then. What else did she say?'

'Norman told her about Susan as well.'

'Who?'

'Susan. Remember? Susan and Amanda?'

'Oh yeah. The English birds. Sure what about her? All you did was nobble her a few times. What's to tell?'

'Yeah, well Ma is looking into wedding rates in Ashford Castle for me now. If it's good enough for Pierce Brosnan, apparently, it's good enough for me. Anyway, I didn't just nobble her a few times. She was nice.'

'Ah go and shite Jimmy. Sure what about Yumiko? You're not exactly hanging around the phone waiting for Susan to call, are you? And that's a good thing, by the way. It's about time you copped on to yourself.'

Jimmy didn't say anything, just took a drink of his pint. He was a bit uncomfortable about all this. Susan was great. It seemed like he'd met someone at the right time in the right place. He really liked her and genuinely did want to give her a call when he got home. The emails were coming in every ten days or so. That was grand too. Nothing too distracting. But since he'd been with her, he was after shagging Yumiko. Twice. In the space of about six hours. That wasn't really him. It made him feel, not dirty, but like he was … well, okay … a bit dirty. And the way Yumiko kept looking at him. He didn't want to mess the girl around and she was a bit smitten. A bit star-struck, even, although Jimmy found that part of it a bit mad. And anyway, when he was alone with Yumiko, they'd barely said anything. She was lovely, but he couldn't exactly see her being a soulmate. That was a thought he decided not to share with Aesop.

'So, did you have a good night?' he said.

'Yeah. It was like riding a bouncy castle.'

'I meant at the gig.'

'Oh, God yeah. That was the best one ever. Did you see Robert getting into Eminem? Pity he couldn't come down into Milk with us afterwards.'

'He was working.'

'You were talking to Johnnie for ages after. What's the story there?'

Jimmy sighed.

'He's very keen on us doing some more stuff before we go home.'

'Brilliant. What's he got in mind?'

'Well, I have to record the English version of "Caillte" anyway. Then he said he'd like to do a few more location shots around Tokyo for the video. Maybe an acoustic version for a DVD single he said he mentioned to Dónal. And then he said he might be able to get us on the bill for this other gig he's organising for some Japanese band.'

'Great. Sounds like it's all happening.'

'Yeah. But I wasn't fucking around with him. I said my job comes first.'

'All right, all right. I think we're all clear on that at this stage, Jimmy. You can take that fuckin look off your face, I'm not going to say anything.'

'Good.'

'Actually, I want to talk to him too.'

'About what?'

'Well … look, Jimmy, I know it hasn't looked like I've been paying for much on this trip. A lot of it has been free. But still, y'know? I don't know where it goes but I've been looking at the receipts that the hole in the wall gives me and it doesn't come to all that much when you see it in yen.'

'You're running out of dosh?'

'Well, not yet. But if I am going to hang about here for another little while, I'm going to start getting short.'

'What's Johnnie meant to do about that?'

'Well, I thought he might be able to get me a bit of session work or something.'

'I s'pose there's no harm in asking.'

'That's what I reckoned.'

'You'd have to play what you're told though. He was pretty impressed last night.'

'With me? What did he say?'

'With all of us. He said we sounded like we knew where we were going.'

'Which we fuckin don't.'

'Yeah. Well, he said he'd never seen anyone do that in a pub gig before. He said we could have played a stadium last night.'

'Johnnie Fingers said that? Brilliant!'

'Ah, I think maybe Dónal told him to say it.'

'Fuck off Jimmy. You were on fire last night. They were eating out of your hand.'

'Ah, it was only a small …'

'Shut up, Jimmy, you gobshite. Look, whatever you decide to do, stop all this false fuckin modesty shit. Go back to your office job if you like. I'm not going to try and change your mind about that anymore. But whatever reason you come up with for doing it, not being good enough to make it in music isn't one of them. And you fuckin know it too.'

'All right Aesop, all right. We weren't going to talk about it, remember?'

'Yeah. Well, stop being an arsehole then. You're good. And I'm fuckin brilliant. And that's a shit-load more than a lot of bands can say.'

'Yeah yeah. Okay. Well what I was going to say before was that I'm not sure Yumiko and me are the best idea in the world.'

'Sure that's grand. I'm hardly going to tell you that you should be shopping for rings, am I?'

'But Susan was different.'

'What, you want to marry Susan?'

'No. But I don't want for Yumiko to get hurt so I'm going to say something to her.'

Aesop laughed and lit up a smoke.

'Of course you are.'

'What?'

'I thought you were finally taking your head out of that dark and dirty place you keep it, Jimmy, but you haven't changed at all, have you?'

'No.'

'And have you thought about Yumiko at all?'

'Who do you think I'm thinking about?'

'The little angel called Jimmy who sits on your shoulder. Same as always.'

'Get fucked. I just don't want her getting upset.'

'And dumping her after one ride isn't going to do that?'

'Look who's talking, Linford fucking Christie. And giving me shit about respect a minute ago.'

'Jimmy, there's a difference between doing a runner like me and hanging around to explain yourself like you want to. Give the girl a bit of credit and let her come up with something for herself. Something that makes sense to her.'

'Are you telling me now it's better to leg it than talk to a girl and finish things properly.'

'First of all, there's nothing to finish, you confused muppet. All you did was ride her. Secondly, the answer is yes. It's better to leg it.'

'Will you explain that to me, please,' said Jimmy, folding his arms. 'This'll be good.'

'Okay. Let's do it my way first. You leg it. Then, best case scenario, right? She never sees you again. At least then she has the option to invent some big pile of bollocks about why you had to leave in a hurry. Maybe you're saving seals or something. Whatever. She'll never know and can think of something that fits in with what she thinks was the real you. Something to remember when she's lying about in her gaff doing her nails with Norah Jones on in the background. Now. Worst case scenario. She does see you again, but you just ignore her. Don't take her calls. Don't answer emails. What does she do? She realises that you're just like all men. A total wanker. That's easy Jimmy. She can wrap that up and put it away with all the other boxes of shit that men have given her over the years. One way, you end up like some complicated hero from a movie. A beautiful memory for her to look back on. The other way, you're just some prick that she can forget about and move on because you weren't worth it in the first place.'

'What a load of …'

'Now let's do it your way. Come on.'

'What?'

'Dump me. Pretend I'm Yumiko and dump me.'

'Fuck off.'

'Go on. Let me down easily. Let's see how you get on.'

'No.'

'Come on, Mr Sensitive. You wanted it explained to you.'

'All right, smartarse. Eh … okay … eh, listen Yumiko …'

'Right. *Oh no. I don't like the sound of that. I know what's coming. I'm sitting here shitting myself. Are you dumping me? But why, for fuck sake? After last night?* Right Jimmy, go on …'

'Are you going to keep interrupting me?'

'I'm just showing you what's going on in her mind. Keep going …'

'Well stop putting on a fucking girl's voice then. Right. Eh. Listen Yumiko, about last night …'

'About last night?! Did you get that off a fuckin t-shirt, Jimmy? Right about now she's going, *Oh God, I've just slept with a western man for the very first time in my life. I've disgraced my father's name. And for what? What's he trying to say to me? Please don't let it be what I think it is …*'

'Aesop …'

'You're doing a great job Jimmy. What are you going to say next? It's not you, it's me?'

'Piss off. I was just going to say that last night was great fun and I really enjoyed being with her …'

'Not that much obviously.'

'… but that I'm only out here for a few weeks and it would be wrong of me to take advantage, so maybe she shouldn't …'

'*Of course you're only out here for a few weeks. I knew that! So you're saying that, even though you know I really like you and would love to spend some more time with you for those few weeks, you'd rather I fucked off? Oh God. What have I done? I just wanted to hang around with you for a while. We had so much fun at the concert. You kept looking at me and smiling. I just wanted to be part of your scene with the band and all that for a few weeks. I thought that spending the night with you would be a good thing. Now you want nothing to do with me. That hurts, oh Jimmy-san that hurts so much. Why don't you just kick me in the tits, you heartless bastard? Yeah, Jimmy. Nice one. Anything you'd like to add to make her feel even better about herself? Bad breath? Big arse? Why don't you just come out and say she's the worst ride you ever had in your life and you'd rather spend the next six weeks at the dentist than go near her mangy pie ever again.*'

Jimmy closed his eyes and put his hands over his ears.

'So that's your way Jimmy. I left her with either a nice memory or a shrug of the shoulders. You left her running down the street in floods of tears and wondering if any man will ever want her if she's that awful to be around. Wondering what kind of a fucking loser she must be if she could repulse you so much in just a few hours. A few hours during which, I might add, she was actually

279

naked and doing everything she thought you wanted her to do. Good man, Jimmy. Well, hopefully she won't kill herself. I mean, she's still got all your ironing to do, right?'

They looked at each other for a minute and then both burst out laughing.

'You're a fuckin eejit Aesop,' said Jimmy, wiping his eyes. 'Her mangy pie ...'

Twenty-four

BY WEDNESDAY there was still no word from Simon. Jimmy was going mad. There was so much going on now. Sakamoto-san was pushing things along much faster than Jimmy would have been able to do on his own and there was no way Jimmy had the authority to call some of the shots that needed calling. He was starting to waffle in meetings and hope that no one noticed, but that would only be good for another day or two. He had three separate threads going out into different project groups and they were all waiting for feedback from him. None of the Japanese lads seemed too fussed or worried about the schedule, but Jimmy had enough shit on his plate without putting all this on the long finger as well. He wanted to nail things down before he moved on to the next batch of issues.

At six o'clock he decided to get out of the office. It was earlier than usual for him, but sitting there looking at the phone wasn't helping and he couldn't concentrate on the documents in front of him anyway. He'd go home and start trying to catch Simon from there. He stepped out of the elevator and decided that he'd get a coffee while he was down there. He went around to Starbucks and found Yuki smiling at him through the window as he got to the sliding doors.

'Hey Yuki.'

'Hi Jimmy. How are you?'

'I'm great. Can I get a skinny latté please? Grande.'

'No plobrem. You and Aesop go out tonight?'

'Ah, I don't think so. I'm working tonight. And Aesop texted me earlier. He's in bed, so I think he must be still feeling a bit tired after the weekend. We'll see you on Friday?'

'Great.'

They both stood there not knowing quite what else to say, but then some guy came in and ordered. Good man. When Jimmy's coffee was ready he grabbed it quickly and headed out with a wave. For some reason, he'd always been crap at talking to women that Aesop had had sex with. He always felt like he should be apologising to them or something.

His phone buzzed in his pocket as he stepped into the courtyard and he stopped at one of the small tables to put his laptop down in case it was Simon. It wasn't. It was a text.

Hi Jimmy. What's going on? Can you call me on my mobile when u get a minute? Tnks. Cathy.

Cathy? In work? What was wrong with her?

He read it again. Fuck it. He'd call her now. Something was up.

'Hello?'

'Cathy? It's Jimmy.'

'Oh Jimmy. Thanks for calling back so quickly. Do you know what's going on around here? Everyone's up to ninety.'

'What do you mean?'

'Have you not heard?'

'Heard what?'

Jimmy was suddenly getting a very bad feeling. His skin started to crawl from his undercarriage right up his back to his neck. His shirt was stuck to him.

'You really don't know?'

'Cathy, you're freaking me out a bit here. What's going on?'

'There's all kinds of rumours going around that we're closing! All the managers have been in meetings with each other for days now and Simon keeps saying it's just a little re-shuffle, but everyone says it's not.'

'What? What exactly did he say?'

'I was hoping you could tell me. He's never here and when he is he practically runs into his office and shuts the door. He didn't come in at all on Monday or yesterday. So you've no idea what's happening?'

'I haven't a clue Cathy. I can't get hold of Simon either. Jesus Christ, where did this rumour come from? We can't be closing.

We're in the middle of a huge deal out here. There's lots of stuff going on. There's no way we're closing. Is Martin there?'

'None of them are saying anything Jimmy. They just keep laughing and telling us everything is grand and not to be worrying.'

'But for fuck sake, someone must know something. Why are people saying we're closing?'

'Well it just started with Simon and Martin and Fiona acting all weird and everything. Cancelling meetings with clients and not turning up to staff ones. Then one of the clients called Marco at eight o'clock this morning and told him that their solicitors want written assurances that the project would be completed because he'd heard we're going under.'

'But that's bollocks! Which client? I'll call them now.'

'I think it was Sony. Call Marco and he'll tell you. But he's on site at the moment. He said he was going to call you later.'

'Fuck sake … listen Cathy, I don't know what's going on, but I'm telling you that we're not going under. We've got some huge contracts coming in, sure. We even own the building there. I saw the books only a couple of months ago and we're in great shape. In six months we'll be fifty per cent bigger again, honestly. It must be just some kind of re-organisation like Simon says. I'm sure it'll be grand. But I'll tell you what I'm going to do. I'm going to keep calling Simon, Martin, Fiona and everyone else in the place until I find out what's happening. As soon as I do, I'll give you a call.'

'Thanks Jimmy. God, we've all been pretty worried.'

'Don't be. I promise I'll find out the story and let you know. But you can tell them all in there from me that Eirotech is definitely not in financial trouble. I know that for a fact. It's probably something stupid and Fiona's just being an eejit about it. You know what she's like. Maybe she's waiting for a big deal to come through or something so she can announce it properly in the trade papers. Remember when we got New York? She wore make-up and everything that day.'

Cathy laughed.

'Yeah. Okay. Well that could be it, but it doesn't feel like that to anyone here. But thanks for calling Jimmy. At least now I know we're not being screwed over if you're in the dark too.'

'Jesus, no. Cathy, I've been with you lot for ten years and I wouldn't act the bollocks with any of you.'

'I know that Jimmy.'

'But I'll have a few words for Simon when I get through to him, I'm telling you. Whatever they're doing, there's no need to be messing people around. Look, I'll go now and try and find him. I'll talk to you soon okay?'

'Okay. Thanks Jimmy. So how's it going out there anyway?'

'What? Oh. Well, it's a bit bloody hectic, Cathy, to be honest. It's good though. Very cool place, Tokyo. All go. A bit hot, but … God, you're after getting me all worked up!'

There were drips of sweat falling off his face now. He wiped at them with his hand.

'I'm sorry Jimmy. But it's just that …'

'I know. It's okay Cathy. I'll sort it out. Right now.'

'Thanks. Right. Well, I'll let you go so. Seeya.'

'Seeya.'

Jimmy pressed the phone off and sat there for a minute looking at it. He found Simon's mobile number and called, but it was out of service.

'Cunt.'

He stood up and walked to the apartment, itchy with the heat and nervous and wondering where he'd put his antacid tablets.

The apartment looked empty when he went in, so he assumed Aesop was either out or in bed like he'd said. He put down the laptop and his coffee and pulled off his tie, throwing it onto the counter. He was all sticky and uncomfortable so he started taking off his shirt to have a shower as he swung open his bedroom door.

The first thing he saw was Aesop's bare backside going up and down on his bed.

'Ugh! Jesus! Ugh! What the fuck?' he said, standing there in shock with his hands to his face. He took in the two slender brown legs bent up alongside Aesop's bony white ones. 'Meatloaf's Underpants' was playing in the background.

Aesop stopped moving.

'Well, holy God. Is that the time?'

'What the fuck are you doing in my bed?'

Aesop lifted his head to look at Jimmy's bedside clock.

'You're early Jimmy.'

He got off the girl and turned around to Jimmy.

'Ugh … you dirty … ugh …'

Jimmy stepped backwards out of the room and slammed the door. He sat on the couch with his arms folded. A couple of minutes later the door opened again and Aesop came out in his shorts. Jimmy didn't look at him at all. He just stared across the room at the wall. Aesop had his t-shirt in his hands and was slowly twisting it into a ball.

'Jimmy?'

Nothing.

'The devil made me do it.'

Jimmy looked over at him.

'Did he? In my bed, you fucking scumbag?'

'Well you're not usually home at this hour, Jimmy.'

'So what? You can't be doing things like that, Aesop. For fuck sake, what kind of knacker are you? You think I need to walk in on that when I come home from work? Christ, I'll be carrying that picture around with me for fucking years, you prick.'

'But I told you what I was doing! I sent you a text, didn't I? Well, I didn't say I was in your bed, but you knew I was with someone. You're supposed to make a bit of noise or something when you walk into a place where you know people are at it.'

'All you said was that you were in bed.'

'Yeah, but I put a winky smiley face on it. Did you not see?'

'That was a sad smiley face, you total fucking moron. I thought you were tired or something. The winky one uses a semi- ... anyway, fuck off! Why were you in my room?'

'Okay Jimmy. I'm sorry. It was a bad thing to do.'

'Why Aesop?'

'Well ... y'see ... Yumiko was after doing all your sheets. They were all nice and clean and soft. Mine are a bit ... eh ... well things got a bit messy there the other night and you can't expect a new girl ... eh, so I put them in the washing machine. And I didn't want to use the couch because I knew you'd freak.'

'So you used my bed instead?! My clean sheets?'

'Mine are in the dryer Jimmy. I was going to put them on your bed when we were done, I swear. I even have a sheet of Bounce in there that your Ma gave you so they'd be nice and fluffy. I wasn't expecting you home, was I? You can't just barge in like that, Jimmy. That's not fair.'

'It's my bleedin room! If you're sharing a place with someone Aesop, there's certain rules that most of us here on planet Earth seem to find fairly reasonable. And that ... that's the biggest one there that you're just after breaking. Jesus, it's one thing to break the toaster and keep drinking all the milk but, for Christ sake Aesop, I sleep in that bed.'

'I know. I won't do it again. I promise.'

'You fucking better not.'

'I won't.'

Aesop looked down at his t-shirt.

'So ... eh, anyway ... well, we weren't quite done, Jimmy. Is it all right if I just, y'know, pop back in so ... eh ... just to finish up, like.'

Jimmy looked at him.

'What do you think?'

'Right. That's fair enough, I s'pose. I'll tell her to go so, will I?'

'If you wouldn't mind. That'd be great.'

'Okay. Right so. I mean ... I could speed things up, like. Be out of there in five, no problem. She won't mind.'

'Aesop, I need to have a shower and find out why everyone in my company in Dublin thinks they're getting the sack. Get you and her out of my fucking sight, will you?'

'What do you mean? What's wrong?'

'I don't know. I need to start making calls. Something's going on.'

'Is it bad?'

'Aesop, are you going to fuck off or are you going to stand there and torment me all evening.'

'No problem Jimmy. Can I use your laptop then, if you're not using it? Eh … right. Maybe I'll just go for a pint?'

'Do that. And who the fuck is she anyway? Yuki's downstairs in Starbucks.'

He pointed at his coffee on the counter.

'Ah yeah. Well, Johnnie called me last night after you went to bed. He had a job for me he said. But it wasn't drumming. He said he could get me into an English school. The dosh was all right.'

'A what?'

'Y'know. Where they teach English. I had to be there at eleven o'clock this morning to meet this bird, Yamaguchi-san, and do a demo class for her.'

'You were teaching English? You?! You can't even speak English!'

'Well, I'm better than average in this country, amn't I? It's only temporary because someone is sick. Well anyway, I went for lunch with Yamaguchi-san and …'

'And you decided to ride your boss? You've never had a job in your life and you ride your boss on the first day?'

'No Jimmy! Jesus, give me a bit of credit will you? That's not Yamaguchi-san in there. It's one of the young ones in the class.'

Jimmy stared at him.

'You rode a pupil?'

'Well, I was trying to, Jimmy. Then you came in and kind of

287

ruined the moment if you don't mind me saying so …'

Jimmy stood up and shook his head.

'I don't have time to listen to this. Just tell me she's older than the dry cleaner will you?'

'What? Ah yeah, it's a proper adult school. Corporate and housewives and that. Yummy mummies, y'know?'

'So she's fucking married?'

'Eh. Well, I didn't ask too many … I'll just go and get rid of her, will I?'

'And what about Yuki?'

'Yuki's up on blocks this week.'

'Jesus fucking … Aesop, I'm going for a smoke on the balcony and when I come back in I don't want to see either of you, right? Whatever's going on at work, it sounds serious and I want to be able to sort it out without wondering if your hairy arse is waiting for me around every corner. Jesus, I'll be having nightmares about that, you fucker.'

A girl's voice called out from the bedroom.

'Jimmy-san? *Do desu ka?*'

Jimmy looked at Aesop.

'Why is she calling me?'

'Actually, she's calling me. I told her me name was Jimmy.'

'What? Why, for fuck sake?'

'Ah, I just do that sometimes. Some birds get a bit weird, y'know? Calling you afterwards and all that. If they look like the type that might start getting clingy, I give them a false name. And she has that head on her, y'know? Jimmy's nice and easy to pronounce for a Japanese bird. I tried using Larry on the girl in McDonalds a few days ago, but that was a fuckin disaster. Y'see …'

'Aesop, I don't want to hear it. Fuck off out of here and I'll see you later.'

Jimmy spent the rest of the evening trying to contact Simon and the rest of the management in Eirotech. He got nowhere.

Marco called at around ten that night and told him pretty much what he'd already gotten from Cathy. He didn't know much more than that. Something was up, but that was the only thing they were sure of. Jimmy sat chewing on a couple of white chalky tablets as he looked vacantly at his inbox on the laptop in front of him, hoping something would come in.

There had to be a reasonable explanation for whatever was happening.

WHEN HE woke up the next morning, he opened his eyes and got his bearings. Almost immediately the previous day filled his head and a lumpy heaviness settled into his belly. He picked up the phone next to his bed, but there were no messages or missed calls. He got up and put the kettle on. Aesop wandered out of his room as he waited for his laptop to boot up.

'Morning.'

'Howarya.'

'Any news from home?'

'No. I'm checking me email here.'

'I'm sure it's grand.'

'Yeah. What are you doing up anyway?'

'Work, Jimmy. Yamaguchi-san called me and said I'd to be in Shinjuku for nine o'clock this morning.'

'Well there's a new experience for you.'

'Yeah. I have to tell you Jimmy, this getting up early lark isn't really me.'

'It's half seven. That's not too bad.'

'It's about five hours earlier than I normally get up.'

'Welcome to the real fucking world, Aesop.'

'I prefer mine.'

'Right. Will you be shagging any pupils today?'

'Well I haven't seen the class yet. Never say never.'

There were some work emails and one each from Dónal and Norman, but nothing from Simon.

'Bastard.'

'Nothing?'

'No. Why can't the fucker just tell me what's going on?'

'I thought yiz were mates.'

'So did I.'

'All right if I use the shower first?'

'Yeah. I'll make coffee.'

'Make mine a big one, will ye? I feel like it's the middle of the night. And you do this every day?'

'Me and the rest of the world.'

'Madness.'

'How much are you getting anyway?'

'Fifteen thousand a day. That's fifteen pints. Not bad. But it's only when she has work for me. I think the regular teachers get less.'

'Well they're not giving the full service are they?'

'True.'

When he got to his desk in work, Jimmy saw a memo on his keyboard. He'd a meeting at nine with Sakamoto-san. He checked his watch. He had thirty minutes. He tried calling Simon again, but still got no answer. The phone was switched off. He pulled out the minutes of the previous meeting he'd had with Sakamoto-san and tried to make some notes to take into this one, but he was having trouble concentrating and kept finding himself staring at the page and tapping his pen against it. He was in the shit. He had no answers for them this morning. The most recent issues had been about financing and he wasn't in a position to make calls at the kinds of levels required. He could try and stall them, he could bullshit them or else he could just come clean and tell them that they needed to talk to Dublin directly. He stood up at five to nine and put everything into a folder. He took a big breath and decided that he'd had just about enough of this shit. He was going to tell Sakamoto-san that it was between him and Simon. Jimmy was going to concentrate on figuring out how to make it work technically, not how to pay for it. Fuck them. He knocked on the meeting room door and pushed it open.

Simon looked up from the table and grinned at him.

'Ah Jimmy! Great to see you.'

Jimmy stood in the doorway and stared.

'Simon …'

'Yeah. Flew in this morning first thing. How's everything?'

'Eh …'

Sakamoto-san was sitting opposite Simon with a few of his managers on either side of him. Jimmy nodded at them and closed the door behind him.

'What's going on?' he said to Simon.

'That's why I'm here Jimmy. Big news. Sit down there.'

Jimmy sat next to Simon and put his folder on the table.

'Simon, I think me and you need to have a quick word without, eh …'

'It's okay Jimmy. Sakamoto-san knows all about it.'

'About what Simon?'

'Jimmy, since you came out here things have kind of changed. Kyotosei and Eirotech have been in negotiations.'

'I know that. We're doing this …'

'No Jimmy. Bigger than that. Kyotosei are buying us out.'

'They what?'

'Yeah. We'll be now working for a new entity. Kyotosei-Eirotech Solutions.'

Jimmy sat back and looked over at Sakamoto-san, who bowed at him with a small smile. What in the name of fuck was going on here? His stomach felt tight.

'Kyotosei-Eirotech? Simon … look Simon, I'd really like to talk to you for a minute.'

'No problem Jimmy. Afterwards, okay? Hanada-san here is going to present the takeover to us all. We've been working on it for a while now. It's pretty much a done deal. We just need to establish a few boundaries.'

Jimmy looked over at Hanada-san. He was one of Sakamoto-san's top men and had great English. Now he stood up and went to the overhead screen where a presentation flashed into view. He grinned down at Jimmy and started talking. It went on for about half an hour, but Jimmy was barely taking it in. It was basically a pile of crap about two great organisations coming together to explore their respective outlooks and forge a new and exciting direction in the area of software outsourcing. The Tokyo office would be handling the project management in Asia, Dublin would be in charge of Europe and they'd partner closely on the best way to break the US financial houses. The main development centre would be in Hyderabad, India. Jimmy watched as each new slide sprung onto the screen in front of him, but nothing that came up told him what he really wanted to know. What about his job? What about Cathy's job? Marco? What was going to happen to them all?

When it was over Hanada-san asked them did they have any questions. Jimmy had a hundred questions, but they weren't for this fucker.

'What do you think Jimmy?' said Simon.

'Simon,' said Jimmy, his voice low. 'I wasn't really expecting this.' He turned to him and looked him in the eye.

'I know Jimmy. There were all kinds of compliance issues that we needed to sort out. It was absolutely imperative that no one knew what was happening until it was ready. We're hoping to sign on it in the next few weeks.'

'I see,' said Jimmy. He was fucking livid, but didn't want to say anything in front of the Japanese lot. 'And staff? Any issues there I should know about now?'

'I won't lie to you Jimmy. There's going to be some re-structuring. But, believe me, you've got nothing to worry about.'

'Does Cathy? Marco? Who should be worried? Because I'm telling you, they're all pretty worried at the moment.'

Simon looked over at Sakamoto-san and gave him an

awkward little smile. Sakamoto-san hadn't said a word yet.

'Maybe Jimmy and I should clear up some of the details on our side since I'm here?'

'Of course,' said Sakamoto-san.

He stood up and bowed, the others jumping to attention. Everyone shook hands, Jimmy's going out automatically to each of them, and then they left and shut the door behind them. Jimmy went around to Sakamoto-san's seat so he could face Simon. He looked across the table and folded his arms, his bottom lip in his teeth and his eyebrows up in a question.

'I know what you're thinking Jimmy.'

'I doubt it.'

'I understand that you're probably a bit upset and want to know where all this leaves you.'

'Among other things.'

'Jimmy, your job is absolutely safe. I can promise you that. In fact, in many ways, it was your performance out here that got us to this point.'

'Really? And yet here I am, the last person in the world to know about it. And I remember the last promise you made me. Y'know, the one about being on the Board. Remember that?'

Simon nodded.

'And that could still happen Jimmy! The landscape has changed, that's all. Sakamoto-san is a huge cheese here and he loves you. In another few years …'

'Another few years? What about six months?'

'Jimmy, you have to understand that we're entering a whole new playing field here with Kyotosei. Things can't just happen overnight. But, really, it's a good thing for all of us.'

'For you and Martin and Fiona, yeah I can see that. What about the rest of us? Everyone was supposed to be getting stock options in January. What's happened to that?'

'Well, obviously Jimmy, that can't happen now. But severance packages are going to be extremely …'

'Severence?! Ah, now we get to it. Come on Simon. Fill me in on the great deal you've cut here.'

'Jimmy, you need to stay calm and see the big picture here.'

'I can see the picture all right. What about the three of you?'

'Well, Martin and Fiona are retiring. I'm staying on the Board but will be giving up operations.'

'Sweet fucking deal, Simon. Nice one.'

'Please Jimmy. You won't help at all if you're going to be like this.'

'Who's getting sacked?'

'Jimmy, nothing is finalised yet. We'll need sales staff in Dublin. Kyotosei are keen to open up some opportunities for the developers to relocate.'

'To where for fuck sake?'

'Hyderabad. And here. Some people will be going in the opposite direction to Dublin.'

'Hyderabad?! Simon, who in the name of Jaysis do we have that will want to live in India? People have families, lives … they're not going to just …'

'I'm just saying that there'll be options, Jimmy, that's all.'

'When are you going to tell everyone what's going on? I was on to Cathy last night and they're all going spare in Dublin. No one is telling them anything and they're not stupid.'

'Fiona's going to call a meeting today. Look Jimmy, nothing's going to actually change for a while yet. Everyone will have time to make arrangements.'

'And me?'

'I told you. You're sweet. Sakamoto-san has a real soft spot for you Jimmy. Once the details are worked out, I guarantee that you'll have a huge role in all this going forward. I mean, we're going to need someone to do my old job, right? We haven't worked it all out, but the way Sakamoto-san talks about you, I think he has his eye on you. It's not the partnership we talked about, I know, but it's a big step up. Chief Operating Officer of what we're going to be is a huge deal.'

'If I get it, Simon.'

'Jimmy, I don't want to tell you one thing and then have to say something else …'

'You don't see the irony in saying that?'

'Jimmy, things are going to work out. You won't be disappointed, I know that.'

'I am disappointed Simon. I'm disappointed that after all these years of breaking my bollocks for you, you went ahead with something like this without at least telling me it was happening. And that's leaving out the fact that I made some very difficult decisions based on what you told me back in Dublin only to find out now that it's all a pile of bollocks.'

'Ah, you're not still talking about the band, are you? Jimmy, that's nothing. I'm telling you, it's only shite-talk to be getting involved in all that. You did the right thing by giving it up, and nothing that's going on here today changes that one little bit.'

'Yeah, well I decided to stick with Eirotech because you convinced me that I was the one who'd be deciding where my career took me. Well I didn't have much say in any of this, did I?'

'This is real life Jimmy. If you can't see that, then I'm sorry but you need to grow up. And I'm telling you that as a friend. There's always things that you can't control. That's just the way it is. This just happened, and the way the timing worked out meant it had to happen now. Come on, Jimmy. Think about it. This is a good thing.'

Jimmy just looked at him. It didn't feel like a good thing. Not one fucking bit.

Twenty-five

THE NEXT weekend Jimmy was still fucked off. Aesop was keeping out of his way. One of the other teachers in the English school was learning *Taiko*, traditional Japanese drumming, and had invited him along to a demo to see what it was all about. It was a Saturday and although Aesop had been looking forward to a nice long kip after his hard first-week-ever as a contributing member of society, he'd managed to fall out of bed at eight in the morning and stumble into the living-room. The prospect of seeing some cool drumming was probably the only thing that could have gotten him there. Jimmy was sitting on the couch with a cup of coffee on the table and his guitar in his lap.

'What are you doing up?' said Aesop.

'I just woke up and couldn't get back to sleep.'

'How long are you sitting there?'

'I don't know. An hour or two.'

'No news?'

'Not really. They're supposed to be coming out with new contracts and redundancy announcements and all that next week.'

'Right. Jimmy, you look a bit rough. Are you okay?'

'Haven't been sleeping great this week.'

Aesop checked his watch and sat down on the armchair. He took a gulp of Jimmy's coffee.

'Ugh. That's cold you fucker.'

'I made it a while ago.'

'Will I put the kettle on?'

'What time is your drumming yoke at?'

'I've a few minutes. I had a shower last night so I'm pretty much good to go.'

'Go on then. I'll have tea. Is there any Barry's left?'

'Any left? We haven't even started into the stash that Peggy gave me when I called around to say goodbye. We'd have to start making tea in the bath to get through it.'

'She gave you some too?'

'Some? Five hundred fuckin teabags she gave me! We could open a shop.'

He went into the kitchen and put the kettle on.

'So,' he said when he came back with two cups and a handful of Jaffa Cakes from the special goodies bag that Peggy had also given him. 'What's going to happen?'

'I don't know. Well, I know that they want me to stay.'

'That's good, isn't it?'

'Yeah. I s'pose. But I still feel like I've been kicked in the nuts. They did all this without saying a word and I was supposed to be on the inside, y'know?'

'Jimmy, I know fuck all about all this stuff. I've only been working a week and I'm already getting stressed. All I have to do is talk to people and I'm getting a pain in me arse with it. One of the blokes in the class yesterday asked me what a subordinate clause was. I didn't have a fuckin clue. I was going to say something about it being one of Santy's helpers, but it couldn't have been that. We were talking about how to make long sentences. Do you know what it is?'

'No. But a clause is usually something legal, isn't it?'

'Yeah, maybe. But he was trying to tell me about his holliers in Hawaii. Unless he got arrested or something over there. Anyway, what I was going to say was that I don't know how all this stuff works, but it seems to me that they're after treating you like a dope. Or maybe that's just normal, y'know? There's three people in it, right? Simon and that other pair. They're just looking after themselves. They're all rich now, right?'

'Yeah. But that's not the point. I was told certain things just a few weeks ago and now I'm left with me balls swinging in the wind. I messed up everything with the band and all because of what they promised me.'

Aesop stuck a few Jaffa Cakes in his mouth.

'Uh too ass.'

'What?'

Aesop held up a hand while he swallowed.

'You're too nice. You're honest and you work hard and you think everyone's like you. But they're not, Jimmy. People are cunts.'

'They are not Aesop.'

'They are!'

'Aesop, they're not. This situation just happened. I'm only pissed off because they kept me in the dark.'

'They kept you in the dark because they needed you. They knew you were thinking of packing it in. What if you'd heard the full story about this Kyotosei thing and then decided that you weren't interested and you'd rather stay with The Grove. They needed you to come out here and do your thing for them. I know you don't think I listen to you, and to be honest I don't a lot of the time, but it seems to me that you've worked your arse off on everything they've ever asked you to do. This big deal comes up, and who do they send out to stitch it together? Mister fuckin Reliable of course. And they didn't want to take a chance that you'd give them the finger and stick with the music, so they come up with this big jackanory of you being one of the directors or whatever they said you'd be.'

'But that didn't happen. The deal with Kyotosei didn't come about until after they said I was up for the promotion.'

'Says who?'

'Simon. He explained it all this week.'

'Jesus, see what I mean? Simon says. Of course he's going to say that!'

'He wasn't just bullshitting me Aesop.'

'Well, you know him better than I do. But it sounds like bollocks to me.'

'No way, Aesop. He wouldn't do that.'

298

'Is he married?'

'Yeah.'

'Kids, mortgage, big car?'

'Yeah.'

'And how much is all this worth to him?'

'I don't know exactly. A lot.'

'Right. So here's this bloke with a chance of setting himself and his family up for life. College for the nippers, gaff paid off, holliers … it's all sorted. Done and dusted. You think he's going to risk that by letting you walk out on him before the deal is done? Is he fuck.'

'Aesop …'

'Okay Jimmy, okay. I'm just saying what I said a minute ago. You're too nice. Maybe this Simon bloke is your best mate, but when it comes down to it he was looking after number one. Maybe he'd even love it if everyone got some of the pie, but, really, why should he give a fuck? In the meantime you're plodding along, doing what you're supposed to be doing, taking care of business and hoping that everyone will do right by you because you deserve it. Which you do by the way.'

'Christ, I thought you said a minute ago that you don't know anything about this stuff.'

'I don't. But I know people, Jimmy. People are greedy fuckers.'

'They're not Aesop! Jesus …'

'They are! We're talking about Ireland here, man. All anyone talks about is big gaffs and new cars and who had the biggest marquee out the back garden for their last fucking cocktail party. Your mate Simon is all set to move up in the world, I'm telling you. He's not going to give that away. Anyway, just answer this for me, okay? Does anything that's happened this week change anything.'

'It changes lots of things.'

'I mean does it change your mind? About The Grove. Are you

still going to work for this crowd or are you going to call Dónal tonight and tell him we'll be back next week and he should be preparing Sparky emotionally for my triumphant return.'

'I thought of that.'

'And?'

'And, there's still Simon's old job. Chief Operating Officer. Everyone's saying it'll be mine. I'm going to stick with it. It's a big job, COO.'

'Okay, and what does it mean exactly?'

'It means I'll be getting a pay rise, more responsibility, more say in things … I'll be basically running the shop day-to-day.'

'But it's not what you were supposed to be getting before?'

'No, they can't do that. There's going to be a whole new Board structure now. But it could still happen down the line.'

'Right. So, if you stay on and get this new job you'll be getting more dosh. You always said it wasn't just about the money, though. You said you loved your work.'

'I do.'

'But your new job will be the same as the old job, except you'll be getting more money. So nothing's changed except this one thing that you said you're not that worried about anyway.'

'Aesop, there you go again not listening to me, you prick. Amn't I only after saying I'll be running the place.'

'But you're running the place now!'

'I'm not! Simon is in charge of …'

'Simon is in charge of asking you to run the place for him. All they'll be doing is cutting out the middleman. A middleman who, according to you, will *still* be on this fuckin Board, whatever it is, and getting paid for doing fuck all if you're running the show.'

'Aesop, look, you don't understand …'

'I know. I told you that already. I'm just trying to see what the difference is between now and before. You said you'd quit the band because all this stuff was happening in work. And now none of it is happening. Nothing important has changed, all these big opportunities are pushed away down the line where they were in the first place, you'll be doing what you always did and the only difference is a few grand a year. And that's assuming you get this Head of Chief Operations thing in the first place. But that shower of James Blunts still managed to get you to stay there and ditch the band.'

'It's not like that. This way I'll be in charge of what happens in the office. Marco and the lads … I can make sure they're not fucked around.'

'Ah, arse biscuits Jimmy. You couldn't even make sure *you* weren't fucked around.'

'But it'll be different next week when I sign the new contract. Look Aesop, I appreciate you trying to cheer me up, if this little fucking lecture is your version of trying to cheer me up, but the COO of a company like Kyotosei-Eirotech is a big deal. I know what I'm talking about. This is still a good move. I promised Dónal a single and a video and a gig out here, and he's got them all. I really fucking hope it helps him get past his money troubles. If it's at all possible to record an album down the road, I'll think about it then. Not now. All this crap scared the shite out of me this week Aesop, I'm telling you. Something I've worked on for a long time suddenly looked a bit wobbly there for a while and I need to get me head down and get things back on track.'

Aesop looked at his watch.

'Listen, I have to head and see what this *Taiko* lark is all about. Just think about it, right? No one's calling you a sucker.'

'What?! Who's calling me a sucker?'

'No one is, Jimmy.'

'I'm not a fucking sucker.'

'I know. Isn't that what I'm after saying? Anyway, what are you doing today?'

'What? Ah, I don't know. I might just go for a wander. Shig-

301

gy's gone to see his folks. I'll probably just explore a bit. I might get the bullet train down to Yokohama and see what it's like.'

'I heard it's rapid.'

'Ha ha.'

'What about tonight?'

'I said I'd meet up with Yumiko for a drink.'

'Good man, Jimmy! So you're not giving her the elbow, then?'

'No. For once in my life, I decided to take your advice and just go with the flow. I just need to forget about all this shite for a few hours and chill out. I talked to her a bit during the week and I think you were right. She just wants to hang around and have some fun. She's a good laugh. Anyway, I'm not able for a big heart-to-heart with her this week. What about you and Yuki?'

'Haven't seen her all week. She's on the rag still, sure. I might head into Sexy Dance Girls. Robert was on to me during the week and said he missed me.'

'He missed you?'

'Well, he said he's having a big party in the club and there'd be a load of new gee in. I'll probably go along and see what the story is.'

'So you won't be home tonight?'

'Nah. Not till late anyway. Why? Are you planning a bit of rumpy pumpy with herself?'

'I'm not planning anything, Aesop.'

'Yes you are, you filthy bastard. Look at the head on you! Dying for some bitty, so you are. I told you, once you start following the Path of Aesop, you never look back. It's not just me saying it, Jimmy. It's biology. And not only that, I was reading on the Interweb there last night that your lad and your nuts are actually programmed to …'

'Ah Aesop shut your hole, will ye? For fuck sake, it's too early in the day to be listening to this shite out of you. But to answer your question, I s'pose there's a chance we'll end up here.'

'A fairly good chance I'd say. So she'll be staying the night?'

'She might be. Why?'

'No reason. Just asking. I don't want to walk in on you or anything, do I?'

'Yeah, right. Well anyway, I'm going for a shower. You'd better head off or you'll be late.'

'Yeah. But I can't be late Jimmy, can I? Sure nothing ever starts till I get there.'

Jimmy stood up and went into his room. Aesop pretended to tidy up the cups and Jaffa Cakes while he watched him come out again and cross the floor to the bathroom with a small wave. As soon as the door closed, Aesop ran into his own room. Two minutes later he arrived out again and tiptoed quickly into Jimmy's bedroom with an armful of his dirty clothes. He threw them into the corner, draped a couple of Jimmy's dirty t-shirts over the pile and then, after a quick glance to make sure the new mound wasn't too obvious, he ran out to catch his train.

JOHNNIE CALLED Jimmy on Sunday afternoon and asked him was he free to record the English vocal for 'Lost' the next evening after work. He had a two-hour spot free in a recording studio that he used and that should be loads of time to get it down with some backing vocals. Jimmy said it was fine. He wasn't really in the mood to do it, but it had to be done and anyway he wasn't about to tell Johnnie Fingers that he couldn't be arsed, was he? They arranged a time and Shiggy and Aesop said they'd meet him afterwards for a scoop. He had a late meeting with Simon, during which he was told his new contract would be ready the following day, and then he headed into Shibuya to meet Johnnie at Hachiko. Hachiko was one of the many exits from Shibuya train station. It was apparently named after a dog that was famously obedient.

'That's not such a big deal, though, is it?' said Jimmy. 'Most dogs are obedient. We've had our dog at home for about six years and he still comes to me Da when he's called, even though half the time all he gets is a kick in the arse for chewing on the rug.'

'The Japanese respect loyalty Jimmy,' said Johnnie, as they stopped to look at the life-sized statue of Hachiko.

'They must do. Jesus … to name a place after a dog just because he had good manners.'

'He used to come here every day with the bloke that owned him. The fella would go to work and when he came back in the evening, he'd find Hachiko still waiting there for him.'

'That's pretty cool.'

'Yeah, but one day didn't the poor bloke die in work. He never came back. But Hachiko still waited for him. He wasn't even two years old, but he still waited for him. Sometimes he wouldn't go home for days. Then he'd go home, get some food, and then come back to wait for his master.'

'Jaysis.'

'He did it for ten years, Jimmy. Just sat down here and waited. Then one day he just keeled over and died on the very spot he last saw his master. Everyone knew him and the story of why he sat there every day just looking at the people coming out of the station. So they put this statue here. That all happened seventy years ago, Jimmy. Hachiko is the most famous dog in Japan. Loyal, faithful, dedicated. The Japanese psyche summed up by this little fella and his waggly tail.'

'Wow. That's … is that a true story or are you winding me up?'

'It's true,' said Johnnie. He reached up and patted the statue. 'You right? We should head.'

'Yeah. Let's go.'

They turned away and walked towards the road.

'Jaysis, it was lucky the bloke owned a dog, wasn't it? Can you imagine a cat doing something like that?'

'A cat?' Johnnie laughed. 'No. I can't see that happening. Mind you, cats are wankers.'

'This is true.'

They walked to the recording studio, Jimmy disturbed to find himself identifying with poor little Hachiko that croaked back there all those years ago. Loyalty, faithfulness, dedication … didn't do the bloody dog much good either, did it? Still, at least he got a fucking statue out of it.

Once they were done in the studio, Johnnie went with Jimmy to meet the others for a drink. Aesop's eyes lit up and he immediately leaned over to Jeremy, the Canadian barman, when he saw the two of them coming through the door. Hanging around with Johnnie was cool.

'Have you any Boomtown Rats?' he said.

'Should do. It's all on a computer. There's about twenty thousand songs on there.'

'Stick it on, will you? That's Johnnie Fingers coming in. He's a good mate of mine.'

'I'll see what we have.'

Johnnie and Jimmy got to the bar.

'Howyis lads,' said Aesop. 'How did Jimmy Silkytones here get on with the singing?'

'Grand,' said Johnnie. 'We've loads on tape. I'll send it all back to Sparky and he'll be able to put it together with the backing. Should be good. I think having some of the Irish cut running through it might be cool as well. I'll talk to him about it. The fade out at the end especially.'

'Great stuff. So are yiz having a pint?'

'Kirin,' said Johnnie.

'Yeah, Kirin,' said Jimmy.

'Two pints of Kirin please Jeremy, when you're ready. And will you ever put on a bit of music while you're messing around back there?'

Jeremy stood up from the laptop that sat next to the cash register and started pulling pints. Before he'd finished the first one, the opening of 'She's So Modern' came out over the speakers. Aesop paid for the drinks and gave Jeremy a quick wink and then turned around to the others with a completely straight face. Johnnie stopped with his glass halfway to his mouth and put it down again.

'That's a bit of a coincidence.'

'What?' said Aesop.

Johnnie pointed towards the ceiling.

'Oh yeah. Jaysis, that's gas, isn't it?'

Next up was 'House on Fire'.

Johnnie looked at Aesop and shook his head with a grin.

'You're a terrible gobshite Aesop.'

'What?'

Johnnie pointed a finger at him.

'Sparky told me all about you, pal. Said it was only a matter of time until you started trying to wind me up.'

'I don't know what you're on about Johnnie. Maybe the barman just likes the Rats.'

'Yeah, maybe. Anyway, I don't care. God, I haven't heard this one in years. There was a lot of ska about then, just after punk. Did you like ska?'

'Jaysis, yeah. It wasn't me favourite, like, but at least they weren't going around the place in a hoor's handbag worth of eyeliner and fucking big pirate blouses on them like some of the muppets. Jimmy got into that shite for a while, didn't you Jimmy?'

'It was a long time ago Aesop. If we're going to start slagging each other off over what we wore twenty years ago, I seem to remember a certain pair of brown cords with plastic patches on the knees that you never took off.'

'Okay, okay. But at least I never bought the Nik Kershaw fanzine. Hey Johnnie, I've been meaning to ask you, when you were a rockstar, were you tripping over gee the whole time?'

'Eh … well, as Jimmy says Aesop, that was a long time ago. I'm a married man now.'

'Yeah, but you weren't then, were you?'

'No.'

'So. What was it like after gigs, backstage and all that. I'd say it was mental.'

'We had a laugh.'

'Yeah … go on …'

'Sure you'll find out for yourself soon enough, won't you?'

'Maybe,' said Aesop, with a quick look at Jimmy.

'Ah right. There's still this thing going on about Jimmy's job, isn't there?'

'Lads, please. I don't want to talk about it,' said Jimmy, putting down his empty glass and beckoning the barman.

'Oh. Is something after happening?' said Johnnie.

'Yeah,' said Aesop.

'No,' said Jimmy.

'Jimmy's after being shafted by his company but he still thinks they're brilliant.'

'Will you shut fucking up Aesop? It's grand Johnnie, just some changes in work.'

'None of my business, lads. These things can get complicated. But remember something …'

The lads all looked at each other and put down their drinks, leaning in.

'It's a lucky man who gets a second chance. If you see something you want – work, music, whatever – you go for it. Ever heard of Machiavelli?'

Aesop nodded. 'The bloke that invented ice-cream?'

'He … eh … I don't know if he did that. But he had some good ideas. Jimmy, you've got a good head on you; you'll be grand. The hard part is figuring out what you want.'

'Thanks Johnnie,' said Jimmy. He turned to Aesop. 'And shut your hole, you. I told you what I'm doing and let's just leave it.'

Aesop picked his pint back up.

'Jimmy gets grumpy sometimes, Johnnie,' he said. 'It's his prostate.'

'Aesop, shut up! Me prostate's grand Johnnie, don't mind him.'

Johnnie looked between them.

'You two spend too much time together,' he said.

WHEN THE lift door opened back at their apartment, Jimmy and Aesop stepped out into the corridor and stopped. Yuki and Yumiko were standing outside their door.

'What the fuck?' said Aesop out of the corner of his mouth. 'Was this your idea, you arsehole?'

'No. I haven't talked to Yumiko since yesterday afternoon and I said I'd call her.'

'So what's going on?'

'I don't bleedin know.'

They started to walk towards them and the two girls turned around. Yuki was crying.

'Oh shite.'

They got to the door.

'What's the matter?' said Jimmy to Yumiko. Yuki wasn't in any state to talk.

'Yuki-chan berry upset. It is Aesop.'

'Eh …'

'What did I do?' said Aesop. He had his keys out and was looking between the door and back at the lift, weighing up his options.

'She say you not call her.'

'Well, I've been busy with work, haven't I? I'm working now. I'm a teacher. Hey Yuki, are you all right?'

Yuki took her hands away from her face and went to him. She put her arms around his waist and sobbed into his shirt.

'Ah Jaysis, stop crying will you? What's the matter? I was going to call you tomorrow when I got home.'

Aesop turned his head to Jimmy. He looked horrified.

'Eh, do you want to come in for a cup of tea?' said Jimmy.

Yumiko nodded and Jimmy opened the door to let them in.

They went straight to the couch and Jimmy went into the kitchen, followed by Aesop.

'Now what, you gobshite?' whispered Jimmy.

Aesop opened the broom cupboard and looked into it.

'Will we hide?'

'You're a fucking dipstick, Aesop.'

'What? I never said I was going to call her or anything. Why did you let them in, you fuckin eejit? What are we supposed to do with them now?'

'I couldn't just tell them to fuck off.'

'Of course you could! Listen, this isn't my scene, man. Fuck this. I'm going to bed and you can …'

'You are in your fuck. Take this tea out to her and make her stop crying. You're not leaving me to deal with that mess out there.'

'You let them in. Jimmy, what do you want me to do? The only way she'll stop crying is if I say a whole bunch of shit to her that isn't true.'

'I thought that was your speciality.'

'Yeah, but I can only use my powers for good. And I know psycho when I see it. If we don't tell them to fuck off right now, this thing is going to come back and bite us on the arse.'

'Us? What are you on about? This has fuck all to do with me, Aesop.'

'It fucking has. Isn't Yumiko out there as well?'

'She's only out there cos you're after upsetting her mate.'

'Get a grip Jimmy. I know what's happening. This is a tag team effort. We go out there and be nice and all of a sudden we'll both find ourselves in a lot deeper than we are now.'

'What are you talking about? You said Yumiko just wanted to hang out.'

'That was before. I see what they're at. This is all planned. They're trying to bully us into something. Do you know fuck all about women? They're trying to spring a mantrap here, I'm fuckin telling you. I've seen it before.'

'Stop talking shite. Yuki's just upset because you didn't call her.'

'All right, Jimmy. I'm taking a risk here, but we'll do it your way just to teach you a lesson.'

'Ah, give over. Take that tea and give it to Yuki and get her to stop crying and fuck off. I'm up early in the morning and I don't need this.'

'I bet you ten thousand yen that Yumiko ends up in your bed tonight.'

'This isn't a fucking game Aesop. The girl is upset. And I'm serious, I need to get to bed.'

'The mid-week ride, Jimmy. That's what they're going for. They're trying to nail the windows shut. This is a lock-down, I'm telling you.'

Jimmy shook his head and handed him two cups.

'Shut your hole and get out there.'

Back in the living-room, Yuki was still blubbering. Yumiko took a cup of tea from Jimmy and smiled at him.

'Sank you Jimmy.'

'Eh, Yuki,' said Aesop. 'You want to come into my room and talk?'

Yuki nodded. She still hadn't said anything. The two of them walked into Aesop's room, leaving Jimmy and Yumiko on the couch.

'So … eh … I hope she's okay,' said Jimmy.

'I sink so. She rike Aesop and he did not call her. She is sad.'

'Right. Will they be long do you think?'

Yumiko shrugged.

'It's just that I've to be up early in the morning and …'

'That is okay. We can just go to bed.'

'Right. Eh … well, the thing is …'

'It is okay. I will be awake early also. I sink Yuki-chan just need some time with Aesop.'

She put her hand on Jimmy's leg.

310

'Sank you Jimmy. You are nice guy.'

'Hmm. Yeah, but …' Jimmy looked at his cup of tea. He couldn't think of anything to say. This was all going to shite and he wanted out. They made some small talk, Jimmy glancing at Aesop's bedroom door in the faint hope that they'd come out. They didn't. Yumiko started to yawn and rub her eyes. Eventually she stood up and went into the bathroom. He took a sup of his tea and waited for her to come back out, but when she did she just smiled at him and went into his bedroom.

Fuck. He really wasn't in the humour for this. He ate a Jaffa Cake while he waited for her to come back out, but after about ten minutes it was fairly clear that she wasn't going to. He went in for a piss and to brush his teeth. It was only as he was about to turn off the light that he noticed the extra toothbrush in the glass on the sink. It hadn't been there this morning. He looked at it for a minute and cursed Aesop for being right. Now what was he supposed to do? Spending the night with her was one thing, but this was all a bit premeditated. Throw in the tears from earlier, and the fact that they'd somehow gotten into the building in the first place, and you ended up with a situation that was starting to get a bit weird.

She was in bed when he went in, smiling up at him.

'Listen Yumiko, I'm very tired and …'

'That is okay. Me too. We sreep.'

'Right. Yeah, sleep.'

He undressed to his boxers and got into bed, turning off the light. She turned onto her side, one arm across his chest and soon nodded off. Jimmy lay staring at the ceiling and wondered what Aesop was doing to get them out of this.

'MORNING JIMMY,' said Aesop, grinning.

'Is it?'

'Not bad. The sun's shining, the birds are singing … all that.'

'I don't hear any birds.'

'You have to listen with your heart.'

'You're a gobshite, Aesop. Is she gone?'

'Yep. Left about six. I heard the front door.'

'Yumiko was gone when I woke up.'

'Grand so. They must have headed out together.'

'Did you sort it all out?'

'For the moment.'

'What do you mean "for the moment"?'

'Well, she calmed down after I rode her.'

'You rode her? You fuckin eejit, how is that going to fix anything?'

'Well, it helped me through the evening, Jimmy.'

'Jesus. So what's going to happen tonight when they're at the fucking door again?'

'Sure that's a problem for tonight. We can worry about that later.'

'You stupid fucker, Aesop. Now it's worse than it was before!'

'You mean you didn't ride Yumiko?'

'Of course I didn't! I want out, Aesop. That pair turning up here and giving it all this weepy shit is the last thing I need right now. It was s'posed to just be a bit of fun. God, I should never have listened to you about Yumiko. I could have ended this ages ago.'

'But I was right last night, wasn't I? Didn't I tell you that they were just trying to use some leverage when we were making the tea. Oldest trick in the book, that. By the way, you owe me ten thousand yen.'

'What? I didn't touch her!'

'I just said she'd end up in your bed. That was the bet.'

'There was no bet, you fucker. Anyway, now what are we going to do?'

'Easy. Don't let them in the next time.'

'That's your solution, is it?'

'If you hadn't let them in last night we wouldn't be in this mess.'

'Aesop, we're in this mess because you have a bollocks for a brain. It's all getting fucked up now. It's only been a couple of weeks and this morning I'm after finding spare knickers in my drawer in there. And there's two jars of stuff in the jacks that I don't even know what they are. Next to her bleedin toothbrush!'

'So you're saying I was a hundred per cent right and you don't have a fuckin clue about anything? That I'm brilliant and …'

Jimmy put down his cup of tea and pointed at him.

'Just stop talking a minute, will you Aesop? I'll take care of Yumiko today. You get rid of Yuki. I don't want them around here again. Look, I wasn't going to say anything after I gave you a bollocking last week, but Yumiko's been rooting around in your room as well.'

'What?'

'On Sunday afternoon after I came back from the shops, there was a pile of your clothes all washed and ironed on the end of my bed. That's just getting too strange, Aesop. Now she's doing your bleedin laundry as well.'

'What? That's fucked up!'

'I know. This has to end, man. Cleaning the gaff, washing me clothes, washing your clothes, making the breakfast, text messages all week, turning up here in the middle of the night in tears. Fuck this. It's not right. I want out.'

'Okay. Listen, I'll call Yuki later.'

'Do. I'll call Yumiko.'

'Did she use Bounce?'

'What?'

'Did she use Bounce in the dryer?'

'I don't know what she fucking used.'

'Cos it makes the clothes all nice and soft.'

'Aesop, just talk to Yuki, right? And don't fucking ride her this time.'

'I'll try, Jimmy. She's just so fuckin … clean. Y'know?'

'Clean?'

'Yeah. These Japanese birds … you could eat your dinner off them. Did you not notice?'

'What are you saying, Aesop? Irish girls are fucking manky now, are they?'

'No, they're not manky. But Japanese birds do seem to go the extra mile, don't they? By the time they come out of jacks and into the sack, they're like a lovely soft little baby or something, all clean and smelling nice.'

'Have you been smoking?'

'No. Sure I can't get any here.'

'Japanese women are not like babies, Aesop. Babies are small and pink.'

'I know that, Jimmy. They're just all nice and clean is what I'm saying. They've got this lovely … hang on … are Japanese babies pink? I would've thought …'

'I don't … oh for fuck sake. I'm not having this conversation, Aesop. But Irish women are clean too. All women are clean. That's what women do.'

'Japanese women are cleaner. That's all. The blokes are clean too, sure. Did you ever see Shiggy when he didn't look like he was only after stepping out of the shower?'

Jimmy looked at him.

'Aesop, I don't know what you're fucking talking about, but I'm going to work.'

He stood up to go and then turned back around.

'Are you saying now that I'm not clean?'

'No. You're grand.'

'But I could be cleaner, is it?'

'I'm not saying that Jimmy. It's just that the Japanese people seem to really get in there with the sponge, y'know? They work it.'

Jimmy grabbed his bag and keys and looked sideways at Aesop as he walked to the door.

'Strange fucker.'

Twenty-six

JIMMY TRIED to stay focused when he got into work. There was so much going on, he didn't want any of it to get in the way of his plan. Aesop had gotten into his head a little bit since his lecture the other day and he'd been mulling over a way to prove to himself that he wasn't being completely fucked around just because he was too nice. It seemed to him that there was only one way to do it. There was only one thing that seemed to really count to everyone. Not him, particularly, but if he was going to close the issue once and for all in his mind, he wanted to be sure that Simon, Martin, Sakamoto-san and the rest of them knew that he wasn't a sap. On their terms as well as his own.

'Fifty grand?!' said Simon.

'In euro,' said Jimmy.

'Christ, Jimmy, what are you talking about? That's insane!'

'I want a signing-on bonus, Simon. I know it's a lot of money, but I think I deserve it.'

'Of course you do, Jimmy. I mean, of course you've always done a great job but you're talking about a hell of a lot of money here.'

'I know. But I'm telling you Simon, it'll really make me feel better about myself.'

'Jimmy, we haven't budgeted for anything like that. The redundancy packages are going to be as generous as we can make them, but the people who are staying with the company will have a whole different set of compensation benefits. We're not doing signing-on bonuses at all.'

'I know that. This is a special case.'

Jimmy was speaking quietly and calmly. He was terrified that his face was all red and he was trying to concentrate on taking deep breaths and looking straight at Simon. Only the two of them were sitting in the meeting room. Simon hadn't even taken the contract out of his briefcase yet. Jimmy had decided to take the initiative as soon as they'd both sat down and had told Simon what he wanted as he was dipping a teabag into his cup.

'Jimmy, I really don't know what to tell you. You're putting me in a very difficult position here.'

'I understand that Simon and I'm sorry. But I don't think I'm being unfair.'

'But why this all of a sudden, Jimmy? You already know how important you are to the whole operation. You have been for years. And we've looked after you, haven't we? Christ, what are you trying to do here? We've always made sure that you were happy. You've been given all the responsibility you wanted, your bonuses have been at the top of the list from day one, anything you wanted you got. Why are you acting now like we've been selling you short? What's going on?'

Jimmy was starting to sweat. When Simon said it, it all sounded true. He rubbed his hands on the fabric on the side of his chair and took another breath.

'Simon, everything's changed now. The whole thing. How long have you been with the company?'

'I started the company, Jimmy. Thirteen years ago.'

'Right. And what was your payout? What's fifty grand as a percentage of what you got?'

'Jimmy, that's not the same thing at all. I put my own money into Eirotech right at the start. I had a lot of exposure, especially in the early years. Jesus, for about six months there Jimmy, the three of us were paying everyone's salary with our credit cards. You had nothing like the risk we had. But that's business. That's how it works. I told you already I'm sorry that we never got the chance to induct you properly, but that was just unfortunate. I can't believe you're coming to me now with this shit after all these years. What's gotten into you?'

'All I'm doing is starting to believe what you've been telling me all this time. All the times you said I was the main man, that

I was doing a great job, all that. I do appreciate everything you've done to help my career, but if I'm going to jump into it all over again, I think I deserve a thank-you too.'

'But Jimmy ...'

'Simon, I'm not just acting the prick here, I swear. This is important. I know it's a lot of money, but I honestly don't think I'm out of line on this. It's fifty thousand euro up front. After tax. I need that to be written into the contract and then I'll sign it and we can all move on.'

'Ah Jimmy, this isn't going to be easy. I need to talk to Sakamoto-san.'

Jimmy said nothing. He'd never felt like this before. Like he was after betraying someone and doing something really good at the same time. Guilty, but totally elated as well. Simon looked at him for another minute and then stood up.

'Let's talk again after lunch.'

'No problem Simon.'

Simon got up and left, closing the door to the room a good bit harder than was necessary. Jimmy sat there and felt his shoulders collapse a little. He really was sweating now, and he wiped his face and forehead with a tissue. That had been the hardest thing he'd ever done in his life. The look on Simon's face, like Jimmy had just told him he'd been shagging his daughter or something. It was awful. He wasn't even sure anymore. All the stuff he'd said; it had all made more sense in his head than it had when it was flowing out of his gob and across the table to Simon. And everything Simon had said was true as well. Eirotech had given him every opportunity. Always had. He'd never stagnated with them. Any time it looked like he was getting comfortable, Simon had thrown him another level of responsibility to see if he could deal with it.

Christ. What had he done?

He tried to focus on all the things that Aesop had said and all the things that had been bouncing around his head over the last week. It had seemed like a good idea this morning. He leaned back in his chair and looked around the office. Fifty grand. Net. Jimmy didn't know anymore. He decided that he'd settle for half that. Fuck, even ten grand was making a point wasn't it? Yeah. Ten grand. If Simon came back and offered him ten grand, he'd be cool with that. Where the fuck had he come up with fifty grand? He couldn't even remember figuring it out. Jimmy stood up and went back to his desk. It was nearly lunchtime, but he knew he wouldn't be eating very much. He was fit to puke as it was. He checked his email quickly and then headed down in the lift to get a bowl of miso soup. As he sat in front of it at the counter of the little restaurant, a million thoughts were lashing through him. He stirred up the soup until it was cloudy and then put the spoon down again and looked at it. Another thought, unexpected, had just bashed its way to the surface … how simple his life would have become if Simon had just told him to fuck off.

ROUND TWO started when Jimmy's phone rang just after half past one. Simon wanted to see him. Jimmy was walking back to the meeting room when the feeling of panic in his guts got the better of him and he made a detour to the toilet to let some of the tension out. He washed his hands and face and looked in the mirror. That fucking rash was back on his neck, but it wasn't as bad as it had been on Samui. He could feel the friction against his collar and he opened his top button, using his tie to hold the shirt closed without it being too tight. When he reckoned that he was looking as normal as possible on the outside, despite shitting two-by-fours on the inside, he walked out of the toilet and down to the conference room where his boss was waiting for him. Simon was wearing his suit jacket now and sitting up dead straight. This wasn't a friendly chat anymore.

'Jimmy.'

'Simon.'

'Well, you're after causing quite a stir, you know that?'

Jimmy nodded but didn't say anything.

'Sakamoto-san had fucking triplets.'

'Did he?'

'He doesn't understand what's going on. He thought everything was cool in the Eirotech camp and then it turns out that our star employee is holding a gun to everyone's head.'

'That's not what I'm trying to do at all Simon. I don't mind talking to Sakamoto-san if that will help him understand where I'm coming from.'

'Well, maybe that might ease his mind. But it doesn't matter. He asked me what I thought.'

'Yeah?'

'Jimmy, I'm going to be honest with you. I told him I thought you were taking the piss. I said we've done everything we could do to make you happy over the years. You were going places and we knew it. So we laid it on for you from the very start. Money, responsibility, everything we were able to do, we did it. For you to come along now and throw it back in our faces was not fucking on. That's what I told him.'

Jimmy's heart seemed to take up his whole chest. It was hammering away inside him. He tried not to think about what his sphincter was doing. This was it. Jesus. After all that. All over red rover.

'Simon, I'm sorry that it looks that way. It's not what I'm doing at all, though. I was only asking for something that I think I deserve.'

'Yeah. Well anyway, Sakamoto-san didn't want to hear it.'

'Right. I see.'

'I mean he didn't want to hear what I had to say.'

'What?'

'He said the money would be in your account the day after you sign the contract. Congratulations Jimmy. I hope you're happy.'

Simon was looking at Jimmy like he didn't even know who he was. Jimmy felt about eight feet tall. Like he'd won the lotto. And it wasn't even the money. Not that Simon seemed to get that.

'That's great Simon. Thanks. I mean it.'

'Don't thank me Jimmy. This has nothing to do with me. And, just between us, I still can't believe you've gone and done this. To put me in that position. Not cool, Jimmy. Not cool at all.'

He shook his head and reached into his folder for Jimmy's contract.

Jimmy's good feeling was starting to disappear. The tiny leaden weight of guilt that had just begun to establish itself in the bottom of his throat disappeared. He was getting pissed off. Who the fuck did Simon think he was? He'd just cleared a share of at least ten million euro by Jimmy's reckoning and here the grumpy bastard was trying to lay shit on Jimmy's paltry fifty grand. That just wasn't fucking fair. He'd spent over ten years helping to build this company for them. They'd no right to try and fuck with his head now just because he wanted a little show of appreciation. He stared back at Simon and said nothing, afraid of what would come out if he did. He was raging.

'Here,' said Simon. He threw the contract across to him. The pages flew out the side of the clear plastic binder and ended up in a mess all over the table in front of Jimmy, a couple of them landing on the floor. They both looked at the sheets and then Jimmy looked up. Simon obviously hadn't meant to do that, but he didn't apologise either.

'Read that, sign it and give it to HR,' he said, standing up. 'You'll get your money then. That signs you up to Kyotosei-Eirotech so you'll be eligible for the COO posting. They'll announce it the day after tomorrow. No doubt your pal Sakamoto-san will step up for you then, too.'

Jimmy suddenly felt boiling hot. He was sure the rash was all over his face now. It felt like a hot hand squeezing him.

'Sit down a minute,' he said slowly, sweat trickling down his back.

'Sorry Jimmy. I've got things to do,' said Simon.

Jimmy stood up.

'Sit *down* Simon!'

Simon stared at him.

'You …'

'I want to say something. Now sit down.'

'You can't …'

'If don't park your arse in that chair right now, I'm walking into Sakamoto-san's office and telling him I'm out of here this afternoon because of what you just did.'

'You wouldn't …'

'I'm serious, Simon. You don't think I can fuck up this deal for you? Because I swear I'll march in there and tell him you just tried to feel my balls if that's what it takes. Now sit down.'

Simon slowly lowered himself into his chair. He looked terrified. Not because of the threat, but because he honestly thought Jimmy was going to give him a box. He'd never seen anyone go that colour before. When he was sitting, still staring and with his mouth hanging open, Jimmy sat too and started to gather the pages together and put them back in the binder. When he was finished he looked up. The red edge of what he'd been feeling had cooled a little but he was still furious.

'I've had just about enough of this shit out of you,' he said. 'Frankly, I don't care what you think anymore. I don't know what particular role you've carved out for yourself on the Board later, but I'm just telling you now that you'd better keep the hell away from me when we're back in Dublin. I've never been treated like that. Not even by a client, much less by someone in my own company.'

'Jimmy, I didn't mean …'

'I don't care Simon. I'm sick of you trying to make me feel like I'm only trying to pull a fast one after everything I did for you. And what you just did with that contract was about the rudest fucking thing I've ever seen in my life.'

He stood up again and grabbed the binder in front of him.

He didn't even look at Simon before heading out the door.

'Disrespectful prick,' he said, over his shoulder.

He gave the door a nice slam.

'TRIED TO feel your balls?' said Aesop. He was laughing his head off.

'It's not funny, Aesop. That was a very stressful day I've just had.'

'It's brilliant. And about bleedin time! What did it feel like?'

'I wasn't really thinking. I was so pissed off that I just gave him a bollocking and stormed out.'

'Hurray for Jimmy!'

Aesop picked up his pint and clinked it against Jimmy's. Jimmy smiled and took a mouthful.

'But you got the cash anyway?' said Aesop.

'Yeah. Well, I have to sign the contract and then I get it.'

'Jaysis. Fifty grand. That's brilliant. What are you going to do with it?'

'Haven't really thought about it. I didn't even really think I'd get it, to be honest. I was just trying to make a point.'

'Yeah right. And all that lovely loot was just an afterthought. Me bollocks!'

'I'm serious. I figured that if money was the only thing they were interested in, then I'd have to use money to see if they were pulling my pud or not. Not, as it turned out.'

'Well, fair play to you Jimmy. I didn't expect you to do anything like that. Very cheeky. But c'mere ... I must be due some of that money, amn't I?'

'You? Why?'

'Because only for me annoying you, you'd never have asked for it.'

Jimmy smiled at him.

'I'll buy you something nice.'

'How nice?'

'What do you want?'

'Halle Berry covered in melted ice-cream and Maltesers.'

'I think she charges sixty grand for that.'

'Okay then, a surprise.'

'Right.'

'Can I have it now?'

'Your surprise? I don't even know what it is yet.'

'I'm crap at waiting for surprises, Jimmy. Come on, can I have it now?'

'No.'

'But …'

'Tough. You'll appreciate it more when you get it.'

'Ooh, you're all hard now, look. That's my influence. I'm shaping you in my image. You're not half as prufrockian as you used to be.'

Jimmy looked sideways at him.

'What?'

'Prufrockian.'

'Which is?'

'I got it last week. It means marked by timidity and beset by unfulfilled aspirations. It comes from a poem.'

'Aesop, what's the point in learning new words that no-one ever uses?'

'I just used it, didn't I?'

Jimmy nodded and caught Mick as he was walking past.

'Two more pints please Mick.'

'No problem, Jimmy.'

'And anyway,' Jimmy went on. 'You're never going to remember them.'

'I will. Sure amn't I very sprachgefuhl these days.'

'If that means "terrible fucking irritating", then yes.'

'That's not what it means.'

'Then I don't know. Did you call Yuki?'

'Yep. Told her to leave us alone. All done.'

'All done? What did you say exactly?'

'That's it. Told her I was seeing someone else and that was that. Twenty seconds. Over. How about you and Yumiko?'

'Eh …'

'Did you not call her?'

'I did.'

'And what did you say?'

'Well … I said … I told her …'

'Yeah … what?'

'I told her I was seeing someone else.'

Aesop roared laughing.

'You see?! We'll have to start calling you Son of Aesop.'

'I'm not proud of it Aesop. It just seemed easier. The way things were getting, I didn't want to meet her again and get involved in a big scene. I feel really bad about it as it is.'

'You'll get over that. You have to train yourself.'

'Anyway, it's kind of true. I got a mail from Susan today.'

'Who?'

'Fucking Susan, Aesop. The girl in Thailand? Jesus, how the fuck are you going to remember all these new words if you can't remember actual people?'

'Years of practice, Jimmy. But when you're a master swords-man like me, it's important to forget about all the girls you've been up on in your past. And giving them false names when you ride them helps too. You disassociate from yourself. It's cathar-tic.'

He winked and ticked a box in the air.

'See? Two in one sentence that time.'

'That was two sentences. Anyway, you weren't up on Susan. You were with Amanda. Do you remember Amanda?'

'La-la-la-la-la …' said Aesop, his hands over his ears and his eyes squeezed shut.

'Well Susan's still writing and we're still getting on grand. I told her I'd pop over when I got back to Dublin.'

'That's not very Son of Aesop, is it?'

'It's not meant to be. She asked me to write a song for her. I've got a few ideas.'

'Oh God. I take it all back, Jimmy. You're still a plonker. Actually I was thinking of writing a song too.'

'I know. Hallewood.'

'No, a different one.'

'About what?'

'Well, I was talking to Robert in Sexy Dance Girls. Did you know he mixes his own music? Does some production too.'

Jimmy shook his head.

'Well he does. So anyway, you know Stevie Wonder?'

'I've heard of him.'

'Well, Robert's a really cool bloke, right? We've been having loads of chats and all. He's deadly. He was telling me all about Nigeria. It sounds amazing. Some of the shit that goes on there reminds me of Ireland.'

'Ireland? How?'

'Ah, the politics and religion and all. It's kind of complicated. The way religion has a hold on people the way it used to at home. And the corruption and all.'

'You're talking about fucking politics and religion now? For fuck sake...'

'Yeah, well we have all these Nigerians in Ireland now, right? And the way they have to put up with shit over there?'

'Aesop, what has this got to do with Stevie Wonder?'

'I'm getting to that. You remember he did Ebony and Ivory with McCartney?'

'Oh Christ ...'

'Shush Jimmy. I was thinking of doing something like that. Updated though. A mixture of hip-hop and Irish death metal. Like Aerosmith did in the eighties, except new and much heavier.'

'Aesop ...'

'I even have a name for the song.'

Jimmy put down his tea.

'Go on then. What's it called?'

'Milk and Cocoa.'

'Right. Milk and Cocoa. And did you mention this to Robert?'

'Not yet. I only thought of it tonight. Because Nigeria is a big exporter of cocoa beans and we have loads of … eh … cows and all, right? And do you know how many of those cocoa beans end up in Cadbury's in Coolock? Loads of them. And it gets mixed with the Irish milk to make Double Deckers and all, right? Y'see? It all makes sense, doesn't it? It'd be a social commentary.'

'Aesop, since when do you give a fuck about society? You've spent your whole life trying to avoid being a member of it.'

'But that's exactly what gives me the subjectivity I need. I can still comment on it, can't I? Would you play guitar on it?'

'Objectivity. But yeah, just try and stop me playing guitar on your new Stevie Wonder song.'

'I'm serious. Nothing gay though. No solos or anything. Just a big riff and we all hammer along like fuck with Robert and me doing the vocals. He speaks Hausa as well from home. It's what they use there. So we'd be mixing it up. What do you think?'

'You write the song and I'm there. Go for it.'

'Thanks. It'll be brilliant, won't it?'

'You're a very peculiar man, Aesop.'

'Thanks. So c'mere to me, when are you going to sign the contract?'

'What? Oh, tonight I s'pose.'

'Have you got it here?'

'It's in with the laptop.'

'Give us a look.'

Jimmy took it out and handed it to him.

'Don't get fucking beer on it. Hold it in your hands.'

Aesop flicked through it. It was about ten pages long. He

suddenly stopped, gasped and looked up.

'You get paid that fuckin much?!'

'Yeah.'

'You jammy cunt!'

'What are you on about? I've been working my arse off for years to get that.'

'You're fuckin loaded!'

'Most of it goes on the gaff.'

'Still, but. Jesus, that's a fortune. No wonder you could afford a new Les Paul. You should get a Tele and an SG as well. Then you could get a nice PRS and a Rickenbacker. And then do you know what you could do?'

'Move back in with Peggy and Seán because I've defaulted on me mortgage payments?'

'You could get rid of the Snot Mobile and get a real car. You'd never be able to spend all that, Jimmy. And, greedy bastard, asking them for another fifty grand like that this morning! I'd have told you to get fucked!'

'Aesop, the taxman gets lumps out of my salary. After the bank gets their bit for me house there's not much left, I'm telling you.'

'Get fucked. You know how much I got on the scratcher?'

'About the exact same as I have to play with every week. Anyway, shut up. You're not supposed to be oogling my salary details.'

'Go on then, sign it.'

'What, here?'

'Yeah, why not?'

'I don't think I have a pen.'

'Hey Mick,' shouted Aesop. 'Do you have the lend of a pen?'

Mick took a pen out of his shirt and handed it over the counter to Aesop.

'Ta. Here you go Jimmy.'

Jimmy took the pen and turned to the back page.

'You know what this means, Aesop?'

'Yep. I get a lovely surprise.'

'You know what else it means? About The Grove?'

'Yeah,' said Aesop, smiling. 'Jimmy I tried me best, but we both know you're going to sign it. I can't spend the rest of me life getting on your wick, can I?'

'If only I could believe that, Aesop.'

'It's true. Anyway, who knows? If we get the album deal you can change your mind later on. And you can still play when you have the time, can't you?'

Jimmy laughed.

'I won't have the time I used to have, Aesop. We'll have to slow down a bit.'

'Sign it Jimmy. I want me pressie.'

Jimmy grinned and signed the back page twice. He wrote the date down and looked at it.

'Well, that feels a bit weird.'

'Why?'

'It's like I'm starting again or something.'

'So what? Look what they're paying you? You're not exactly starting from scratch for fuck sake, are you?'

'No. Actually, that's the COO salary they're giving me. It's about twenty per cent more than what I was on before.'

'You absolute geebag!'

Jimmy laughed.

'It's not about the money, Aesop.'

'My hairy arse it's not, Jimmy.'

'Whatever. Anyway, it's done now.'

'Cool. Will we celebrate?'

'I've work tomorrow, Aesop.'

'Ah, you're always working. Come on. Let's get shitfaced.'

'Maybe a few more pints just …'

THEY STUMBLED out of the lift, giggling and shushing each other, at half two in the morning. Straight away they both stopped dead and looked down the corridor to see if any surprises were waiting for them. There weren't. They looked at each other and burst out laughing.

'The scaredy head on you.'

'Piss off! I saw you eyeing up the fire escape.'

They sat up drinking tea and eating chocolate-covered Kimberley bikkies for another hour and talking shite. Jimmy played a few of the pieces he had in mind for Susan's song.

'So, you reckon she's Superchick, Jimmy?'

Jimmy looked over at him.

'Are you going to start giving me shite at this hour of the night, Aesop?'

'No, really. I'm serious.'

'I don't know. She's really fucking nice, though. It's a start, right?'

'Can you tell me something Jimmy?'

Aesop put down his cup and leaned forward, frowning.

'What?' said Jimmy.

'Why is it so important to you to have a girl?'

Jimmy picked up his guitar again as he thought about it and Aesop held up his hand and ran into his bedroom. He came back with the camcorder.

'I want to get this.'

'Fuck off! You're not recording me when I'm drunk.'

'Come on. I'll only forget what you said. I want to put this on the website and it'll save me writing it down.'

'Why for fuck sake?'

'Rockstars are always being asked questions like this. The fans want to know this shit Jimmy.'

'I'm not saying anything until you put that down.'

'Chicken.'

'Every time I look at you, you have that fucking thing out.'

'It's for the site. I'm making a video diary of the trip so I don't forget any of it. The early days, y'know? Before we go platinum.'

'I don't care.'

'Okay, okay. Look, it's turned off. I'll remember. Now come on. Why is it so important that you have a girl?'

'It's not that important.'

'But it is! You're always serious about it. It always has to be just right. Dicking around the way I do is just a waste of time for you. You have to have a proper bird there with you all the time. Are you afraid of being old and lonely or something?'

'No. Well … I mean, who wants to be lonely? But it's not that. It's just … when I'm on me own I … I s'pose I think too much. I get selfish.'

'You? You're not selfish. You're always buying the *Big Issue* and everything.'

'I don't mean I turn into a scabby bastard. I just end up thinking about myself all the time. I write songs that are all heavy and personal. I don't really enjoy myself, y'know? I'm happier when I've got someone there with me. It makes everything seem … like there's more point to it. I mean, if it's just me – on me own – then what's the point?'

'So you want someone there all the time to tell you you're brilliant?'

'No. It's not like that, you fuckin eejit. Look … okay, it's as if I'm not really a proper person when I'm on me own. I know that sounds stupid, but that's what it's like. There's too many things about me that are all fucked up and confused. Things I think about. Having someone really close to you means you don't spend all your time in your own head, thinking about what an arsehole you are.'

'I'm always on my own Jimmy, and I think I'm brilliant. And without meaning to sound like I'm sniffing your jocks here, you're not an arsehole.'

'Look, I don't need a woman here right this second. Susan and me will see what happens when I get home. I better get some kip, though. Look at the time.'

'Yeah. I've to get to Chiba tomorrow morning. Some shitebag is sick this week and I've to cover for him. Lazy bastard.'

'If he wasn't sick, Aesop, you wouldn't have any work.'

'Still. I don't think I'm cut out to be a teacher, Jimmy.'

'Well I won't argue with that. Where's Chiba anyway?'

'Somewhere near the airport.'

'Christ, you better get to bed too then.'

'Yeah. By the way Jimmy, you did the right thing today.'

'Asking for the money?'

'Signing the contract. Don't mind the money. You did the right thing.'

'Thanks.'

'Jaysis. Look at us being nice to each other and all. I'd give you a hug only I'd be afraid of what it might lead to after all the gargle. Anyway, congratulations.'

'Thanks man.'

'No problem.'

'No. So c'mere, what ever happened with you and Katie that time by the way? Y'know, Jennifer's mate ...'

'La-la-la-la-la ...'

Twenty-seven

ROUND THREE didn't go well for Jimmy. He wasn't even expecting there to be a Round Three. Round Three was supposed to be a formality. He looked across the table at Simon as Sakamoto-san led the applause. The wind seemed to be sucked out of him and every inch of his skin was prickling and hot. Simon didn't look back. He just stared up at Sakamoto-san and kept clapping. Jimmy's hands made a token effort at doing the same, but they were suddenly so clammy that they probably only made a squelching splat as they met. Jimmy turned to Shiggy opposite him. He was also just sitting there, stunned. They'd given him the job. Shigenori 'Shiggy' Tsujita-san was to be the new COO of Kyotosei-Eirotech Solutions. He'd be based in Dublin, flying over in a few weeks to take up the position. Shiggy was Jimmy's new boss. Jimmy swallowed as best he could with a throat that was completely dry and smiled at him. Shiggy didn't smile. He didn't look like he could. He just stared back at Jimmy.

Sakamoto-san started talking again and announced that Jimmy would be one of six new Assistant Vice Presidents of the company. It was all part of the new structure. As well as being COO in Dublin, Shiggy would be a Vice President. Jimmy got a clap from everyone and a smile from Sakamoto-san, the new CEO, but he was barely following what was going on anymore. Then Simon got up and started talking about dotted lines and shared responsibilities and Jimmy stopped listening altogether. He'd been fucked again. It had practically been a given that he'd be the new COO. Everyone had said it. He'd been given the pay rise and everything. He didn't even know anyone else was in the running. Where did that leave him? AVP was just a title. A new way of putting people on different tiers for the purposes of salaries and promotions. Officially it meant that he was a Level Three employee. He was a number. He was fucking Patrick McGoohan.

After the meeting Jimmy went back to his desk and sat in front of his computer. He looked through his inbox and read a few mails, but nothing was registering with him and he spent half an hour just clicking, scrolling and gazing and feeling like the whole world was having a laugh at him. Then the phone rang.

'Jimmy?'

It was Shiggy.

'Hiya Shiggy. Congratulations, man. Sorry I had to run out after the meeting. I was in the middle of something here.'

'You want coffee?'

Jimmy didn't really feel like talking. 'I'm a bit busy Shiggy.'

'Come on. See you downstairs in robby.'

'Ah, I'm kind of … oh, okay. Okay Shiggy. Seeya there.'

Shiggy was already waiting for him when the lift opened. They walked out of the building and around to a coffee shop a couple of blocks away.

'Jimmy, I am sorry. I didn't know,' said Shiggy as they waited at their table for the waiter to bring their coffee.

'Shiggy, you don't have to apologise. You're perfect for the job.'

'They never say anysing to me. I find out same time as you.'

'Really Shiggy, it doesn't matter. To be honest, I should have expected something like this. The way things have been going lately, I'm amazed I wasn't told they were shipping me off to India for a few years.'

'Jimmy, I can't say no to job.'

'What? Of course you can't! Don't even think about it, Shiggy. Look, this is a great opportunity for you. Don't mind me. I didn't get the job and you did. That's life. You'll be great. God, and you'll be back in Ireland again. We'll have a laugh. My Ma will be delighted.'

The coffee arrived and Shiggy stirred his with a cinnamon stick.

'Don't feel rike raughing. See the Japanese way? They never ask me do I rike to live in Ireland again. Just say I have to go. So I have to go. Work hard for the company.'

'Is it that bad?'

'No. Job is great of course. And I rike Ireland. But not the point, Jimmy. They just send me. I have to go. No choice.'

'Listen Shiggy, these things just happen. I won't act the prick with you in work just cos we're mates. We just have our jobs to do and we'll do them. Same as before.'

'I know that. But still I sink it will be strange.'

'Shiggy, I'm still running the information systems right? You'll have all the other shit on your plate to take care of. We'll make a great team. Don't worry about it.'

'Sanks Jimmy. Jimmy, I am grad that you still work for Eiro-tech. To try and do this job in Ireland without you would be so compricated.'

'We'll be grand Shiggy, watch. It's a new company now. All kinds of things will be happening. We'll blow them all away. Don't be worrying about it. We'll even get to play together again, won't we? We never found a replacement for you.'

Shiggy nodded and looked down into his cup.

'Sorry Jimmy,' he said again. 'Reery.'

'Shut up, you fucking big girl. It's cool, I'm telling you.'

Shiggy gave a little laugh.

'Sanks.'

'For what?'

'Because at reast I know we still friends. You call me fucking big girl. Fart head.'

Back in the office it was Simon's turn to ring Jimmy's extension. He wanted to talk to him before he headed off the next day. Jimmy trudged the by-now familiar steps to the conference room and went in. Simon was standing up and gestured to the seat opposite, waiting until Jimmy sat down before he sat down himself.

'Jimmy, I just wanted to say that we only made the decision yesterday. I didn't know Tsujita-san was going to get the job. I swear to God. And Sakamoto-san insisted that no-one be told before today's meeting.'

'Yeah. Well, it doesn't make any difference now, does it?'

'It does if it's going to affect your job.'

'It won't. Tsujita-san is a great guy. He'll do a brilliant job.'

'I'm glad to hear you say that. And you're okay?'

'Well … no, not really.'

'Jimmy, I know we've had a bit of a rough time of it the last while, you and me. I want to apologise properly for what happened on Tuesday. I didn't mean to throw the contract at you and I shouldn't have done it. I'm sorry.'

'Okay.'

'Are you sure?'

'Simon, it's done. Let's just get on with what we have to do. We're all going to be pretty busy from now on, yeah? No one has time for things to get personal. Let's just forget it.'

'Good. Thanks. Listen, for what it's worth, despite everything that happened, I still thought that you should have gotten COO. There were about half a dozen names in the pot and in the end it came down to you and Tsujita-san. The new Board just reckoned that you're too good an engineer to waste on Operations. We couldn't afford to lose you in that role. That's why you still got the pay rise. There was also the matter of Japanese. Tsujita-san is bilingual and Sakamoto-san felt strongly that that was going to be important down the line. And besides anything else, having both of you running the show for us together will be perfect. But listen, you'll have complete control on any aspect of IT, our own systems of course as well as the client projects. Infrastructure, development, support; the whole thing. It's not just the same as before either. This time you'll be building a full development centre in Hyderabad and liasing between Tokyo and Dublin. Any projects we take on have to go through you. It's big, Jimmy.

I hope you can see that. If anything, it's as important a role as Tsujita-san's. In this industry especially, he'll be depending on you completely to do his job. By the way, I think we can get Sakamoto-san to change your title. How does CIO sound? Chief Information Officer. There's a good chance that you'll be made a full VP next March too at the AGM.'

'Sounds okay.'

It was just more promises and acronyms. More putting things on the long finger, out of his reach where he had no control over them.

'It's all been a bit mad around here,' said Simon. 'But where you're going to be is still a big step up from where you were. Considering all that's happened, I think that's pretty good.'

'Yeah. I s'pose. Look Simon, this hasn't really sunk in yet. Every time I think I know where I stand, the goalposts move.'

'I understand Jimmy. Actually, on that subject, there's something else I need to mention before this is all done and dusted.'

'What?'

'It's your music.'

'What about it?'

'I know you played a concert out here a couple of weeks ago.'

Jimmy went red but didn't say anything.

'It got a mention at home in one of the magazines and Martin's youngfella saw it. He's a bit of a fan of yours, apparently. I'm just going to say this one more time. This has to stop, Jimmy. It has to. It's not why we paid for you to come out here. I even heard that there's someone staying with you in your apartment. Someone from your band? We're expected to pay for that too, are we? Okay Jimmy, that's the way it is now and let's say no more about it. But with the responsibilities ahead of you, we can't afford to only have half of your attention. You understand that, don't you? I mean, come on Jimmy. This is a multi-million dollar operation we're after putting together. You have to be one hundred per cent on board or this is not going to work.'

'Simon, I've already told the band that anything I do with them will be part-time. Work comes first from now on. Absolutely. They know that.'

'I'm afraid that's not good enough, Jimmy. We're not talking about you doing your party piece when you have a few beers in you. You've already had a record playing on the radio at home for God sake. What's next? MTV? We can't have that. Whatever about Eirotech giving you a bit of leeway, Kyotosei is a very old Japanese company and having you prancing about on the telly and making the papers and then coming in the next day trying to negotiate some big deal or other … the image and credibility of the whole company is what's at issue here. You do a concert in Tokyo one week, and it's all over the newsagents in Dublin the next week. That actually happened, Jimmy. It's not on. Do you see what I'm saying?'

Jimmy felt stuck to the seat. What was he saying exactly?

'So what does that mean? What am I not allowed do?'

'Okay Jimmy, as far as I'm concerned I don't care if you play in some pub on a Sunday afternoon if that's what floats your boat. But the whole band thing has to finish. No more television and radio and write-ups about what you were bloody doing on Saturday night. No more records and doing concerts in town. I'm sorry Jimmy. It has to be that way. That's the kind of publicity we can do without when we're trying to get this thing off the ground. It's not like you're singing Dana songs, y'know? There's swearing and everything.'

'But Simon, what I do in my free time is my business. Everyone in this company, in every company, has a life outside work. You can't try and make me stop playing music when I'm not in the office.'

'I'm not trying to do that. I'm trying to protect the credibility of the firm. This isn't a hobby with you. It's much bigger than that.'

'I don't know if I can agree to that Simon. That's a huge encroachment into my personal life.'

Simon sighed and leaned back in his chair.

'Please Jimmy. Think about what I've just said.'

'I don't need to think about it. I can't just completely give up music. I've been doing it since I was a kid, Simon.'

Simon took some tea and nodded slowly.

'All right, Jimmy. I didn't want to do this, but if I have to spell it out to you I will. You signed a contract with us. One of the clauses states that you can't be involved in any other businesses.'

'What are you talking about?'

'Your band is a business Jimmy. It generates income.'

'You know bloody well that that's not what the contract is saying! It means I can't work for any competitors or for any other business in this industry. It doesn't mean I can't play music in my spare time.'

'In this instance, it does. Jimmy, technically, you could be classified as a professional musician. Our lawyers already confirmed that for us. By signing that contract on Tuesday, you quit the band. Completely. It's as simple as that. If you try and keep playing, we'll be obliged to let you go and start legal proceedings against you personally as well as the people you work for. There's just too much money at stake now, Jimmy. I'm very sorry you made me say it, but that's the way it is. This whole thing is at a very early stage and we absolutely can't have anything get in the way. As of now, millions of dollars are directly dependant on your application to the job at hand. It's a huge risk for us and an enormous responsibility for you but I mean it when I say this, Jimmy ... that was a legally binding contract and you're going to have your hands completely full with Kyotosei-Eirotech. At the end of it you'll be a very successful man, but in the meantime there's just no room for that band. It's over. It has to be, end of story.'

Jimmy had his head in his hands now. Jesus H. Christ, would this never fucking end? His phone beeped on table in front of him. He picked it up absently and checked the message. It was from Aesop, who'd obviously given up on trying to find where the semi-colon was on his phone.

'Wink wink.'

'For fuck sake …'

'What's wrong?' said Simon.

'Eh … nothing.'

'Jimmy, look, I'm running late for another meeting. We'll talk again in the morning before I head off, right? I'll be back in a couple of weeks. When I come back, you'll be giving the biggest presentation of your life to some of the most important people you'll ever meet. I'll be with a trade delegation from Ireland and we're going to announce the new company then at a major function. The Irish ambassador and everything will be there. And the Minister for Trade. You'll be the star of the show, Jimmy. The man who's going to make it all happen. I'll explain all about it tomorrow. And Jimmy, I'm not bullshitting you here. You work for us now. You need to get your head together and see what a great opportunity it is for you. No more distractions, okay? We've all got to knuckle down here and take this thing to the next level. Which is going to be huge, by the way. Forgetting about that band is the best thing you'll ever do. I'll see you tomorrow.'

Jimmy watched him go out and picked up his phone again, fingering the buttons for a minute. In the end he just shook his head and replied.

'Just tell me it's not Yuki.'

A minute later another message popped up.

'Nope. Domino delivery girl frm lst week. Wanted to try Irish sausage variety. Think she likes it. All about cultural exchange this week, amn't I? Hows ur day going?'

Jimmy read it and smiled to himself.

'Gr8.'

THE NEXT three weeks were tough on Jimmy. Everything was in a kind of limbo. He was still working on the Hyderabad project, but now he had to completely re-think the issues of who was going to be doing what. The redundancy announcements had been put back until the big press release and announcement that Jimmy would be overseeing when Simon got back to Tokyo. He hadn't told Aesop or Dónal about the contract. He was waiting for the right time, hoping that there'd be one.

The single was pretty much in the bag. They couldn't make him stop that. He probably couldn't even stop it if he wanted to. Sparky and Dónal had almost finished editing the video and they'd already sent the English version of 'Lost' back to him so he could hear it. It was great. Sparky had added some Irish overdubbing to the fade out, just as Johnnie had suggested, and it made it sound very cool. Plaintive and lamenting, which of course just happened to suit Jimmy's new frame of mind. He hadn't told Simon about the song being released the next month, but Simon could blow it out his arse. It had happened before the contract so it wasn't part of the deal. As swan songs went, it wasn't a bad way to bring the curtain down.

Jimmy tried to be as upbeat as he could in work and when he was out with Aesop and Shiggy, but when he allowed himself to wallow he couldn't help feeling like he was after getting boxed in. The fifty grand meant nothing much except the fact that they'd given it to him. And Simon really wasn't talking shite about the job. It was a great opportunity and even the first phase was at least twelve month's worth of new and exciting projects. But still. This wasn't the closure he was after.

Aesop was also struggling. He was getting more and more pissed off with being an English teacher.

'They won't talk Jimmy!'

'What do they do?'

'They sit and take notes and ask me all these grammar questions that I haven't got a bleedin clue about. I keep trying to just sit and have a chat with them, but they're too shy, most of them. They want to learn how the language works, y'know? How the fuck do I know? It just does. If they'd talk they'd get better at it, but they want to know all the rules first so they don't make any mistakes. I mean, it's obvious when they make a mistake, but I can't just correct them. It's always *why, why, why*? I'm going mad.'

'Well Aesop, you're not being paid to shoot the breeze with them, are you? You're s'posed to be a teacher.'

'But I'm not a fuckin teacher, Jimmy. I don't even like teachers! They ruined my fuckin childhood, the bastards. And this lot don't even mess. They're all sitting up straight and paying attention and listening to everything I say. I've been with the same class of swots now for nearly a month. Three times a week. It's a nightmare.'

'I don't know what to tell you Aesop. No one ever said being a teacher was easy, did they? All those obedient pricks sitting there quietly, wanting to learn and understand what you're telling them. It's a tough job.'

'Yeah. Well anyway, only for the dosh I'd be packing it in.'

'Why don't you try getting them away from the classroom? They might loosen up a bit.'

'Where am I s'posed to bring them?'

'I don't know. The zoo or something.'

'The zoo? It's not a fuckin playschool, Jimmy.'

'At least it'll give them something to talk about, won't it?'

'Me arse. They'll just follow me around for the whole day, asking me questions and fuckin getting on me wick.'

'Oh God. Well at least you got a couple of rides out of it, didn't you?'

'Yeah. Four actually, including the receptionist. But even that wasn't worth it. One of the young ones I porked stopped talking in class altogether the next day. She hasn't said a word in two weeks. It's freaking me out.'

'Maybe she was disappointed with your sensitive approach to love-making.'

'Very unlikely, Jimmy. She nearly fainted when I took himself out and gave her the waggle. Look, I'm just … I don't know. When are we going home?'

'What? You want to go home? Are all the Jaffa Cakes gone? I can't go yet Aesop. I've probably got another month here the way things are going. You can go though.'

'I was thinking of it. It's just … I've been really getting into this *Taiko* thing. I thought I might try and hang on for a concert they're putting on in a few weeks.'

'Well you should definitely hang around for that. It'll be a great way to end the trip.'

'Yeah.'

Aesop suddenly looked thoughtful.

'What's wrong?' said Jimmy.

'Nothing. Well … now you have me thinking about Jaffa Cakes again. I forgot we were out. Fuck it anyway.'

Twenty-eight

JIMMY WAS chatting to Shiggy at the bar in Foley's on Friday night when Aesop swaggered in like it was his living-room. There were half a dozen Japanese people trailing behind him. He marched up to the lads and clapped Shiggy on the back.

'Howya lads.'

'Aesop. Who's this lot?'

'This is my class I was telling you about. Well, some of them. We're on a field trip.'

Jimmy looked at the clock over the bar.

'At half eight on a Friday night?'

'Yeah. They wouldn't let me bring them out during school, so I thought I'd invite them out anyway. We've just had our dinner in Noshinoya down the road. A bit rough, but I forced it down.'

Aesop turned back to the Japanese behind him and made the introductions. They all seemed a bit nervous, bowing and shaking hands with Shiggy and Jimmy.

Shiggy started talking to the one nearest him.

'No Shiggy,' said Aesop. 'No Japanese tonight. This is an English lesson, okay? We're all going to have a few pints and get to know each other. Isn't that right Ohno-san?'

Ohno-san went red and gave a kind of nod-bow. Jimmy looked them over. They'd already had a drink or two, he could see. They had that red Japanese beer-face thing going on. There were four girls and two guys, the girls dressed like they were going to a wedding. Aesop stepped closer to Jimmy and muttered under his breath.

'See the one in the pink? Suzuki-san. Vroom vroom, y'know? She's the one that hasn't said a word since I showed her me baby's arm. I threw two small glasses of Sapporo into her in the restaurant and I think she's coming out of her shell.'

'You're trying to get her drunk? Aesop, leave her alone for God sake.'

'I'm not trying to ride her again or anything. I just want her to open her gob for fuck sake. All of them. If we have a good session here tonight, then next week we'll all be mates in school and I can stop hearing about their crap hobbies and how much they like to watch fuckin telly at the weekend. We can have a laugh.'

'And when did this brainwave occur to you?'

'It's your brainwave, Jimmy. Well, it is if you just replace the word "zoo" with the word "pub".'

'I'm not sure about this Aesop. Japanese people don't really do sessions like you and me do them.'

'Stop being a homo. It's a brilliant plan. Now get friendly, right? I want them yapping their holes off in ten minutes.'

He called to Mick.

'Nine pints of Guinness please, Mick.'

'On the way, Aesop.'

Aesop turned back to Jimmy.

'Got paid today. I'm a bit wary about getting into a round with them. A couple of the girls don't look like they're up for a feed of pints. But I'm thinking, fuck it, I'll buy the first round anyway and see what happens. It'll be worth it if I can go through the whole of next week without wanting to strangle any of them.'

Mick put the pints up on the counter in a big line and Aesop paid for them and took a step back to admire the view.

'Did you ever see anything as beautiful in your life, Jimmy?'

'The Cliffs of Moher were nice.'

'The what?'

'Look them up.'

He started to hand the drinks around to lots of oohs and ahs. The girls all giggled at each other and the two guys looked a bit worried.

'Here you go everyone, look …' said Aesop. He put his pint to his mouth and took three inches off it before putting it back down on the counter and blessing himself. 'Now you go.'

They all took small sips and looked back at him.

'You like it?'

'Berry good,' said Ohno-san.

He looked around awkwardly and then blessed himself. The others were still looking at their glasses and wondering how in the name of Buddha they were going to be able to drink all that beer. Aesop grinned at them all.

'See? Isn't this fun? This is how we do it in Ireland. We're all friends here. So tell me, eh, Sato-san, do you like learning English?'

'Ah yes. I rike.'

'Great. Why?'

'Ah …'

'Come on. We're just talking. Say whatever you want.'

'Ah …'

'Everyone else keep drinking. Go on, get it down you. That's right, Suzuki-san, you drink up. Sato-san?'

'Ah … I … ah …'

'Okay, why do you want to learn English?'

'Ah … my company say … *anno* …'

'Yeah? What do they say?'

'Ah …'

'Okay, it's for work. Watanabe-san, why do you want to learn English?'

'*Anno*, I rike to American TV.'

'So you can watch telly? Okay. Fair enough. What's your favourite show?'

'Show?'

'Your favourite programme. Do you like, eh … *Friends*?'

'Ah yes. I rike.'

'Okay. Who's your favourite character in *Friends*?'

'Cha … char.'

'Do you like Rachel?'

'Ah yes. Rachel. I rike.'

'Yeah. She's nice, isn't she? Who else?'

'Who … ?'

'Do you like … eh … Joey?'

'Joey. I rike.'

'Good. Anyone else like *Friends*?'

They all looked at each other and then down at their drinks.

Aesop took another huge gulp of his pint. Jimmy could see beads of sweat on his forehead.

'So, does anyone here play the *Taiko* drums?' said Aesop. 'Hands up. Anyone?' He put his own hand up and looked around at them. The Japanese stared at his hand.

'Eh … that's a no, then. So, anyway … eh … you all met Jimmy here, right? Jimmy, is there anything you want to ask the lads?'

'Do you think Aesop is a good teacher?' said Jimmy.

Silence.

'Speak slowly Jimmy,' said Aesop. 'You have to speak slowly to them.'

'I think they understood.'

'They didn't. Shut up. Okay … oh look, my drink is nearly gone. I'll just buy myself another one, will I?'

Nothing.

'Right so. Here I go, I'm going to buy another drink. Does anyone else want one?'

'I'll have one,' said Jimmy.

'Fuck up, you. Anyone? No? Okay so, I'll just get the one so.'

Ohno-san was making a gallant effort at his pint, but was still only halfway down. His face was now edging into beetroot territory. The rest of them had barely broken the head on theirs.

'This isn't working, is it?' said Aesop to Jimmy, as he turned around again to catch Mick's attention.

'You're putting too much pressure on them, Aesop. Just leave them alone and let them relax before you start giving them the third degree. They'll be grand.'

'But this is what they're always like Jimmy. It's fuckin painful.'

'Are you always grilling them like this?'

'I'm only trying to get them going! We should … they … ah, fuck this for a Friday night. Here, you talk to them. I've got a pain in me arse with the fuckers.'

'You've only been in the place five minutes! And you're not leaving me with them all night either, you bollocks. Try and be a bit more patient and they'll be grand.'

'Fuck them. I'm going for a piss. Get me a pint there, will you?'

'I think I see why you're not enjoying being a teacher, Aesop.'

'I know. It's the dopey bastard students they keep giving me. This is s'posed to be a cultural exchange. I even tried talking about *Taiko* and got fuck all, did you see that? How am I s'posed to get them talking about Ireland? They're looking at their pints like I gobbed in them.'

'Aesop, there's more to Irish culture than getting gee-eyed on Guinness.'

'Is there?'

'Why don't you try talking about Joyce or something?'

'Joyce who?'

'James fucking Joyce. They're learning English. He's a famous writer. Maybe they'll be interested in that.'

'What did he write?'

'Are you serious? He wrote *Ulysses*. It's the most famous book in the world!'

'*Ulysses*? That doesn't sound very Irish.'

'He named it after the Greek Ulysses. Y'know? The great hero that travelled around the Mediterranean and had all these adventures?'

'Oh right. Yeah. That rings a bell. Hang on, is he the bloke that had the run-in with the Cyclops?'

'There. See? You have heard of him. But Joyce's *Ulysses* wasn't …'

'Oh yeah. I remember him now. He had a genie too, didn't he?'

Jimmy looked at him, puzzled.

'A genie?'

'Yeah. Remember? The mad magician shrunk his bird and he had to go and rescue her. Then he had to fight all them skeletons.'

Jimmy sighed. 'That was Sinbad the Sailor, Aesop.'

'Different bloke?'

'Just go and have your piss, will ye? You're a fuckin eejit.'

THINGS PICKED up over the next hour or so, but Shiggy leaned in to Jimmy and whispered as they both watched Aesop explain to his pupils how Irish monks invented whiskey to keep them warm when they were hiding in towers from Vikings in the winter. He'd bought everyone a glass of Bushmills Malt.

'Jimmy, don't sink this is good idea.'

'Which part?'

'Whiskey part. Already drunk. Rook.'

It was true. They'd all finished their first pint and were nursing fresh ones. Ohno-san and Suzuki-san were on their third pint and they were both starting to wobble a bit. On the upside, everyone was getting chattier.

Ohno-san stepped up to the bar and called one of the Japanese barmen over.

'Ooh, look,' said Aesop to the lads. 'Ohno-san is getting a round in. Good man Ohno-san!'

But Ohno-san wasn't buying a round. He handed over his tumbler of neat whiskey and waited until the barman gave it back to him, now filled with water and a hunk of ice the size of a tennis ball. He grinned and turned around with it, showing it to Aesop.

'Japanese style,' he said.

Aesop gaped at him.

'You're after fuckin murdering it Ohno-san, you dopey bastard.'

'Aesop …' said Jimmy.

'Look what he's after doing to it, Jimmy. It's not bleedin Jack

348

Daniels I'm after giving him.'

'Leave him alone. It's his drink.'

'It'll only be all pissy now on him.'

'Aesop, let him drink it his way. Cultural exchange, remember?'

'Bollocks to that! You can't …'

'Shut up, Aesop. You'll embarrass him.'

Ohno-san wasn't following the conversation anyway, but he was grinning now and starting to dance along with the music on the house system. They were playing Abba and he was obviously a bit of a closet fan. He danced over to Aesop and took his drink off him. Aesop looked on in horror as he handed it over the counter to the barman. Back it came, swimming in ice and water. Ohno-san gave it back to him and raised his own glass, his hips and shoulders bobbing away to 'Angel Eyes'.

'*Kampai*, Murray-sensei!'

Aesop looked at his glass like he was going to cry.

'Yeah. *Kampai*. Fuck.'

Five minutes later the countertop was full of watered down whiskey and half-finished pints. The Japanese crowd were all talking away to each other in Japanese and dancing along to whatever came on. Jimmy and Shiggy were still sitting at the bar, watching, and Aesop was standing with his back to them, looking at his newly-animated charges. He turned around.

'This wasn't the plan.'

'Well, you wanted them to loosen up, didn't you? Look at them. They're having a ball.'

'Yeah, but they're not talking to me, are they? We're s'posed to be bonding.'

'Aesop,' said Shiggy. 'I sink I know plobrem.'

'What?'

'I talk to Saito-san.'

'What did she say?'

'She say she don't understand you. Nobody can.'

'When?'

'All the time.'

'What?'

'She say you have funny accent. No one can understand when you talk.'

'Ah, that's just because it's noisy in here.'

'No no. In school tsoo. Understand maybe twenty per cent. Rest of time, no crue what you are talking about.'

'But ... but ... why didn't they say something?'

'You are *sensei*, Aesop.'

'So what?'

'In Japan, *sensei* berry important person. Must respect.'

'What's the point in that if it means I'm talking to the fuckin wall?'

Shiggy shrugged.

'Japanese way.'

'I don't believe this! Well then they must be the dopiest students in the world!'

'No, Aesop. You are just shit teacher. Sorry.'

Aesop opened his mouth to say something, but then just looked down at his whiskey and water and closed it again.

'Come on Aesop,' said Jimmy. 'How disappointed can you be? Being a teacher isn't for everyone. You have other talents.'

'I really tried, Jimmy.'

'It's not your fault. You're just ... well ... you're fucking crap at it, aren't you?'

'Why did she hire me then?'

'I don't know. Maybe she fancied you?'

'Fuck sake, Jimmy. That's not fair. You can't give someone a job just because you fancy them.'

'Really?'

'Of course not. That's shit. I thought I was doing something important. It felt good, y'know? I mean, sometimes I got a pain in the arse and all, but I was trying me best and it felt good when

I saw people using new words that I'd taught them and all that. And now it turns out that I'm fuckin useless and all Yamaguchi-san wanted was to get me into the sack. That's fuckin … that's so … disrespectful.'

Jimmy and Shiggy roared laughing.

'What?' said Aesop.

'If you do any more growing up on this trip,' said Jimmy, 'you'll start growing pubes.'

'Piss off. God, look at them.'

His class were having a really good time.

'What's the problem? They're loving it.'

'But they're talking Japanese. I might as well not even be here.'

Another hour went by and only three of them were left: Ohno-san, Suzuki-san and one of the other girls, Watanabe-san.

'Eh, Aesop, I think this is getting a bit messy,' said Jimmy.

'What?'

'Look at Ohno-san.'

Ohno-san had his shirt off and was standing up in the corner on one of the benches, belting out a very off-key version of 'Daydream Believer'. He was rubbing the head of an Irish girl who was sitting a little bit down from him. She pulled away from him and Jimmy caught the look in her eye. Either she wasn't a Monkees fan or else she was about to punch the fucking head off Ohno-san. Jimmy suspected the latter.

'Aesop, get him down off there before he gets into trouble.'

'Yeah. Christ, look at him.'

Aesop went over and tried to talk Ohno-san down from the chair. He wasn't having any of it. He shook his head and then roared again as Neil Diamond came on.

'Come on, Ohno-san. Time for beddie-byes for you.'

'*Sweeet Carorine! Du-du-du …*'

'Ohno-san, you're making a show of yourself. Get down, will you?'

Ohno-san shifted down the bench a little to get away from him.

'*I be incrined! Du-du-du* ...'

'For fuck sake, man. You're going to ...'

It happened. The pint in front of the girl next to him got the tip of his foot as he kicked out the chorus and it went spinning around the table, spraying lager everywhere.

'Jesus!' shouted the girl, jumping up and away from the table. 'You fucking eejit!'

Ohno-san giggled, his hand over his mouth.

'So sorry!' he said, laughing and bowing.

'I'm very sorry about this,' said Aesop. 'I'll get you another drink. What was it?'

'Tell your friend to feck off home before someone kills him.'

'I will. I'm trying to. Ohno-san, get down!'

Aesop looked around to Jimmy for help. Everyone in the bar was watching now.

'Jimmy ...'

'You're doing a great job, Aesop.'

'Bastard.'

He turned back and reached up to pull at one of Ohno-san's arms. Ohno-san struggled and started to hit Aesop on the head with his umbrella.

'You fucker. Stop that!'

Ohno-san was screaming laughing now, pulling his arm back away from Aesop, his other hand tapping the umbrella off his head and shoulders. He gave a final yank and Aesop lost his grip on him. Ohno-san's arm went flying back and his elbow went through the small window behind him.

'Oh fuck.'

The window, about ten inches across, was shattered with most of the glass falling outside. Ohno-san wasn't hurt, but he stopped singing and dancing, checking his arm for blood.

'See what happens when you act the prick?' said Aesop. 'Now

get fuckin down before you break something else.'

Ohno-san nodded and got down slowly. He looked subdued now and glanced around him. He bowed a few times at the rest of the bar.

'*Gomen-nasi* … sorry … *shitsurei-shimasu* …'

'Don't mind all that. Put your shirt on …'

'*Who the fuck did that?*'

A guy had come storming in from the small courtyard outside and marched straight over to Aesop.

'Was that you?'

'Eh, well … it was just an accident.'

The guy pushed him.

'That glass went all over my girlfriend.'

'I'm very sorry about that. Eh, the window just kind of gave way …'

'Did it? How about I make your fuckin teeth just kind of give way, ye fuckin prick.'

His girlfriend came running in.

'Rob, it's fine. Leave him alone.'

'No, I won't leave him alone. That could have gone in your eye.'

'I'm grand, really.'

The guy pushed Aesop again.

'What are you going to do about it, pal?'

'Look, I'm sorry. We were just … eh …'

Ohno-san stepped in front of Aesop and shouted.

'No!'

'What's your fuckin problem?' said the guy, shifting his attention.

'Fuck off,' said Ohno-san.

The guy pushed Ohno-san, sending him careering back into another table and sending more drinks flying. The bouncer pushed his way from the back of the bar and grabbed the guy from behind.

'All right. Calm down, calm down.'

'Get the fuck off me you, ye big fuckin gorilla.'

'You're out of here. Come on.'

'Get off. I'll fuckin batter ye. You too, you little fucker.'

'Let's go.'

The bouncer bundled him out the door, his girlfriend following him.

'Fuck off!' yelled Ohno-san after him, getting off the floor and running to try and catch up to him.

Jimmy grabbed him as he tried to go past.

'Aesop, get this fucker into a taxi, will ye?'

'Right.'

Aesop took one arm, Shiggy took the other one and they got him out the door and up the stairs. Jimmy followed with the shirt and the umbrella. They saw the other guy walking down the road and arguing with his girlfriend. Jimmy whistled for a taxi to stop and they quickly bundled Ohno-san into it. They threw in the shirt and umbrella after him, slamming the door and watching it take off towards Roppongi Crossing.

'Could've done without that,' said Jimmy, scratching his head.

'Yeah. Oh fuck. We're not done yet,' said Aesop.

'What?'

'Look.'

Their friend from earlier had heard them whistle and saw them out on the street. He wanted to settle up. His bird was trying to drag him by the arm in the opposite direction, but he kept shaking her off and broke into a trot.

'Right, you,' he said to Aesop when he reached them. 'Let's go.'

'Listen man, I didn't do that to the window. It was the bloke in the taxi.'

'Me hole. I know it was you.'

He shoved Aesop in the chest, knocking him backwards

until he tramped on Shiggy's foot. Shiggy yelled; a peculiar high-pitched screech. They all stopped and looked around at him.

'Arrgh! *Itai*!!' he roared. He had his head right back, contorted in pain. Then he straightened up and stepped in front of Aesop, his face a picture of fury.

'Okay,' he said. 'Ret's go.'

The guy looked at him. Shiggy was half his size.

'It wasn't you. It was this fucker.'

'Now is me. Come on.'

Shiggy took a step back and went into a fighting, Bruce Lee stance. He bounced up and down on his toes and put his arms out in front of him into two fists. It looked pretty impressive. He whipped his head to the side and back to loosen up. The guy's girlfriend caught up to them.

'Rob, stop it! Come on. Let's just go home.'

'Hang on … I … I was talking to this bloke, not you. What's your problem?'

'You are my ploblem.'

Jimmy and Aesop looked at each other. They'd never even seen Shiggy raise his voice before. What was with the Jackie Chan shapes?

The guy put his hands down and looked at them all. The fight was gone out of him.

'Rob, please?'

She had his hand again now, pulling him away.

'Next time, pal,' he said to Aesop, pointing at him.

Aesop was going to say something smart, but he caught Jimmy's eye and shut his mouth again. The girl pulled him away and they walked off.

Shiggy relaxed and looked around at the others. They all let out a huge sigh.

'Nice one, Aesop,' said Jimmy.

'You can't blame me for that.'

'You got him drunk.'

'He got himself drunk. I'm not his Mammy.'

'Come on. Let's just go back in.'

Back in the pub, two of the wait staff were clearing up the mess. Jimmy looked around. Watanabe-san and Suzuki-san were exactly where they'd left them. Aesop went to the bar. He brought a pint of lager over to the girl who'd lost her pint and apologised again. Then he bought drinks for the table that had gone flying when Ohno-san was pushed into it.

'It's your round,' said Jimmy, smiling at him, when he came back to get his own drink.

'So much for getting paid today,' said Aesop, looking in his wallet. 'I've blown three hundred euro already tonight.'

'Well at least I think this pair are done for the night.'

'Yeah. I should probably get them a taxi as well. Christ, what a fuckin disaster.'

He started tapping the girls on the shoulder. They were both fast asleep.

'Suzuki-san? Suzuki-san? Time to go home.'

She didn't move.

'Fuck sake. Watanabe-san? Hey, Watanabe-san? You ready to go home?'

Watanabe-san mumbled something.

'Come on. That's right. Time to go home. Will we get you a taxi? Watanabe-san?'

She raised her head without opening her eyes and vomited two pints of Guinness all over his jeans and shoes before resting her head back down on the bar.

Aesop stood there, dripping, and looking down at himself.

'Fuck.'

The other two were creased up laughing.

'Fuck.'

He looked at the two of them, sighed and then headed off to the toilet.

'Hey Shiggy,' said Jimmy, when he stopped laughing. 'Since when do you know karate?'

'Karate? I don't know.'

'But what was all that poncing around up on the street there? I thought you were going to kill him.'

Shiggy laughed.

'No Jimmy. Only pretend.'

'What? You can't fight?'

'No. Big chicken.'

'But the guy was huge! What would you have done if he'd wanted to fight?'

Shiggy shrugged.

'Don't know, Jimmy. Shit pants, plobabry.'

Twenty-nine

MONDAY MORNING in Tokyo, hot and shitty. Jimmy checked his inbox as he supped on a huge paper cup of cappuccino and saw the mail from Simon. It was the list of people who were to be made redundant in Dublin. He'd worked with most of them for the best part of ten years. Jimmy scanned the document twice more and read Simon's accompanying email half a dozen times. The whole thing was gone to shit. The company had been completely re-moulded to fit with how Kyotosei wanted to do things. Jimmy himself would be spending the next two years flying between Dublin, Hyderabad and Tokyo and when he wasn't doing that, he'd be in New York with the new sales staff trying to pitch to the big financial houses there. It was as though his career had changed completely overnight. He'd be working with new people, doing a different job for new clients and very little of what had been important just a few weeks ago now counted for anything at all. He sat and stared at the computer monitor and felt completely depressed as he read the names again. Marco and Cathy were getting the boot.

The real pox of it, though, was what Simon said in the email. He, Jimmy, was to go back to Ireland in two weeks to announce the redundancies. Simon wouldn't be there; he was going on vacation after he'd finished travelling with the trade delegation from the Irish government. He was in Bangalore at the moment with a bunch of other 'industry leaders' and half the bloody *Dáil*. Once he'd fired everyone, Jimmy would then fly back out to Tokyo for what would probably be at least a six-month stretch while he got up to speed with the Japanese operations. He'd also be put on an intensive Japanese language course to help him communicate with his new colleagues. Instead of the apartment, he'd be doing a home-stay with a Japanese family for those six months. He'd be living with them as a boarder and was expected to immerse himself in Japanese life.

Jimmy read the mail again in a daze. This was it – the very reason he wanted to stay with the company was that he wanted control over what happened to his career, something he didn't have with fickle music fans. But what kind of fucking control did he have now? Six months in a Japanese homestay? For fuck sake. He was supposed to be like that poor little dog, Hachiko. Obedient, dedicated, devoted. He was supposed to go home and fire his friends – while Simon ponced around the Seychelles – without ever having been given the chance to plead a case for keeping them on, or negotiate better packages if they decided to leave.

Jimmy clicked the email shut and bit at the end of his pen. He knew he didn't want this anymore. He'd made a terrible fucking mistake. Everyone had gotten a raw deal. Cathy and Marco ... Dónal and Aesop ... Jimmy himself. The only ones who were really ahead were the management of Kyotosei-Eirotech. Jimmy stood up and went down the lift to the lobby. He went outside and walked up the road for about fifteen minutes. He stopped outside a sandwich shop and looked in the window. Something about his reflection caught his eye and when he bent in to take a closer look, he could see the red mark on his neck again. It tingled and prickled in the heat. He touched it with his fingers for a second, noticing that his old friend heartburn was back as well, and then turned around and walked back to the office. A new mail had come in while he was out. It was from Dónal. Sparky had put together a first cut of the video. They'd just finished it and Dónal wanted to show Jimmy immediately. Jimmy looked at the clock on the wall opposite him. It was two in the morning in Dublin. Sunday night. They must have been working at it all weekend.

He plugged in his headphones and watched and listened. It was amazing. Totally professional-looking. A real video. And the sound was great too. Jimmy sat and smiled to himself as he played it two more times. When it cut to the gig footage in What the Dickens, it might as well have been in the Albert Hall. It looked huge and Sparky had added lots of blurred edges and atmospheric fades. It finished with a close-up along Jimmy's mike stand and into his face with a blue spotlight shining on his profile. It looked absolutely fucking brilliant. Eventually he stopped it. He was still grinning away to himself like a fool. Then he clicked back to the email from Simon and his face fixed itself into a cold stare again. He thought about calling Dónal at the studio, but then decided against it. He didn't know what to tell him, how to tell him what he'd done. All he knew was that he'd fucked up. The mark on his neck burned and seemed to be crawling up his cheek as he looked back at the laptop and made a decision.

Fuck this job. He didn't want this. He wanted out.

THE REST of the week was totally depressing. It was wet and hot and Jimmy just felt weighed down by everything, not least the heavy humid air that seemed to settle on him every time he stepped outside. Aesop was even worse. He'd been fired from his teaching job. Yamaguchi-san had found out from someone that he'd been riding pupils. She'd called him into her office on Wednesday morning and told him he wouldn't be needed anymore.

'Sorry to hear that, man,' said Jimmy.

'Yeah. Well, to be honest, I was starting to really fuckin hate it.'

'But did it not go better after your little field trip?'

'Fuck no. They didn't mention it on Monday morning. Not a single fucking word. Can you believe it?'

'Well, Shiggy was saying the Japanese don't harp on about it when they get drunk. They just forget about it the next day and no one takes the piss.'

'Well it's true. I went in and started the lesson as normal, and they just did the usual. Ohno-san watched baseball on Saturday,

Saito-san played with her cat. Blah blah. So I asked them did they enjoy the pub? They nod. Grand. So wasn't it funny when Ohno-san was singing? Nothing. They all went quiet and didn't say another word except to answer questions from their workbooks. A complete waste of time, Jimmy. And fuckin money.'

'What did Yamaguchi-san say?'

'About bringing them on the piss?'

'About you riding pupils.'

'Ah, she just said it was inappropriate behaviour.'

'That's fair enough. It *was* pretty inappropriate, Aesop.'

'But you're not supposed to go ratting to the principal, Jimmy.'

'Well, you said they were swots …'

'Still. Anyway I think it was the receptionist that told her, not one of the students.'

'It was going to happen sooner or later, Aesop. What did Johnnie say?'

'Haven't spoken to him yet.'

'Right.'

'Fuck all this anyway.'

Aesop looked pretty down.

'The video's cool, though, isn't it?' said Jimmy, trying to cheer him up.

'Jaysis, yeah. Deadly. I know it's us on there, but it feels like it's someone else, doesn't it?'

'Yeah, a bit.'

'I've got a really good feeling about it, Jimmy. I think we're going to make it, y'know?'

Jimmy said nothing.

'Really. When I saw it, I just thought … fuck it, that's a really good song and a really good video and we've got as much right to be rockstars as anyone else. If that crowd get behind it in England …'

'Yeah. Hang on, I thought you hated the song?'

'Well, I do. But it'll sell, man. Get us on the map, y'know? I mean, Lizzy's first single was "Whiskey in the Jar", wasn't it? It wasn't like they kept making trad songs after that. The album will have "Meatloaf's Underpants" on it, won't it?'

'Aesop, it's not good to assume there's going to be an album.'

'There will, Jimmy. I feel it in me water. We're going to be huge.'

JIMMY COULDN'T put it off any longer. He called Dónal on Thursday when he got home.

'You signed a contract?'

'Yeah.'

'Jesus. What does it say?'

'Well, it just means I'm tied in to Eirotech.'

'Well, that's just like it was before, right? I said we'd work around you. We'll manage, Jimmy, don't be worrying about it. Listen, I sent the video to Sultan and they nearly pissed themselves when they saw it. They're all over it, Jimmy, I'm telling you. They're putting it out next month. Jimmy, I know you'll be busy when you get back and it'll be hard work, but I'm nearly sure they'll go for the album now. All we need is a few more songs maybe, just to give us some room to play with. Sparky can do all the mixing during the week when you're not here. If the album comes out I just know it'll blow everyone away, then you can look at what you're going to do about all this work stuff. I was thinking about it, and …'

'Dónal, listen a minute.'

'What?'

Jimmy took a deep breath.

'There's a bit of a problem.'

'Jimmy, don't fuck with me now.'

'I'm not. Listen, the contract I signed says I can't work for anyone else.'

'What do you mean?'

'They're saying I can't keep playing with The Grove. They want me to stop.'

'What?!'

'That's what they said. No gigs, albums, me being on the telly … they want me to give it up.'

'Tell them to fuck off!'

'I can't Dónal. It's in the contract.'

Dónal went quiet.

'Listen, I'm really sorry about this,' said Jimmy. 'I fucked up.'

'Yeah. Sounds like you did, Jimmy. What does the contract say exactly?'

'Well, it says … mainly it says … eh …'

'Oh fuck it. Fax it to me. Now.'

'I can't do it from here.'

'Well do it from work tomorrow.'

'Dónal, they said their lawyers looked it over. I'm stuck. He said they'd sue me if I tried to play or left the company.'

'Jimmy, fax me the contract. But c'mere, you need to tell me something before I get involved in all this. What do you want? What do you want to happen? I really can't afford to fuck around anymore, man. You understand that, right? Things are …'

'I want out of that contract. I'm after making a complete fucking balls of everything Dónal. I just want to play music. That company is fucked up. I don't want to be there anymore. They want me to fire my mates, man.'

'Right. Leave it to me. Send me the contract. I'll talk to you when I look at it.'

'Dónal, I'm really sorry about this. I thought I was doing the right thing. I just got fucked.'

'Well, that happens. But I wish you'd come to me, you gobshite.'

'I know. Look, I've been thinking about nothing else for months now. I kept trying to stick with things here, but they just kept changing everything around. Now I'm locked into this. The whole deal with Kyotosei was closed because of me. I nailed it for them. They're not going to let me go. Dónal, I'm due home in a couple of weeks, but they want me back out here for six months after that.'

'Six months? No fucking way, Jimmy. What if we got an album deal? Maybe you could record it out there, but … actually no. Fuck that. That's a shit way to try and do it. Leave it with me, Jimmy.'

'Thanks Dónal.'

'Yeah. Well, just do me a favour will you? Don't dig yourself any more holes out there.'

'I won't.'

'Good. How's Johnnie?'

'He's grand. Said he might have another gig for us, but I don't think I'll be here for it. I hope he hasn't gone to too much trouble or …'

'Don't worry about gigs out there for the moment. We've got other stuff to sort out. I'll talk to Johnnie. Look, I'll talk to you tomorrow, right?'

'Yeah. Seeya Dónal.'

'Cheers.'

Thirty

JIMMY LOOKED up from his notes at the telly.

'Seven hundred,' he said.

Aesop was on the couch. It was pretty much all he did now, lying there and watching telly and messing about with the camcorder and the computer. Funds were low again since he'd been sacked and he was doing his best not to go to Foley's until Happy Hour kicked in. They were both feeling a little bit deflated. Their Excellent Adventure was coming to an end and they didn't really know where they stood, where things were going or even what the fuck they'd be doing this time next month. The only thing they were sure of – the only good thing – was that the single would be out by then. In the meantime, when Jimmy wasn't in work or working his bollocks off on the speech he had to give Simon's trade delegation from Ireland on Monday night, they were just hanging about in the apartment and waiting and watching BBC World. And getting on each other's nerves.

'Jimmy, who's that bloke talking to the lady?'

'Michael Aspel.'

'Right. And what does Michael Aspel know about antiques?'

'He presents the show, doesn't he?'

'If she's showing him her plates, then they're not worth a wank. If they *were* worth a wank, she'd be showing one of the experts.'

'But …'

'Come on Jimmy, no wonder you never win. You don't even know the format of the show. Will you ever pay attention? Good stuff equals experts. Shite stuff or background on the venue equals Michael Aspel.'

'I don't want to play this stupid fucking game anymore. Anyway, I can't concentrate on this with the telly on.'

'Well turn it off then. For fuck sake … you're no fun anymore.'

Jimmy picked up the remote and switched off the television.

He shoved Aesop out of the way so he could check his email and make sure the flights were confirmed.

'All good?' said Aesop.

'Yeah. I got Shiggy to sort it out. The three of us are on the same flight. Tuesday evening. We've two hours' wait in Bangkok and then home through Amsterdam.'

'Can we not hang about Bangkok for the night and go the next day?'

'For what?'

'Well, y'know … it'd be like the song. Anyway, there's something I missed on the island, and I heard you can do it in Bangkok.'

'What?'

'I'm not sure what it is exactly, but Andy mentioned it. Something called the Ping Pong Show. Have you heard of it?'

'No. Is it like a cabaret or something?'

'I think so.'

'Doesn't sound like you. Or Andy.'

'Yeah, but he said I should definitely see it.'

'Well you'll have to do it next time Aesop. We're just passing through.'

'Yeah. It's probably just something stupid.'

'Right. Well … I s'pose that's about it then.'

Jimmy looked around the apartment. It seemed like they'd been living there for years. Thailand was a distant memory. And Dublin? Like they'd only read about the place.

'Yeah. Jaysis,' said Aesop. 'This was some trip, wasn't it?'

'Yeah. But … ah shite … I'm all nervous waiting around to see how the contract stuff works out. And I still have to work on this presentation in case it doesn't. It's a bit of a bummer.'

'How? Are you not happy with how things turned out?'

'What?' said Jimmy, looking at him.

'Well, this was a big trip for you. All the stuff you had to do … the band, work, all that. Are you happy with how it went?'

'Am I happy? Were you not listening to me in the pub the other night when I told you I was fucking totally depressed, that work had completely turned to shite and that now I was depending on Dónal to get me out of the whole fucking big mess?'

'Well ...'

'Remember when I said everything I've worked for since I left college was up in smoke and I had to go home and fire Marco and Cathy? And the only thing I had left in the world, now that the fruits of twelve years' hard slog was nothing but bitter fucking disillusionment, was the faint hope that I can get released from the contract and somehow – *somehow* – make it in the music business.'

'I thought you were just having a rant.'

'I *was* having a fucking rant! You were s'posed to be listening to it.'

'I was listening Jimmy, but you just seemed very down and all and ... I ... kind of got a bit bored.'

'Jesus ...'

'I got the general idea though, Jimmy.'

'Fuck sake.'

'What did Dónal say anyway?'

'I'm still waiting for him to call. He said he'd call tonight. But the last time I spoke to him, he said it didn't look too bad. It just depends on what they decide to do if I want to get out of it.'

'What could they do?'

'Well, they'll probably just tell me to go. I mean, it's not worth anyone's hassle to have me there if I don't want to be, right? Dónal reckons it'll be fine.'

'So why don't you just quit now?'

'I have to wait till I see Simon, don't I? He's in China now. He'll be back Monday morning and then the big press release is on Monday night. I can bring someone, by the way. I s'pose you're up for free beer and food? Just don't do anything stupid, you hear me? Anyway, I wanted to see if I can do anything about

Marco and Cathy and a couple more of the heads in there before I take my leave of the place. The deal they got was a bit shit.'

'Vintage fuckin Jimmy.'

'What?'

'Up to your beanbag in all this crap, and you're still thinking of everyone else.'

'Aesop, Marco is trying to start a new life with your sister, remember? Of course I'm going to try and get him a few extra quid.'

'What about Shiggy? Does he know you're trying to get out of Dodge?'

'I haven't told him yet. I haven't seen him, sure. The poor bastard is really up to his goolies now. He has to walk into the office in Dublin next week and take over the place. First order of business, "Jimmy, can you escort the following people out to the carpark". They're after putting a lot of pressure on him, Aesop. I'll tell him over the weekend.'

'What's he going to say?'

'I don't know. But he won't be doing fucking cartwhee …'

The phone rang and Jimmy jumped on it.

'Dónal? Oh thank fuck …' he said.

'What?' said Dónal. 'What's wrong?'

'Everything! I was on to Simon during the week. He's flying in on Monday with this trade delegation thing.'

'So what?'

'Dónal, they're putting on a big reception in the Irish ambassador's gaff. Everyone is going to be there. I thought he was just talking big before, but it's all true. The Minister for bloody Trade and everything! All these journalists are travelling with them too. About forty delegates, including trade heads and Enterprise Ireland, civil servants and who the fuck knows else. They've already been to India and China and now they're coming to Tokyo.'

'Jimmy, what's that got to do with you?'

'The reception has to do with me. It's the big official announcement. Kyotosei-Eirotech is officially signed into existence. Sign the deal, shake hands, smile for the camera. A triumph for everybody involved and all that shite. A shining example of how two pioneering companies can overcome cultural differences to forge deep and long-lasting ties in the twenty-first century. Dónal, I'm actually reading that off the fucking invitation! I'm s'posed to be giving the keynote speech on the whole thing. And that's after Simon and the bleedin ambassador unveil me and Shiggy as the new fucking poster boys for Japan-Ireland relations!'

'Oh. Right.'

'Please tell me you found a way out. I can't do it. I can't go up there and tell everyone how brilliant it all is and then have them find out that I'm packing it in. Shiggy should do it on his own or with Simon. I have to get out before Monday, Dónal. I fucking *have* to! This is getting too big. He says it might be covered by the fucking news at home for Christ sake! I need to let Simon know that I'm getting out.'

'Afraid it's not that simple, Jimmy.'

'What?! You said it'd be cool!'

'I checked with a couple of mates and that contract you signed is airtight. There's only two ways out of it. Either they just let you go because they're being nice, or you buy yourself out – if they let you.'

'Buy myself out? How?'

'You give them money. Specifically, you have to negotiate your way out of it. I don't think they're just going to let you walk. This merger they're doing is all over the papers here. My mate works in this area. He says that if you leave, they'll probably have to replace you for at least six months with some big-name consultants. It could be as long as a year. They'd need to do that to maintain full continuity for existing clients as well as keep up appearances, especially with all this publicity. Consultants cost money, Jimmy. You'll have to come up with the value of the contract in euro terms. Three years' salary my mate reckons, two if you're lucky. Plus, I'm guessing that they'll want something on top of that for the hassle, and possibly the finder's fee to replace you. I'm estimating here, but you'll need to come up with around three hundred grand to end this thing.'

'Three hun …'

'That includes the fifty they gave you for signing it in the first place. They'll obviously want that back.'

'But … where would I get that much money?'

'I don't know. I really wish you'd spoken to me before you signed, Jimmy. I think we're fucked. I might have been able to cover some of it as a loan from Sin Bin. But this? No way. We're a little bit strapped for cash just at the moment. I can try Sultan, but they're obviously going to tell me to fuck off. Maybe if the album was already flying high, but with only a single … no chance.'

'I'd have to completely re-mortgage the house! I'd be up to my bollocks in debt. It'd take me ten years to recover from it. And that's if I had a fucking job like the one I do now!'

'Jimmy, they mightn't even accept money. Or if they did, you don't know what the figure might be. There's still the other way.'

'Which one?'

'You ask them to let you go.'

'Just ask them?'

'Yep. Maybe they'll do it. Unlikely, but you never know, right?'

'Dónal, did you not hear what I just said? Me and Shiggy *are* the company in Ireland.'

'Jimmy, I'm just saying that the contract is solid. I was hoping we'd get them on misrepresentation, but that won't work. You've been with them for years and involved in the formation of this whole new entity. You can't pretend you didn't know what was going on. Cooling-off is no good either. Man, you have to talk to them. Ask them to let you go. If they do, great. If they want money, you have to pay them. That's really all there is to it, unless they fire you or something and I don't see that happening, do you?'

'No.'

'Well then. Get onto your boss and tell him you've changed your mind. When are you back in Ireland?'

'Wednesday. We fly out on Tuesday night.'

'Good. Okay, well all I can say is good luck Jimmy.'

'Yeah. Thanks.'

'Call me as soon as you know anything. 'Lost' is supposed to be released the week after next. I need to know what's going on before that happens.'

'Why?'

'Jimmy, we can't put the single out while you're working there.'

'What?! I thought …'

'No way would Sultan take the risk. They'd be leaving themselves open to huge losses if they had to pull it off the shelves while you were tied up in a court case.'

'Fucking hell … a court case?! But …'

'You beginning to see how big all this is, Jimmy?'

'Fuck. Yeah. I am.'

'Good. It's not looking too pretty right now, Jimmy. If that single doesn't go out, there'll be … repercussions. Talk to them, Jimmy. Be nice and hope for the best. Otherwise I don't know what we're going to bloody do. Fuck it anyway … we were so close. Listen man, I have to head. I've a meeting. I'll talk to you later, right? Let me know what they say.'

Jimmy hung up and bit at his thumb. He felt sick. Aesop looked up from the couch, where he was messing about with the computer again.

'Wrong number?'

'He can't get me out of the contract.'

'Bollocks.'

'He says I'll have to try and blag my way out of it myself.'

'Can I help? I'm good at stuff like that.'

'I don't think so, Aesop.'

'You never let me help, Jimmy. Come on.'

'Aesop, this is serious. If I can't get out of the contract then it's all over. Everything.'

'But the single …'

'No! There won't be a single! It might be illegal for them to release a single while I'm contracted to someone else.'

Aesop stood up. 'But … but … fuck that, Jimmy! The single was always fine! Why has that changed?'

'Because of the contract I signed.'

'Why did you sign it then, you fuckin eejit?'

'You fuckin handed it to me and gave me a pen.'

'Well you never said it was going to affect the fuckin single.'

'I didn't know!'

'Dopey cunt!'

'Fuck off! I've enough on me mind without you starting in on me as well.'

'There has to be a single,' said Aesop. 'Jimmy, there has to be.'

'I'll talk to Simon.'

'Ride him if you have to. Jimmy, this was s'posed to be it, man. Everything was cool … we were … everything was …'

'Well, I'm sorry if this inconveniences you, Aesop!'

'Fuck sorry! What are we going to do about it? I'm not going back on the scratcher, Jimmy, I don't care. No fuckin way am I going back to that. Let me help, Jimmy. I must be able to do something. C'mon …'

'Like what, Aesop? What are you going to do? What are you doing now, for fuck sake?'

Jimmy walked over to the table and looked at the computer.

'See?' he said, pointing at the screen. 'Some bird with her tits out. That's your contribution, is it? This is serious Aesop, and you're sitting there downloading this shit off the Web. On my fucking company's computer, by the way. Get rid of it, will you?

I'm in enough fucking trouble as it is. Where do you find that crap anyway? Christ, you've a whole folder full of it, look.'

'I was looking at a celebrity lookalike site. Lots of girls that look like Halle Berry. I was using it for inspiration. But once you're at a site like that, you're just a couple of clicks away from all kinds of filth, Jimmy. It's shocking the stuff they have on there. So I just downloaded some of it and …'

'Fuck sake, Aesop. Can you not see what's going on here? This isn't Aesop-land we're in. This is real.'

Aesop looked down at the computer but didn't say anything.

Jimmy took out his phone. What was he meant to say to Simon to get out of this mess? Monday night was the night. The night that Simon showed off his new baby to the world, and Jimmy was supposed to be the one wheeling it around in a pram. He couldn't leave things till he got to Dublin. He had to do something now, before it was all official and public. He dialled. Then he pressed the off button. Simon wouldn't let him go. Not in a million fucking years. Jesus, what was he going to do? He had to come up with something.

'I need to go for a walk,' he said.

WHEN HE got back two and a half hours later and saw that the light was off in the living-room, he assumed Aesop was probably out somewhere on the piss. He flicked on the switch and then saw Aesop move. He was lying on the couch. There was music playing softly on the laptop.

'Oh. You're here.'

Silence.

'Jaysis, it's windy out there. I think there's a typhoon coming in.'

'*Orrrrr … laaaa …*' mumbled Aesop. '*Orrrr … laaa …*' Then he giggled.

He sat up and looked over at Jimmy, squinting in the light. Jimmy stood at the door and stared at him.

'What's wrong?'

Aesop's eyes were puffy and red and the front of his shirt was stained.

'Nothing.'

'What? Something's fucking wrong. What is it? Is it Jennifer? Your Da? Jesus, Aesop, tell me what's up!'

Jimmy shut the door and walked over to Aesop. Then he saw the bottle on the table. It was a two-litre bottle of *sake*. Or, at least, it used to be. There was only a couple of inches left in the bottom of it.

'Tell me you didn't drink all that.'

'Not yet. There's a bit in it still.'

'Oh God. Why? For fuck sake Aesop, will you tell me what happened?'

'Nothing fuckin happened Jimmy.'

'Well why are you fucking crying then?'

'I'm not crying. I just … have something in me eye.'

'Your shirt is soaking, you eejit.'

'That's *sake*.'

He stood up and went into the kitchen. He was out of his face with the drink and stumbled against the table on the way in and then fell over a chair and landed on the floor. Jimmy ran in and helped him up. He led him back out to the couch and then went and got him a glass of water.

'Here.'

'Thanks.'

Aesop drank the water, spilling some of it down his front, and handed the glass back to Jimmy.

'Aesop, why did you drink all that shit?'

'I just did.'

'You don't just sit on your own in an apartment and drink two litres of *sake*. Even you don't do that.'

Aesop leaned over and turned up the volume on the laptop and then pointed at it.

Jimmy listened. Christy Moore was singing 'Nancy Spain'.

'So what?' he said.

'They said I could do a solo at the *Taiko* gig. But I don't know any of the Japanese pieces well enough and they all work so hard on them I didn't want to just ad-lib something or chance me arm, so the *sensei* said I could do an Irish piece. I borrowed a *bodhrán* off Mick in Paddy's and was looking for something I could do. I started off with the drum bits from *Riverdance*, and then I started to find other bits and I was putting together some ideas. But while I was doing that, I left the thing playing in the background like a fuckin eejit, didn't I? Your trad playlist.'

'But you don't even like trad.'

'I know. But I had a couple of glasses from the bottle you got as a welcome present. Then I listened a bit more. A few more ballads. A few more glasses. The next thing I know, I'm staring into space, drinking the bottle from the neck and getting drunker and sadder until I'm completely locked and wondering why I'm all the way out here in Asia instead of back home looking at the Mountains of Mourne sweeping down to the fucking sea. I was thinking of McGuigans and the lads and ... even me Da and Jennifer and Peggy's dinners. Taking the piss out of Sparky and Norman and ... and Irish girls, Jimmy. I miss Irish girls, man. Jimmy, every song on that yoke has some fucker bawling his eyes out over something. Every song Jimmy! Every one of them is either away from Ireland and wants to go home, or else he's in love with someone who's dead or married or has a gammy fuckin leg. And that's not even including the songs where it's the English that are acting the prick.'

'You fucking absolute idiot, Aesop!'

'What?'

'You can't drink a big bottle of piss and then listen to two hours of Irish ballads on your own, you gobshite. Everyone knows that. Especially when you're not used to it. What did you expect?'

'I was just listening to it and then it started to get in on me.'

'Stupid bastard. Of course it's going to get in on you. Aesop, you're lucky you didn't stick your head in the oven.'

'I wasn't planning on doing it, was I? The bastards get into your brain and start poking and poking away at you until you start asking yourself what the fucking point is of being alive at all if you're Irish. Anyway, the oven is bollixed. The knob fell off.'

Jimmy shook his head and went in to the fridge to get a beer.

'Will you get me one?' called Aesop.

'Have you not done enough damage to yourself for one day?'

'Just to get the taste of this shite out of my mouth.'

Jimmy brought back two beers and they sat listening to the laptop. Eventually they stopped talking and just looked through the gloom at the screen. 'Nothing But the Same Old Story', 'The Town I Loved So Well', 'Ordinary Man' … they went on and on … 'From Clare to Here', 'Slievenamon', 'Scorn Not His Simplicity' – a right fucking tear-jerker that one, 'The Rare Oul Times', 'The Fields of Athenry' …

Eventually Eleanor McEvoy started singing 'A Woman's Heart' and Aesop turned to Jimmy and grinned.

'Now that's what I call fuckin sad.'

Jimmy laughed.

Aesop reached over to the computer and pulled it towards him.

'I made you a present, look. A peace offering after you got your knickers in a twist earlier.'

'Is it a naked woman? Because …'

'No. Actually, I've been working on it for a few days. It's a new screensaver, look.'

Aesop clicked to preview the screensaver and straight away the video for 'Lost' came on and filled the screen and speakers.

'What do you think?'

'It's brilliant!' said Jimmy. 'How did you do that?'

'Took me fuckin ages. But I found something on the Web that

let me use movies as screensavers, so I thought it'd be a laugh.'

'It's cool. Thanks.'

'No problem.'

When the song was over, the screen went black and they just looked at it for a minute.

'Me Mam's song is on there too,' said Aesop, quietly.

'What?'

Aesop found it on the computer and clicked play.

'She used to sing this when I was small.'

Luke Kelly came on, singing 'Raglan Road'. They sat in silence, listening. Jesus, the man's voice sent a chill up your back. It was amazing.

'Do you know what the words mean?' said Aesop, looking up.

'Not really,' said Jimmy. 'But I think it's from a poem. Patrick Kavanagh or Brendan Behan or someone like that.'

'Da always said only two people in the world could sing that song. Luke Kelly and Mam.'

Jimmy looked over at him. Aesop was staring at the computer screen, his head still swaying slightly from the *sake*.

'I must've got me Da's voice, mustn't I?'

'It's a great song,' said Jimmy.

'They let me in to say goodbye to her. I didn't know I was saying goodbye, but I s'pose she did. I was only eight. She told me to look after Jennifer.'

Fuck. Jimmy reached for the bottle and took a huge mouthful. Aesop never talked about his Mam.

'She said to do me best in school and be good for me Da. And always to remember that I was special and that she loved me.'

The song shimmered through the room like an echo.

'I didn't want to stay. She had all these tubes and wires coming out of her. I was afraid. I think I started to cry.'

'You were only a kid.'

'I remember being at the door and she called me back to give her another hug, but I just ran out to me nanny in the hall.'

'Fuck. Aesop, you were only …'

'That was it. I think she died the next day or the day after. Nanny looked after us. And Peggy of course. We have loads of photos and all in the house, but it's only when I hear Luke Kelly singing that I really remember her properly. Her face … her voice … y'know?'

'Jesus, Aesop. I'm sorry.'

'But sometimes when I hear the song, I … I realise that … what a fuckin waster I ended up being on her. I never did anything for her, Jimmy. She's up there, looking at me, and all I've ever done was make her worry about me. I was shit in school, I tormented me Da, never had a job, got fired out here from teaching, I'm always fucking around with women. I'm fuckin crap at everything. Except this.' He pointed at the *bodhrán*. 'That's it.'

'Aesop …'

'Jimmy, please. Try and fix this thing with your boss, will ye? Anything I can do …'

Jimmy opened his mouth to say something and then just sighed.

'I swear, Jimmy. If I don't do this, I don't …'

He shrugged. His eyes were bleary and tired and his face flushed, but he didn't even look sad. He looked scared.

'I'll try,' said Jimmy.

Aesop nodded.

Jimmy looked down at the computer.

'Look, go to bed. You can read all about him tomorrow. I need to do a bit of work on this presentation.'

'You'll talk to your boss tomorrow?'

'Yeah. I'll try. Fuck knows what I'm going to say to him, but …'

The screensaver came back on then and they both looked at it. There they were on the screen. Being rockstars.

'Think of something,' said Aesop.

Jimmy nodded and bit at his thumb.

Thirty-one

THE PHONE on Jimmy's desk rang just after six on Monday evening. He was about to pick it up and then noticed what time it was.

'Fuck,' he said quietly. He didn't have time for it, whatever it was. The reception was at eight and he was running very late. He gathered his speech into a pile and stuffed it into his briefcase, letting the phone ring out. He looked around his desk to make sure he hadn't forgotten anything and then stood up and grabbed his jacket. He had to get home, shower and then get to the ambassador's residence to set up the presentation. He'd have to be there early to make sure everything was absolutely ready to go.

In the lift down to the lobby he cursed Simon. He hadn't been able to get hold of him all weekend. He'd been in China, only arriving in Tokyo this morning. And when he got to Tokyo, he was caught up in meetings, sight-seeing and some big lunch with the rest of the delegation and a couple of Japanese ministers. Jimmy had managed to get him on the phone for just two minutes at about three o'clock.

'Jimmy, how're things?'

'Eh, grand. Look …'

'Are we all set for tonight? This is going to be huge Jimmy. Everyone's going to be there. Is your presentation all ready?'

'Yeah, I was working on it all weekend.'

'Great stuff. Tsujita-san's going to translate for you, right? He knows that?'

'Yeah, I've gone over the whole thing with him.'

'Perfect. Jimmy, I can't even tell you what tonight is going to do for your career. This is going to be the biggest thing you've ever done.'

'Yeah, I know. Look, Simon …'

'When this is all over, every systems integrator and consulting firm in the country is going to want a piece of you. Just as well for us we got you first, isn't it? You got all the graphics I sent?'

'Yeah, I have them. It's all ready. Simon, I need …'

'Look Jimmy, they're bringing us to the Meiji Shrine now. I can't talk. They're all waiting to head off. I'll see you at the ambassador's right? We've got some drinks function on beforehand, but I'll be there by eight. Everything's set, right? You need anything?'

Jimmy was walking towards the meeting room with the phone held to his ear. He'd wanted some privacy for what he was going to say. Before he had a chance to answer Simon, he heard someone in the background calling him.

'Sorry Jimmy. I've to go. I'll see you later, right?'

'Eh … right. Seeya.'

'This is going to be a huge night, Jimmy, watch.'

Jimmy hung up. That was probably his last chance to do it properly. To ask Simon to let him go before the presentation. He let out a huge sigh and went back to his desk. He was out of options. He shook his head as he sat down and thought about all the people who would be there later on in the ambassador's residence. He had to go through with the whole thing. Fuck. He had no choice anymore.

He ran into the apartment. Aesop was at the dining table eating cornflakes in his underpants.

'What the fuck are you doing?' said Jimmy, putting down his stuff and running into his bedroom.

'What?'

Jimmy stuck his head out the door to look at him.

'What are you doing?'

Aesop looked down at his bowl and back up at Jimmy.

'I'm learning to play the bagpipes. What are you doing?'

'We've to be there in half an hour! You're not even dressed.'

'You said eight o'clock.'

'I've to get there early to set everything up.'

'What's that got to do with me?'

Jimmy was back in his room again and shouting out at Aesop.

'I thought you were going to help me carry the stuff.'

'What stuff?'

'The projector and the computer and everything.'

'But I'm not dressed.'

'I fucking know! Get dressed.'

'I need a shower.'

'Jesus, Aesop, will you hurry up and have one.'

'You're a bit on edge Jimmy. You need to let a bit of air out of your balloons there, so you do. Everything all right?'

'No! I'm fucking late and you're still sitting there in your …'

He came out of his room and took another look at Aesop.

'What the fuck are they?' he said, pointing.

'They're me new underpants. The disposable ones. Remember Shiggy said they all wear them here?'

'They don't look like underpants, Aesop.'

'Yeah, they're not the most fashionable scanty in the world, but it saves on washing now that the girls are gone.'

'Aesop, do you know what they are?'

'I just told you. Shiggy gave me them. Said they were exactly what I was after.'

'Aesop, they're incontinence jocks.'

'What?'

'For old men. You're wearing an old man's nappy, ye fuckin eejit.'

'I am in me arse.'

'You are!'

'But Shiggy said … you don't think … oh Christ. I'll fuckin kill him!'

Jimmy shook his head and ran back into his room.

'Will you get a move on, you gobshite? There's no such thing as disposable underpants.'

'He wouldn't do that to me, Jimmy.'

'He just did it, you stupid gullible bastard. Now will you plug in the laptop? I want to be sure that the battery's full, just in case.'

'Did you talk to Simon?'

'No. I wasn't able to get him properly.'

'So what's going to happen?'

'I don't know. Maybe I'll get a chance to talk to him at the reception.'

'That's cutting it a bit fine, isn't it?'

'Do you reckon?'

'Ah yeah, Jimmy. Sure you're supposed to be telling everyone how much you love your company at that thing tonight and how marvellous it's all going to be.'

'Is that what I'm s'posed to be doing? Jaysis, isn't it great that you're here, isn't it Aesop?'

'You can't say all that shit to everyone and then turn around and quit, Jimmy. You'd look like a spa. Do you want a quick bowl of cornflakes?'

'Will you fuck off Aesop? And I don't have time for cornflakes.'

He came out of his room again in a towel. 'Will you plug in … ugh! What are you doing?'

'I'm not wearing a fuckin nappy, Jimmy.'

'Can you not do that in your room?'

'Which is better? Me in a nappy, or me in the buff?'

'I'm going for a shower, Aesop. Plug that thing in and get ready, will you? Come on. Chop chop. We're really fucking late here!'

He disappeared into the bathroom.

'I told you Jimmy,' Aesop called after him. 'I can't be late. Nothing ever starts till I get there.'

The bathroom door opened again and Jimmy looked out.

Aesop looked back at him.

'I'll just get ready then, will I?'

JIMMY AND Aesop were escorted up the elevator to the ambassador's residence by one of the girls from the embassy. She seemed as preoccupied as Jimmy.

'Big night tonight,' she said, checking again through her to-do list.

'Yeah,' said Jimmy. He wasn't really paying attention. The lift wasn't air-conditioned and he was all hot after the dash to get a taxi.

'A lot of big names will be along. Do you know the British ambassador and his wife will be here as well?'

'Will they?'

'Two Japanese ministers too. And representatives from all the universities.'

'Right.'

'What are you doing here tonight?'

'I've to give a talk.'

She looked at her list again.

'Oh yes. Jimmy Collins from Eirotech. That's the main event, isn't it?'

'Eh …'

'Jimmy's a little bit nervous,' said Aesop.

'Oh don't be. The crowd that's in here tonight go to these things all the time. They're well used to it.'

'I'll be grand.'

'Not used to standing up before a crowd?'

'Actually, I … eh … no. Not really.'

'You'll be fine.'

'Thanks.'

'Hey Clodagh,' said Aesop. 'What's the food like at these things?'

'Lovely. It's all freshly made especially. The ambassador's got a proper chef. Brown bread and everything.'

'Really? Jimmy, did you hear that?'

'Yeah.'

'We've been out here for a couple of months now,' said Aesop. He winked at Jimmy. 'I'm gagging for a bit of brown.'

'They've Guinness on draft too. Paddy Foley's do it. You know Paddy's?'

'I've heard of the place.'

'The manager is up there now setting up the taps.'

'Mick?'

'You know him?'

'He's been looking after us out here.'

'Oh. Are you staying with him?'

'Kind of.'

The door opened up into a big foyer, which was essentially the entrance to the ambassador's home. Clodagh directed Jimmy into the living-room and showed him where the presentation was going to take place. Then she left them and went down to the lobby again.

'Fuckin hell,' said Aesop, taking it all in. 'The size of it! Who pays for this?'

'You do. Or, at least, you would if you paid tax.'

They looked around. The living-room was about the same area as Jimmy's entire house back home. Beautifully decorated with comfortable furniture and huge expensive-looking pictures hanging on the walls. The main floor area was cleared, leaving room for the hundred or more people who'd be coming tonight to stand around. A baby grand piano stood in one corner and a wooden lectern occupied another. An enormous viewing screen had already been pulled down from the ceiling to the right of the lectern. A small table was sitting there, ready for the projector.

'I guess that's where we'll be doing it. Come on. Let's get this sorted out. I'm going to need a drink before all this.'

'It's not a gig you're doing, Jimmy.'

'It feels like it. Put the laptop on the occasional table there.'

'Where?'

'The occasional table.'

'What's that?'

'That fucking table there,' said Jimmy, pointing at it.

'Occasional table?'

'Yes.'

'What is it the rest of the time?'

'It's a fucking bunch of bananas, Aesop. Now will you put the computer down and give me a hand. I need to find the outlets.'

The two long wooden sliding doors that served as one of the walls to the room opened behind them and they spun around.

'Lads,' said Mick, grinning at them.

'Mick! I believe you're in charge of the beer tonight.'

'That's right. Do you want a pint? I've it all set up in here, ready for testing.'

'What's in there?'

'The dining-room.'

'There's more to this place?'

'Yeah! Look …' Mick pulled open the doors some more and showed them. The dining-room was about half the size of the living-room.

'Is that where they keep the …'

Aesop walked over and looked around the dining-room.

'Fuckin hell! Look at this spread!'

'Yeah. The ambassador likes to put on a good show. Other ambassadors have bigger gaffs, but no one does better parties than the Irish ambassador. The man's a legend.'

'Jesus. Look at all that food!'

A dining table about the size of two full snooker tables was packed with the most gorgeous-looking food Aesop had ever seen. Mountains of brown bread, about a dozen poached salmon, lots of assorted potato and pasta salads, cold cuts of meat fresh off the bone … Aesop walked over and looked around in amazement.

'Aesop,' said Jimmy back in the living-room. 'Do you mind? I'm under a bit of pressure here.'

'Be with you in a minute, Jimmy. Christ, look at this!'

He put a handful of individually-wrapped miniature Foxes Glacier Mints in his pocket and scanned the table once more.

'They have After Eights too, Jimmy, look.'

'Aesop, I don't give a wank what they have. Are you going to help me?'

'See this Mick? Thinks I'm his bleedin lackey. C'mere, are the pints tonight really free?'

'As much as you can drink Aesop.'

'Ooh Jaysis. Payback time, Mick. You're going down tonight.'

'Aesop!' called Jimmy. He was on his knees, looking around the back of the sofa next to the lectern.

'I'm coming, I'm coming. Jesus …'

Aesop winked at Mick.

'Stick a pint on there for us, will ya Mick?'

'On the way Aesop.'

A bell clanged and Clodagh showed four more people in. The guests were starting to arrive. Jimmy looked around at them from his position on the floor and then back at Aesop, his face red from exertion. He roared in a whisper to him.

'Will you get over here you useless fuck and give me a hand? Everyone's coming and I can't find the sockets!'

Aesop wandered over, nodding and grinning at the new arrivals as they took off their coats.

'Maybe they only have occasional sockets,' he said to Jimmy.

Half an hour later there was a respectable crowd of about thirty people mingling and chatting and taking drinks from the liveried wait staff that flitted between them with trays. Aesop didn't like the look of the small glasses of Guinness that were on offer, so when he was ready for a drink he opened the sliding door a bit and poked his head in.

'Pint, Mick.'

Jimmy caught him.

'What are you doing?'

'I'm getting a pint.'

'The dining-room isn't open yet. We're s'posed to be mingling, not getting gee-eyed on pints.'

'Sure I don't know any of these fuckers.'

'That's what mingling is, Aesop. You get to know them.'

'But they're not my kind of people, Jimmy. They keep giving me business cards and then looking at me like I'm peculiar because I don't have any.'

'Just say you're out of them.'

'But then they ask me what I do. You said to keep my mouth shut about that.'

'Tell them you're an English teacher.'

'But I got fired.'

'Lie, Aesop. It's what you fucking do, remember?'

'Where's your boss?'

'I don't know. They haven't arrived yet. It's nearly eight. They should be in soon.'

'Are you going to tell him?'

Jimmy watched as a camera crew set up at the back of the room.

'I … I can't. Look at this place. It'll be packed with … hey, there's Johnnie!'

Aesop looked around. Johnnie Fingers had just walked in and was waving at them.

'What's he doing here?' said Jimmy.

'I invited him yesterday. Why? Is that a problem?'

'Well … no, I s'pose it isn't. Everyone else is here. He might as well be here too.'

'Hey Johnnie,' called Aesop.

'Hi guys,' said Johnnie, coming over. 'Thanks for the invite Jimmy.'

'Eh, no problem. How's things?'

'Grand. I was talking to Dónal last night. Told me all the news. A bit of a pickle you're after getting yourself into here.'

'Fucking tell me about it.'

'Yeah, sounds like you'll have your work cut out for you convincing them to let you leave. He said it would cost around three hundred big ones? Jesus. How the hell are you going to get out of that? Have you talked to your boss yet?'

'No,' said Aesop. 'He keeps chickening out.'

'Fuck off Aesop, I'm not chickening out. I haven't seen him in two weeks sure. And look at this place. I can't go telling him tonight, can I? The world and its granny is here to witness his big day. I thought I'd get a quiet moment but that's not going to happen now, is it? No, maybe I'll just get through tonight and … see what happens.'

Aesop started making chicken noises.

'Will you shut up, you wanker? Jesus, there's enough pressure on me tonight without you here acting the clown as well. I should've told you there was a cover charge.'

'Well, good luck Jimmy,' said Johnnie. 'Break a leg.'

'Thanks.'

'Don't be too impressive though. Remember you're trying to get out of all this. The better you do, the harder it'll be afterwards! Hey Aesop, where did you get that pint?'

Aesop winked at him.

'See that sliding door? Well pull it open and a little Guinness pixie called Mick will jump out and give you a pint. Tell him I sent you.'

'Grand. See you in a minute.'

Johnnie headed over to the sliding doors and pulled one of them back. Jimmy watched him, but didn't say anything.

'Oh I see,' said Aesop. 'It's okay for Johnnie Fingers to get pints off Mick, but I'm not allowed to, am I?'

'Stop annoying me Aesop. I'm very nervous tonight.'

'Sure, what difference does it make to you if you're going to quit?'

Jimmy looked at him.

'Are you completely fucking oblivious to what's going on around here?'

'What do you mean?'

'Do you know why we're all here tonight?'

'The poached salmon?'

'This is a huge deal, Aesop. The celebration of a big fucking success story worth tens of millions of dollars. And I'm the one who's meant to explain to all these people how it happened.'

'You've played bigger crowds in McGuigans.'

'This is nothing like that, Aesop! The room will be full of dignitaries and industry leaders and journalists. Look at that camera for fuck sake. That's RTÉ over there.'

'Is it? Will I go over and say hello? Could be good publicity for the band.'

He turned to go but Jimmy grabbed his arm.

'Stay the fuck put. Don't mention the band to anyone here tonight no matter how drunk you get, which you're not to do either. You're an English teacher from Dublin, you hear me? No band, no music, no getting drunk and no fucking annoying anyone. Right? I know this isn't your scene, Aesop, but this is very, very, very fucking important. Don't do anything tonight that will embarrass me, right? Anything you think might be a laugh, won't be. Look at me and promise me that you won't take the piss tonight. Please?'

'Jesus, Jimmy. Will you relax? I won't embarrass you.'

'Swear.'

'I swear! Look, I'll tell you what. I'll go over and talk to that oul nun in the corner, right? What harm can come from that?'

'Do. Thanks.'

'Don't sweat it Jimmy. I keep telling you, I only want to help.'

'Well you can help by being nice to the Sister and leaving everyone else alone.'

'Done.'

Jimmy looked over Aesop's shoulder.

'Oh fuck. Here they are …'

The trade delegation had just arrived. Forty very important people poured into forty suits. Jimmy swallowed and left Aesop, running back and switching on the computer to make sure everything was okay. He looked around him. The room was suddenly packed. He saw Shiggy come in behind the huge group and smile at him, giving him a big wink. He tried to smile back but his face felt frozen. Then he saw Simon smile and wave over. He gave a little wave and then turned back to the computer, sweating. He was shitting planks now. He had to do this thing properly. This would have to be the biggest performance of his life. He stood up straight and walked over to Simon, who immediately introduced him to the Irish ambassador. Jimmy flashed his grin and did the firm handshake thing with a small bow. It was showtime.

For the next hour or so, Jimmy was on fire. He couldn't help it; he was the star of the show. Simon gushed and beamed and steered him around the room so that he could meet everyone. They all knew who he was; Simon had been talking him up for most of the week. The British ambassador oozed charm. Jimmy loved talking to him. He was obviously an old hand at this type of thing.

'Oh, yes, it's a pleasure to meet you at last Jimmy. Simon has been telling us all about you. I believe you're the man who's going to show us how it's all done?'

'Ah now. Simon's just being very generous. Eirotech has some of the best people in Ireland and Kyotosei has all the experience and skills we'll need to make it work. Very much a team effort.'

'Not at all. According to Simon, you're the technical architect who's going to build the whole thing.'

'Ah, Simon. You shouldn't be saying things like that. We're all in this together, your Excellency.'

'Please, call me Andrew.'

'Thank you Andrew. Well, as I say, it's a very exciting time for us all. Please God it'll be a great success.'

'I'm sure it will. Your colleagues in the industry who I've spoken to tonight all seem very impressed.'

'We're very much looking forward to it.'

He managed to give Simon a nudge when the British ambassador looked around for a waiter to take his empty glass. One more try.

'Listen Simon, do you have a minute? I've got to …'

'Jimmy, I'll talk to you later okay? I've got a lot on my plate just at the moment. Sakamoto-san has to meet the Minister for Trade.'

Simon patted Jimmy on the shoulder and went off to find Sakamoto-san.

'Fucker,' muttered Jimmy to himself. That was his last chance.

Aesop came up to him shortly before nine.

'Jimmy, I can't take it anymore. I had to leave Sr Breege with Johnnie.'

'Did you?'

'Man, nuns give me the willies big time.'

'She looks harmless enough. She's about ninety.'

'She said she's been here for fifty-seven years Jimmy. And apparently she wasn't a fuckin spring chicken when she arrived.'

'Ah she's grand.'

'No way. Nuns are scary. They know what you're thinking.'

'Just be polite.'

'I'm telling you, nuns can spot bullshit from ten miles. She knows fucking well what kind of person I am. She can sense it. I'm her natural enemy.'

'Look Aesop, I'm a bit busy here, yeah? Talk to someone else if you have to. Just don't do anything stupid. I'm trying to …'

'Jimmy!'

Simon was back again with more people for Jimmy to meet.

'Hi Simon. Eh … this is … em … Paul Murray.'

'Hello Paul.'

'Hiya Simon. Nice to meet you,' said Aesop.

'Oh, you're from Dublin? Great. Jimmy, Paul, this is Michael from Enterprise Ireland and this is the cultural attaché from the French embassy, Loic.'

'Hello.'

'Hello.'

'Jimmy is our main guy, our problem solver. He'll be giving the keynote speech later on.'

'Ah yes, it's a pleasure to meet you, Jimmy.'

'And what do you do Paul?'

'I'm a plastic surgeon.'

Jimmy closed his eyes and took a deep breath. He just couldn't fucking help himself, could he?'

'Really? And where do you practise?'

'Ah, I don't really practise so much anymore. I just kind of get in there and go for it, y'know?'

They looked at each other and Jimmy forced a laugh.

'Don't mind him,' he said. 'He was just telling me that he's got a place in Harajuku.'

'Oh … I see.'

'Is that Clodagh?' Jimmy went on desperately. 'Have you met Clodagh, Simon? She's with the embassy here. Excuse us Paul …'

He glared at a grinning Aesop and then started to manoeuvre the others towards Clodagh, who was chatting to another girl nearby.

'Fucker,' he mouthed over his shoulder as he left.

'I'll be glad to have a look at your nose for you Jimmy,' called Aesop after them. 'Call the office tomorrow and we'll see what we can do about it.'

Before Jimmy could go back and tell him what a geebag he was, the Irish ambassador started speaking from the lectern. Everyone stopped what they were doing and turned to face him. He welcomed them all to the reception and then started to point out the various ministers and other dignitaries who were in attendance and everyone clapped.

'Actually, I've also just had the pleasure of meeting someone for the first time tonight who I've long had a great respect for,' said the ambassador. 'Ladies and gentlemen, we're privileged to have one of the original Irish popstars with us tonight. Johnnie Fingers of the Boomtown Rats is here.'

More clapping.

'I don't mind telling you that a younger and probably much more trendy college student than the person you're listening to at the moment once had quite a collection of Boomtown Rats records.'

Jimmy looked over at Johnnie, who grinned and raised his glass as the ambassador gestured to him. The nun beside him was now appraising him again with her arms folded. This was a level of debauchery she'd never had the opportunity of putting in its place before.

'Maybe Johnnie will give us a song later?' said the ambassador.

Johnnie shrugged and smiled.

'Okay, well if you'd like to make your way into the dining-room, Claude has excelled himself once more. We'll have some speeches after dinner and then of course a very special deal will be signed between Kyotosei and our own Eirotech Solutions that promises to herald a new era of collaboration between the technology industries of both countries, so that'll be a nice photo opportunity I'm sure.'

A final clap and then everyone turned to face the sliding doors, which were immediately pulled apart to reveal the smorgasbord in the other room. Jimmy stared and shook his head again with a quiet curse. Aesop was already in there on his own. He looked up in surprise as the doors opened and then grinned out at everyone, half a poached salmon balanced on his plate and mayonnaise all over his mouth.

'Hurray for Claude!' he said.

Everyone laughed except Jimmy.

Johnnie found him ten minutes later trying to steady a small plate on his knee as he tried to butter some brown bread.

'Going well, isn't it?' said Johnnie.

Jimmy looked up.

'Oh, hiya Johnnie. Yeah, seems to be.'

'Everyone's talking about you. That's pretty cool considering who else is in the room.'

'Yeah. It's a bit nerve-wracking.'

'You must be pretty good at this job of yours.'

'Ah, this is all for show, Johnnie. It's not a very glamorous job most of the time, I can tell you.'

'I don't know what you're going to tell your boss. I was talking to him earlier. I didn't say I knew you or anything, but I think he wants to have your babies.'

'Shite.'

'Yeah. Well, you'd better think of something good to get out of it. You're right up on a pedestal at the moment.'

'Don't bleedin remind me.'

'Listen, the ambassador's mad for me to sing a song after dinner.'

'I heard. Are you going to do it?'

'I'd rather not to be honest. Not really my crowd, is it?'

'I know. You could just play something on the piano. An instrumental? Something classical or something?'

'I thought of that, but he wants a Rats song.'

'So what are you going to do?'

'I was hoping you might help me out, Jimmy.'

'How?'

'Would you sing?'

'What? Ah Jesus, Johnnie. I can't sing tonight. I'm a bit busy with all this shite, amn't I? And anyway, Simon will have fucking conniptions if I get up there. The rows we're after having over all this? Christ, he'll go mad. Sorry man.'

'All right Jimmy. I understand. I won't hassle you. I can see you've got your plate full.'

Johnnie smiled down at Jimmy's knee. There was half a loaf of brown bread on it.

'Yeah,' laughed Jimmy. 'I had to grab some before Aesop bloody ate it all.'

'He's some man for taking the piss, isn't he?'

'Will you stop? He's got a neck like a jockey's bollocks.'

Simon and the Irish ambassador walked over.

'Oh Jimmy, I see you've met Johnnie Fingers.'

'Eh, yeah. I was just telling him I was a big fan of his.'

'Jimmy plays music too,' said Simon to both of them. 'He used to be in a band in Dublin.'

'Really?' said Johnnie, smiling at Jimmy.

'Ah, eh …' said Jimmy.

'Maybe the two of you could sing us a song together?' said the ambassador. 'When everyone's finished eating? Before the speeches?'

'Well …' said Jimmy, looking at Simon. 'I'm not sure …'

'Of course he would,' said Simon. 'Jimmy's a great singer.'

'But … I mean …'

'You can't say no to the ambassador, Jimmy, can you? After he put on this big party for us all?'

'What do you think, Johnnie?' said the ambassador.

'Sure. Why not? If Jimmy doesn't mind …'

'Well, that's settled then,' said Simon. 'It'll be a fun way to introduce yourself before your presentation, won't it? This is a celebration after all, right? Oh look … Ambassador, I don't think you've met Sakamoto-san properly, have you? He's going to be running the new enterprise here in Japan …'

The two of them walked off, Jimmy staring at them. Then he looked back at Johnnie.

'Cheeky bastard!' he said.

'Who, me?'

'No no, of course not you. That cheeky fucker Simon. Did you see that? All the shit he's been giving me over the band and now he wants me to sing just because he wants to show off to the ambassador. You'd swear I was his fucking party piece, taking me out whenever he feels like it. Wind me up and off I go. Jesus, it's one thing working for the wanker, but now he's telling me when I'm to sing! I can't believe he just did that. Who does he think he is? *That settles it* … he didn't even wait for me to answer!'

'Listen Jimmy, I don't mind if you don't want to do it. I'll just say I have to head off and …'

'No, fuck him. We'll do it.'

'Okay. If you're sure. What do you want to sing?'

'What do you want to play? Did you get a look at the piano?'

'Sounds fine. That young one's been playing The Corrs on it all night and it has a bit of grunt to it.'

'Mondays?' said Jimmy.

'Yeah? If you like. You know the words?'

'Of course. Jesus, it's a classic.'

'Right then, we'll do it.'

It was one of the most surreal experiences of Jimmy's life. He stood next to the piano when the ambassador finished introducing them and put one hand on it. Then he took it off again, worried that he looked too much like Frank Sinatra. He turned around to Johnnie and smiled.

'This is a good song for a Monday,' he said then to the waiting crowd.

Johnnie winked and started the intro to 'I Don't Like Mondays' and everyone gasped. It was the coolest piano intro in the world, and Johnnie had played it like he was putting sugar in his tea. Jimmy looked out and grinned. Talk about fucking weird. Singing this song with Johnnie Fingers playing the keyboards would have been up there in the top-three all-time dreams come true. But here he was doing it in front of a bunch of middle-aged men in suits who were standing around and sipping on wine. He caught sight of Aesop, who was laughing and moving his head from side-to-side, a plate of cheesecake in one hand and a pint in the other. Jimmy didn't know what to do with his hands. He had no guitar and no mike stand and so put them in his pockets. He was sure it looked stupid but singing the Rats in a room like this was hard enough without worrying about it. He closed his eyes and sang as loud as he could to be heard over Johnnie as he pounded out the piano runs. He tried a bit of audience participation on the 'tell me why' lines, waving out to them to join in, but only Aesop, Clodagh, Mick, the Irish ambassador and another couple of people got the idea. The rest of them stood around, bemused, and nodded along. Jimmy saw the Japanese girl who had been playing The Corrs earlier looking at Johnnie with her mouth open.

When it was over they got a huge clap and cheer and Jimmy pulled Johnnie around to the side of the piano to him, where they bowed together.

'That was fucking weird,' said Jimmy, out of the side of his mouth.

'You don't need to tell me,' said Johnnie, smiling and waving. 'I was getting the hairy eyeball off Sr Breege for the whole song.'

'Yeah, I saw her. Listen, besides that being a completely psycho experience, thanks.'

'For what?'

'I just sang with Johnnie Fingers!'

'Hey, I just played with Jimmy Collins.'

They grinned at each other.

'I think I win,' said Jimmy.

The ambassador called for quiet and asked Simon up to the stand to give his speech.

'Well, I don't know if I can top that,' said Simon, adjusting his tie. 'Unless you all want me to sing Molly Malone?'

'Yes!' shouted Aesop from the back.

'Ah, I don't think so,' said Simon, craning his neck to try and see who the funny fucker was.

He spoke for about ten minutes about the new company and how important its formation was as an example of what could be done if everyone pulled together. He thanked everyone for being there and the ambassador for being such a wonderful host and then went on to talk about all the talented and hard-working people who'd made the whole thing possible.

'And, of course, right at the top of that list is a man, some of whose talents you've already heard here tonight …'

'Johnnie Fingers!' yelled Aesop from deep in the crowd. He was on his eighth pint.

Simon frowned and tried to find the comedian again.

'Actually, I was thinking of Mr Jimmy Collins …'

He clapped to get everyone started and then moved away from the lectern to let Jimmy step up. Shiggy was beside him, smiling, and Jimmy introduced him and thanked him for acting as his translator. Once Jimmy had the projector switched on and the first slide swept into view, it all went smoothly. Even Aesop managed to shut his arse. The background music was a mixture of Celtic and Japanese sounds and Jimmy didn't even need to check the notes in front of him. He'd gone over this about twenty times and had it in the bag. He was Jimmy Collins, Head of Information Systems, Chief Project Manager, future Chief Information Officer. He spoke easily for about twenty-five minutes, describing the various cultural, technological and financial obstacles that they'd had to overcome to put in place a project of this scale. He made sure to mention lots of people in the room and thank them for the various roles they'd played in allowing it to happen and then he congratulated Shiggy and Sakamoto-san on their new positions. When he was done, he got a huge round of applause. Simon, standing only a few feet away, nodded and clapped at him like he'd just won the Tour de France for Team Eirotech. Then Jimmy introduced Sakamoto-san to the lectern and shook his hand, bowing low and getting out of the way. He'd nailed it again. He'd managed to make them all look brilliant. Like forming a new company across three countries was a piece of piss.

Once the speeches were over, Jimmy came away from the front of the crowd and started mixing with everyone again. He made his way into the dining-room to get himself a pint. Aesop was propped up against the table, talking to Mick.

'Mick, will you stop serving that fucking eejit?'

'Ah Jimmy, there you are. Sorry, I popped in to see Mick. The speeches were getting a bit boring.'

'Are you going to behave yourself?'

'Yep. I'm tired now anyway. When is this thing over?'

'They're setting up a table so that Simon and Sakamoto-san can sign in the new company for the cameras. Should be done in half an hour.'

'Grand. Everything go well?'

'Yep. I'm a genius.'

'So you told the boss you were quitting?'

'Jesus no. That can wait till tomorrow.'

'They're never going to let you go, Jimmy. Isn't that right Mick?'

'All I know is, everyone that comes up here for a drink is talking about Jimmy Collins,' said Mick.

'Ah, I'm just flavour of the month, that's all.'

Johnnie came over to join them.

'It's a pity you've to head home,' he said.

'Yeah.'

'There's a couple of good gigs coming up and I was talking you up for a support slot.'

'Sorry Johnnie,' said Jimmy. 'It just didn't work out. Maybe another time.'

'Yeah. Well, I s'pose you've got all this stuff to sort out first.'

'I know.'

'Who were the bands Johnnie?' said Aesop.

'Ah, it doesn't matter. No point in upsetting you, is there?'

'What? Don't tell me it was someone cool!'

'Sure what other kind of band do you think I'd be involved with, Aesop?'

'You hear this, Jimmy? You're after fucking every …'

'Drink your pint, Aesop,' said Jimmy. 'I've had a long day and the last …'

He suddenly noticed it had become very quiet in the other room. Johnnie was staring at him and Aesop had gone completely pale.

'What's wrong?'

Then he heard it. He looked around. Almost everyone there was now glued to the front of the room. A few people were looking at Jimmy. Every face was a picture of horror.

He looked up at the screen.

It was Aesop. He was on top of a woman, giving it loads, with 'Meatloaf's Underpants' playing in the background. Jen's camcorder had obviously been on the dresser at the end of Jimmy's bed and was pointing up along it. You couldn't see anyone's face, but you could see Jimmy's guitar next to the bed. One of his Eirotech polo shirts was draped over the dresser where he'd thrown it. What you could see of Aesop was more than anyone had probably ever seen before, certainly from that angle, and way more than anyone would want to. The bed shook and rattled as he pounded up and down on top of the girl, slapping her arse in time with the music with one hand. The other hand was punching the air. The girl was shouting too as her head bounced off the headboard.

Jimmy turned and bolted through the crowd, knocking elbows and spilling drinks. He eventually reached the computer and smashed a fist down on the keyboard to turn off the screensaver. When he did, the spectacle of Aesop's jackhammering was immediately replaced by a huge blue Eirotech logo on the screen, just like the one on the polo shirt in the video. Jimmy's heart had stopped beating by the time he stood up and looked around the ambassador's living-room. His chest ached and his face was dripping. Simon stood about twenty feet away, ashen and sick looking. Johnnie was now standing in another corner, holding up Sr Breege who had apparently fainted. He was looking between the screen and Jimmy as he patted the back of her wrist.

Jimmy took in the rest of the crowd as he fumbled with his tie. He was rooted to the spot, two hundred shocked eyes boring in on him. He turned and looked over at Aesop who by now was green in the face. Jimmy glanced around the room again. There was total silence but the Japanese girl's words – screeched out in rhythm to her head crashing the headboard into the wall – were still echoing around through the stillness …

Oh Jimmy-san. You so big. Hung rike moose … oh Jimmy-san …

He closed his eyes and when he opened them Simon was standing next to him, snarling and poking his finger into his chest and saying stuff that Jimmy couldn't even hear with the whooshing noises that were gushing around in his head.

Aesop inched over to Johnnie, who was now standing there with Shiggy. Sr Breege had been brought into the kitchen by one of the staff so she could sit down away from the crowd. The three of them looked on as Jimmy stood in the middle of the floor, his arms down by his side and his head hanging low. Simon was standing in front of him. They couldn't hear what was being said, but they got the general idea. Johnnie looked around at Aesop.

'That was you up there, wasn't it?'

'Yeah. Oh God, I'm going to hell. Oh Jesus … what did I do? Oh holy fuck … the screensaver … I must have …'

'Christ. Poor Jimmy,' said Johnnie. 'This must be the worst thing you've ever done, Aesop.'

Aesop nodded. He looked like he was about to cry.

'It's up there, Johnnie. It's definitely up there …'

IRELAND

Thirty-two

Jimmy, Dónal and Sparky were in Sin Bin two days later. Sparky was already working on the guitar parts for Susan's song that Jimmy had recorded onto his laptop. Dónal reckoned it would be a perfect follow-up single to 'Lost'. They sat around then, drinking tea and talking. Dónal wanted to know about what had happened, but Jimmy just shook his head. He didn't want to talk about it.

'Anyway, fuck it. It's done. I wanted to be famous, didn't I?'

He had his elbows on his lap and his face in his hands.

'They'll stop writing about it soon enough,' said Dónal.

Jimmy nodded.

'Really, Jimmy. Most people don't read the business section anyway.'

Another nod.

'Come on, man. I know you're …'

Aesop walked in and stopped at the door. He saw the three of them and walked over slowly.

'Howyis lads,' he said.

'Aesop,' said Dónal.

Jimmy didn't even look up.

'Jimmy?' said Aesop. 'Jimmy, are you not going to talk to me? Listen, I don't know what happened. I'm really sorry. It was an accident.'

'You're a bleedin accident,' said Jimmy.

'I know. I shouldn't be let near computers.'

'You shouldn't be let out of the house.'

No one said anything for a minute.

'You're definitely fired?' said Aesop.

'What do you think?'

'Did they not believe it was me?'

'Did they not believe that my mate regularly uses my name when he scores chicks because he doesn't want them to find him afterwards? And that he rides them in my bedroom. No Aesop, they didn't. Isn't that funny? And when they took back their computer that night, they found it full of porn.'

'I meant to delete all that stuff when you told me, I swear! I just forgot cos I was so pissed that night.'

'Jesus, all that time you were on the Internet, I thought you were trying to better your mind. Or researching one of your musical masterpieces.'

'I was! I was … well, some of the stuff I was doing was …'

'They checked the logs of the sites you were on and showed me a fucking list of them.'

'Ah come on, Jimmy. It wasn't that bad. You should see some of the stuff they have. Chickens and horses and everything. I'm not into that shite. It was all consenting adults.'

'I wasn't consenting, was I? Sakamoto-san wasn't consenting. Sr Breege ended up in hospital, Aesop. Was she consenting?'

'But she was grand the next day.'

'That's not the fucking point!'

'Ah Jimmy, I know how it looks now, but … y'know … for a rockstar, a bit of scandal like that is a good thing. They expect that in the music industry. Don't they Dónal?'

'Leave me out of this Aesop.'

'Well, it's just as well Aesop, isn't it?' said Jimmy. 'Because I'll never be able to get a job in any other industry.'

'I don't know what to say, Jimmy. It must have been the screen-saver thing I got. I was taking everything off the camcorder and putting it on the computer cos I had to give it back to Jennifer. I must have clicked the wrong button or something and the screen-saver found that movie. I don't know how it fuckin happened. It wasn't even my idea, Jimmy. I was showing her some of the gig on the camcorder and she said she wanted me to tape us. I'm so, so fucking sorry man. Is there anything I can do? I'll talk to them, tell them it was all me. I'll go around to your office and …'

'You weren't even s'posed to be staying in the apartment, Aesop. It's too late for all that. Man, you fucking crucified me out there.'

Aesop's face looked like nothing was holding it up.

'I'm sorry Jimmy.'

Jimmy sighed. 'Ah … just fuckin forget about it, right? It's done. Go and put the kettle on, ye fuckin eejit.'

Aesop nodded and went into the kitchen. No one spoke for a while.

'So the single's out next week?' said Jimmy eventually, looking up.

'Yeah. All ready. Everyone's very excited about it. But Jimmy, there's something you need to know. Listen man, things are really tight here. I didn't want to say anything before, y'know, with all the stuff you had going on, but even if the single does well we're on very thin fucking ice with the landlord in this place. I'm not sure that me and Sparky are going to have the resources if the time comes to start working on the album. The bank is starting to get nervous and I don't think I'm the manager's best mate anymore. I might have to find someone else to record the album for you. I mean, we'll get something from Sultan up front but that won't happen until …'

'Dónal, I know about all that. The gobshite in the kitchen told me.'

'He what? The fucking little …'

'It's fine Dónal. I'm glad I know. Listen, they let me keep the fifty grand. I had to sign a non-disclosure agreement to say I wouldn't talk to the press about what happened. They just want it to go away and don't need me giving interviews.'

'I can't imagine you'd want to.'

'Yeah, but they weren't taking any chances. They felt they didn't really know what I was capable of anymore, which is fair enough I s'pose. Dónal, I want to give you the fifty grand.'

'You what?'

'I know a few of the investors pulled out of Sin Bin and I want to buy in. I know you're tight for cash and if music is the only way for me to make a living now, thanks to fuckin Bill Gates in there, I'd like to be a partner with you. I don't just want to be a musician, I want to be in on the business side. I know the score with Sin Bin. We need some dosh to keep things going while we're waiting for Sultan to come up with some cash. What do you think? Would fifty cover us? Sparky?'

Dónal and Sparky looked at each other. Sparky was grinning.

'Jesus, Jimmy, that would buy us four months. Maybe five! But … are you sure?' said Dónal.

'Absolutely. But I need to have a say. And not just with The Grove. Other bands too. Music is all I've got now. I want to know everything there is to know. That's the only way it can work. I'm pissed off with other people running my life. You're still the boss around here and that's cool. If I have to have a fucking boss I want it to be you. What do you think? We can work out the details later, but I just want to know if you're cool with the idea.'

'Do you know what you're saying Jimmy?' said Dónal. 'This business is a tough bastard. The way things are now, you just need to play. Get involved in this side of it and that's a whole new ball game. I can't guarantee a return on your fifty grand. I can't even guarantee the fifty grand back. You'll be putting all your money on the success of the single.'

'Exactly, Dónal. My money, my song. That's the way I want it. I know it's a risk, but you took enough of them for me, didn't you? So how do you feel about having a new apprentice? What do you reckon? Ready to bet the farm?'

Sparky and Dónal exchanged glances again.

'Mine's already in the pot, Jimmy,' said Dónal, grinning. 'Are you ready?'

'Yeah. Fuck yeah.'

Dónal stuck out his hand and Jimmy shook it. Then Sparky leaned over and punched him on the shoulder, all teeth and beard and wrinkles.

Then they heard the faint sound of Meatloaf's Underpants. It was low and tinny over Jimmy's laptop speakers.

'Jesus,' said Jimmy, looking around at the desk. 'There it is again. I didn't even have a chance to get rid of the screensaver I was so freaked out.'

Sparky was closest and went over to the table, tutting, to turn it off.

'Hang on Sparky,' said Dónal. 'I want to see this.'

They both went over to Jimmy's laptop to see Aesop in all his glory. Jimmy looked over and gave a little smile. They were both staring at it with their faces scrunched up, like they'd just taken a bite out of a lemon.

'Not pretty, is it?' he said.

'Jesus, he's a disgusting little bastard,' said Sparky. 'That poor girl …'

He turned off the computer and they came back to Jimmy, Dónal laughing and shaking his head and Sparky looking over at the kitchen like Beelzebub himself was in there making the tea.

'Well, now you know,' said Jimmy, with a sigh. 'That's what Aesop's arse looks like. You couldn't see it properly on the telly.'

'Where is he anyway?' said Dónal, looking around. 'How long does it take to make a pot of tea?'

He called in to the kitchen.

'Aesop! What's the story with the tea?'

They heard Aesop cursing through the door.

'I can't … where's the … this fuckin thing won't …'

'He's not good with kettles,' said Jimmy. 'You might want to go in there and show him how to use it.'

Dónal stood up and crossed the floor to the kitchen.

'It's only new, the eejit. He better not break it.'

Jimmy picked up his cup, but it was cold now on him. He looked up and saw Sparky staring at him.

'What's up?'

Sparky shook his head. 'Nothing.'

He fished a banana out of his breast pocket and started to peel it.

'So what happened with the big business deal out there?' he said.

'Postponed. They're still going ahead, but before Kyotosei signs anything they're insisting that Eirotech puts up the cash for a huge publicity campaign to try and paint over all this. Won't be cheap. Looks like Simon might have to hold off on that castle he had his eye on. Putting me out there was all his idea. He's got a fair bit of work ahead of him now, so he does. Anyway, they're looking at trying to put it all together again next year when I'm just a bad dream. In the meantime, everything goes back to the way it was while it's sorted out. Marco has my old job.'

'That's good. So I s'pose you might say that, in a way, it all worked out for the best then? You got out of the contract, you were allowed keep the dosh and then your mate got a promotion. Aesop's fuck-up didn't turn out as bad as it could have, did it?'

'Well, he kept saying he wanted to help.'

'Yeah. Jesus, I'd say that Japanese crowd were pissed off when they found all that stuff on their computer.'

'They went fucking ape. The screensaver was only the start of it.'

'Right. Yeah. C'mere, isn't it funny how he managed to do it twice?'

'What? What do you mean?'

'Well, it's one thing to do it on the company's computer, right? But how come it fucking happened on your computer as well?' Sparky pointed over to the table behind them. 'I mean, it just happened again, didn't it?'

Jimmy felt himself going red.

'I … eh … what do you … I don't …'

'It's almost as if he was just trying it out first, to see if it would work, isn't it? Before he put it on the proper computer, like.'

'I … I don't know what you …'

'He must have got fierce brainy out there in Japan to do something like that. Eat a lot of fish, did he?'

He was staring at Jimmy again, his mouth full of banana.

'He doesn't like fish,' said Jimmy, quietly.

'By Jaysis, a man who'd do something like that in front of all those people must want something very badly. If I didn't know any better, Jimmy, I'd say it'd take someone with a bigger brain than Aesop to come up with that, fish or no fish. Would you say?'

Jimmy nodded slowly. He was boiling hot. Even his ears felt red.

'Maybe …'

Aesop called out from the kitchen.

'Do you want Jaffa Cakes, Jimmy? They've loads here.'

'No, I'm grand,' answered Jimmy, still puce and looking at Sparky.

'Sparky?' shouted Aesop. 'Jaffa Cakes?'

'No! Don't you know I don't eat fuckin bikkies, sure.'

'Oh right. Sorry.'

Sparky finished his banana and put the skin down on the table before sitting back in his chair with his hands behind his head.

'God, he's got fuckin manners on him now and everything, the guilty little shite. Yeah, I'd say things worked out. Considering it was all an accident pure and simple, like. Would you?'

Jimmy looked down into his lap. 'Ever heard of Machiavelli, Sparky?'

'Was he one of the Three Musketeers?'

Jimmy shook his head.

'So … now you know. Are you going to say anything?'

Aesop arrived out of the kitchen and put a tray of tea down in front of them. He took up the pot and started to pour Sparky's tea, splashing some onto the table.

'Ah shite. Sorry Sparky. Hang on, there's a cloth in the kitchen …'

He ran off to get it. Sparky watched him in amazement and then picked up his tea to taste it. It was lovely. Perfect. Just how he liked it. He looked up.

'Say anything, Jimmy? About what?'

'Thanks, man,' said Jimmy. 'I might tell him anyway when all this good behaviour wears off.'

'Yeah. And I want to be there for that, right? C'mere, poor Shiggy must have been upset about the whole thing, was he?'

'Oh, he was fucking livid. Raging. He was the one who insisted I had to go. He point-blank refused to work with me anymore after the shame I brought on everyone. I disgraced him personally, as well as the company he's worked for all his life.'

Sparky grinned. 'He's a good bloke, Shiggy.'

'Man, he's the fucking best,' said Jimmy.

おわり

(The End)

どうも...

A lot of people weighed in with encouragement over the last couple of years and I just wanted to say that every kind word was note d and appreciated more than I could possibly articulate here without writing a nice poem about it – which I'll spare you as a gesture of how much your support meant. Thanks everyone.

It would probably be wrong of me to plug my first novel (ahem-*Superchick*-ahem) here, but I have to extend my heartfelt thanks and admiration to Laura Kennedy who did so much to make it a reality, and then a success, with the enthusiastic backing of Mercier Press.

One way to write a book is to methodically research and verify facts and details until you have an enormous store of knowledge on which to draw. Another way – and I'm a big fan of this one – is to pester people who already have an enormous store of knowledge and then get them to tell you things. This brazen indolence on my part was facilitated by Niall McCarthy in Dublin; Colman Murray in New York; Seán Furlong, Jem Dykes, Simon Cahill, Martin Clarke and Rob Wrixon in Sydney; Angelika Burke in Hong Kong; Tommie Mullarkey in Auckland; Mick Shannon in Beijing and Séamus Hanly, Neil Day, John Coyle, Patrick Tierney, Rajiv Trehan and Masayuki 'Spike' Kishi in Tokyo. Special thanks to Andy 'Jock' Plester, who dived in to give me a bunt over the last hurdle.

And, of course, thanks heaps to the brilliant Johnnie Fingers … for not telling me where to go with myself.

Getting to the pointy end of a book is always the hard bit. It's around then that you really need some cool counsel before you can send it off on its way. I would have been in trouble without Joe Burke, Brian Dolan, Ruth Kelly, Fiona Lodge and Stewart Ward – all of whom were a huge help, as well as being generous to a fault with their time.

Mercier Press have been behind me since the beginning and my editor, Aisling Lyons, has managed to counter all my whinging with boundless reserves of professionalism, patience and good humour. *Rock and a Hard Place* and its author owe an enormous debt of gratitude to her.

And more than anyone ... thanks, love and all respect, to Ruth ...

SJM
Sydney, 2006

Superchick
Stephen J. Martin

ISBN: 978 1 85635 464 6

'All women are bastards …'

JIMMY COLLINS – competent middle manager by day, suburban rockstar by night – has just been dumped and he's not taking it very well. Even a visit to his stylist can't cheer him up.

He decides to take control of the situation, convincing his friends to help him find the perfect girl – beautiful (but loyal), smart (but not too smart), confident (without being feminist), an expert bun-maker, who's indifferent about shopping, enthusiastic about *Star Trek* and scornful of self-help books.

As lead singer and guitarist with one of Dublin's best-known pub bands, The Grove, Jimmy decides to kick things off by writing a song for her; the mythical babe who's got it all – Superchick.

Ride On
Stephen J. Martin

ISBN: 978 1 85635 529 2

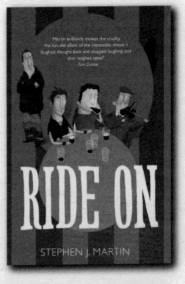

JIMMY COLLINS and his band have made it – with two chart-topping singles they are suddenly famous rock stars. While Jimmy isn't too keen on all the attention, his drummer Aesop is lapping it up and taking full advantage of the legions of female fans clamouring for his attention. Which means there are an awful lot of suspects when one of them turns into a stalker.

The Grove need to find a bodyguard. But where are you meant to find a professional who'll put up with someone like Aesop? Who knows what he's like, has extensive Special Forces experience and, most importantly, the patience of a saint? There's only one man for the job and there is only one way to make sure Aesop's really safe. But living in secluded isolation in Co. Cork with only Norman for company is not Aesop's idea of a good time …